Debra Webb is the award-winning *USA TODAY* best-selling author of more than one hundred novels, including those in reader-favourite series Faces of Evil, the Colby Agency and Shades of Death. With more than four million books sold in numerous languages and countries, Debra has a love of storytelling that goes back to her childhood on a farm in Alabama. Visit Debra at www.debrawebb.com

Rachel Lee was hooked on writing by the age of twelve and practised her craft as she moved from place to place all over the United States. This *New York Times* best-selling author now resides in Florida and has the joy of writing full-time.

THE SAFEST
LIES

DEBRA WEBB

MURDERED IN
CONARD COUNTY

RACHEL LEE

MILLS & BOON

First Published in Great Britain 2019
by Mills & Boon, an imprint of HarperCollins*Publishers*
1 London Bridge Street, London, SE1 9GF

The Safest Lies © 2019 Debra Webb
Murdered in Conard County © 2018 Susan Civil Brown

ISBN: 978-0-263-27436-3

0919

Printed and bound in Spain
by CPI, Barcelona

THE SAFEST LIES

DEBRA WEBB

This book is dedicated to
my two beautiful daughters.
Like the heroine in this book,
you are strong, amazing women!

Chapter One

Sadie Buchanan had never been to Winchester before. The closest she'd come was Tullahoma and that had been years ago when she was first assigned to the Nashville area. A joint task force conference at the Arnold Air Force base had required her attendance for a day. Frankly, it was unusual for an agent to end up in this area, much less request a retrieval. The kind of trouble that required her participation rarely happened in small towns. Most of her assignments took her to the larger metropolitan areas around the state or deep into the desert or the mountains.

In any event, whenever an agent was in trouble, she went in.

She parked in front of the Franklin County sheriff's office. Extracting agents from dangerous situations hadn't exactly been a part of her plan when she started her career, but within two years of her first field assignment she found herself doing exactly that after one particular mission. The assignment as well as the agent involved had been high profile, garnering her the full attention of the powers that be. During that fateful mission she as well as the Bureau discovered her knack for getting in and out with particular ease. From that point forward, she had been focused on training for moments like this one. It wasn't the sort of task just any agent felt comfortable doing. Success required a very particular skill set.

Go in, attain the target and get out alive.

Her father always said that everyone had a gift. Evidently, this was hers. It hadn't failed her yet. She had no intention of allowing it to start today.

Inside the brick building that housed the sheriff's department and county jail, a female desk sergeant greeted her.

"Special Agent Sadie Buchanan." Sadie showed her credentials to the other woman. "I'm here to see Sheriff Tanner and Agent Ross."

"Good morning, Agent Buchanan. Down the hall and to the left," Sergeant Rodriquez said with a gesture toward the long corridor beyond her desk. "They're waiting for you in the conference room, ma'am."

Sadie thanked the sergeant and headed in the direction she'd indicated. One thing she had noticed about Winchester already and it was barely ten o'clock in the morning—it was a couple of degrees hotter than Nashville. The town was attractive in a quaint sort of way, surrounded by a lake and bordered by hills and woods. Most folks would see those hills and woods as nature's perfect landscape. What Sadie saw in all that natural beauty were places to hide. Lots and lots of potential hiding places.

Not a good thing when attempting to locate a target.

She opened the door to the conference room and walked in. Four people waited for her but only one that she recognized: Special Agent Deacon Ross. He, too, was assigned to Nashville. They'd only worked together on one occasion, but he had a stellar reputation. The last she'd heard he had taken an extended leave of absence.

Maybe the rumors that he might not be coming back were just that—rumors. He certainly appeared to be involved in this case.

"Agent Buchanan," a tall, dark-haired man at the head of the table said as he stood, "I'm Sheriff Colt Tanner. We're glad you could come." He extended his hand.

Sadie gave his hand a shake. "Happy to help, Sheriff."

"This is Chief of Police Billy Brannigan." Tanner gestured to another man. This one had brown hair and eyes and looked as much like a cowboy as the sheriff.

Brannigan extended his hand across the conference table. "Good to meet you, Agent Buchanan."

"Likewise, Chief." Sadie accepted the gesture and turned to the next man in the room. "Agent Ross." She offered her hand.

Ross gave her hand a shake and then turned to the woman at his side. "This is Cecelia Winters."

Sadie extended her hand once more, this time toward the petite woman with the fiery mane of red hair. "Ms. Winters."

Winters brushed her palm briefly against Sadie's

but didn't speak. Since she had the same last name as the target, Sadie assumed she was a wife or other family member.

"Why don't we have a seat and get started," Ross suggested.

Sadie pulled out a chair and sat down as the others resumed their seats. A couple of files and a stack of maps lay on the table. Not exactly the typical setup for a tactical mission briefing but she'd gotten the impression this one was different than her usual assignment. She didn't have a problem with different. As long as it didn't get anyone killed. Sadie was yet to lose a target once she had attained him or her.

"I imagine," Ross said, "you were briefed on the situation we have."

"I only just returned to Nashville late last night from an assignment in Memphis. I'm afraid the details I received are sketchy at best. I assumed I would be fully briefed when I arrived."

This would certainly be her first briefing with a civilian present who was totally unrelated to the official aspects of the investigation. She had a feeling this assignment was going to become more and more unusual.

"A particular group of extremists in the Franklin County area was pinpointed more than two decades ago. Gunrunning was suspected to be a major part of this group's activities. Over the past few years suspicions of their involvement with kidnapping, possibly related to human trafficking, have surfaced. My former partner, Jack Kemp, investigated this group when it was first discovered but at the time there was not enough substantial evidence that the members were involved in anything criminal or illegal to pursue any sort of operation. Just over nine years ago that status changed, and Jack came back for a second look. During the course of that assignment he disappeared. Recently, new information about what happened to him has come to light. In part, that information was obtained through a civilian informant. Like most of us, Jack worked with a number of civilian informants."

"One of those informants is Levi Winters," Sheriff Tanner added. "Levi has recently gone missing and we suspect this group may be involved."

Brannigan didn't add anything. Sadie was undecided as to whether his continued silence was a good thing. Perhaps his involvement was only for informational purposes. The target was likely outside his official jurisdiction.

"Is the Bureau opening a new case in the area?" Seemed a no-brainer. But Sadie was not up to speed on the happenings in Franklin County. The more Ross talked, the more she understood that he had friends in high places and that was why she was here. "Or is this one off the record?"

The men in the room exchanged a look, which answered the question without anyone having to say a word.

"To a degree," Ross admitted, "the retrieval is off the record. There appears to be some hesitation about reopening the case involving the group known as Resurrection. Personally, I think we're caught in the middle of a war between the Bureau and the ATF, leaving us blind. We're hoping any information Levi may have will help pull this all together. But," he qualified, "finding him is our primary goal."

Making it doubly important that she brought him back alive. Sadie considered the other woman at the table. The hope in her eyes was impossible to miss. Right now, Sadie could walk away and that decision would not adversely affect her career since this mission was off the record. She could stand up, walk out that door and never look back rather than risk her life for some informant whom she did not know and had no idea if he was actually credible.

Chances were, if she made that decision, the informant would die.

And though that decision would not prove unfavorable to her career, it would prove immensely unfavorable to her conscience.

"Let's have a look at what I'm up against."

Tanner went first. He explained that he had not encountered any trouble with members of this group—at least none of which he was aware. The members of the so-called Resurrection group were anonymous. Any who lived amid the community kept quiet about their involvement. Neighbors, friends, possibly even family had no idea about their participation. The tactic was actually fairly common and had been used for centuries by one secret group or another.

Brannigan spoke for the first time, agreeing with Tanner's summation. The Winchester Police Department had not run into trouble with anyone who claimed to be or who was thought to be involved with this extremist group. The crime rate in the county was comparatively low. Rumors regarding the group known as Resurrection leaned toward the idea of extreme or doomsday-type preppers. Part of the problem was that there appeared to be an offshoot fringe group known only as the *others* who were far more dangerous. More primitive and violent.

Ross took over from there. "We've contacted a source within the ATF but we don't have anything back from him just yet. He can only help us so much without crossing a line. Whatever else we do, we can't keep waiting and risk losing Winters. Ultimately, the hope is that the Bureau and the ATF will initiate a joint task force, along with local law enforcement, to look more thoroughly into what this group is doing. As I said, for now, our immediate focus is on extracting Winters."

Sadie understood perfectly. "If the Resurrection or this offshoot group has him, we need to get their attention. Obviously—" she scanned the faces at the table "—you don't have the location where he's being held."

Tanner tapped the stacks of maps. "There are certain areas we feel are the more likely places but, no, we don't have a damned clue."

"And there's no time to conduct the kind of search required to locate a needle in a haystack," Sadie suggested. "Time is our enemy." She set her gaze on Ross's, knowing he would understand the goal. "We need their attention. I would recommend a news bulletin about a missing federal agent last seen in the Winchester area. Keep it ambiguous for obvious reasons. Give my description but not my name." She shifted her attention to Tanner. "I'll start with the most likely place and beat the bushes until they find me."

"You want them to find you?" Tanner looked uneasy as he asked the question.

"We don't have time to locate and infiltrate any other way. Prompting them to find me will be much faster and far more efficient."

"Isn't that far more dangerous, as well?" Brannigan asked.

"Yes." Sadie saw no point in whitewashing the answer. "But it's the only way to accomplish our goal in a timely manner."

"Agent Buchanan is highly trained for exactly these sorts of situations," Ross assured all present.

Judging by the expressions Tanner and Brannigan wore, his assurance did little to alleviate their reservations.

"You're suggesting going in without backup," Brannigan argued. "The only thing I see coming of that is two hostages needing extraction."

Sadie acknowledged his assessment with a nod. "That is a possibility. But, Chief, you can trust me when I say, if I wasn't experienced and completely confident about this situation, we wouldn't be having this conversation. I know what I'm doing. I understand the risk and, based on what I've heard so far, I am not overly concerned."

"I may be able to help."

All gathered around the table turned to the woman who had spoken. Cecelia Winters looked directly at

Sadie even as the men in the room started to argue with her announcement.

"Not happening," Ross stated unconditionally, tension in his voice, his posture and the set of his jaw.

"He's right," Tanner agreed with a firm shake of his head.

"This whole thing is far too risky as it is," Brannigan added.

Sadie ignored them all. Instead, she focused on the woman who had made the statement. "How do you believe you can help?"

Cecelia blinked at Sadie's question. "The people in this town know me. They know what happened to me— to my family. Nothing is secret anymore. If I spread the news, they'll believe me. They will pass it along far more quickly than something reported in the news. Not everyone around here trusts the news."

"Cece," Ross argued, "your getting involved could only complicate matters."

Sadie got the picture now. Ross and Cecelia were a couple. He didn't want her anywhere near the line of fire. A personal connection more often than not spelled trouble when it came to an assignment like this one.

"Help from most any source can be useful, but Ross could be right," Sadie said, not to change the woman's mind but because it was true.

The hard look Ross sent her way shouted loud and clear that he wasn't happy with how she had responded to the offer. Too bad. He wanted Sadie to do a job, an extraction—a very risky extraction. Why wouldn't she use any available resources?

"Levi is my brother," Cecelia said. "I want to help." She glanced at Ross. "I need to help."

"You understand that when this is over, there could be a backlash?" Sadie needed her to comprehend the long-term ramifications of any step she might opt to take. Sadie didn't like getting civilians involved but it seemed as if this one was already eyeball deep in the situation.

"I do. The past decade of my life has been one long backlash. I think I can handle a little more."

Ross obviously didn't think so.

Sadie stared directly at him. "Is this going to be a problem for you?"

She didn't like problems. Especially those that came from the people who were supposed to be on her side.

He held her gaze for a moment before saying, "I guess not."

"Good." Sadie turned back to Cecelia. "You tell whomever you believe will get the word out the fastest that the agent who was working with your brother showed up and was going around town asking questions." She shrugged. "Trying to help, but now she's suddenly gone missing and you're worried about her."

Cecelia nodded. "I can do that."

"The most likely starting place?" Sadie asked, looking from one man to the next.

"The church," Ross said. He glanced at Cecelia as he spoke. "We have reason to believe the Salvation Survivalists were working with the primary group in some capacity. They were housing weapons most likely intended for the Resurrection group, but we don't have solid evidence of that conclusion. The ATF is looking at that aspect along with numerous others but, as we've established, they're taking too damned long and they're not sharing."

"But you're certain the two are or were connected."

"We are," Ross said.

Tanner and Brannigan agreed, as well.

"Then that's where I'll start." To Cecelia she said, "You put the word out about me asking questions." She shifted her attention to Tanner. "Make sure the local news reports a missing federal agent. No name, just a description," she reminded.

Tanner nodded. "I can make that happen."

"I'd like to familiarize myself with maps of the area, particularly around the church."

Ross spread the maps on the conference table and started the briefing regarding landscape. Sadie took her time and carefully committed the maps to memory. One of the things that made her good at her job was her ability to memorize maps and recall landmarks. For a girl who grew up in the city, she was a damned good tracker. As good as any hunter she'd ever worked with and she'd worked with a few.

More than anything, she paid attention. The old saying that it was all in the details was more often true than not. The details were crucial. One didn't need a photographic memory to recall the details. She just had to pay attention.

"What about the church?" Sadie considered the map of the area around the church, which appeared to be well outside town. "I need some additional history on the church."

"My father started the church about thirty-five years ago," Cecelia explained. "He was a very cruel man, capable of anything. He had many devoted followers who turned to my older brother, Marcus, after our father's murder. There are those who still believe one or both to be messiahs of a sort. I'm confident the most deeply devoted know far more than they've shared. If they hear about you, you better believe the word will go where you want it."

Ross pushed a folder in Sadie's direction. "This will give you a good overview of what we know. It's not complete by any means, but it's as much as anyone knows."

Sadie opened the file and skimmed the first page. "I'd like some time to go over what you have and then I'll drive out to the church, hide my car and start digging around. If I'm lucky, someone will come looking for me in short order."

"For the record," Chief of Police Brannigan spoke up again, "I still think this is a bad idea."

Sadie wished she could convince him otherwise but to an extent he was correct. This was most likely a bad idea.

But their options were limited. Sometimes the bad ideas were the only feasible ones.

Chapter Two

Dusk was settling way too fast. Sadie had knocked on doors in the vicinity of the church—not that there were that many. She'd asked straightforward questions, calling the group she sought by name. Then she'd driven to the now-defunct church of the Salvation Survivalists and she'd started poking around.

Breaking in had been a breeze. The ATF and the FBI had gone through the building numerous times and though every entrance had been secured, the lock on the back door was damaged. All of ten seconds were required to rip the crime scene seal away and finagle the thing open. As easy as taking candy from a baby.

It was possible a couple of days might be required to garner the attention she sought. Not good for her target. Levi Winters might not have a couple of days. On the other hand, it was possible he wasn't a hostage at all and was happily ensconced among friends deep within this suspicious group. His sister, Cecelia, was convinced he was a hostage, but sisters didn't always know the whole story.

Sadie's sister certainly did not.

She and her sister had never been friends. Maybe it was the ten years that separated them in age or the fact that her sister had chosen a path Sadie despised. Pricilla Buchanan was a criminal defense attorney. Her entire existence was focused on undoing what law enforcement personnel like Sadie risked their lives to do. Of course their mother insisted they were both angels, but she was wrong. Their mother wanted to see good in everyone. Pricilla was not good. She was self-centered, self-serving and indifferent when it came to justice.

Sadie kicked aside thoughts of her older sister as she strolled the halls of the extremist church whose followers still refused to speak ill of their most recent infamous leader. The man, Cecelia Winters's older brother as it turned out, had been hiding smuggled guns. He'd sworn he had no idea how the weapons had ended up in the secret underground hiding place beneath the church. He'd gone so far as to attempt to claim the weapons had been there since before his father died almost nine years ago. Talk about a scumbag. Then again, apparently his father had been an even bigger lowlife.

Ross and the others suspected Marcus Winters had been holding the stockpile of weapons for the Resurrection. Despite the seriousness of the charges he faced, Winters refused to spill his guts. Whomever Marcus Winters was protecting he was too damned afraid to make a deal, even for the promise of a new life in witness protection.

The moment he'd been arrested he had shut down like a dying cell phone battery and hadn't spoken since. Anything that might provide clues about a connection between the church and the gunrunning extremist prepper group was long gone. The tunnel between the church and the Winters home was set for demolition. Cecelia mentioned that she intended to sell the place the moment it was released from evidence. She wanted to wash her hands of that ugly past as soon as possible and who could blame her? Based on what Ross had told Sadie, the woman had already paid a high price for standing up against her family.

Sadie followed the directions she'd been given to find the tunnel area. Mostly she was killing time. The longer she hung out in the area the more likely she was to run into what she was looking for. At least that was the hope. If she were really lucky things would happen as quickly as she hoped.

Ross had given her a piece of information to use as leverage once she had infiltrated the group. His contact from the ATF insisted this would be immensely useful. She'd gone into missions with less, but this felt a little slim by any measure.

The entrance to the tunnel was barricaded. Sadie turned and headed back in the direction she'd come. She took the stairs two at a time and returned to the church's main sanctuary.

There was nothing else to be done here. She turned for the front entrance and stalled. A man sat on the very back pew. His hair was gray—not the white gray, the silver gray. It poked from beneath a fedora. A full beard did a hell of a job of camouflaging his face. He wore overalls and a button-down, long-sleeved shirt, no matter that it was as hot as hell outside. It was difficult to assess if he was armed. Her view of him from the chest down was blocked by the back of the pew in front of him. From a merely visual perspective he appeared reasonably harmless.

Sadie, however, was too smart to assume any such thing based on appearances.

"You must be that missing fed."

Though he said this in a low, rusty-with-age voice, it seemed to echo in the hollow sanctuary. Not particularly threatening and yet with simmering power.

"That's me. Sadie Buchanan."

"I hear you and a fed friend of yours have been looking for me."

Obviously, he meant Deacon Ross. "I don't know about anyone else and I definitely don't have any friends around here, but I've been looking for someone. That's a fact. Can't say whether that someone is you."

She dared to walk toward him, one step at a time down that long center aisle. The rubber soles of her hiking boots were quiet on the wood floor.

"What is it you think you're looking for, Ms. Buchanan? Or should I call you Agent Buchanan?"

Sadie sat down at the pew in front of him, turned in the hard seat to face him. "Sadie is fine. After yesterday, I doubt that anyone considers me an agent anymore—except maybe for the purposes of prosecution."

The story that she was an agent on the run was the best cover she could come up with given the circumstances and the shortness of time.

"Nine years. Stellar record. Up for promotion," he said, his gaze steady on hers, "the way I hear it. That's a lot to give up for whatever it is that brought you here, Sadie."

So the man had friends in the right places. Only a handful of people in this town knew her name and none beyond the four with whom she had met in the sheriff's conference room were aware of her background. She shrugged. "I should have gotten that promotion two years ago. And you're right, nine years is a long time to watch men like my SAIC write his own definition of justice. Besides, my daddy was a firm believer in a man—or woman—having the right to live his life the way he wanted and to bear arms. I suppose I have him to thank for my hardheadedness."

The man's gaze hardened. "As interesting as this conversation might prove to be, I don't like wasting my time, Sadie. Why don't you tell me what it is you think I need to hear?"

"I appreciate that you looked me up, Mister…?"

"Prentiss," he said, "Rayford Prentiss."

"Mr. Prentiss," she acknowledged. "The trouble is— and I mean no offense to you—I really need to speak with the man in charge. It's urgent. We don't have a lot of time."

He held her gaze for a long moment of thickening silence. "You don't look like the sort with a death wish," he finally said.

Sadie smiled. "Not if I can help it. What I have, Mr. Prentiss, is some information about a joint task force mission that will prove more than a little devastating to the Resurrection. If you and your friends take me in, I'll give you the heads-up you need to survive the storm that's coming—assuming you know what I'm talking about and have the authority to take me where I need to go."

A crooked smile lifted one corner of his bearded mouth. "First, I know precisely what you mean and I have all the authority I need. The real question is, why on God's green earth would I believe that foolish story?"

"Well, my motive is somewhat personal, Mr. Prentiss. I will tell you that I've gotten myself into a bit of trouble and I don't see any ready way out, so this looks like as good an option as any other. My daddy always said planning for the future was smart business. I need to disappear for a little while, Mr. Prentiss. I think you and your friends can make that happen. You do me a favor and I'll do one for you."

Prentiss chuckled. "I really am flummoxed, Sadie. You appear quite sincere and yet I'm not certain I believe you. Be that as it may, we'll play your little game. After all, it took considerable courage to start this thing." His gaze settled heavily on her and this time there was no mistaking the promise there. "Rest assured, whatever this is, if you're lying to me, you will not like how this ends."

"Great." Sadie pushed a smile into place and sat up straight. "Then we have a deal."

Another of those long moments of silence elapsed with him staring at her. "It appears we do."

He raised a hand and people seemed to come out of the woodwork. Four men, all armed. "My friends will see to your transportation. Goodbye, Sadie."

When he stood and walked away, she couldn't help

wondering if this mission would end right here, right now. These guys could kill her and no one would ever know exactly what happened, much less who did the deed.

Wasn't that the way it always was?

The door closed behind Prentiss and she stood, glanced from fierce face to fierce face. "So, who's driving?"

"Take off your clothes," the one nearest her said.

She laughed. "I never take off my clothes on the first date."

He aimed his weapon at her. "Take them off now."

One of his pals stepped forward and tossed a bag on the floor at the end of her pew.

"There are clothes in the bag," the one who appeared to be in charge and who held his aim steady on her announced.

"Well, if you insist."

Taking her time she toed off her boots, peeled off her socks, then unbuttoned her shirt. When the shirt, the boots and socks were in a neat pile next to the provided bag, she shucked her jeans and added them to the pile next.

When she reached for the bag, the man with the gun at the ready protested, "Everything comes off."

She figured that would be his next order. Sadie reached behind her and unhooked her bra. She allowed it to fall forward and drop to the pile. Then she swooped off her panties and added them unceremoniously to the rest.

The man nodded and she reached for the bag. Inside was a pair of gray sweatpants and a white tee. No underwear. No socks. Thankfully there was a pair of plastic flip-flops. The cheap kind found in bins near the checkout counter at discount stores. She donned the provided outfit and slipped her feet into the flip-flops.

The man who'd brought the bag grabbed her things and put them into the empty bag. She hated that her cell phone was in that bag. Besides a gun, it was the asset she depended upon most.

Oh well.

"Let's go." The man with a bead on her motioned with the barrel of his weapon toward the back of the church.

"What about my car?" she asked as they marched toward the rear exit.

"A friend will pick it up and dismantle it for parts."

She stalled and glared at the man. Was he out of his mind? "Wait just a minute. That car cost—"

"You won't need it where you're going."

THE DRIVE TO their destination took half an hour, give or take a minute.

Sadie had counted off the seconds and minutes, in part to distract herself from the sorts of thoughts that wanted to crowd into her brain. But mostly because it was important to maintain a sense of location. Half an hour from the church was a reference anyone coming to her rescue could use to facilitate the task.

Except there was no one coming. This mission was basically off the books. Ross and his friends would get worried when they didn't hear from her in a couple of days but there wasn't a whole lot they could do other than beat the bushes and rattle a few cages looking for her. Finding her would be difficult if not impossible. The tracking devices in her cell phone, in the soles of her shoes and in her bra were who knew where. Unless someone had been watching her and followed this caravan, she was probably out of luck as far as backup was concerned.

Frankly, she had been surprised by their vehicles. She'd expected big four-wheel-drive trucks caked with mud and decked out with gun racks. But that wasn't the case at all. The two vehicles were both new top-of-the-line SUVs. Sure, they were four-wheel drive, but they were sleek and almost elegant looking—unlike the men inside.

The younger of the group had been tasked with her personal security. He'd secured her hands behind her back and dropped a cloth bag over her head. He sat in the back seat with her. Another one drove. The other two men were in the second vehicle, with Prentiss, no doubt. No one in this vehicle had said a word en route. Music had played just loud enough to prevent her from noting another reference—any sounds in the areas they drove through. Animals, trains, construction, whatever.

When the vehicle rolled to a stop and the engine cut off, the music died. The doors opened and low voices rumbled around her. Beyond the voices was quiet. No city sounds. No traffic sounds. Not even any animals.

Fingers wrapped around her upper arm and tugged her from the center section of the back seat. A hand guided her feet so she wouldn't break her neck climbing out. When she was steady on the ground the sack was dragged from her head.

Her first thought was that she had gone back in time. The towering stone walls made her think of the ones surrounding a castle she'd visited in Edinburgh, Scotland. The walls were massive, at least thirty feet high. There were what appeared to be guard towers built into the wall. A large, square stone structure stood in the center of the expansive grounds that were like a quad on a college campus without all the fancy landscape. Like the primitive keeps she'd seen in her travels, the windows were tiny in proportion. There were other buildings beyond the larger one, but she could only see the rooftops in the distance.

She stared overhead. Frowned. There was no sky.

She scanned what should have been the sky for as far as she could see. Steel and some sort of panels stood high above her. Reminded her of a massive warehouse. But no clouds or sun or anything else that said *sky*.

Wherever they were, they were not outside. But the SUVs had rolled to a stop right here. She glanced over her shoulder at the one she'd only just emerged from. The ride had seemed to stay on level ground. There had been no downhill or uphill movement. The ride had been smooth but not so smooth that she wouldn't have noticed a change in elevation. There could have been an elevator somewhere that brought them below ground. But that didn't seem right, either, since they hadn't stopped long enough to roll into any sort of elevator until a minute ago, when the engines shut off and they got out.

The man behind her nudged her forward with the muzzle of his weapon. She took in as much of what she could see as possible, committed it to memory as they moved forward. Wherever they were, the place was certainly fortified for battle. If they were underground as she suspected, she supposed the purpose was for surviving a nuclear attack. Additionally, being underground would explain why the feds and local law enforcement hadn't already spotted the compound from the air.

By the time they rounded the corner of the largest building she'd seen so far, only two of the men remained with her. Prentiss and the other two had gone in a different direction. The one with the gun at her back kept her moving forward with the occasional nudge. Beyond the large building were increasingly smaller ones. Along the east side of the wall the smallest structures were numbered. They sat in a long row like cabin rentals at the lake. Only there was no lake—not that she'd seen so far anyway—and this was no vacation. The long, low building that stood the farthest west from the center of the grounds had no windows and appeared to be their destination. The squat roofline told her it was one story. She saw only one entrance along the front, assuming what she was looking at was the front.

The second of the two guards unlocked and opened the door. Number one nudged her to go in. The guards followed close behind her. An immediate left took them down a long white corridor lined with doors on either side. No windows on the doors, either. Midway down the corridor, they stopped at a door and number two guard unlocked it with a few clicks of the keys on the control pad. Once the thick door pulled outward, Sadie understood this would be her accommodations for now. Until they decided what to do with her, she imagined.

"I'm supposed to be meeting with the man in charge," she reminded number one.

"Tomorrow."

The door slammed in her face.

She turned around. A dim light came from around the perimeter of the room. There was a steel cot, a toilet hanging on the wall with a sink formed in the tank. Just like the ones she had seen in the few prison cells she'd visited.

With a quick drawing back of the covers, she checked the mattress, ensured the sheets weren't tainted with anything she could see or smell. Fabric smelled clean enough. She paced the small room and considered her options. There had been four men with Prentiss. She hadn't seen any others when they arrived but that didn't mean there weren't hundreds around here somewhere. There was no accurate body count for this group.

If the Resurrection was like most of these extremist groups, there would be several hundred on-site. This was obviously a headquarters. The setup was too good to be anything else. The Bureau had been gathering information on extremist groups like this for decades. But this one had somehow managed to stay under the radar. The members didn't talk. Fear, she imagined. It was human nature to talk about the things in which one was interested. Being a part of something like Resurrection would typically provide bragging rights for those who had a penchant for the extreme. But there was no bragging from these members.

Their silence made them even more dangerous. Restricted the available intelligence to gather, making the jobs of Sadie and others like her far more difficult. Law enforcement personnel depended upon informants and the information garnered on the streets. When information stopped flowing, it was impossible to find footing in a given situation.

Sadie braced her hands on her hips and moved around the room again, this time more slowly. She considered the walls, thought about the door when it had opened. The walls were likely made of concrete just as the door was. Thick concrete, eight inches at least. The floor and ceiling of this building appeared to be the same as the walls. The smooth, cold finish of the concrete was interrupted only by the small blocks of light around the walls near the floor. The cot was metal, the sheets a thin material more like paper than fabric. No good for constructing a hangman's noose. She turned back to the door. The lock wasn't the usual residential sort. It was electronic and required a code.

Getting out of here wouldn't be easy. If she was really lucky, Levi Winters was in this same building. Assuming he was a hostage. Hopefully, he would know a way out and would be willing to go with her.

That was the problem with being underground or, perhaps, burrowed into a mountainside. Getting out was generally somewhat complicated.

She'd been in tighter spots, Sadie reminded herself.

All she had to do was find her target and she would locate a way out of here.

It was what she did.

Chapter Three

The woman was trouble.

Smith Flynn studied the screen monitoring her movements. She paced the six-by-eight cell as if the journey might end some other way the next time she turned around. She hadn't stopped since being placed inside. This restless behavior was for the benefit of anyone observing.

He had watched her arrival. She had walked into the compound, shoulders back, chin held high, all the while discreetly surveying everything in her field of vision. Sadie Buchanan was neither afraid nor uncertain. Her arrival at this compound was not by accident any more than was the timing of her appearance. She was on a mission.

Whatever she was doing here, unfortunately she was his issue now.

He did not like unexpected issues. Even fearless, attractive ones like Sadie Buchanan.

"What's your take on this new development?"

The voice drew Smith from his musings. He turned to Prentiss. The older man had been running the group known as the Resurrection for a very long time. He rarely had much to say but when he spoke anyone within hearing distance listened—not because he was so articulate or interesting, but because they wanted to live. Prentiss did not take disrespect well.

"She has an agenda," Smith said, not telling the other man anything he didn't already know. "It'll take some time to determine what that agenda is."

Prentiss nodded, his attention fixed on the screen. "I don't like killing women. There's something innately wrong with a man killing a woman. It's a sin like no other, except for killing a child. Any man who would kill a woman or a child is lower than low." His gaze swung to Smith. "But, if you tell me she's lying, I will kill her."

Smith didn't waste time pretending to consider the situation. "I can tell you right now that she *is* lying. No question there." He turned his attention back to the screen. "The question is why. We'll need that answer before you kill her."

Prentiss nodded. "You're right. Until we have the answer, she belongs to you. Do with her what you will, just get the truth for me."

"I always do."

The old man stood and headed for the door. Smith waited until the door closed before turning back to the screen. He wondered if this woman had any idea just how much trouble she was in. Whatever she thought she'd come here to do, she had made a most regrettable mistake.

He exited his cabin, locking the door behind him,

and crossed to the detention center. No one questioned his movements. They knew better. The door was unlocked and opened for him as if he was a king. Once inside he said to the guard, "I'll be using interview room two for an hour or so. Bring me Levi Winters."

"Yes, sir."

The guard hustled away to do Smith's bidding. Smith took the short corridor on the right and then an immediate left where six interview rooms waited. Each room was equipped with very specific instruments for persuading answers from those who had the misfortune of ending up in one of the spaces. Before going to interview room two, he stepped into the observation room and checked the monitoring system.

Two minutes elapsed before the guard entered interview room two. He settled the prisoner Levi Winters into the chair on the side of the metal table facing the hidden camera. Once Winters was secured to the bolt in the concrete floor, the guard exited. Smith considered Winters for a longer moment. He was younger than this woman who'd gotten herself invited to this ultrasecure place.

More important than any other aspect of this prisoner, he was scared. Scared to death.

THEY WERE PROBABLY going to kill him now.

Levi's whole body felt as cold as ice. There was no telling what they had planned for him this time. That bastard Flynn had done things to him, made him talk when he didn't want to talk.

Levi closed his eyes and lowered his head. He was

doomed. All he'd wanted was to find the truth. To prove to his sister that he wasn't a bad guy like their brother, Marcus. He'd let her down so badly already it hurt to think about it. Even under the circumstances. He hadn't helped Cece the way he should have so he'd decided to prove the whole truth about their daddy and all that he and Marcus had done, like ordering the death of the FBI guy, Jack Kemp.

Jack had been good to Levi. He'd made him feel like his life mattered—like he mattered. Levi had wanted to be like him. And then the guy had disappeared.

What nobody knew was that Levi remembered the night their mother had died, no matter that he'd been nothing but a little kid. She and that bastard who was their father had been arguing so loudly and so desperately—arguing, screaming and crying. Then suddenly the arguing had stopped. Levi had crept out of his bedroom and to the top of the stairs. Their momma had lain at the bottom of the stairs. The crying had started again, only that time it was Levi. The only thing he remembered after that was Cece holding him and their grandmother screaming. Eventually she had calmed down and taken them home with her.

The certainty and hatred that had sprouted that night had grown and grown but before Levi could work up the courage to do what needed to be done, their younger sister, Sierra, had killed the old bastard. It should have been Levi. He should have killed that devil and taken care of the family when their older brother, Marcus, had not. But Levi had been weak. He'd been weak and afraid. He'd let Cece down and now he was going to die without having made up for the past.

He wished he could see Cece one more time and tell her how sorry he was. She had paid the price for all of them.

The door opened and Levi froze. It would be him— the one the other prisoners called the Interrogator. Levi's body shuddered at the idea of what he might have planned for him this time. Why had he screwed up so badly yet again? All he wanted at this point was to go home. To show his sister how much he loved her and to start doing the right thing with his life.

He wasn't like his father or his older brother. Evil didn't swim in his blood.

He just wanted to go home.

Smith Flynn walked into the room. He had the lightest gray eyes, almost transparent. That and his blond hair almost made him look like some guy from Norway or Sweden or something. He didn't look like anyone from around here. He was tall, six-four at least. And strong. You could tell he pumped iron. But he hadn't laid a hand on Levi. He had other ways to induce pain. He used equipment and his words. He knew the things to say to strike terror in a man.

Before Levi could stop himself, his gaze flitted to the far end of the room where the metal cabinets stood. Inside those locked doors were instruments he hoped to never see again. Evidently he wasn't going to be so lucky. Flynn wouldn't be here otherwise.

The worst part about the whole damned mess was that this guy wanted some truth from Levi, but he didn't have anything to trade for his life or even for a little more time free of torture. Levi had nothing. He had come to this place to prove something. All those years ago when he'd first joined the Resurrection so Jack Kemp would see how smart he was, he'd made a mistake. Truth was he'd let Jack use him. He'd needed that father figure Jack represented so badly. Levi would have done anything to impress him. But he'd gone too far.

All he'd done was gotten into trouble. Now he was likely going to get dead the same way Jack had.

Levi would end up in hell with his damned daddy.

"We have a new problem, Levi."

Fear tightened around his neck. Even the man's voice had a way of terrifying anyone who happened to be stuck in the room with him. Deep, dark, dangerous. Fear twisted inside Levi. Why didn't this Interrogator just kill him and get it over with? He didn't want to die but he couldn't take this much longer.

"I already told you I don't know anything. I only came here to find the truth about an old friend. I swear that's it. The whole story. The truth. There's nothing else."

"Jack Kemp," Flynn said. "You told me that before. Tell me again why you think Kemp came here?"

"He was from the FBI," Levi said. No point pretending he could hide anything from this bastard. The Interrogator had ways of digging stuff out of him. "He asked me to help him get information about the group called the Resurrection, but I went too far."

"Meaning you joined the calling all those years ago?

Nine or so years ago, am I right? You did this to help your friend."

Levi nodded. "But Jack disappeared before I could tell him anything. I figured y'all found out what he was up to and got rid of him."

"Your brother, Marcus, was responsible for what happened to him, Levi. If you had seen the news recently, you would know this. He confessed."

Levi was surprised that Marcus confessed to giving Jack to those crazy people. The only way he would have admitted to anything was to save his sorry ass. Hurt twisted in Levi's chest. "What about my sisters? Did you see anything about my sisters?"

Flynn directed that icy glare at him. "Do I look like I would waste my time keeping up with your sisters?"

Levi blinked, bit his tongue so hard he tasted blood. He wanted to hurt this guy. But he'd heard all about him—the Interrogator. The one who got the answers for the Council. The one who knew how to cause pain. Fear snaked through Levi. He shouldn't have come back here. He'd wanted to help…but he'd just made another mistake. Jack was dead by now, no question. Marcus was in jail. God only knew about Sierra. Hopefully Cece was okay.

Flynn placed a photo of a woman on the table. "Do you know her?"

The woman had black hair and eyes nearly as dark, like a raven. Her skin was dark, like she'd lain on a beach all summer. She was pretty but he hadn't seen her before. He shook his head. Prayed that was the right answer because it was the only one he had. "No. She doesn't look familiar."

"Are you certain? Think carefully, Levi. If you lie to me, it will be much worse for you."

"I swear to God I don't know the woman. I have never seen her before."

Flynn said nothing for a long moment. Levi's chest felt ready to explode with tension. Why the hell didn't the bastard just go ahead and tell him he was a dead man? If death was coming, he'd rather know now and brace for it. He was sick of these games. He did not know this woman. He did not know any other information related to the FBI or this damned place or any damned thing else that mattered. His foot started to bounce, making his shackles rattle. He forced himself to still. Losing it wouldn't help his situation.

"I believe you, Levi." Flynn withdrew the photo, tucked it away in a folder. "My true concern is that she appeared here only a few days after you."

Agony welled inside Levi. "I don't know why. I don't know her. Why don't you ask her?"

"Not to worry, I certainly will. I think I might know why she's here but I need to be certain."

Levi blinked. He didn't have a damned clue where this was going or what this woman had to do with him. He just wanted to go back to his cell and be left alone. He didn't want the Interrogator opening up those cabinets over there the way he'd done before. Pulling out his torture tools and making Levi nearly piss his pants.

Ever since he was a teenager, Levi had thought that to some degree he was brave. He'd thought he was the kind of man who did the right thing. A sort of hero. At least he'd wanted to be. He'd hoped he could be a hero for his sister Cece and help her prove her innocence… but he hadn't helped. And he damned sure wasn't a hero. He wasn't even brave.

He was a coward.

Nothing but a stinking coward.

"Can I count on your help, Levi?"

Levi snapped his focus back to the man. He swallowed back the bile that had risen in his throat and tried to slow his pounding heart. "Yeah, sure. What do I have to do?"

"I haven't worked out all the details just yet. We'll talk again soon."

The man stood and walked out.

Levi sagged in his chair. Squeezed his eyes shut and thanked God he'd survived a second encounter with the Interrogator.

Whatever he wanted, Levi could do it. He would do it. At this point obedience was probably the only way to stay alive. Cece would want him to stay alive. She would. He knew this without question. His sister would absolutely want him to do whatever necessary to stay alive.

Even if he was the worst kind of coward.

SMITH RETURNED TO his cabin and turned on the security feed to watch the woman.

She had stopped her pacing. Had decided to conserve her energy. He suspected she was above average in intelligence. Certainly she was cockier than the average agent. Her dark hair and eyes, the olive skin, gave her an exotic appearance. Beyond the superficial, she looked strong. Undeniable curves, but not soft. Lean. Toned muscle. This was a woman who worked hard to be prepared.

Her claim of possessing useful information was not a particularly original tactic. Her methods of getting their attention, however, were damned original. To garner the attention of Prentiss himself, then get herself picked up by members and brought here this way was ingenious. And extremely risky. Whatever she wanted, it was important. Important enough to risk her life.

Reconnaissance teams had been doubled and were out there now, patrolling and watching for trouble. No matter that the team that had brought her here had ensured they weren't followed. Her clothes and personal items had been removed before she left that godforsaken church. That level of motivation demanded careful consideration.

It was possible a tracking device was implanted somewhere on her slim body but the initial scan had not picked up on anything close to the surface. Her clothes and cell phone had been cleaned. As he'd anticipated, her phone was more or less a blank slate. Anything incriminating had been wiped. It had been reduced to a mere tracking device. This was a very well-trained agent.

Rather than take the risk the initial scan had missed something, he picked up a secure internal line and called Medical. "Run deep scans on Prisoner Buchanan. Send the results to me ASAP."

Smith ended the call, his attention still focused on the woman. He watched as she whirled around at the sound of her cell door opening. She didn't resist when the guard cuffed her hands behind her back and then escorted her out of the confining space. Smith followed the monitors, watching her move down the long white corridor and out onto the quad. The two crossed the common area and entered the smaller medical building. Smith switched to another camera and followed their movements inside.

The guard took a position at the door leading to Imaging while the waiting technician assumed custody of the prisoner.

"Remove your clothing," the tech ordered.

Buchanan glanced around the room, noted the imaging equipment and then did as he asked without question. The top came off first, revealing high, firm breasts and a narrow waist. As the sweatpants slid down her hips and thighs, Smith's gaze followed. Despite his own training, his body tightened. Her shape was undeniably attractive. Gently rounded hips and long legs sculpted by hours of running. Her long hair hung around her shoulders, the only remaining shield she possessed.

The quality he found most surprising and interesting was that she stared square at the male technician without the slightest flinch. She was not shy or afraid.

Smith continued to observe as the scans were accomplished. On a second screen, he monitored the results. There was no indication a tracking device or other electronic object had been inserted or implanted. She was clean.

His curiosity roused. This woman—this Federal Bureau of Investigation agent—had walked into a compound filled with heavily armed and well-trained extremists. In truth, the people here were more mercenaries than preppers. She had done this while completely unarmed and with no way to call for backup or hope to escape.

Sadie Buchanan was either telling the truth about her agenda for being here or she was completely insane.

He would know the answer soon enough.

Chapter Four

Saturday, August 4

Sadie opened her eyes. Darkness crowded in around her, jolting her heart into a frantic run.

For a moment her brain couldn't assimilate where she was. Air refused to fill her lungs.

Then she remembered. Compound. *Resurrection.*

Trouble.

She froze.

What had awakened her so abruptly? A sound. The slightest brushing of fabric against fabric as if someone had come far too close to her huddled position on this rock-hard cot.

She dared to take a breath and the subtle scent of leather and wood whispered against her senses. Adrenaline burned through her once more.

She was not alone.

Forcing herself to relax, she peered into the darkness. Slowly but surely her eyes filled in the dark form sitting on the edge of the thin mattress, barely centimeters away. Whoever it was sat perfectly still, didn't even breathe.

Someone had come into her cell, had walked the half-dozen steps across the small concrete room and sat down on the edge of her cot. The door opening should have awakened her but it had not. Had they put something into her food?

She never slept so heavily.

"What do you want?" She said the words then waited for a response, holding her breath for fear she would miss some part of the answer, assuming an answer came.

"Why are you here, Sadie Buchanan?"

Male. His voice was intensely deep, and...*dangerous*. She couldn't stop the shiver the sound elicited.

Grabbing back her usual unflappability, she fired back, "You already know the answer to that question."

A grunt was his immediate reaction.

She ordered herself to relax. Where was her usual fearlessness? It was something for which she didn't typically have to search. Granted he had startled her from sleep in the middle of the night. Then again, she couldn't be sure what time it was. It could be morning for all she knew. Without a window with which to judge, she couldn't make an accurate assessment. There had to be something in the food she had dared to nibble at. She had known better but hunger sometimes overrode experience.

"Why are you here, Sadie Buchanan?" he said once more.

The words were harsher this time. His patience was

thinning, and he obviously didn't like repeating himself. Well, she didn't, either.

"Like I told your friends, I have information that could help your cause. I came to make a deal."

He laughed. There was zero humor in the rough noise. "If you were half as smart as you apparently believe you are, Sadie Buchanan, you would know that people like us don't make deals."

The full depth and breadth of her courage finally reared its head. About time. "Well, now, that's not entirely true, Mister...?"

"Flynn. Smith Flynn."

Her brain instinctively searched her memory banks. No Smith Flynn was found there. "Perhaps you're unaware of the deals those in charge make quite often. Deals with a certain South American gunrunning cartel. The recent shipment was detained by the feds and local authorities right here in Winchester—assuming we're still in the Winchester area. And that's only the beginning of your troubles. Things are not going to go so well for your friends if you refuse my generous offer of help."

He appeared to contemplate her warning for a time. If she was really lucky, his curiosity would trump his logic.

"What happened recently," he said, his voice still somehow disturbing to her senses, "was an unforeseeable stroke of good fortune for *your* friends, but it won't happen again."

Sadie was the one who laughed this time. "You really believe all those stored weapons were found in those underground tunnels at the church by accident? A lucky break for the feds?"

His tension shifted to the next level; she felt it in his posture even if she couldn't see him in the darkness. Though their bodies weren't touching, tension crackled between them. He was as edgy as she was. She squinted, peered harder through the darkness. Her eyes had adjusted more fully to the darkness allowing her to see that he had lighter hair. Blond, she calculated. Maybe gray. She couldn't say for certain.

"You have proof it wasn't?"

The next step was a risky one. Other than Levi Winters, she had no names of members except the one she was saving as the ace up her sleeve. "I know what the local authorities said. A heads-up took them to the church. The Winters family meltdown was secondary. They were already going there anyway. The church had been on their radar for a while. The goal was to hit when it counted. We both know how that turned out."

He considered her statement for long enough to make her doubt herself.

"I can't decide, Sadie Buchanan, whether you actually have relevant information or if you simply have a somewhat complicated death wish. If exiting this world is your goal, putting your service weapon to your temple would have been far easier."

"I can assure you, Mr. Flynn, I do not have a death wish." She was winning this round. "What I have is information you and your friends can use. But I can't force your interest." She relaxed into the thin mattress as if she'd said all she had to say.

"I will be watching you, Sadie Buchanan. If you're lying, you will regret your actions far more than you can imagine."

She reached out, her hand landing on what felt like his upper arm. The muscles there were like steel but she suspected that had nothing to do with him not being relaxed and everything to do with serious workouts.

"Tell me about you, Smith Flynn. What's your story? What are you running away from?"

He snagged her hand, clutched it in his own. "Why would you think I'm running from something?" His thumb found her palm and stroked the tender flesh there. "You don't know me."

His touch unnerved her, which was the point. "How can you be certain I don't know you? No one is invisible, Mr. Flynn."

The mattress shifted and fabric rustled as he leaned close. His face came so near to hers she could feel his breath on her skin. Her own ability to breathe stalled.

"I know this because you have never seen my face. A name is only a name. It's the face—the eyes—that tell the story, and I will know yours."

With every ounce of courage she possessed, she forced herself to turn fully toward him, putting their mouths mere millimeters apart. "Then show me your face and we'll know for certain."

She felt his smile. "You are very brave, Sadie Buchanan. Or perhaps you are more naive than I thought."

"I thought you had me all figured out, Mr. Flynn."

"So did I."

He drew away and she dared to breathe again.

"You have a command performance this morning, Ms. Buchanan." The mattress shifted again as he stood. "I hope for your sake you pass the series of tests you are about to encounter. If some part of you recognizes that you're in over your head, you might consider quitting now. I'm confident the Council would be willing to permit a quick, merciful death if you confessed the truth before wasting more of their time."

"I'm not a quitter, Mr. Flynn." Sadie dropped her feet to the floor. "If you knew me at all, you would know this."

The next sound she heard was the door closing and then locking.

Just to be sure he was actually gone and not waiting in the darkness, she stood and moved around the walls of the room, reaching out to ensure he wasn't standing in the center of the dark space.

She leaned against the door and closed her eyes. He might be right about one thing—there was a very strong possibility she was in over her head.

THE GUARD USHERED her out the exit. This one, like the ones yesterday and the men who had accompanied Prentiss, wore a camouflage military uniform. The boots were military style, as well. Outside, Sadie squinted at the light. It seemed so bright she had to remind herself it wasn't the sun. There was no sky because this place was underground somehow.

"Where is this place?" she asked the man ushering her along. "Underground? In a cave?" If it was a cave, it was a really large cave. Maybe it was built into a mountainside. That would explain how they'd driven directly in and why the facility had not been located by any sort of aerial surveillance.

As usual, the man ushering her along said nothing. Even when he'd opened her cell a few minutes ago, he hadn't spoken. She had gotten up from the cot and walked out, grateful to escape the concrete box.

"If we're underground…" Sadie stopped, causing him to almost trip over her. "Technically I don't need these cuffs. Where would I go if I ran?"

He glared at her, grabbed her by the upper arm and steered her forward.

"Where are we going?"

Still not a word.

The smaller buildings, almost like cabins, captured her attention again. Living quarters for those in charge, she surmised. Somewhere around here there would be a barracks for those members like the one escorting her this morning. She wondered about the man who had come to her cell sometime during the night. He probably lived in one of those private quarters.

"Were you on duty all night?"

Still no answer. He walked forward, his gaze straight ahead.

"A man came into my cell." She almost stumbled trying to look back over her shoulder at the mute guard as she spoke. But she was glad she did. He made the slightest little flinch in response but quickly schooled his face. She couldn't decide if he'd felt a fleeting hint of concern that she might fall or if the idea of the man who visited her unsettled him somehow.

"He tried to scare me."

No reaction.

"But he didn't scare me. If he'd intended to kill me, he would have."

"There are worse things than dying."

His fingers wrapped around her upper arm once more and ushered her toward a building on the left. The sign posted by the door read Clinic. She wanted to question him about the comment, but he ushered her through the entrance and walked away before she could. A woman wearing a white uniform took charge of Sadie.

"The guard will wait for you outside," the nurse, doctor, whatever she was, explained.

The woman, her black hair slicked back in a tight bun, led the way to a plain white room with an exam table as well as a side table loaded with medical equipment. Sadie decided the woman was a nurse or technician. She checked Sadie's temperature and then led the way back into the corridor.

In the next room, there was yet another examination table. A stack of neatly folded sweatpants and a tee sat on the table. Beyond that was a curtain—the type that would hang over a shower.

The nurse pulled a key from her pocket and removed the cuffs, then gestured to the curtain. "Take off your clothes and shower. Use the soap in the bottle."

Sadie didn't argue. She took off her clothes, got into the shower and washed her hair and body as instructed. When she'd finished and stepped out of the shower, the woman—nurse, whatever she was—waited by the exam table. She wore an apron, a face mask and gloves. Stirrups now extended from one end of the table.

"We'll do your exam now."

No point in arguing. Sadie climbed onto the exam table and placed her feet in the stirrups. A close physical examination followed. She rolled Sadie onto her side and checked her back and buttocks. She scanned her arms and legs, hands and feet. Her face and scalp. Then she did a pelvic exam.

Sadie grimaced. "You looking for anything in particular?"

They had scanned her thoroughly yesterday. This seemed a bit overkill.

The woman peeled off her gloves and tossed them into a trash receptacle. "Put on your clothes."

Sadie complied. When the fresh sweats and tee hung on her body, the nurse recuffed her and led her back out the front entrance to where the guard waited. From there, he led Sadie toward yet another building, this one about the same size as the clinic. The sign on the door read Council. The building was like all the rest, gray, like concrete. Austere. This one was a one-story like the clinic and the detention center.

As soon as they stepped inside the building Sadie understood this was a place of importance. The floor was carpeted. Something commercial with low pile, but enough to quiet footsteps. The walls weren't a stark white as all the others had been. This was more of a beige.

"What did you mean when you said there were worse things than dying?"

"Wait here." He steered her toward the waiting bench. "Maybe you won't have to find out."

Sadie sat on the bench against the wall and watched as he walked away. She ignored the idea that he had a point about there being some things worse than dying. For now, she preferred to focus on more optimistic scenarios. She had a feeling she was on a dangerous precipice. Whatever happened in the next few minutes would determine her future. One slip either way and she could go over the edge completely.

Minutes passed. Three, then four and five. Eventually ten. Sadie crossed her legs, uncrossed them and then crossed them again. She swung her foot up and down. Someone in this place was watching her. She might as well show them how thoroughly unimpressed and utterly bored she was.

A door on the opposite side of the corridor, a few yards beyond where she sat, opened. A different guard—she recognized the camo uniform but not the face—strode to her, pulled her to her feet and shepherded her toward the door he'd exited. The room was fairly large. A long table stood across the far end; seven, no eight men were seated on the other side. One chair sat on this side of the table. Sadie suspected that chair was for her. The guard nudged her forward, confirming her suspicion. When she'd taken a seat, he waited behind her.

Most of the men were old and Caucasian. Not a particularly big surprise. There was one, however, who was not so old. A few years older than Sadie. Maybe forty. Blond hair. Piercing gray eyes. He stared at her, as did the others, but there was something about his stare that penetrated far deeper. They wore civilian clothes. Jeans, short-sleeved shirts—some button-down, others pullovers—and hiking boots. Except for one.

Of all those present, the only person among them she had seen before was the man named Prentiss. He wore the same style overalls and long-sleeved shirt he'd worn in their first meeting. No fedora this time.

He spoke first. "Agent Buchanan, you've created quite a stir around here." He glanced side to side, acknowledging his colleagues. "We're mostly in agreement as to what should become of you. There's a single holdout, preventing a final decision."

Sadie made a face. "I'm not sure I understand, Mr. Prentiss. You haven't heard what I have to say. Maybe you're not interested in protecting your assets and followers."

He stared directly at her, his glare as deadly as any weapon she'd ever faced. "I don't think you understand, Agent Buchanan. We have no interest in anything you have to say. We have our doubts as to the worth of anything you might have to offer and we've decided we have no patience for whatever game you're playing."

Not exactly the reaction she'd hoped for. Time to throw out the ace up her sleeve. "Mr. Trenton Pollard." She scanned the faces as she said the name, looking for a reaction or some indication that one or more of those present recognized the name. Everyone seated at the table—except the younger man—had shoulder-length hair, a full beard and mustache, hiding a good portion of their faces, but not one of them outwardly flinched, grimaced or so much as batted an eye.

"The Bureau and the ATF," she went on, "have targeted Resurrection with the intention of taking down those in power, starting with you, Mr. Prentiss. They consider you the weak link in this group. The necessary information to accomplish this feat will be provided by Mr. Pollard. It's my understanding there's more than simply your location, far more, he plans to share."

All eyes stared at her.

Good or bad, she'd shown her hand—her only hand. Now the ball was in their court.

She had nothing else.

Except what she could make up as she went along. She'd always been fairly good at improvising.

The men whispered among themselves, save the younger one. He sat staring at Sadie without saying a word or even glancing at anyone else. That he still watched her so closely had begun to get under her skin. She kept her attention on the others, hoping all that going back and forth was in her best interest.

Finally, a hush fell over the group and Prentiss settled his attention on her once more. "Agent Buchanan, we still have reservations about your decision to come here with this so-called warning. Though I will give you this, you have our attention. Still, my question to you is what could you possibly hope to gain?"

Now for the improvising. "I screwed up." She shrugged. "I had an opportunity to pad my bank account and I took it. I see no reason to share the dirty details. Sadly, two days ago I found out an investigation had been opened and my assets were about to be frozen. I moved a few things around but there was no way I was going to be able to disappear quickly enough. I needed someplace to go ASAP. Someplace they wouldn't be able to find me. Since they haven't been able to find you in all this time, I figured we could help each other out. The information would buy my way in. Then I found out Pollard is about to spill his guts. I'm assuming your organization has a backup plan for disappearing."

"I fear you have overestimated your worth, Agent Buchanan."

Well, hell.

"I regret that you feel that way." She stood.

There it was. The no-go she had hoped wouldn't be thrown out. Still, he had mentioned a holdout. Maybe, just maybe the game wasn't over yet.

When no one said anything else, she offered, "Since there's no place for me here, I guess I'll just have to take my chances trying to outrun the Bureau's reach. I wish you well in doing the same. They are coming, Mr. Prentiss. Trust me on that one."

A remote smile tugged at the old man's face. "Perhaps you should have done your due diligence when weighing your options, Agent. You see, once you're here, there's only one way to leave."

She didn't need a more detailed explanation.

The Council had decided her fate.

Death.

Chapter Five

"What happens now?"

As usual, the guard said nothing while he steered Sadie out of the building. She hadn't actually expected him to answer her question, but she needed to try. He was the one person who had spoken to her besides Prentiss, even if it had been only once.

And there was the man who had visited her in the dark of her cell.

Definitely wasn't the guard. His voice was different. He smelled different, too. This close it was obvious her guard wasn't freshly showered like the man who'd sneaked into her cell. The stranger who'd made that middle-of-the-night appearance had smelled clean, like soap—the kind of soap used by a man who cared how he smelled. His hair had been lighter, as well; a blond or maybe a gray.

Frankly, she hadn't encountered anyone else who met the smell-good criteria. She thought of the blond man in the room where her appearance before the powers that be had taken place. He had seemed nearer to her age. Considering his light-colored hair, he could have been the one, though she hadn't been close enough to him during the questioning to pick up on his scent.

Didn't matter, she supposed. They hadn't bought her story so living past this moment was growing more and more unlikely. Not exactly the way she had seen things going. She was still breathing so no need to give up just yet. There might be time to turn this around.

"Are you supposed to kill me?"

Her guard just kept walking, shepherding her along as he went. He wasn't so old. Early forties, maybe. It was difficult to tell. He was tall, reasonably muscled. He looked fit. The woodland greens uniform molded to strong arms and legs and a broad chest. His complexion wasn't as pale as she would have expected considering this place—wherever the hell it was—appeared to be sheltered from the sun. Now that she thought about it, the old men who'd sat around the table, the younger one, as well, had good coloring. They either had tanning beds around here someplace or these people spent time in the sun outside these walls.

But where?

Gardens? Fields? Wasn't part of the doomsday prepper thing attaining self-sufficiency? They either raised their own food or bartered with others of like mind.

"If I'm going to die, why not talk to me? It won't matter in a little while anyway, right?"

Despite her urging, he kept his mouth shut. He led her beyond the quad and all the buildings that seemed to circle the place where she'd been questioned by the group of elders or leaders. The final building they approached wasn't really a building. It was more like a massive carport. SUVs and trucks and a couple of military-type vehicles were parked beneath its expansive canopy. On the far end a long low building with half a dozen overhead doors connected to the covered parking. Vehicle maintenance, she supposed.

The guard didn't stop dragging her along until they were beyond the parked vehicles. Several small metal domes dotted the ground. At first she thought of underground gasoline tanks, but that didn't make sense since four huge tanks stood next to the maintenance building. Maybe the aboveground ones were water tanks. There had to be a water supply in here somewhere.

Her guard ushered her to the nearest dome and opened it. Beneath the metal dome was a steel wheel, the kind you would see on a submarine door. Grunting with the effort, he twisted it to the right and then raised the lid-like door upward. Beyond the door was a ladder that disappeared into the ground.

The guard straightened and reached for her secured hands. When he'd removed her restraints, he gestured to the ladder. "You go on now."

She looked from the hole in the ground to him. "What's down there?"

He stared at her a moment. "You'll see."

"Really? You couldn't think of anything more original than *you'll see*?" She ordered her heart to slow its galloping. This was that moment, the one where she had to decide if she was going to cooperate or make a run for it.

She glanced around. There was no readily visible place to run. Her guard didn't appear to be armed but that didn't mean that others who were close by weren't. Besides, where the hell would she go? And there were those guard towers.

"Running won't do you no good."

He didn't need a crystal ball or to be a mind reader to recognize what she had on her mind. "Tell me what's down there and I'll get out of your hair."

With a big put-upon breath, he said, "There are people like you down there."

"Prisoners?" She stared him directly in the eyes.

He nodded.

"Are they dead or alive?" That was the big question now.

He shrugged. "Does it matter? Like I told you, there's some things worse than dying. This is one of them."

He said a mouthful with that. So much for rescuing Levi Winters. Then again, maybe he was down there, too. "Well, thanks for the heads-up."

It was now or never. If she was going to make a run for it—

"You see that hole in the wall to your right?"

His words yanked her attention back to him. "What hole?"

Even as she asked the question, a small square opened and the barrel of a rifle extended from the wall. Apparently there were guards monitoring the walls of this place from numerous vantage points, not just the obvious towers she had seen. Running would definitely be a waste of time.

"If you run, you're dead."

Made her decision considerably easier. "Got it."

Sadie put a hand on the ladder and swung one foot, then the other onto a rung. When she'd scaled down about four rungs, the squeak of metal on metal drew her attention upward as the hatch-type door closed. She drew in a big breath and let it go. Nothing to do now but see if there were any other living humans down here.

Thankfully it wasn't completely dark. Emergency-type lighting, dim though it might be, was placed along the downward path. When she reached the bottom of the ladder, a good twenty feet below the hatch, a long tunnel lay ahead of her. More of that dim recessed lighting kept the darkness at bay. The temperature was far cooler down here and there was that earthy, musty smell in the air.

Speaking of air, it was obviously pumped down here somehow. She took another breath. Hoped like hell it was anyway.

"You're the first female we've had down here."

Sadie whipped around at the muttered words. The man stood only inches from her. How had he sneaked up on her like that? Her instincts were generally far more in tune with her surroundings.

"Who are you?" She kept her shoulders square and met his curious gaze without flinching.

Unlike the men in the compound, this man was as pale as a ghost. His hair was a stringy brown and hung down around his hunched shoulders. His clothes were like hers, sweats and a tee, only his looked old and were filthy and ragged. His feet were bare and dirty.

"George." He licked his lips. "What about you? Got a name?"

"Sadie." She braced to make a run for it but decided to hold off until she got a better indication of his intentions. It wasn't as if there was any real place to go and George here likely knew the place like the back of his hand.

"Sadie." He rolled her name around in his mouth as if he were tasting it.

She glanced around again. "What is this place?"

"The big dig." He chuckled, the sound as rusty as his teeth.

She forced her lips into a smile. "Like in Boston. I gotcha. Where are you digging to, George?"

He shrugged one of those bony shoulders. "Wherever they tell us to."

"They tell you things?" She jerked her head up toward the hatch at the top of the ladder.

"Orders. Yeah. They send 'em down along with food and water."

Thank God. That was her next concern. "So they feed you. That's good."

Another of those spasmodic shrugs. "Enough to survive. Most of the time anyway."

Well, great. Just great. "What now, George?"

"Can't say for sure. You work until we hear different." He started forward into the tunnel.

"Work?" Sadie walked alongside him. The tunnel was wide, plenty wide enough for about three people to walk side by side. Overhead, wood and steel supports kept the ground from caving in. This was no slipshod operation. Some amount of engineering know-how had gone into what they were doing.

"On the dig, of course. We're working on a tunnel headed south to Huntland. Already got one finished to Winchester."

"Sounds like a sizable operation."

He croaked another of those rusty laughs. "The Resurrection's got big plans, Sadie."

Clearly. "How many workers are down here?"

"About twenty."

"They're all prisoners?"

"Yep. Some of us were part of them before we screwed up. I guess getting put down here was better than the alternative."

That remained debatable. "What about those who weren't part of the Resurrection?"

"Some were taken from the outside for their knowledge or skill and put down here."

"Knowledge?"

"Contractors. You know, builders. A couple ex-military guys who were assigned to the air force base."

A point she would need to pass along if she ever got out of here. "You have tools and equipment?"

"Sure." He glanced at her, his brown eyes sunken and hollow. "Lots of tools."

Sadie followed him down the length of the first tunnel and then they hit a sort of fork in the road, except there were about four different ways to go. He took the fork farthest to the left.

"Do you dig up to the surface, creating an egress or access point?" This could be a good thing.

He shook his head, deflating her hopes. "Only so

far up. The rest is up to them. They do that part from above. We're not allowed to get too close to the surface."

Nevertheless, that meant those areas were closer to freedom. "Sounds like they've got it all figured out."

Her escort grunted an agreement.

The sounds of metal clanging and low voices rumbled in the distance. "We're almost to the dig where we're working now."

Ahead, the outline of bodies moving came into focus. Men wore helmets with attached lights. They swung pickaxes, hefted shovels and other digging tools. A battery-operated jackhammer rattled off. Sadie surveyed the cacophony of activity.

"This is what I'll be doing?"

George stopped and faced her. She did the same. "You give me those flip-flops you're wearing and I'll tell you."

She could do that. They were a sort of one-size-fits-all and pretty much worthless as foot protection went. "Sure."

As soon as she kicked off the footwear, he snatched the thongs and tugged them onto his grimy feet. When he'd finished, he looked directly at her and held up his end of the bargain. "We'll get the word—usually don't take long, I'd say between now and tomorrow—then we'll know whether you're a worker or supplies."

"Supplies?" A frown creased its way across her forehead. Deep inside she had a very bad feeling this was the worse-than-dying thing the guard had mentioned.

"Sometimes they stop feeding us. Like when we don't get as much done as they want. Some of us get sick and can't work as fast. They punish us then. If you're supplies, then you'll be the emergency food."

Oh hell.

He shrugged those bony shoulders again. "You'd be surprised how long even someone as skinny as you will last."

She glanced around. Said the only thing she could think to say in response to that unnerving statement. "Doesn't seem as though you have any way to keep your *supplies* from going bad."

"No need. We wouldn't eat you all at once. We always keep supplies alive as long as possible. Take an arm or a leg, then another when that one is gone. It works out pretty good. By the time the supplies is dead, we can finish off the edible parts before they start to rot."

Made an eerie kind of sense, she supposed. Unless you happen to be the main course.

No one paid much attention to them as they arrived at the worksite. The man who'd served as her guide—George—handed her a pickax and motioned to a spot for her to start. Sadie walked wide around the other workers and started hefting the ax. She couldn't help glancing over her shoulder now and then just to make sure no one was watching her. Most of the group looked like the man who now sported her flip-flops. Baggy, ragged clothes. Long, stringy hair. Filthy. Pale and weary looking.

Now that she had arrived they didn't talk so the only sounds were the pecking and scraping at the earth. The rattling jackhammer. And in those rare moments of silence, the breathing and grunting. During the next few minutes several things crossed her mind. Where did they sleep? Relieve themselves? And if she was the only female to show up, would she be raped if she tried to sleep?

Maybe she would ask George the next chance she got.

A loud sound like the single dong of a doorbell echoed through the rhythmic poking and pecking and grunting. She glanced around, her attention settling on George. He put down his shovel and started back the way they had come. The other workers looked from George to her before going back to work.

Apparently the news had arrived. Maybe dropped down from the top of that ladder the way she basically had been.

Her fingers tightened on the handle of the ax.

She supposed she would know soon enough if she was to be a permanent worker or emergency supplies.

SMITH WAITED FOR Prentiss to show up.

He'd asked for a meeting with the man immediately after the Council questioned Buchanan. The old man had decided to take his time. He knew Smith was not happy with the decision and he wanted him to wallow in his frustration.

Smith crossed the Council's private meeting room and stared out the window. For more than three decades the Resurrection had been clawing its way into this mountainside. Back then there had been only whispers about a group of doomsday survivalists sprouting up in Franklin County. No one really knew or understood what they were. Smith wasn't sure if even those early leaders of the small group understood what they would become over time.

Smith shook his head. They had become something entirely different from what they once were—from what they were supposed to be. Preparing to survive mankind's destruction of himself was one thing, preparing for a war with those not like-minded was something else altogether.

But things had escalated in the past decade. Now it was about power and greed for the few rather than the safety and survival of the many.

"Making you wait was unavoidable."

Smith turned to face the man who had entered the room. Rayford Prentiss was an old man now, but that didn't stop him from being utterly ruthless. Age had not mellowed him at all—in fact, it had done the opposite. He was as mean as hell and cared nothing for human life.

Prentiss poured himself a hefty serving of bourbon and lifted the glass to his lips. Smith watched, his patience thinning all the more with each passing moment. But he would not allow this bastard to see his mounting discontent. He couldn't let that happen until the time was right.

Soon, very soon. Sooner than Smith had anticipated.

The Buchanan woman's arrival and the name she had tossed about was a warning. Something was about to go down. Smith needed to prepare. To do that, information was required—information from Buchanan. Dropping her into the hole had been premature. The move was a blatant challenge against what Smith had suggested.

"You're displeased with my decision about the woman," Prentiss announced as he poured himself a second drink.

"She obviously has connections. Those connections could prove to be valuable."

Prentiss sat the bottle of bourbon back onto the credenza and belted out a laugh. "Because she spouted the name of a man who has been gone from here for years? If she had connections, she would know that Pollard is likely dead and buried. Of no use or threat to anyone."

"Maybe, maybe not. Either way, you're missing the big picture, old man." Smith strode toward him. "How much longer do you believe you can continue to rule these people like a dictator?"

"You believe you would be better as the head of Council."

It wasn't a question. Smith purposely made no bones about his feelings. He wanted Prentiss to know that his days were numbered. Far more so than he realized. Smith had to bite back the smile. Everything was going to change and this greedy bastard had no idea what was coming.

"You're the only one left who believes in your vision. No one on the Council agrees with your methods. They merely tolerate you out of respect for what once was."

Anger sparked in the old man's eyes. "You mean your father? I've gone too far beyond *his* vision of what the Resurrection was?"

Smith gritted his teeth for a moment. "Don't compare yourself to my father."

Prentiss moved in closer, glared up at Smith, his fury barely held in check. "You were gone for ten years. You only came back when you heard he was dead. If he hadn't named you to the Council with his dying breath, you would be in the tunnels where you belong."

The one thing that had gotten Smith through the past two years was knowing that in the end—when this was all over—he would be able to look Rayford Prentiss in the eyes and tell him the truth that no one else could know. The shock alone would likely kill the old son of a bitch.

Smith lived for that day.

Prentiss cleared his face of emotion. "You would have me change my decision about the woman."

Another statement. "You can do as you please, including change your mind."

No one questioned Prentiss. At least no one except Smith. His first month here, Smith had drawn the line in the sand. So far, Prentiss had not crossed it. He blustered and stomped all around it, but he was careful not to push too far. There were too many who remained faithful to the memory of Avery Flynn. Prentiss wouldn't risk a rebellion. Not at this crucial juncture.

"And why would I change my mind?"

"Buchanan could prove useful," Smith said. "She didn't pull that name out of thin air. Consider how few people know what that name stands for."

Smith had him there and he knew it. Trenton Pollard had been an ATF agent. He was the only one to burrow in so deeply without being discovered. Fury roared through Smith at the memory. Pollard had burrowed deep into Resurrection. Almost took them down and then he disappeared. Except he hadn't gone far. Like the FBI agent Jack Kemp. He'd ended up buried not far from here. But Prentiss didn't know that for sure. No one except Smith knew. Although Kemp had been a casualty of the Winters family, he and Pollard had been after the same goal: the end of the Resurrection.

They weren't the first but they were the most memorable—the ones who had infiltrated the deepest.

Until now.

Prentiss made a face of dismissal. "I have my doubts as to any potential use she might prove to have."

"Are you willing to take that risk?" He wasn't. Smith was well aware that his bravado was merely for show. Particularly now that the possibility had been publicly brought to his attention. He would never give Smith that kind of ammunition to use against him if he turned out to be wrong. "At the very least she could prove a valuable bargaining chip in the future."

"Very well. For you, I will change my mind. But the risk is yours. If she becomes a liability, she will be your liability."

The two stared at each other for a long moment. Smith imagined Prentiss wished him dead. The feeling was mutual.

But not just yet.

"One day, old man, you'll learn to trust my judgment."

Prentiss made a scoffing sound. "Perhaps."

The old man walked out, leaving Smith staring after him. Rayford Prentiss would know soon enough.

Smith summoned the guard who had been assigned to Buchanan's security. He wondered if she would ever understand that she owed her life to him. If the two of them survived what was to come, he would see that she recognized what a serious error in judgment she had made coming to this place.

What the hell had she been thinking?

What had the Bureau been thinking?

He supposed it was possible this was some sort of rescue mission. Maybe for Levi Winters, though Smith didn't see him as a valuable enough target to risk the life of an agent.

Whatever had brought her here, she had put a kink in his timeline.

Now he was left with no choice but to make drastic adjustments. Otherwise everything could go wrong. The past two years of his life would be wasted.

That could not happen.

Chapter Six

Sadie did as she had been ordered and kept digging but part of her attention remained on the man coming toward her. Most of the other workers glanced her way but none dared to stop and stare. They wouldn't risk being caught slacking. The men in charge, George and three others, didn't mind bopping a slacker on the head with a shovel or nudging them in the kidneys with an ax handle. Judging by the scars on some of the workers, things could get a lot worse.

Whether it was survival or just the hint of control that came with being in charge, George and his peers appeared to take their positions very seriously. Maybe there were perks not readily visible. Obviously it wasn't clothes or a good hot bath or more to eat. Everyone in this hole looked the same as far as their state of health, ragged attire and level of filth went.

George stopped a couple of steps from her. "Come with me."

The best she could estimate she'd climbed down that ladder about two hours ago. Already blisters were forming on her hands and her muscles ached from hefting the ax. As much as she didn't look forward to days or weeks or months of this sort of hard labor, she would take that any day of the week over becoming the rest of the crew's dinner.

"Why?" Might as well know now. The whole crew would hear the news soon enough. Why keep everyone in suspense?

"They want you back up there." He jerked his head upward.

Sadie's knees almost gave way on her. "I have to go back up the ladder?"

She framed the question in a less than optimistic manner since the rest of the workers were listening. No need to rub in the idea that she was out of here. If she sounded hesitant or worried maybe they wouldn't feel so bad that they weren't the ones climbing out of this hole. Then again, there was no way to guess what waited for her up there.

There are some things worse than dying.

Still, she preferred continuing to breathe over the alternative.

"Let's go," George said rather than answer her question.

She tossed her pickax to the ground and followed the man back through the long, dimly lit tunnel. He didn't speak, just walked along, his newly attained flip-flops clacking in the silence.

When they reached the ladder, he squinted his eyes to look at her. "Somebody up there must have plans for you. Once you're down here, you don't usually go back up."

She thought of the man who had visited her in the dark and then of Prentiss. If either of them wanted her back, it couldn't be good. She would know soon enough, she supposed. If Levi Winters was still alive, he was obviously up there. She hadn't seen him down here.

"Guess so." She shrugged.

He nodded toward the ladder. "Thanks for the flip-flops."

She resisted the urge to tell him that if she had anything to do with it, he and the others would not be down here much longer. But she couldn't take the risk. Not to mention, at this point she couldn't guarantee anything. So far this mission had been an epic failure.

"Sure."

She climbed the ladder. As she reached the upper rungs the hatch-type door opened. The guard—the same one from before—waited for her. She blinked repeatedly, then squinted against the brighter light. Maybe it was coming up from the dim lighting, but she realized that the lighting was very similar to sunlight. More so than she had realized. Maybe there were solar tubes or some other discreet way of pumping in sunlight without being easily detected by anyone flying over the area.

The guard closed the hatch and glanced at her feet. He didn't ask what happened to her footwear. He probably had a good idea.

He ushered her away from the small field of domes. She decided since she'd only seen one access point while she was down there, all the other domes must be for pumping air into the tunnels.

"Where am I going now?"

He probably wouldn't tell her but it didn't hurt to ask.

As she'd expected, they continued forward without him responding. When they reached the detention center, they kept walking. Once they were beyond the Council building where she'd been questioned, they reached the area with the row of smaller buildings. He steered her toward the one marked with a number nine. At the door, he knocked and waited.

Sadie's fingers and palms burned and she wished she could wash her hands. The blisters stung. Her gaze drifted down to her feet. And they were filthy. Her pink toenails looked out of place on those feet.

The door opened and the blond man from the group who'd questioned her today stood in the threshold.

He nodded and the guard walked away. "Come inside."

This he said to Sadie. His voice was deep, curt. His silvery gaze unflinching.

Sadie did as he ordered, crossing the threshold and entering unknown territory. Nothing new. Encountering the unexpected was a major part of her mission history. If she and Levi Winters were lucky, this mission would flounder its way to success while they were both still breathing.

Her host closed the door behind her. The cabin-like structure was basically one room. A bed, table and chairs, and a small sofa were the only furnishings. On the far side of the room was a small kitchenette. A door beyond the kitchenette likely led to a bathroom. Next to the bed was a smaller table that appeared to serve as a desk since a laptop sat atop it. All the comforts of home, she mused.

He pulled out a chair from the larger, round table. "Sit."

She sat.

Rather than secure her in some manner as she'd expected, he moved to the other side of the table and sat down, his clasped hands settled on the tabletop.

"You present quite the quandary, Sadie Buchanan."

She had been told this more than once, usually by a superior at the Bureau. The words rarely turned out to be a compliment. More often, she was reminded of proper procedure and other prescribed protocols.

"Tell me what I need to do to rectify whatever the problem is." She placed her hands on the table, wanted him to see the blisters. "I'd like to know I have a place here."

He stared at her for a long while without saying more. She decided he was even closer to her age than she'd first thought. Thirty-five or thirty-six, maybe. He was tall, looked strong and his skin was unmarred by scars, unlike many of those she'd seen above and below ground in this compound. Obviously, he'd never been in a lower-level position.

"I don't trust you."

He said this in scarcely more than a whisper and still the sound startled her. He hadn't spoken in so long, she was caught completely off guard. And there was something else. The harsh whisper was somehow familiar. She studied his blond hair and then she leaned forward, putting her face closer to his, and she inhaled deeply, drawing in his scent.

It was him.

The man who had visited her in the darkness. *Smith Flynn.*

She eased back into her seat. "If it makes you feel any better, I don't trust you, either, Mr. Flynn."

He smiled. The expression was so scant she might not have noticed had she not been staring at him so intently.

"You would be wise to be grateful for my intervention on your behalf."

She met his intent stare with one of her own. "So you're the one who had me yanked back out of that hole." She hummed a note of surprise. "Interesting."

Made sense, she supposed, since she'd been brought directly here.

"Is that your way of saying thank you?"

She stared directly into those silvery eyes for a long moment before she answered, opting to give him a taste of his own medicine. "Should I be thankful?"

He glanced at her blistered palms. "I can send you back, if you prefer. The rest of the Council recommended you for emergency supplies."

Damn. She moistened her lips, tried her best not to show how immensely grateful she was not to still be in that hole. "That won't be necessary. I am thankful you rescued me, Mr. Flynn. I suppose I'm a little worried about why you would go against all the others."

"You need a bath, Agent Buchanan."

He pushed back from the table and walked to the

door. When he opened it, her guard still waited on the other side. "Get her cleaned up and put back in her cell," Flynn ordered.

"Yes, sir."

Sadie didn't wait to be told what to do next. She pushed to her feet and headed for the door. When she stood next to this man who had saved her for now, she hesitated. "Will I see you again?"

"If you do as you're told, you will see me again."

She walked out, followed the guard in his camo uniform. As usual, he said nothing. Relief sagged her shoulders. She was tired and hungry. Maybe after the bath she would be allowed to eat.

She decided to go broke on information. "I haven't seen Levi Winters. Is he in solitary or something?"

The guard didn't respond.

"He's been here longer than me," she went on, as if he'd spoken. "Maybe he's already assigned to a job. I didn't see him at the big dig."

At the door to the detention center, he finally looked at her. "You don't need to worry about anyone but yourself. That's the way you stay alive. You do what you're told and you don't ask questions."

She nodded. "Got it."

Inside, he took her to another room, not her cell, and ordered the female in the white uniform there to see that she got cleaned up. This was only the second time she'd seen another woman. When her guard had left, Sadie turned to the other woman. "Hi."

The woman looked her up and down. "After your bath we'll do something for those blisters."

Sadie followed her to a large room that was mostly a huge shower. Three freestanding tubs sat to one side. Hooks along the wall were likely for towels. The other woman turned on the water in one of the tubs and then she left the room. More than ready for cleaning up, Sadie walked over to the tub and started to undress.

The woman returned with a towel, more of the ugly sweats and a pair of sneakers. "Size seven?" She glanced at Sadie's feet as she asked the question.

Sadie nodded. "Yes, thanks."

"Don't linger too long," the woman said. "When you're done, come back to my office."

Sadie nodded and thanked her again. The woman disappeared.

The extra-warm water felt amazing as she stepped into it. She ignored the burn when it covered her hands. A sigh slipped from her lips as she permitted herself a moment to relax. She had earned it by God. The woman had said not to linger so she didn't. She washed her hair and smoothed what appeared to be homemade soap over her skin. When she was finished, she dried off and pulled on the clothes. Still no underwear and no socks, but she was grateful for something more than flip-flops.

She exited the shower room and walked in the direction she'd come. The only other door went into the woman's office. It looked more like an exam room. The woman got up from her desk and gestured for Sadie to sit in the only other chair.

Sadie watched as she gathered gauze, tape and some sort of salve. "You're a nurse?"

The woman glanced at her. "I am."

She was young. Midtwenties, Sadie decided. "They let you go to nursing school?"

The woman paused in her work of applying salve to Sadie's palms.

Damn, she'd obviously asked a question she shouldn't have. "Sorry. I was just curious."

"I had just finished nursing school in Tullahoma when they brought me back here."

Sadie held her gaze. "Oh."

The other woman's attention flitted away as she wrapped gauze around Sadie's right hand. "I thought I didn't want to come back but then they told me I'm getting married this year." Her face lit with a smile. "I was happy then."

Sadie moistened her dry lips. The young woman had gotten a taste of freedom during nursing school and she hadn't wanted to come back so they had dangled a carrot. "Who's the lucky guy?"

"His name is Levi. We met a long time ago but then he left. I never forgot him. I always told my father I missed him."

"Levi Winters?" Was that possible?

She nodded. "You know him?"

Sadie gave her head a slight nod rather than flat-out lie. "Who's your father?"

"Rayford Prentiss." She beamed another smile. "The head of the Council. He has many children here. Of course, we're all grown up now. My father says it's time for more children."

The picture cleared for Sadie. The Resurrection numbers were dwindling and Prentiss intended to plump up the population.

"Are there lots of married couples here?"

"Some, yes. But more are getting married this year. Some of us will be moving out, integrating into the outside communities. It's—" She snapped her mouth shut and her face paled as if she'd only just realized she had said way too much to a prisoner.

"I understand," Sadie said quickly. "It's a great plan. Mr. Prentiss is a visionary."

The other woman's smile returned. "He is. I didn't want to see it when I was younger, but I see it clearly now."

Sadie wondered if the powers that be at the Bureau and the ATF had any idea what Prentiss was planning.

The man had his sights set on far more than this compound.

SMITH RAN HARD, pushing for another mile. There were times when he left the compound for Council business but this was the only way he left the compound on a daily basis. He ran six miles every day. Did the rest of his workout in the rec center at the compound. But when he ran he needed the freedom he couldn't get within the center running around and around a track. To find that freedom he ran through the woods. He had a route that took him through the areas where he was less likely to run into another human. Only once had he encountered another man and he'd been a hunter with no desire for small talk. He'd been on a mission that involved prey of the four-legged kind.

Smith made his usual quick stops. Leaned against a tree in one location and pretended to check his right shoe. There was nothing on the ground at the base of the tree. Nothing tucked into the moss. Then he moved on. His next stop was the sparkling stream that bubbled out from the mountainside. He knelt on one knee and cupped his hand for a drink. The water was crystal clear and cool despite the heat of the late summer days. He scanned the rocky bottom of the stream as he drank. Nothing. He sipped the water and then moved on. There was one final stop, the rocky ridge where he stopped again. This time he tied his shoe. There was nothing tucked between the stones.

No message.

He had been certain there would be something. A warning of some trouble headed his way. Or of some planned rebel uprising. The one time that had happened had secured once and for all his position on the Council. This time, however, he'd expected news of Sadie Buchanan's true mission. Some word of other trouble he should anticipate. But no message had been sent.

There could be only one explanation. Buchanan's mission was off the books, in all probability unsanctioned.

She was on her own.

Damn it. He couldn't take care of a rogue federal agent and complete his own mission. He was already on thin ice with Prentiss.

The memory of Avery Flynn carried a great deal of weight, as did his warning when a rebel faction had planned a takeover. But Prentiss remained more respected. If a choice had to be made between the two of them, Smith would not likely come out on top.

There was one other thing he could do. He could go down to the church and find the most recent newspaper. A message went into the classifieds only if there was no other option. If his contact had felt he was being watched in the woods, he would not leave a message at any of the regular drops.

Smith headed in that direction at a steady pace. His destination was just over three miles so less than half an hour was required to make the journey. He would have been able to go much faster if not for the winding, rocky paths through the woods. The paths were ones used by hunters and hikers, nothing made by anyone who belonged to the Resurrection.

He and the others were careful not to make new paths and to stay on the ones made by others. Slowing as he approached the church, Smith surveyed the area to ensure no one was about. The church was now defunct. Marcus Winters and his sister Sierra had been outed by their sister, who had recently been released from prison.

That was the way of secrets. They could only be kept for so long before they were found out.

His secret wouldn't keep much longer. He could not accommodate this unforeseen hitch. There was no leeway in his schedule for Sadie Buchanan and whatever trouble she had dragged in with her.

The church was empty as he'd expected. He walked to the road and checked the paper box that hung beneath the official mailbox. With the local newspaper in hand, he strode back to the church and sat down on the front steps. He opened the paper and carefully skimmed the classifieds. Nothing.

But the name Trenton Pollard had been a clear warning. He tossed the paper aside and stood. Something was happening and he needed to be able to prepare for whatever that something was.

What if his contact had been compromised?

There was no way to know.

Smith heaved a breath and returned to the woods. He picked his way back to a familiar path and jogged for a couple of miles. In the two years since going undercover he had not been faced with a situation like this one. But he'd understood this time could come. His contact could be compromised. The man was older; he could very well have fallen ill or died. Time would be required for a replacement to be situated.

The only question was whether or not Smith had the time.

He slowed to a walk when he was within a mile of the compound. For now there was little he could do beyond moving forward as if Sadie Buchanan had not suddenly appeared.

The Levi Winters issue had apparently been rectified. Prentiss had decided to use him as a breeder. Smith still found that abrupt decision strange. Had that been the beginning of whatever was happening? Perhaps Sadie Buchanan was not the real problem. Maybe it was Winters.

His brother, Marcus, had been a reliable ally for many years. Levi had been an on-again, off-again dabbler. He had been involved with Jack Kemp—yet another reason Smith couldn't understand Prentiss's sudden decision to keep him for any purpose.

Smith ensured he was not being followed as he ducked into the camouflaged pedestrian entrance to the compound. Whatever Prentiss was up to, he would keep it to himself until he was ready to move. He never shared a strategic move that involved security with any of the other Council members, much less Smith. He was far too paranoid.

There was nothing to do but remain vigilant and see how the situation played out.

Prentiss was a very astute man. He had not hung on to his position as leader of the Council by being naive or weak.

Smith supposed he should be grateful he had managed to abide the man this long. Certainly he could claim at least one record.

No one else had ever lived a lie right in front of Rayford Prentiss for this long.

Chapter Seven

"Where are we going now?"

Sadie felt grateful for the bath and the clean clothes and in particular for the salve and the bandages on her hands. But she still had a mission to attempt completing. She needed to find Levi Winters. Obviously he was still alive if Prentiss had planned his marriage to one of his daughters. Sadie decided not to try to figure out if the woman was his biological child. The idea that the old man could have dozens of children by different women made her feel ill, especially if the women had not been willing participants in the endeavors.

"The cafeteria."

Her attention slid back to the man at her side. The rumble in her stomach warned that it had been way too long since she had fueled up. No question. But maybe the trip to the cafeteria was about a new job for her. Just because she was being taken there didn't mean she would be allowed to eat.

"To work?" she asked since her guard seemed a bit more receptive to answering questions now.

"To eat."

This time her stomach growled loud enough for him to hear, too.

He grunted. She supposed that was as close to a laugh as he would permit, but she didn't miss the glint of humor in his eyes.

They entered the detention center. This time their journey took them to the left when they reached the connecting corridor that led to the cells on the right. At the end of the left corridor a set of double doors stood, the word *Cafeteria* emblazoned across the pair.

At the doors he hesitated. "Go to the serving line. Get your food and sit down. Eat and don't get into trouble. I'll be back for you in fifteen minutes."

She nodded her understanding and walked through the doors. Her guard didn't follow. There was probably a separate cafeteria for the people who belonged. There were maybe a dozen people, all wearing the same attire as she did, seated around the four tables. When she stepped up to the serving line, the man behind the counter grabbed a plastic tray and dumped beans, bread and something not readily identifiable but green in color onto the tray.

Sadie accepted the tray and walked toward the tables. Stainless steel water pitchers and cups sat on each table. The other prisoners were male. Not surprising since the number of females she had met were few and far between. The other prisoners eyed her suspiciously as she passed. She caught snatches of conversation about working in the fields or the laundry facility. There was one who sat alone at the table farthest from the serving line. He stared at his plate, visibly forcing his spoon to his mouth, chewing and then repeating.

Relief swam through Sadie. It was Levi Winters. Even in the baggy sweats and with his head bowed, she recognized him. She headed for his table, pulled out a chair and sat. Before she spoke, she reached for the pitcher and poured herself a glass of what appeared to be water. Just plain water, she hoped. Hopefully not laced with some drug to keep them under control. She still believed the man—Flynn—who had come into her room in the middle of the night had only been able to do so without her knowledge because she had been drugged with a mild sedative.

When she had downed a bite of bland-tasting beans and dry bread, she glanced at her tablemate. "You okay, Levi?"

He glanced up at the use of his name, stared at her for a moment. "Do I know you?"

She shook her head. "My name is Sadie. Your sister Cece sent me."

Hope lit in his eyes. "Is she okay?"

Sadie smiled. "She's doing great. Her name has been cleared and they've sorted the truth about what really happened when your father was murdered."

Cece had given Sadie a specific message for Levi. "Cece wanted you to know that everything is fine and none of what happened was your fault. She just wants you safe and back home."

His hopeful expression fell, and he stared at his plate once more. "They'll never let me go."

"Do you want to marry the girl?"

His head came up, his fearful gaze colliding with Sadie's. "I don't even know her. Prentiss said when I was a kid my father promised me to him for one of his daughters. He said if I didn't do exactly what was expected of me they'd put me in the tunnels." He shook his head, shuddered visibly. "I've heard about what happens to the folks who end up down there."

Nothing good. Sadie knew this firsthand. She glanced around. "Don't worry. I'll get you out of here. Just stay calm and trust me."

A frown furrowed his brow. "I don't know who you are but you're crazy if you think we'll get out of here alive. No one does. You either do what they say, or you're never seen again."

Sadie gave him a reassuring smile. "Like I said, just stay calm. Do as you're told until I tell you different."

His eyes rounded, his attention shifting over her shoulder.

Sadie glanced back just in time to see a man coming toward her. He didn't look happy. In fact, he looked angry. She stood, putting herself between Levi and the threat. "You have a problem, pal?"

The man stopped, evidently surprised that she stood up and faced him. He glared at her. "I'm going into the tunnels, because of you." He stabbed a finger into her chest. "You're damn right I have a problem."

He called her one of those truly ugly names that no woman ever wanted to be called and then he spit in her face.

Sadie swiped away the spittle with the sleeve of her sweatshirt. "I hate to hear that, but I didn't make the decision. Mr. Prentiss probably did. Why don't you take it up with him?"

His face blanched at the mention of Prentiss's name. Sadie gave herself a mental pat on the back for the quick thinking.

The man glared at her a moment longer, then walked back to his table. Sadie dragged her chair around to the end of the table and sat where she could see the rest of the people in the room. She snagged her tray and pulled it down to where she sat and forced herself to eat. Food was necessary to survival. She tasted the water—it seemed okay so she drank it down, quenching the thirst that had been dogging her since she arrived.

One by one the other prisoners in the cafeteria got up, tray in hand, and readied to leave. On their way to the tray drop, they passed Sadie, flinging whatever food they hadn't eaten at her.

She ignored them, kept shoving beans and bread into her mouth. From time to time when the food hit her in the face she flinched, but otherwise she showed no outward sign of discomfort or fear. They were all ticked off at her now. She had been pulled back from the tunnels and one of them was going in. They likely believed it was only because she was a woman. The truth of the matter was, Sadie had no idea why she'd been pulled out of the tunnels. Luck? Not likely.

"I wish I was as brave as you."

Sadie glanced at Levi. She gave him a reassuring smile. "You're doing pretty damned good, Levi. Cut yourself some slack. And don't worry, we'll be out of here before you know it."

He shook his head. "You don't understand."

Judging by his defeated expression he was more worried than relieved to know she was here. "What is it that I don't understand? I came here to find you and get you out. I will make it happen."

He swallowed hard, his throat seizing with the effort. "They're listening. I couldn't tell you. I had to do what I was told." He stood, picked up his tray. "I'm sorry. Really sorry."

As Levi walked away Sadie wondered how she had allowed her defenses and her instincts to fail her so thoroughly. She'd made an elementary mistake. One that would likely carry a heavy cost—like her life. She should have considered that Winters would have been brainwashed or indoctrinated to some degree by now.

"Well, hell."

She stood to take her tray to the drop zone but her guard appeared. "Leave it," he said, his expression as unreadable as his tone.

Sadie deposited the tray back on the table and followed the guard out of the cafeteria. The corridor was empty. The prisoners who had thrown food at her had either returned to their cells or were back at work. The guard led her back to her cell. He held her gaze a moment before he closed and locked the door. She could swear she saw a glimmer of regret in his eyes.

If the guard was feeling sorry for her, she was definitely screwed.

SMITH STEPPED OUT of the shower and dried his body. There had to be a reason he hadn't been given additional intelligence about Sadie Buchanan via his contact. The name she had tossed out, Trenton Pollard, was a code phrase warning that trouble was headed Smith's way. But there was nothing else. No message at any of the usual drop sites.

He pulled on clean jeans and a freshly laundered shirt. The dress code was fairly simple for Council members. They wore whatever they liked. Most moved back and forth between the compound and the outside community. But not Smith. He stayed here. Didn't take chances by lingering in the community.

The guards wore the camo while the workers were issued the sweats. Only those in supervisory positions or who served on the Council were allowed to wear civilian attire. The clear distinction was one of the things Flynn hated most about this place…this life.

No one should be made to feel inferior to others. One's way of life should be based on choice, not a dictatorship led by one insane, self-centered man. How the hell had so many been drawn into this life? Then again, the world was changing, and those interested numbers were dwindling.

A knock at his door drew his attention there. He finished lacing his boots and stood. "Enter."

The door opened and one of Prentiss's personal bodyguards, this one named Mitchell, stepped inside.

"Mr. Prentiss would like to see you in his private quarters."

The old man rarely summoned Smith unless there was a Council meeting…or trouble. Smith's gut said this was the latter.

"Tell him I'll be there shortly."

Mitchell gave a quick nod, then left, closing the door behind him.

Smith walked to his desk and checked the monitor on his laptop. Buchanan was in her cell. Her bandaged hands and clean sweats told him she'd behaved herself during her cleanup. There were no posted complaints of trouble involving her.

She presented a conundrum. Did he tell her who he was or did he wait for her to admit why she was really here? Her provided story wasn't cutting it for him. There was something more she was hiding.

Prentiss hadn't swallowed it, either. Smith's move this morning had bought Buchanan a little more time, but he couldn't be certain how long that time would last. He had hoped to receive word from his contact this morning to give him some sense of direction. His best course of action at this point was to hold out for any intelligence that filtered in over the next few days, assuming the trouble he worried was coming didn't show first.

Taking his time, he walked to the final cabin on Council Row and knocked on the door. When his father had been alive, he had lived in cabin one. Prentiss didn't like the idea of being that available. He wanted the rest of the Council in front of him, like a wall, protecting him from any danger that forced its way into the compound.

The bastard was a coward.

"Come in."

Smith went inside. The old man sat at his table, a steaming cup of tea in front of him.

"Join me," he offered with a wave of his hand.

Smith pulled out the chair opposite him and settled into it. "I'm good, thanks," he said, declining the tea.

Prentiss sipped his tea for a half a minute before saying, "The Council has had a change of heart."

Smith remained still, his face clean of tells. "Has there been a vote I wasn't informed about?"

Of course there had been. This was how Prentiss conducted business when he wanted something his way. He didn't bother arguing his point, he simply left out the people he felt would vote against him.

"It was an emergency and you weren't available." His gaze locked with Smith's. "Apparently you were on a run or a hike. Some communing with nature."

"I do the same thing every day," Smith reminded him. "Today was no different. You're well aware of my personal schedule."

"Except something occurred while you were out," Prentiss countered. "Your new pet project, Sadie Buchanan, confessed her real reason for being here and it was not that she required sanctuary. She has infiltrated our walls under false pretenses. She represents a threat to our security."

Dread coiled inside Smith. Buchanan hadn't looked as if she'd suffered any torture for information. He couldn't see her voluntarily coming forward with this new and startling information, particularly if it cast her in a negative light.

"Really. That's an interesting development. Why don't you tell me what happened?"

"She told Levi Winters that his sister had sent her

here. Buchanan was tasked with coming here to rescue him. The information she fed us was nothing more than a distraction to cover her real mission."

"I'd like to question her again," Smith said. He stood as if the recommendation had already been approved. "I'm confident I can get her full story."

Prentiss held up a hand. "No need. A final decision has already been reached. We're turning her over to the *others*. Levi Winters, as well."

Smith kept his surprise to himself. "You selected Winters for your daughter—"

"The choice was premature. He failed his final test. We don't need his kind here."

"We do need more females. Buchanan wouldn't be the first one we've swayed to our way of thinking." It was the best argument and the most logical one he could come up with at the moment.

The old man eyed him for a long while before he spoke again. "You've been her champion since she arrived. Are you suggesting you've selected her as a wife?"

Before he could answer, Prentiss went on. "You've snubbed each of my daughters, but you would have this traitor? This outlander?"

"As I said—" Smith ignored his suggestions "—she may prove useful in a future negotiation. I have not considered her as a wife, only as a bartering asset."

Prentiss announced, "The Council wants her out of our midst."

"I don't agree, and I have an equal say on Council matters." Smith held his ground. He had a vote in all matters. Prentiss understood this, no matter that he despised the idea. The bastard would not force his hand.

Prentiss stood and walked over to his desk. He picked up a document. "It is decided. The decree is signed, and the message conveyed to the *others*. There is nothing further to discuss. You missed a great deal by being out of pocket this morning, Smith. Perhaps you should rethink your schedule in the future."

"Decrees can be overturned," Smith said, dismissing the other man's declaration. "I'll speak to the Council members."

"There will be no further discussion on the matter. You will escort Buchanan and Winters personally. Tomorrow morning."

Smith stared long and hard at him. "What are you up to, old man?"

He held Smith's gaze, then he smiled. "We make our own beds, Smith. And in the end, we have no one to blame but ourselves for the lack of comfort."

The slightest hint of uneasiness trickled through Smith's veins. This was something more than Sadie Buchanan or Levi Winters at play here.

"At sunrise in the morning you will depart," Prentiss repeated. "You should be back before dark."

Smith didn't waste any more time arguing. Instead, he left and walked straight to the detention center. The guards didn't question him as he entered, nor did anyone attempt to stop him when he walked straight to Buchanan's cell and unlocked the door.

Buchanan turned to face him. She stood on the far side of the small cell as if she'd been pacing the too-confined space. Before she could school the reaction, uncertainly flared in her dark eyes.

He went straight to the point. "What happened today?"

There were ears everywhere on this compound but questioning her was not going to change what had already been done. As a Council member he had a right to know all the facts.

"What do you mean?" She shrugged. "I was pulled back from the tunnels, given an opportunity to bathe and then taken to the cafeteria."

His irritation flared. "Do not waste my time. What happened?"

Her arms folded over her chest. "I ran into an old friend. Gave him a message from his sister. She's been worried about him."

"What exactly did you say?" Fury had him clenching his jaw to prevent saying more than he should.

She heaved a big breath as if he were the one trampling on her last nerve. "I told him who I was and that his sister had sent me to rescue him. I also told him not to worry because I would be getting him out of here."

Well, that sure as hell explained a lot. He stared directly into those dark eyes. "So you lied. Your story was a cover for your real mission."

She gave a succinct nod. "I lied."

"Get some sleep. We leave at sunrise."

He turned his back on her but before he was through the door she asked, "Where are we going?"

He didn't bother glancing back. "To trade a mole for a lost rabbit."

Chapter Eight

They knew.

What was worse, she had told the enemy herself.

Sadie closed her eyes and shook her head. She had royally screwed up this one. Flynn had called her a mole. He was taking her from the compound today to trade her for a lost rabbit. One of the Resurrection's own, obviously, who had been taken by another group or some other faction involved with their mutual black market business dealings.

Considering she was FBI, it was possible the lost rabbit was in holding with some branch of law enforcement. The local cops? The feds? She had gotten the impression that as far as Winchester and Franklin County law enforcement were concerned—at least until the takedown at the Salvation Survivalist church—the Resurrection was more a local legend than anything else. A bunch of local yokels with guns they picked up at gun shows and MREs they ordered from the internet.

But that was not the case at all. The Resurrection was

a long-term, well-planned and -operated organization with powerful contacts and an extensive reach. At this point, local law enforcement was well aware that gun-running was involved. In Sadie's experience, drugs and human trafficking oftentimes went hand in hand with the smuggling of weapons. Maybe these daughters of Prentiss's weren't his biological children. Maybe they were stolen children he'd raised in this damned compound.

Sadie paced the few steps to the other side of her concrete cell. She had to finagle an escape. There were people in this place who needed rescuing. There was Levi and the ones in the tunnels. And possibly all the women. Though she had only seen a couple, she suspected there were more. She exhaled a big breath. This situation was far bigger and more complicated than she or anyone else had initially speculated.

It was possible another federal agency, like the ATF or the DEA, knew more than the Bureau about this group. The sharing of information was limited to a need-to-know basis for the safety of any ongoing operations and embedded agents.

She needed more information. She exhaled a resigned breath. What she really needed was backup.

The swish and whir of the lock snapped her attention to the door.

Sunrise had arrived.

The door opened and Smith Flynn met her gaze. He didn't mince words. "Let's go."

She walked toward him, expecting the broad-shouldered man to step aside so she could move through the door but he didn't. He held his ground, staring down at her.

Apparently he had more to say before this party got started.

"From this moment until I tell you otherwise you will do no thinking for yourself. You will do exactly as I say, when I say. Understood?"

Anything to get out of this prison. "Understood."

"We walk out of here, you don't look at anyone, you don't say anything. You follow me and you do exactly as I tell you."

"I can do that."

He turned and headed along the corridor. She followed. As they left the cell behind and reached the exit of the detention center, she didn't spot her guard or any others for that matter. Outside was the same. Her instincts urged her to look back over her shoulder, to look around, but she resisted the impulse. Flynn had told her not to look at anyone. She decided not to test him this early in today's game. Whatever was going to happen from this point forward, she needed to proceed with extreme caution.

She had resigned herself to the idea that she might not be able to escape this place on her own. If she couldn't get out, she couldn't get Levi out. At least if she managed to lose Flynn at some point, she had a chance of getting help back here to rescue Levi.

At this point she was more than a little surprised that Flynn hadn't restrained her hands. They headed in the direction of where she had spotted all those vehicles parked. The tunnels were in that direction, as well. Her heart instantly started to pound. She did not want to end up back down there. If that was what was about to happen, she had to do something. At least try to escape. A final ambitious effort even if she was shot for her trouble.

She bit her lips together to prevent asking him if that was his intent, simultaneously bracing for fight or flight. He'd said she was being traded. Surely that meant they were leaving the compound. Then again, the guy in the cafeteria had been fired up because he was being sent to the tunnels in her stead. That was a trade, wasn't it?

Damn it. A rush of dread roared through her veins.

She was stronger than this. If she allowed the dread and uncertainty to get to her now, she would lose all semblance of control over the situation. She might not have much as it was, but she was still hanging on to a sliver. Whatever happened, she had to cling to that modicum of control.

When they reached the motor pool, he opened the rear passenger door of a black SUV. He reached inside for something. When he drew back he had two things, nylon wrist restraints and a black hood like the one she'd worn on the way here with Prentiss and his thugs.

Movement inside the vehicle had her leaning forward just a little. Someone was already in there. The black hood concealed everything from the shoulders up, making it impossible to say if the passenger was male or female.

Flynn held out the nylon restraint and she offered her hands, wrists together, for him to do what he had to do. When her wrists were bound tightly together, he dropped the hood over her head. A hand rested against her upper arm, ushering her toward the open SUV door. She climbed in and settled into the seat.

"Where are we going?" the other prisoner asked.

Sadie recognized the voice. *Levi.* Apparently, he either hadn't received the same lecture she had or he chose to ignore the order.

The door closed and a few moments later the front driver's-side door opened, the SUV shifted slightly and then the door closed again. She resisted the urge to lift her hood and make sure it was Flynn who had climbed behind the steering wheel. He'd secured her hands in front of her so she could certainly do so but, again, she resisted the impulse. If the situation went downhill from here it wasn't going to be because she gave it a shove.

She wanted out of here far more than she wanted to satisfy her curiosity. That Levi was with her was a genuine stroke of luck. If she could salvage this rescue operation, all the better.

The vehicle started to move. About a minute later there was a brief stop, then they were moving forward again. Sadie imagined they had stopped long enough for the doors or gate or whatever to open, allowing them out of the compound. Though she couldn't see to confirm the conclusion, her heart hammered at the idea that they could very well be beyond those suffocating walls.

For the next ten minutes by Sadie's count, they drove fairly slowly. The ride was smooth, making her judgment of the speed not as reliable as it could be. Again, the urge to lift the hood and look around nudged her. She wrestled it away.

At least for now.

"Get down on the floorboard!"

The shouted order startled Sadie and for a split second she couldn't move.

"Get down!"

She tugged at Levi's arm and then scrambled onto the floorboard. Thankfully he did the same.

The shattering of glass and the pop of metal warned they were under assault.

"Stay down as low to the floor as possible," she whispered to Levi. She felt his body flatten in an attempt to do as she said.

The SUV's engine roared and the vehicle rocketed forward. The momentum of the driver's evasive maneuvers swung their weight side to side, made staying down increasingly difficult.

"Stay down," she urged the man hunkered between the seats with her.

The SUV barreled forward, swaying and bumping over the road. Sadie concentrated on keeping her body as low and small as possible. This vehicle likely wasn't bulletproof. The shattered glass she'd heard earlier all but confirmed as much. A stray bullet could end up killing one of them.

If the driver was hit...they would probably all die.

The SUV suddenly braked to a hard, rocking stop.

Another shot exploded through the rear windshield and then a detonation of new sounds. Ripping, cracking...then a hard crash.

The SUV suddenly lunged forward.

"You can get up now."

Flynn's voice, definitely his voice though it sounded muffled. Sadie recognized it was the blood pounding in her ears that smothered his words. She scrambled upward, swept the glass she felt from the seat and then righted herself there.

"We okay now?" she asked. After what they had just gone through, she figured the rules had changed. Asking if they were out of danger seemed reasonable.

"For now."

"What's happening?" Levi demanded, his voice high-pitched and clearly agitated.

"We're okay," Sadie told him, hoping he would calm down rather than grow more distressed.

She felt his arm go up. She grabbed it, hung on. "Don't do anything until he gives the order," she reminded. "We need to get through this."

At this point, she trusted Flynn on some level whether he deserved that trust or not. But they weren't in the clear yet. She couldn't be sure of his ultimate intent. There was a strong possibility that she and Levi were only valuable if they were still alive. His risky protection measures might be self-serving.

The SUV braked to another sudden stop. Sadie's pulse sped up again.

The hood covering her head was abruptly yanked off. "Get out," Flynn ordered.

He whipped Levi's hood off next and issued the same order to him. Sadie hurried out of the SUV. Levi came out behind her rather than getting out on the other side.

The road was not paved. Dirt and gravel. Muddy. It must have rained last night.

She looked up, squinted at the rays of sunlight filtering through the thick canopy of trees overhead. They were deep in the woods but they were out of that damned prison. The dirt road seemed to cut around the edge of the mountain. To their backs was the mountainside, in front of them was a steep drop-off. As she and Levi watched, Flynn stood outside the driver's-side door and guided the still-running SUV to the edge of the road. He jumped back as the engine roared and the vehicle bumped over the edge of the road, crashing through the trees.

Exactly like the one that had been firing at them, she realized, as the familiar sounds echoed around them. That was the reason for his sudden stop back there. The other driver instinctively attempted to avoid the collision, whipped the steering wheel and ended up going over the edge of the road and down the mountainside.

Sadie watched the man walking toward them. It wasn't until that moment that she noticed the backpack hanging from one shoulder. She didn't have a clue what was in that backpack, but what she did know was that they had no transportation.

She asked, "What now?"

"Now." He pulled a knife from his pocket and sliced through the restraints on her wrists and then did the same to Levi's nylon cuffs. Flynn's gaze locked back on hers. "We run."

THE COUNCIL HAD VOTED.

Fury roared through Smith as he moved through the

dense underbrush as quickly as he dared. Buchanan had no trouble keeping up with him, but Winters was slowing them down more than anticipated.

"Keep up," he shouted over his shoulder. Buchanan shot him an annoyed look.

He imagined she had some idea that they were in trouble but he doubted she fully comprehended the magnitude of the situation. The Council had decided to terminate Smith's position within their ranks and, apparently, him. They would want him and the people with him dead as quickly as possible. No loose ends. No way to trace the murders back to them.

This was Prentiss's doing. No one else on the Council would have dared to speak against Smith. The old man had grown worried that the rest of the members preferred Smith's style of progressive leadership.

He had suspected this was coming. Smith had kept his cover intact far longer than anyone expected. Funny thing was, it wasn't until Buchanan showed up that Prentiss found the perfect leverage to use toward this very end.

Smith had two choices: save Agent Sadie Buchanan's life or attempt to salvage his cover.

His cover was shot to hell.

He led them deeper into the woods. Merging into the landscape was the only way they would make it off this mountain alive. For now, they had a head start. The three-man crew Prentiss had sent after them was down. If one or more survived, it was only a matter of time before he climbed up that ravine and called for backup. Staying on the road was out of the question. There were lookouts at certain points along this stretch of road and there was no other drivable egress in the close vicinity. Disappearing between scout stations was the only option. Moving back and forth and in a zigzag pattern was their only hope of outmaneuvering the enemy.

Reinforcements would come like panthers after prey. Until then, they needed to put as much distance between them and this location as possible. Prentiss would send his team of trackers and they would bring the dogs. Time was of the essence.

Smith knew these woods. He had grown up here and he'd spent most of his time cutting paths through this dense foliage. Over the past two years he had planned for this very moment. There was never any doubt about this moment. It would come and he would need an emergency egress. He just hadn't expected to be bringing two others along with him.

There were answers he would need eventually but there was no time for that now.

"Where exactly are we headed?"

Buchanan pushed up behind him. She was strong, fit. The only good thing about the additional luggage with which he was saddled.

"You'll know when we get there."

"Those were your friends back there, right?"

Before he bothered with an answer, she fell back a few steps. "Hang in there, Levi. We have to keep going."

"Why the hell are we following him?" Winters shouted. "He's one of them."

"That's a good point."

It was the total lack of sound after Buchanan's statement that warned Smith the two had stopped.

He did the same and swung around to face the latest hurdle in this unfortunate turn of events. He visually measured Buchanan before shifting his focus to Winters. "Do you know your way out of here?" He waved an arm to the junglelike growth around them. "We're a lot of miles from the nearest house. You'll need water. I have water. A limited supply, but I have it."

Buchanan glanced at Winters, who now stood beside her. Then she looked up, probably searching for enough of the sky to see in which direction the sun was rising.

"We're heading south," Smith advised. "And we have a long way to go. When my *friends* back there—assuming there are survivors—get a call through to Prentiss... Even without survivors, he'll be expecting a check-in. When that call doesn't come, they'll pour out in droves to find us and they'll bring the dogs. We have to move as fast and as far as possible before that happens."

"Why should we trust you?" Buchanan asked.

She was no fool. She was ready to go but she held out, no doubt to prove to Winters that she was ultimately on his side. She hoped her support would gain his cooperation. If rescuing him had been her original mission, she likely wanted to make that happen. Understandable.

Smith shrugged. "You have no reason to trust me. But I'm going. I know the way. I have the necessary supplies. You can either follow me or you can find your own way. Makes no difference to me."

He pivoted and continued his trek through the shoulder-deep underbrush.

Fifteen seconds later he heard the two coming behind him. They were moving fast, trying to catch up. Whatever Buchanan had said to Winters, she had lit a fire under him. Good. Smith had no desire to end up dead before he'd finished his own mission.

THEY WALKED FOR another three hours before he felt comfortable allowing a water break. There was a small overhang of rocks just up ahead. They would duck under there. It would be cooler close to the earth beneath the outcropping and their position would be hidden from anyone who might be catching up to them. So far he hadn't heard the dogs but that didn't mean someone wasn't out there on the trail. Prentiss would use every method available to him. Losing more control was not an option. Smith almost wished he could see the bastard's face.

He had his doubts about the physical condition of the three who had gone over the mountainside in the other SUV. He doubted any one of them would be capable of giving chase. A call for backup would require time. Forty minutes to an hour to prepare and reach the point where the three of them had abandoned the SUV.

He scanned the trees beyond their hidden position and listened intently. By now, it was more likely than not that search parties were out there. The dogs would ensure they moved in the right direction. The head start Smith had gained was the one thing he had on his side.

Smith downed the last of his water and tucked the empty bottle back into his pack.

"Where are we going?" Buchanan asked.

"To the river. The water is low this time of year but that will work to our advantage. We'll use the water to throw the dogs off our scent."

"I haven't heard any dogs," Winters argued. "Wouldn't they be after us by now?"

"When you hear them," Smith warned, "it'll be too late." He pushed up from the rock he'd used as a seat. "Let's get moving."

He held out his hand for their water bottles. He tucked each one into his pack and headed out. Buchanan didn't hesitate. Winters did but not for long.

Rested, Smith pushed a little faster. He wanted over this ridge and to the water's edge within the hour. He wouldn't rest easy until they'd put a mile or so wading through the water behind them.

Mosquitoes swarmed when he pushed through the foliage. He ignored the occasional bite. Behind him he heard his followers swatting at the irritating insects. The ground was rockier here, making him less sure-footed. Still he pushed as fast as he dared.

By dark he would reach the safe place where he would be able to use the emergency device that would summon backup. Smith had nothing against local law enforcement in Franklin County, or the neighboring counties, for that matter, but he had an obligation to ensure there was no breach in security. The only way to do that was to use the communication device he had hidden and to call his contact and no one else.

The rumble of curt conversation droned behind him. He didn't slow down or bother to look back. He couldn't force either of them to follow him. More important, he could not share who he was or his mission with either of them, either. If they were captured, Buchanan might survive torture without talking but Winters would not.

Besides, Smith saw no reason to share that information until absolutely necessary for his own protection, as well.

"Why did my sister send you to find me?" Winters asked the woman two or three steps in front of him.

Evidently, Winters had decided to question all aspects of his good fortune. Some people just couldn't be satisfied by merely being rescued from certain death.

Buchanan kept her voice low as she answered the question. Smith didn't catch all that she told the ungrateful man. Something about his sister being worried and the local police being concerned that the Resurrection group were a more considerable threat than they had estimated.

Smith could tell them exactly how big the threat was, but he had to get out of this situation first.

"Why you?" was Winters's next question.

Smith slowed, diminishing the distance between them. He would like to hear the answer to that one.

"That's what I do," Buchanan said, practically under her breath. "I rescue other agents or assets who get themselves into trouble."

Well, well, he'd known the lady wasn't the average federal agent. Interesting that she was a rescue and retrieval specialist.

"I guess this time isn't working out so well," Winters said with a dry laugh. "Just my luck."

"We're not beaten yet," she protested. "I've never failed before. I don't intend to start now."

Smith hoped the lady was right.

Failure would mean a very bad end for all of them.

Chapter Nine

They had been walking for most of the day. Her sneakers were still wet from the slog through a mile or more in that narrow river. The water level had been low but hopefully it was enough to throw the trackers and their dogs off their scent.

The sun was going down and the trees were thick but it was still as hot as hell. Sweat beaded on Sadie's forehead. Her legs ached. She was in damned good physical condition but this went way beyond her usual workout. This was grueling. They'd been going uphill until the past hour. The downhill journey wasn't much better, just used a different muscle group. The under-canopy brush remained thick and the landscape was rocky.

She had tried to keep Levi calm and focused on moving forward but he was resisting more and more the farther they went on the desperate journey. She wasn't sure how much longer she could keep him cooperative. His misgivings were understandable, reasonable even. But they had little choice. Keeping ahead of the enemy had to be their priority.

So far they hadn't heard any sign of the dogs Flynn

had worried about. Thank God. Their stoic leader had stopped several times and listened for anyone who might be following them. He hadn't heard or spotted anyone yet. She hadn't, either, and she was keeping her eyes and ears tuned in as keenly as possible. She did not want to be captured by those bastards. Chances of surviving beyond the trip back to the compound were way less than zero.

If they were caught, they were dead.

"How far now to the destination you've targeted?" She had to admit, she was damned tired, not only physically but of blindly following orders. But she would keep going until they reached some semblance of safety or until she found reason to do otherwise.

"It's a ways yet."

Flynn said this without looking back.

Something about his nonchalance bugged the hell out of her. "Define *a ways*."

He stopped. She almost bumped into his broad back. He wheeled around, his glare arrowing in on her and she stumbled back a step.

"We've been lucky so far, let's not screw that up now. We'll get there when we get there. Just keep moving and stay quiet."

He gave her his back and started forward again.

So much for getting an update. Sadie trudged after him.

"I'm done." Levi glanced covertly at her. "I know where we are now. I just want to go home." He jerked his head toward the faint path Flynn left in his wake. "We can't be sure what he's got planned. I'd feel better taking my chances on my own from here. I can do it. You should go with me."

Sadie slowed, keeping pace with Levi. She glanced at the man disappearing deeper into the woods. "You sure about that, Levi? If they catch us, it's doubtful we would survive. Let's get through this night and we can decide how we want to move forward in the morning."

"Just let me go." He started backing away from her. "Hell, the best I can tell, he's leading us away from Winchester. My sister and the people I trust are that way." He jerked a thumb to his left.

"Let's catch up with him and confront him about your concerns." She had a bad, bad feeling about this. "We'll figure out the best option. We're safer in a group."

Levi shook his head and took off in another direction. West, Sadie decided. She went after him. As curious as she was about whatever Flynn had in mind, Levi was the one she'd come to rescue. She had a duty to keep him safe, even when he made it difficult.

She wanted to call out to Levi but she couldn't risk that the enemy was close. The last thing she wanted was to draw Prentiss's people.

She pushed harder to catch up with him. All this time he'd dragged behind. Apparently he'd gotten his second wind. They hadn't made it far when she heard someone behind them. Adrenaline fired through her veins. She glanced over her shoulder and spotted Flynn.

Levi ran harder. Sadie did the same. But Flynn was gaining on them.

In the next moment Sadie had to decide whether to

keep going with Levi or to distract Flynn, giving the younger man an opportunity to reach his sister and help. If Flynn had no real interest in what happened to them, why come after them? Why not just let them go?

Something was wrong with this scenario.

And if Levi was familiar with the area and knew the way home, why not give him a chance to make it?

Decision made, she zigzagged, heading south once more. She held her breath until Flynn shifted his direction and came after her.

She ran harder still, determined not to make it easy for him to catch her.

She sidled between two trees; her shoulder scraped hard against one. She cringed. That would leave a mark. *Keep going.*

Maintaining her balance at this speed and along this rough terrain as she plowed through brush and dodged the bigger trees was not an easy task, especially downhill.

No slowing down! He was close. Only steps behind her. She could hear him breathing.

Damn, she needed to go faster.

Fingers grabbed the back of her sweatshirt. Yanked her off her feet.

They went down together, rolled in the brush. A limb poked her cheek. She grimaced.

Flynn landed on top of her, his bigger body grinding her into the brush and dirt.

"What the hell are you trying to do? Guarantee we end up dead?"

She tried to scramble away. Screaming was not an

option. If there was anyone out there on their trail, they would hear.

Better the devil she knew…

"Get off me," she growled.

He glared at her for a long moment, those silver eyes icy with fury.

Then he got up, pulled her up with him and kept a death grip on her arm. He had no intention of allowing her to run again.

"That little move you pulled back there, allowing your friend—your rescue target—a chance to run, likely put a bullet in his brain or worse."

Uncertainty trickled into her chest as she struggled to catch her breath. "He knows how to get home from here. He said you're taking us in the wrong direction. Is that true?"

Frustration hardened his face. "That depends on where you think the right direction is. He's going home to Winchester? To his friends?" He laughed, shook his head. "I hope he makes it, but that's highly unlikely. They have watchers in town. Those watchers will be on the lookout for all of us. The possibility that he'll make it to help before someone nabs him right off the street is about the same as Santa paying him a visit early this year. He won't make it. Do you hear me? He. Will. Not. Make. It. Which is why we're not going directly to Winchester. I have a safe place to wait for help."

That trickle of uncertainty turned into a river. "Then I have to go after him."

When she would have headed back in the direction she'd come, he held on to her more tightly.

"You're going to draw them right to us. We have to go. We've wasted too much time already. The only way you can help Levi now is by doing exactly what I say."

She stared at him, tried to see beyond that iron mask of his. "Who are you?" She had no real reason to trust this man and yet every instinct screamed at her to do exactly that.

"You already know the answer to that question. Right now, I'm the man who's trying his best to save your life."

"How can I be sure?"

She waited for an answer, held his gaze. He needed to give her something concrete. Why would a man so high up the food chain in the Resurrection organization suddenly throw everything away and run just to save her or anyone else?

"You answer a question for me and I'll answer one for you," he countered.

"Quid pro quo," she suggested.

He gave a succinct nod.

She could do that. He pretty much already knew all there was to know about her anyway. She'd owned being a federal agent. She'd made the mistake of spilling her true mission to Levi. Beyond her last boyfriend, this guy probably knew everything there was to know about her, including her favorite college professor's name.

"All right." She braced for his question.

"Why did you use the Trenton Pollard cover story? Where did you get that name?"

"That's actually two questions," she pointed out.

He gave her a look that said he was running out of patience.

"That was the name I was told to toss out if I needed more leverage in a dicey situation."

"Who gave you the name?"

"My point of contact."

More of that frustration tightened on his face. "He or she has a name?"

She nodded. "But I'm not giving that name to you until I see where this journey ends."

He shrugged. "Fine. Let's get moving."

"Wait a minute. I get a question, too."

"So ask your question so we can go."

"Why does the Pollard name mean so much to you?"

"He's a friend of mine and I don't see how you or your point of contact could know him."

Done talking, he started forward again. She glanced over her shoulder. Hoped like hell Levi knew what he was doing. She followed Flynn. If Flynn was truly on the run, her money was on Prentiss and his people coming after him first. Finding him and Sadie was likely far higher on their priority list than finding Levi.

Hopefully that would work in his favor until he reached help.

Either way, he'd made his decision and she'd done the only thing she could: helped him escape an unknown situation.

THEY WERE CLOSE. Smith was relieved. He wasn't sure how much longer Buchanan would last. She'd held up far longer than he'd expected as it was. She was strong but they were both tired.

The safe place he'd prepared wasn't far now.

"Give me a minute."

Smith stopped, sized her up as she leaned against a tree. He shrugged off the pack and removed the last bottle of water. "We can share this one," he offered, passing the bottle to her.

This last one would have been for Winters but he'd cut out on them without any supplies. Smith wondered how far he would get before a member of Prentiss's posse caught him. Not all the way into town for sure.

He watched as she opened the bottle and downed a long swallow. When she came up for air, he said, "We're almost there."

She choked out a dry laugh. "That's what you said an hour ago. I'm beginning to think you're lost, Flynn." Her gaze locked with his. "I hope that's not the case."

"Being lost is one thing you do not have to worry about, Buchanan."

He knew this place inside and out. He'd explored every square mile in his youth. Always looking for something different, something else. He'd never found it here. Leaving had been the only way to escape this life and the people he had grown to hate. His father had been the only voice of reason among the group of preppers who had started the Resurrection. When Avery Flynn had fallen ill, Prentiss had taken over and changed things without his knowledge. He'd started to dabble in criminal activities. Smith's father had never wanted to cross that line. There had been fringes of his followers who'd gotten caught up in the black market-ing of weapons and even in transporting drugs, but he'd always weeded them out in time.

But when his father lost control, it all went to hell.

Smith hadn't come back to make things right. It was too late for that. Too many of the old-timers were gone and too much of the younger blood was greedy and power hungry. The extremists without conscience had taken over. He'd come back to take them down. It wasn't what his father would have wanted but his father had been wrong. Anywhere those with extreme attitudes and beliefs gathered, nothing good came of it.

Ever.

"Fifteen minutes," he assured her. "We'll reach our destination in fifteen minutes—barring any unfore-seen events."

She screwed the cap onto the water bottle and tossed it to him. "I'm holding you to that."

He downed a long swallow and put the remaining water away. Before he could stop himself, he licked his lips and savored the taste of her. Sadie was differ-ent from any woman he'd ever met. She was stronger, determined, loyal. Intelligent. Unconditionally fearless. She stirred his interest in numerous ways.

Shaking off the distraction, he started moving for-ward again. "Let's go. We don't want to fall behind schedule since you're holding me to it."

She laughed again. He liked the sound of it. "You're a smart guy, Flynn."

Maybe. He hadn't considered himself smart in a long time. The truth was, he hadn't even considered the future until very recently. He had resigned himself to the idea that he would likely die getting this done.

Still could. It wasn't over yet.

The underbrush was thinner here in the rockier soil. Made going a little easier. Being physically exhausted, however, made just moving a chore. It had been a long day. Buchanan wasn't the only one who was beat.

They made the fifteen-minute timeline with a couple of minutes to spare. He pointed to a copse of trees that hugged the mountainside maybe ten yards below their position. The relief on Buchanan's face was palpable.

The overgrowth was thick around the cave opening. He carefully pushed the limbs aside and ducked inside first. There were times when a man should go first—like when he needed to ensure there were no wild animals, no den of snakes holed up in his safe place. Buchanan would likely argue the point with him but there were some things his father had taught him that stuck. *Always protect those under your care.*

Something else she would argue. Fiercely, no doubt.

He tugged the flashlight from its holder on the side of his pack and scanned the small shelter. Clear. No sign of animals. As often as he could get out here he sprayed the area with repellant to ward off animals but some critters weren't so easily put off. Thankfully the place was clean, no animal droppings. No snakes.

"You can come in." He held back the limbs, ensuring he didn't break any. Those limbs acted like a curtain, providing a layer of camouflage.

Once she was inside, he used his flashlight to locate his stored supplies. The cave was only about fifteen feet deep and the last five or six feet narrowed down to the point where crawling was the only option. He'd banged his head plenty of times. At the very back, he carefully moved the stacked stones he'd gathered in the immediate area. All looked exactly as if they'd always been right here in this pile. He'd gone to a great deal of trouble to ensure no one who might stumble upon this place noticed his stored goods.

Beneath the stack was a nylon bag, pale gray in color, nearly as large as his pack. It was sealed in a clear plastic over bag. Inside he kept his emergency supplies. The plastic was to better protect them from the elements and to ensure the bears and wolves didn't pick up on any scents.

His gut growled as he set the ready-to-eat packets aside. They'd only had a couple of protein bars today. It was time for something a little more substantial.

"What's all this?" Buchanan moved in next to him, sat back on her knees.

"Dinner. A burner phone. Weapon. First-aid supplies." Not so much of the latter but enough to get by in a minor emergency. A packet of blood-clotting agent, a suture kit. Antibiotic salve and a few bandages. "Water. A small blanket. Emergency light. You know, the usual."

There was also a backup plan, which he pocketed without mentioning. He tucked the nine millimeter into his waistband and loaded most of the other supplies into his pack. "You want beef or chicken?"

She studied the two packs of ready-to-eat meals. "I'll take the chicken."

"Good choice." He passed it to her and grabbed the beef.

He moved back to the roomier portion of the cave and opened up the small emergency light. He sat it on the ground. The lumens were low but he didn't want it glowing beyond the cave opening. It was enough. He tossed his guest the thin blanket. It wasn't much but it was better than nothing when one was sleeping on the ground.

"You can use that tonight. I'll use my pack for a pillow. I don't mind sleeping on the ground."

"So we're staying the night here?"

He shrugged. "If that's what it takes."

While she opened the food pack and ate, he fired up the burner phone. Once it was on, he moved to the cave opening to get better service. With a few taps, he sent the necessary message. The phone's battery was way too low. He'd charged it the last time he was here. With it turned off it should have maintained the charge. When the message had been delivered, he relaxed. He returned to where Buchanan sat and settled in for however long they had to wait.

He opened his meal pack and ate slowly, more slowly than he wanted to but it would satisfy him better that way. Buchanan did the same. She'd likely had similar training and understood the need to adapt to extreme change. Being a field agent required a degree of flexibility. That she consumed every bite of the less-than-tasty meal confirmed his conclusion.

When she'd finished, she said, "Tell me about the message and why we may be here all night."

"The message goes into a pipeline of sorts. It takes a while to get to the intended recipient. Once he has it, he'll make arrangements for a pickup. When the pickup is ready, we'll go to the designated location. There are several good options within two miles of our position."

She sipped on the packet of water. "The contact is aware of this location?"

He shook his head. "No one knows this location. It's a security precaution in case there's ever a breach in our communications. I selected this location based on my knowledge of the area and the best egress routes. We agreed upon designated pickup points. The gap allows for a degree of separation between me and any trouble that might crop up. As I'm sure you're well aware, advance preparation is key."

She nodded but then frowned. "What if you're injured? You might not be able to make it to the pickup point."

"That's where my backup plan comes into play." He patted his pocket. "I have a beacon, the same technology skiers use. If necessary, I turn it on and they can find me."

Her expression told him she was impressed. "You've got all the bases covered."

He focused on his food for a while, let the silence fill the space. It would be dark soon. Since there was no way to know what time they would have to move, it would be best to get some sleep now while they had the opportunity.

When he'd finished his meal, he put the packaging

into his pack. "Sleep if you can. We may have to move again at any time."

He checked the screen on the burner phone before sliding it into his shirt pocket. With the phone on vibrate and the pack as a pillow, he stretched out for a quick nap, braced his arms over his face. He hoped like hell the charge lasted until he had a response.

He listened as Buchanan spread the thin blanket out on the ground and did the same. She lay there quietly for about a half a minute. He was surprised she lasted that long.

"What are you, Flynn? If you tell me you're just a run-of-the-mill member of that group we escaped, I'm going to know you're lying."

At this point he didn't see any reason to keep her in the dark. "I'm like you."

She rolled onto her stomach. He felt more than saw the move. "Only way different."

He chuckled and lowered his arms. "Not so different."

"Come on. You don't work for the Bureau or I would know. The ATF didn't claim you. Neither did the DEA. Since when does Homeland Security embed agents in the middle of nowhere like this?"

This time he outright laughed. "I'm not with Homeland Security. I'm with the ATF."

She lay there for a moment seeming to mull over what she'd learned. It wouldn't be unusual for an embedded agent to be denied for the purposes of protecting the mission. Like the military, need to know was the motto for most federal agencies.

Finally she asked, "How did that happen? Did someone recruit you?"

"No. I recruited myself."

She waited for him to go on but he didn't. He should have realized she would want his story as soon as she knew the truth about who he really was, but he wasn't sure he wanted to share it. It felt too intimate.

Or maybe he was afraid it would turn the *moment* into something intimate. It was essential that they stayed focused. Emotions could not get tangled up in this precarious situation.

"I'm waiting for the rest of the story, Flynn. Don't leave me hanging like this."

"I grew up in Franklin County. My father was one of them, only not like what you see today. It didn't start out that way. But I watched it happen and I hated it, hated the men who made it happen. I made my way into the ATF for the sole purpose of coming back here and taking Resurrection down. For years I pretended that wasn't my motive. I tried to be a good agent, take the assignments given. Do the job to the best of my ability—whatever that job might be. But I couldn't forget. Two years ago when my father died, I approached the top brass with an offer. They accepted and I came back to do what needed to be done."

"Wow. That's a hell of a story, Flynn. You must have incredible restraint. You've had to pretend to be one of them for two whole years."

He rolled over her comment for a time and then he said, "I've always been one of them. I'm just not like them. That's the difference."

She nodded. "I get it."

"What about you, Agent Buchanan? How did you become a rescue and retrieval specialist?"

"Growing up in Montana I always said I wanted to work where the sun shines all the time and there's no snow so I ended up in Miami. I was so new it was painful but because of my obvious Hispanic heritage, I was needed for a particularly high-profile assignment right off the bat. They wanted me to get inside and evaluate the situation with a deep-cover agent who had gone silent. Getting in was easy. I have a knack for putting people at ease and making them believe what I want them to believe."

"You do." If it hadn't been for her using the Trenton Pollard name, he could have fallen for her story. She was good.

"Not only did I find the guy but I got him out using my favorite bait-and-switch tactic. It almost never fails."

"Is that right?"

"That's right. I make the bad guy believe he's going to get one thing and then I do exactly the opposite of what he expects."

He chuckled, couldn't help himself. This was a woman who enjoyed her work.

"Turns out my target was the grandson of a former director. He was so impressed with my work, he urged the powers that be to make better use of my skill set. So here I am. This was basically a favor. An off-the-record mission."

"Well, Agent Buchanan, it's a pleasure to make your acquaintance." He thrust his hand at her.

She grinned and gave it a shake. "Ditto, Agent Flynn."

Now if they could only get themselves out of this thorny situation, maybe he'd ask her out to dinner.

A frown furrowed his brow. The beef jerky obviously hadn't done its job or he wouldn't still be thinking about food.

Then again, maybe it wasn't food on his mind.

He peeked at the lady lying so close.

Too dangerous, he reminded himself.

Maybe another time when they weren't both targeted for execution.

Chapter Ten

Monday, August 12

The way Flynn kept checking the burner phone, Sadie was reasonably confident he was worried more than he wanted her to know that there had been no response from his contact and the phone's battery was dying.

He hadn't said as much but she was no fool. There was no way a crucial reaction to a critical situation would take this long. She pulled her fingers through her hair, wished she had a brush. She shifted her position a bit—this rock was not made for comfort. Being stuck in this cave all night was even less so. She was thankful for the protection from the elements and the enemy but even when she slept, fitfully to say the least, she was aware of *him* next to her. The smell of his skin, the heat emanating from his body. Not helpful when trying to sleep. At least not when she wanted desperately to do something entirely unrelated to sleeping.

Not smart, Sadie.

The situation wasn't completely unexpected. She had been so focused on her career for years now that she'd

totally ignored her personal life. Sure, she had the occasional date with some guy a friend insisted she so
needed to meet. Very rarely did that develop into physical gratification. Apparently, that was an issue. She was
like a starving animal now, desperate...

She rubbed her hands over her face and wished for
a long, hot bath. Maybe a trip to the spa the way she'd
done years ago—before her career took over her life.
There, she decided, was the real source of the rub. All
her female friends—the ones with whom she'd done
lunch and spa days—were married. Most had children.
They all thought because Sadie was approaching thirty-
five that she should be doing the same. It wasn't really
because they were old-fashioned or had narrow views,
it was just human nature. The heightening urge to pro-
create as one reached thirty.

Sadie had passed thirty several years ago and not
once had she thought about a permanent relationship,
much less kids.

She worked. Work was her constant companion, her
best friend, her lover.

Her traitorous eyes stole a glance at the man packing
up their sparse campsite. But this man had her dwelling on her most basic instincts. Of all the times for an
attraction to form, this was the absolute worst possible one.

The guy was a stranger—no matter that she now
knew he wasn't a criminal—and their situation was
dire at best.

Before daylight he'd gone outside their hiding place
and checked the area. When he'd returned, she had

taken a turn slipping out of the cave to go for a necessary break, as well. Flynn was good at concealing his concern but she hadn't missed his mounting tension. It was in the set of his broad shoulders, the lines across his handsome forehead.

He was worried.

Which made her worry.

It was possible, she supposed, that there had been a delay due to some unpredicted issue. But they had gone well beyond that possibility now. This was not just a delay, this was a total breakdown in the link between a deep undercover agent and his primary support contact.

When Flynn pulled on the pack, she asked the question burning in her brain. "What's the plan now?"

"No response from my contact. The phone's battery is dead. We move on. Staying here any longer would be a mistake. As well hidden as we are, the dogs could pick up our scent again."

"Agreed." For the first time this morning she thought of Levi. She hoped he had made it to someplace where he could call someone he trusted. Things would have been a lot simpler if he'd stayed with them. She glanced at the man towering over her. A lot simpler on numerous levels.

"Stay close," he reminded her, "and move as quietly and quickly as possible. We'll head off this mountain and into town via trails that keep us out of sight and away from where we would most likely run into people."

Which meant they would be hiking a lot of miles, taking the longer, tougher routes. The blisters forming on her feet ached. They weren't as bad as the ones on her hands, but they were getting there. She glanced at the bandages, considered discarding them but decided against it for now.

At the opening that would take them out of the shallow cave, he hesitated. "We'll save the backup plan for later. I have no way of knowing what's gone wrong with my communication link so I don't want to give anyone our location until we know whether the one who receives the signal is friend or foe."

So, she'd been right.

He parted the thick foliage and made his exit. Sadie followed.

Whatever happened now, they were on their own.

SMITH HAD NO choice at this point but to admit that his contact was either dead or he'd turned.

He had known the man who was his primary backup for a decade. He found it difficult to believe he could be turned. Odds were, he was dead. The mistake was Smith's. He had insisted on only one person having knowledge of his egress options. He should have known better than to rely on only one man. Humans were not immortal. Accidents happened, health issues cropped up. One or both stealing lives at inopportune moments. Things happened, infusing desperation, weakening even the strongest man.

Choices at this juncture were extremely limited but at least they still had a couple.

Smith had decided that they would keep moving. Yesterday had been spent traveling in wide circles up and then down the mountain. No express routes. Today would be somewhat more direct. He would use a scatter pattern to prevent leaving a straightforward trail to follow. However hard he tried not to leave signs of their presence, it was impossible not to break the occasional small branch or trample plants.

Their path wouldn't be difficult for a trained tracker to follow. The dogs wouldn't need anything but their scent.

Frankly, Smith was surprised he hadn't heard the dogs at some point yesterday. Particularly after Winters separated from them.

This, too, was cause for concern.

Was Prentiss so certain he would win that he didn't bother sending a search party?

The idea hadn't crossed Smith's mind until his contact failed to come through and time had continued to lapse without trouble finding them.

Now that he considered the possibility, Prentiss had been the one to insist Smith take Buchanan and Winters to the *others*. If he'd discovered Smith's secret, why not kill him at the compound? Was the old bastard's intent to make an example out of him? Show his followers who their true protector was?

This was more wrong than he had realized.

There was a mole all right, but it wasn't Buchanan. It was someone on Smith's home team. Someone in the ATF with clearance to this mission. Only a handful of people knew about this cleanup and infiltration detail. Still, that didn't mean someone with the opportunity hadn't found a way to access the files. The world was one big electronic filing cabinet these days. Nothing was unattainable if one knew in which drawer to look and possessed the skill to open it.

Had Prentiss turned someone with that kind of know-how?

The only way to be sure was to get Buchanan to safety and then for him to return to the compound for Prentiss. This was a finale that required an up close encounter.

He had spent the past two years of his life digging deeply into the Resurrection. He was not going to walk away without eliminating the organization, even if that meant taking matters into his own hands.

The compound had been built into the mountain-side. It was completely camouflaged and protected by the earth itself. Over and over he had mentally plotted where and how the explosives would need to be planted to destroy the place—to bring down the entire moun-tainside. The problem was, as gratifying as that result would be, it wouldn't change anything. Some of the powers that be lived outside the compound. They hid themselves among the locals to stay aware of whatever was going on in the rest of the world. Having every-one with power, reach and contacts in the same place at the same time for elimination would be virtually impossible.

Smith had toyed with that scenario a thousand times.

Once the compound was destroyed, those who sur-vived would go into hiding. He knew them all—every single one. But sending them to prison for their crimi-nal activities required solid evidence, none of which he possessed outside that compound. Even lining them up for vigilante-style termination would require an army. The moment one was taken out, the rest would scatter like crows. Since he didn't have an army prepared to commit cold-blooded murder, he needed a better plan.

A laugh tugged at his gut. In two years he hadn't been able to come up with a workable strategy.

He could sever the head of the snake, Prentiss, but another one would sprout in his place.

Unless…he found a more lethal snake willing to swallow up the competition entirely.

A new plan started to form. Smith had a feeling this one might even work. But to make that happen he would need to enter the territory of that lethal snake.

It was a good plan. He thought of the woman right behind him. Rather than attempt to explain the intricate details and to persuade Sadie to go along, he decided to keep her in the dark. She would be mad as hell when she found out, but if he accomplished his ultimate goal, she would forgive him.

He hoped.

Altering his course, he headed for dangerous territory. He readied for trouble, exiling all distraction in order to focus fully on his surroundings, listening and watching. Within the hour they would cross into territory ruled by another group. They couldn't really be called an organization since they weren't technically organized. These people didn't even have a name, much less a motto. Anyone who knew them merely called them the *others*. The one thing Smith knew for certain about them was that they were dangerous. Cunning and methodical.

Maybe clinically insane. Certainly crazy by anyone's measure.

Crazy was what he needed at the moment.

All he had to do was find it without getting Buchanan or himself killed.

THEY WERE TRAVELING in a different direction now. Yesterday he had done the same. Flynn had wound back and forth around this mountain. She'd figured his goal was to make their path more difficult to find and follow. With no response from his contact and no sign of Prentiss's people or dogs, she had expected he would take a more direct route today.

Maybe not.

She wanted to ask him about his plan, but he'd reiterated that silence was particularly important today. Rather than risk making too much noise, she'd kept her questions to herself for now and followed his lead. If she had to find the way out of here they would likely end up bear bait in these damned woods.

Not that she'd spotted any bears or bear tracks but there could be bears, coyotes or wolves, to name a few predators who would present a problem.

There was the gun he'd had hidden in the cave. But she didn't have any idea how much ammunition Flynn had on him. Maybe only what was in the weapon. Maybe not enough to survive if they were attacked by man or beast.

But they had their wits, no shortage of determination and Flynn's extensive knowledge of the area.

The situation could be a lot worse.

A muzzle jammed into the back of her skull. Before her brain had time to analyze how it happened so fast without her noticing someone was closing in on her, her body instinctively froze.

"Don't move."

Somehow she had known the person—man obviously—on the other end of that barrel was going to say those two words.

Smith spun around, his weapon leveled on the threat. "Back off," he warned.

Before his growled words stopped reverberating in the air, three more men stepped forward, rifles aimed at him.

Sadie blinked, startled when she'd thought nothing else could shock her. The men wore paint, like body paint—nothing else as far as she could tell. They had melted into the landscape and only when they moved had their presence become visible. She blinked again to ensure she wasn't seeing things.

"Back off," Flynn repeated. "Aikman is expecting me."

If these were more of his friends, it would have been nice if he'd given her a heads-up before the one behind her startled the hell out of her.

One of the three fanned out around Flynn stepped forward, moving closer to him. "Drop the gun."

Sadie held her breath. Agents were trained never to relinquish their weapons but sometimes there simply was no other choice. An agent learned through experience when it was time to forget the classroom training and do what had to be done.

Flynn tossed the weapon to the ground and raised his hands. "My name is Smith Flynn. Take me to Aikman."

The guy behind Sadie shoved a bag at her. "Put this on."

Sadie took the bag and tugged it onto her head. The last thing she saw before the black fabric fell over her eyes was Flynn with the business end of a rifle stuck to his forehead.

The nearest muzzle nudged her back. "Start walking."

She did as she was told, hoping like hell she didn't trip over a tree root or a rock. No one talked but she heard the faint sounds of their new friends moving through the underbrush. She suddenly wondered if the painted guys wore shoes or boots or something on their feet. She hadn't noticed. The guy behind her was probably painted, too. He was, she decided as she recalled the arm that had thrust the bag at her.

The only good thing was that Flynn appeared to know who these people were. This Aikman, she assumed, was someone in charge. Hopefully someone high enough up the food chain to keep them from becoming "emergency supplies."

Her toe snagged on a root or a rock and she almost face-planted. Thankfully, she managed to grab back her balance. Her sudden stop to capture her equilibrium won her another nudge from the muzzle.

Sadie counted off the seconds and minutes. By her

estimate, they walked for half an hour. The terrain didn't change much. Brush, rocks, moving sometimes up, sometimes down. The scent of food cooking told her they had reached a camp of some sort. She doubted it was noon yet but it was past midmorning. No matter that she'd had a protein bar very early that morning, her stomach sent her a warning that she needed to eat again soon.

And coffee. What she would give for a big, steaming cup of coffee.

She wondered if this group would have a compound built into the mountainside like the Resurrection. She had to admit, the idea had been ingenious. A hand suddenly rested on her left shoulder. She stopped, braced to either fight or run like hell. The bag whipped up and off her head.

She blinked twice, three times, and surveyed the area. There was a canopy of green overhead. A combination of trees and vines and other plant life she couldn't readily identify. Sunlight filtered through, making her blink with its brightness after wearing the bag. There were shacks made of branches, twigs and brush. This didn't look anything like a compound. These were like primitive huts that flowed seamlessly with the brush and trees. She looked upward again, spotted similar builds in the trees. The tree houses were also constructed with limbs and other pieces of the surrounding natural resources, making them almost like an extension of the trees.

Another nudge in the back and she started walking again. Flynn walked ahead of her, a painted man on either side of him. They moved deeper into the trees. Finally they reached an area that looked very much like the place against the mountainside where they'd slept last night. Brush and branches hid a narrow cave opening. They were escorted inside where two more men, these wearing dark clothes similar to SWAT gear, took over escort duty. The man who'd been behind Sadie all that time and his friends slipped back out the way they had come.

Beyond the opening, the cave widened into a room. There were lights in the cave but not electric lights. The lanterns looked like the old oil type. The cave floor was rocky. Water trickled from the walls here and there. Smelled musty. No more food smells. Whoever had been cooking, they were outside in the rustic camp they'd passed through.

This cave was far larger than the one they'd called home last night. The ceiling zoomed several feet overhead and the width of the space was five or so yards. They moved downward from there. Maybe a more elaborate compound had been built deeper in the cave.

The wide tunnel divided and they took the left fork. A few yards in they passed another wide room-size section on the left. Rows of rustic tables filled that space. Dozens of oil lamps lit the area. People dressed in white coveralls like painters and wearing paper face masks were frantically packing some sort of product.

Oh hell.

Drugs.

Her stomach sank. This was one of those things you

couldn't unsee. People in this business didn't allow out-
siders to see their work and walk away.

This was bad.

She hoped like hell Flynn knew what he was doing.
She also hoped he knew these people really well—well
enough to share dark secrets.

Otherwise they were goners.

Once they had moved beyond the workers in the
white suits, they passed a number of large round stones
that sat on either side of the corridor. The lead man
stopped. With obvious effort he pushed one of the stones
aside, revealing a hole in the rock wall, like a large
round doggie door without the flap.

Not exactly a user-friendly entrance to wherever they
were going next.

"Inside." The man looked at Sadie as he said this.

She glanced from him to the hole. Was he serious?
She shifted her gaze to Flynn. "I'm supposed to go in
there?"

"For now. Don't worry."

He couldn't be serious.

The man with the gun waved it as if he was running
out of patience.

Great. She squatted, then dropped onto her hands
and knees. She poked her head far enough through the
opening to see what was inside. Nothing. As best she
could determine it was just an empty, small, cube-like
rock room. She crawled inside. Squinted to get a better look at the space. She shifted, scanning all the way
around while there was still light filtering in from the
open hole. In the corner to the left of the hole she'd just

entered her gaze snagged on a form. She crawled closer, her eyes adjusting to the even dimmer light.

Bones.

Not just bones. An intact skeleton.

The rotting clothing suggested the owner of the bones had been male.

She swallowed back a sound, not exactly a scream but something on that order.

The noise from the stone rolling in front of the hole once more rumbled around her. She sat down on her bottom and stared at the only exit from this new prison. A dim outline of light from the lanterns in the corridor slipped in past the stone now blocking that exit.

Her gaze shifted back to the bones. She couldn't really see them now but her brain filled in the details from the picture seared into her memory.

Whoever had been stuck in here before had died in this place.

Without water or food it wouldn't take that long.

She thought of the lack of tissue on the bones. The person had been trapped in this place for a very long time. Years. Maybe as much as a decade considering the deteriorated state of the clothing he wore.

Sadie sat in the middle of that musty, dark space and replayed the past decade of her life. She had graduated with a master's degree and some big plans. Two summer internships with the Bureau and she was accepted as soon as she reached the age requirement. Her parents had been so proud. Her mother had been a little concerned about her daughter going into law enforcement, but she'd come to terms with the decision after the first year. Maybe it had been Sadie's excitement that had won over her mom.

Sadie had ended the relationship with her hometown boyfriend before entering training. The long-distance relationship had basically been over since undergrad school anyway. They were going in different directions with changing objectives. Why prolong the misery by watching the relationship they had once believed would go on forever shrivel up and die? Strange, she never once considered when the relationship ended that it would be her last one.

Dates, never more than three, maybe four with the same guy. Her social calendar consisted more of bridal showers, weddings and baby showers for friends than dates for herself.

If she died in this dark, dank place her parents would be devastated.

A life half lived.

Not true, she decided. If she died in this place, she would be dying young, for certain. But it wasn't a life half lived. She had lived every single day to its fullest. She had loved the hell out of her work. She had helped to bring down numerous bad guys and she had rescued more than her share of good guys.

"Get over it, Sadie. You are not going to die in this hole in the ground."

She pulled up a knee and rested her chin there. She would find a way out of here. It was what she did. And she was really, really good at it…usually.

As soon as Flynn finished his meeting with this Aikman person and was brought here, they would put their heads together and come up with an escape plan.

Flynn had a contact with these people. He hadn't appeared worried when they were captured. She shouldn't be worried, either. Then again, Flynn's record with his contacts hadn't actually been a reassuring experience so far.

Maybe it was time to get worried.

Chapter Eleven

Smith had waited a half hour. The cuckoo clock on the wall counted off every second with a loud tick-tock. Any minute now the bird would slide past its door and count off the hour: 11:00 a.m.

He forced himself to relax. He possessed as good an understanding of these people as anyone. They did things their way in their time. Making him wait was a way of showing dominance. As long as he was still breathing there was reason to believe an arrangement could be reached.

This move had been a risk. A risk he was wagering everything would work out. Unfortunately, the wager involved Buchanan's life as well as his own. If things didn't work out as he intended, her death would be on him. That was the one part that didn't sit well with him. But they were in a no-win situation. As a trained agent, she would understand the need to take drastic measures.

Smith drew in a deep breath and reminded himself to be patient. To play the game.

The tunnel where Buchanan had been secured had forked again, leading to the outside once more. Another campsite had been built against that side of the mountain. Again, using elements that blended in with the environment to keep them off the radar of reconnaissance flyovers.

Aikman's office was like any other with a desk, chairs and electricity. The electricity was furnished by a generator. The primary difference between this place and that of the Resurrection as far as Smith could see was the absence of electronics. The *others* didn't use electronics with the exception of burner phones, which they used sparingly. They stayed as far off the grid as possible.

The door behind Smith opened and Aikman entered, minus his usual bodyguards. They no doubt waited outside the door. No matter that he was well aware that Smith was unarmed, he would never take the risk of being alone in a room with a known follower of the Resurrection without backup close by.

"You got some nerve coming here after what you did, Flynn." Aikman sat down behind his desk. "I was expecting you to deliver two packages yesterday. Prentiss and I had a deal. First, you don't show, then I get word you've dropped off the grid. Now you waltz in here with only one package." He shook his head. "This is not good."

Draven Aikman was younger than Smith. His rusty-brown hair was kept skinhead short but his beard was long, at least ten or twelve inches. He wore the same dark uniform as his soldiers. He'd killed the old man who held the position as leader before him. The story was that the old man was sick, practically on his death-bed and making bad decisions. Aikman claimed he took care of the failing part for the good of the whole. Whatever his motive, he now held the highest position among this closed, clannish group known only as the *others* by the few who were aware of their existence.

Aikman propped his feet on the desk and leaned back in the chair, eliciting a squeak of protest from the base. The desk and chair, like the rest of the furnishings, might have been unwanted castoffs picked up from the side of the road on garbage day. The *others* had a reputation for living free of excessive material burdens. Survival of the coming human self-annihilation was their singular goal. Still, they were only human and not completely immune to power and greed. In any group there was always someone who couldn't resist the temptation of *more*.

"You suddenly develop a death wish?" Aikman asked. "Coming here, throwing my name around like we're friends. I could get the wrong idea."

"The deal Prentiss made is off. I'm here with a different offer."

Aikman lifted his brows. "This better be good."

"There are other names on my list," Smith warned, "but I chose to bring this offer to you first."

The other man's gaze narrowed. "What kind of offer?"

"We both know the Resurrection is your primary competition. We've blocked your every attempt to expand your operation into other areas. You've been stuck making the drugs no one else wants to make unless they have no other choice. We've pushed you out of the arms business. Basically, we've kept you down for decades."

"If you're supposed to be buttering me up for some proposition," he laughed, a rusty sound, "you're falling way short of the mark."

This was the mistake most people made. To look at the *others* and how they lived, one would automatically think uneducated, backwoods hillbillies. But that was not the case at all with the ones like Aikman. According to Smith's sources, the man had a master's degree in business administration. He was smart. Allowing you to believe he wasn't automatically put you at a disadvantage in any negotiation.

"I'm sure you get my meaning," Smith said, ignoring his dig. "I've decided it would be in both our best interests to join forces. We both have our resources. If we pool those resources, we could expand our operations and take over the Southeast."

Aikman dropped his feet to the floor. "You want me to believe that you're ready to abandon your loyalties to the Resurrection—an organization that runs in your blood? You would trample on your daddy's memory?" He grunted a sound of disbelief. "Pardon me if I don't believe you. What're you up to, Flynn?"

This was the risky part. It would have been easier for Smith to keep walking. To climb down this damned mountain and turn himself over to local law enforcement. He would have been sent back to where he belonged ASAP. The mission would have been over and the goal he'd dedicated his entire existence to for the past two years would have been lost forever.

He would have been alive, safe and free of this nightmare.

Except Prentiss would have gotten away. He and his Council of ruthless killers would have relocated and continued doing whatever they pleased with no care of the human cost. No worry about what the guns and the drugs were doing to society.

Smith was left with one option—finish this in the only way possible: light the fuse of the Resurrection's number one enemy.

Start a war.

"Prentiss sold me out," Smith confessed. That part was true. Rumor of the shake-up would get around soon enough if it hadn't already.

There was no other explanation for the trio who'd showed up behind them on that mountain road after they left the compound. Prentiss had intended to wash his hands of Winters, Buchanan and Smith. End of story. To believe they had appeared for any other reason would be foolish. Somehow Prentiss knew. Which would also explain the sudden drop in communications with Smith's contact.

Whatever had gone wrong, Smith was on his own. He had few options if he wanted to finish his mission and this was the best one.

Aikman reared his head back and considered the announcement for a moment as if he didn't quite believe what he'd heard. He pursed his lips then rocked forward, propping his forearms on his desktop. "You actually expect me to believe that Prentiss dared to attempt a coup so he could be rid of you?"

"Believe what you want." Smith turned his palms up. "I came here to give you the first dibs on *my* coup. If you're not interested, then I overestimated your ability to see the bigger picture. I won't waste your time. I have other options."

Aikman's gaze narrowed once more. "What other options? We own this mountain. My people and yours. There's no one else."

Smith smiled. "If that's what you believe, then I really did overestimate you, Aikman."

The statement was a direct insult but it also made the other man think. "You're talking about that Hispanic gang, aren't you? They've been inching their way up the food chain for years, but they're not organized enough or financially flush enough to be more than a nuisance." He hesitated. "What is it you know that I don't?"

There was no time to go there. "We have to act fast, Aikman. We can't sit around discussing the politics of the region. Prentiss is out there looking for me right now."

Aikman scrubbed a hand over his jaw. "What is it you've got to offer?"

"You get me and my friend off this mountain and I'll give you everything you need to take down the Council. Locations, security codes. Everything. The Resurrection and all it entails will be yours for the taking."

"Where do you come back into the picture?" He

shrugged. "Doesn't sound like we're doing anything. Sounds more like I'm doing and you're cutting out."

Smith shook his head. "I'll be back. There's a personal matter I have to take care of first."

Aikman grinned. "Are you referring to the woman?"

Tension slid through Smith. "I am."

Aikman scratched at his thick beard some more. "You see, that's where we have a bartering issue."

Smith's instincts stirred. "What does that mean, Aikman?"

He leaned back in his chair, his hands on the worn arms. "To tell you the truth, things get a little lonely out here from time to time. Sure there's women, but not one I've cared to take for more than a little bump and grind. There's definitely none like her. I need someone who presents a challenge. The ones I've run up on so far bore me."

Smith's gut clenched at the idea of what this bastard had in mind. The *others* were known for staying to themselves. They had no use for those who were different, whether that difference was as simple as skin color or went way deeper. The man's fascination with Buchanan would be short-lived and then she'd end up a curiosity or, worse, a sex slave.

"I don't see how that's my problem. This is business. Important business," Smith warned. "You should keep that in mind as you decide your next move."

Aikman grinned. "I'm making it your problem, Flynn. You brought this problem between you and Prentiss to my door, now I'm bringing mine to you.

I want the woman. You give me the woman and we'll have a deal."

"Not happening." Smith stood. "Let's not waste each other's time with games. We'll be on our way to the next prospect if this is your final answer."

The other man stood, leaned over his desk, bracing his hands on the worn surface. "Do you really think I'm going to let you just walk back out of here?" He moved his head slowly from side to side. "This was a no-turning-back meeting, Flynn. You don't get to sit in my office and then just walk away. You think Prentiss would watch me walk away if I paid him a visit?" Aikman angled his head and studied Smith. "Then again, he might if I told him I had a gift for him. What you think you're worth to the old bastard?"

Smith smiled. "Not nearly as much as you are."

Aikman reared back, then laughed as if Smith's statement hadn't startled him. "I gave you a chance, Flynn. I guess you aren't as smart as you think. What woman is worth dying for?"

"I could ask you the same thing."

Aikman didn't flinch, but Smith saw the glimmer of uncertainty in his eyes before he blinked it away. "My people appreciate tangible proof they're being protected. With that in mind, from time to time a public display is required to keep them reassured. At dawn, we'll give them something to feel good about. Maybe the two of you will be worth all the distraction you've caused after all. You wouldn't believe what organs go for on the black market."

Smith ignored the threat, turned his back and walked

out of the man's office. The guards grabbed him by the arms and jerked him forward.

Not exactly the news he'd hoped to take back to Buchanan.

SADIE HAD MOVED around the entire space and found no openings, not even a crack, except for the small round opening she'd been forced to crawl through to get in here. She couldn't help wondering if the owner of the remains in the corner had done the same thing—searched for some way to escape, wondering what would happen next—before he died here.

Whatever he'd had planned, it hadn't worked out for him.

For the first time on a mission, her mind wandered to her folks and she tried to remember the last time she'd spoken with her parents. Had she said the right things? Told them she loved them? She couldn't see her sister being there for them in their time of grief if Sadie never made it out of this place.

Don't even go there, Sadie.

Moving around the perimeter of the room once more, she closed her eyes and listened for any sort of sound. The soft whisper of words slipped beyond the crack between the stone that made a door and the hole in the wall that it covered. She couldn't say if the voices were those of the guards outside the room or people walking past in the long corridor.

The lives of these people likely revolved around the preparing and packaging of drugs. Survival. They lived to please their leader, this Aikman that Flynn asked to see. There was no logical reason why they would concern themselves with her or her survival.

Lines creased her forehead, nagging at the ache that had begun there. How long had Flynn been gone? An hour? An hour and a half? He could be dead by now for all she knew. She hugged her arms around herself, feeling oddly chilled. It would be bad enough to be stuck here with him. The concept of ending up alone in this hole—her gaze drifted across the darkness—was far worse.

Movement near the small opening drew her attention there. The rock rolled away and light poured in. Sadie stood back and waited to see what would happen. She held her breath, hoped it was Flynn and not the guards ready to drag her away to some torture chamber.

When Flynn popped up through the hole, relief rushed through her and she drew in a lungful of air.

Before he could speak, she asked, "What happened? Did you talk to Aikman?"

The stone was rolled back over the hole, blocking all but that narrow crack of light. Flynn hesitated, waiting for the guards to lose interest and wander back to their posts.

"I did. He was intrigued by my offer."

His tone told her that wasn't the whole story by any means but it might very well be the best part of it. "What was your offer?"

"The information he would need to take over the Resurrection."

No surprise there. Flynn was worried that Prentiss

would get away. He didn't want that to happen. "What did you ask for in return?"

"Safe transport off this mountain."

Made sense, she supposed. If his ultimate goal was to stop Prentiss and his followers, giving away his secrets to an enemy would certainly do the trick. Not exactly the usual protocol for a federal agent, but desperate times called for desperate measures. She couldn't fault him for wanting to see his primary mission accomplished no matter that his cover was blown.

She sat down on the floor. No need to keep standing. She'd walked this space a thousand times. Exhaustion and hunger were nagging at her. "When do we leave?"

He didn't sit. Instead, he kept moving around the space as if he was agitated or frustrated. Either would be understandable under the circumstances.

"Watch for the bones on the left of the door," she warned.

Still, he said nothing, just kept moving through the near total darkness. After five minutes, his movements had grown unnerving with her sitting so still. Finally, she stood and demanded some answers. "So what's the rest of the story?"

He stopped, turned to her. She couldn't see his face, certainly couldn't read his expression, so she waited for him to explain.

"I took a calculated risk coming here. I put my offer on the table and it didn't go the way I expected."

"Can you be a little more specific?" He'd told her a considerable amount with those two statements and yet nothing at all.

"The only way he's prepared to accept my offer is if he gets *you* in the bargain."

Sadie barked out a laugh. "Are you serious?"

"Unfortunately, I am." He heaved a frustrated breath.

The idea of where they were and those bones over in the corner slammed into her midsection like a sucker punch. "How did you respond?"

On one level she could see how he might want to agree. After all, at least one of them needed to get out of here alive. It was the only way the people expecting their return would ever know what took place on this mountain. No matter that she comprehended the logic, she struggled to maintain her objectivity. Agreeing to the man's terms would be the reasonable thing to do.

At least that way Flynn could go for help. Assuming she survived whatever came after that, she could still be alive when help came.

But on a whole other level, she wanted to kick his ass for coming up with this insane idea in the first place. Fury burst through her.

As if he'd read her mind or felt her mixed emotions, he said, "I told him no way. If I go, you go."

Her heart skipped and then sank just a little. "What good does it do for both of us to be stuck here?" Or end up like the guy in the corner? She exhaled a chest full of exasperation and crossed her arms. "Tell him you changed your mind. Tell him," she added firmly, "he has a deal. You go and I'll stay."

"No way."

His hands were on his hips and she could feel his glare even if she couldn't see it.

"It's the right thing to do, Flynn. One of us needs to get down this damned mountain."

She hoped Levi Winters had found help. Maybe she would have been smarter to go with him. Except it was better that she and Flynn drew the danger away from him and let him get away. At least he could tell Ross and the others all that he knew. That was something.

"I got you into this," Flynn said, his voice low, fierce. "I'll get you out."

"How do you plan on doing that?"

He moved in closer, put his face near enough to hers that his lips brushed her ear. She shivered in spite of her best efforts not to react.

"He's not going to pass on this deal. He just wants us ready to do whatever he asks when he pretends to have a change of heart."

The feel of his breath on her skin made her want to lean into him. She pushed the idea away. "What do you think he'll want us to do?"

"He'll want us to act as a distraction while he carries out his coup."

"What kind of distraction?"

"The kind that gets captured and taken back to the compound and to Prentiss."

She jerked away from him. "What? Why the hell would we do that?"

"Because he's not a fool. He knows it won't be easy getting in even with the information I can give him. If that's what he requires, we have to be prepared to go. Are you with me?"

She wasn't so sure this plan was any better than the first one he walked in here telling her about.

But that was irrelevant.

"I'm in," she said finally. "At least we won't end up like the guy in the corner."

How had this mission turned so completely upside down?

Chapter Twelve

Sadie woke, her body shivering. A moment was required for her to orient herself.

Cave. Aikman. The *others*.

She sat up, scrubbed at her cheek where her face had been pressed to the cold ground. She'd been curled into a ball on the cold rock floor. She peered through the darkness, scanning the room as best she could. Listening for any sound, including breathing, she heard nothing.

Where was Flynn?

Memories of him pulling her against him in the night invaded her thoughts. She'd shivered from the cold invading her very bones and he'd pulled her against his big body to keep her warm. Several times during the night she had awakened to the feel of his protective arms around her, his shoulder like a pillow and the length of his body radiating heat into hers.

"Flynn?"

She got to her feet, dusted herself off for the good it

would do. No answer. She ran her fingers through her hair. Apparently she'd slept through him being taken away.

Had Aikman summoned him for another meeting?

Her heart kicked into a faster rhythm. Maybe they'd already taken him off this damned mountain. Maybe she wasn't going anywhere.

Aikman had requested to keep her.

She chafed her arms to create some heat with the friction. Flynn would never go for it. He'd said so last night. He wasn't going without her.

Then again, it was possible he hadn't been given a choice this time.

For a few minutes she walked around, warming up her stiff, aching muscles. She really needed to use a bathroom but she doubted she would be permitted to leave her small prison. A few more minutes and she decided she couldn't wait any longer. She chose the corner the farthest away from the remains and relieved herself. The dead guy had likely been forced to do this for days or weeks before his body could no longer resist death.

Another ten or so minutes elapsed with her walking back and forth across the center of her prison cell when the stone suddenly rolled away from the opening. She moved to the wall and braced for whatever trouble might be coming. If one of the guards came in for her, she could fight him off for a while. As weary as her body was, the battle might not last long.

"Out!"

The voice was male but not one she recognized. She didn't move.

"Come out!" the man demanded. "Time to eat."

Her stomach rumbled. Getting out of here was better than staying. If it involved food, that was all the better. She pushed away from the wall and moved to the opening. On her hands and knees she scurried out as quickly as possible and shot to her feet. She didn't like being in a vulnerable position. She looked up, and two men—guards she presumed—stared down at her as if she were some sort of alien.

She blinked repeatedly to help her eyes adjust to the light. It wasn't that bright but it was a hell of a lot brighter than inside that hole she'd been stuck in all night. The two stared at her for a moment longer, then gestured for her to go to the left. Her gait was a little off at first but she soon found her rhythm. One of the guards ambled in front of her, the other behind her. They led her back the way she'd originally come into this cold, dark place. Once they were outside the cave, she squinted against the way brighter light. The sun was up but it was still early. She was escorted to one of the twig shacks and ushered through the primitive door.

A woman waited inside the shack.

"Take off your clothes and get into the tub."

She stared at Sadie, waiting for her to obey the issued command. Her hair was long and dark like Sadie's but her skin was pale. If a bath was on the agenda, Sadie wasn't about to argue with her. She stripped off her clothes and toed off her shoes. Once she was in the tub the woman peeled the bandages from her hands and ordered her to sit. Sadie complied.

It was at precisely that moment that she considered

maybe she was to be the morning kill. Maybe she was breakfast. She jerked her attention to the left just in time for a pail of water to be poured over her head. Surprisingly it was warm. A bar of soap was tossed into the tub with her and she went to work washing her face and body. It felt so good. More water poured over her and the woman started washing her hair. Sadie didn't complain. It felt amazing to have her scalp massaged. She could sit here and savor the attention for hours.

Then came more water, only this time it was cold. When she was thoroughly rinsed, the woman helped her towel off and provided a pair of blue cotton shorts and a white tee. Sadie had no idea where the clothes came from but they fit and she was glad to be out of the days-old sweats. She tugged on the same shoes she'd been wearing since her time at the compound. They were finally dry after their trek through the water. The blisters on her hands and feet were still tender but there was nothing she could do about that.

The woman ushered her over to a table and chairs and prepared food for her. The plate was metal, more like a pie tin. Scrambled eggs and toast were heaped onto the plate. A tin of water stood next to it. Sadie didn't wait to be told—she dove in. She was starving. She hoped Flynn was given food before he was taken to wherever he had gone. The food suddenly felt like a lump of cement in her stomach. She felt guilty about the nice bath and the hot food considering she had no idea where he was or what might be happening to him.

Focus, Sadie. You can't stay strong and be of any use to anyone if you don't eat.

As she forced bite after bite into her mouth, first one and then another woman came into the tiny shack and climbed into the tub of water she'd used. After five women had bathed, they shared the duty of carrying out pails of the dirty water.

Sadie understood the concept of conservation but she was immensely grateful she'd been first this morning.

The woman with the long dark hair led her back outside. One of the guards who'd escorted her from her cell was waiting. He led Sadie through the woods and to yet another shack-like house, this one larger. Once they were inside, she could see that this one was built into the mountainside and the interior was more like an actual house. A long corridor led to another door. The guard opened this door and urged her inside.

"And here she is. The woman we've been waiting for."

The man behind the desk stared at her, a grin on his face. Another man stood, rising above the chair that had prevented her from seeing him.

Flynn.

The relief that gushed through her made her knees weak. He was still here. More important, he was alive.

Rather than aim her question at Flynn, she stared directly at the other man. "What happens now?"

"Now, the two of you head out."

So Flynn had been right. This man—Aikman, she presumed—had never intended to keep her. The threat was nothing more than leverage to garner their cooperation.

"We'll take you as far as the road where you dumped

the SUV. You'll be on your own from there." Aikman turned to Flynn. "As you know, I'll have eyes on you at all times. Once you're inside, I'll wait for your signal to make my move."

Sadie kept her thoughts to herself. There was no point in asking questions until she and Flynn were alone.

Flynn nodded. "On my signal."

Aikman nodded and with that gesture they were escorted from the man's office and back outside his rustic dwelling. Two all-terrain vehicles waited. One guard climbed aboard each vehicle and ordered Sadie and Flynn to do the same. Once she climbed on behind a guard and Flynn did the same with the other, a third guard dropped the black cloth bags over their heads. Aikman intended to keep their location a secret.

The vehicle bumped over roots and rocks and God only knew what else. Sadie held on tight no matter that she'd just as soon not touch the guy driving. Holding on to the enemy was better than risking a potentially fatal injury from bouncing off this rocky ride. She focused on counting off the minutes.

Half an hour later the vehicles stopped.

"Get off," the driver shouted over his shoulder at her.

Sadie reached up and removed the bag, then climbed off the ATV. The guard snatched the hood back from her as if he feared it might carry his fingerprints. She smoothed a hand over her hair as she watched the two drive away, bouncing and bumping over the terrain. When they were out of sight, she scanned the area. Woods. So thick they almost blocked the sky.

She turned to Flynn. "You're still sure about this plan?"

"I don't have an option."

She turned all the way around, surveyed the woods once more. Nothing but trees and brush. "The way I see it, we can go in whatever direction we like." Her gaze settled on him once more. "You don't have to finish this if it means you'll end up dead."

Flynn held her gaze for a long moment before he finally spoke. "You go. Stay south and you'll find your way to the main road running into Winchester. If I still had the emergency beacon you could use that, but they took it so you'll be on your own. Keep your movements quiet and you'll be fine."

Sadie was shaking her head before he finished talking. "Either way we go, we go together."

"They have Winters," he said, his tone grave. "I have two hours to show up or he's dead."

Son of a bitch. Frustration, then fury tore through Sadie. "He should have listened to you." To both of them for that matter.

Flynn shook his head. "Doesn't matter. Prentiss had learned my identity before I left the compound with the two of you. We were never getting off this mountain without doing this or something like this."

"In that case, I guess we should get moving." Damn it all to hell. "We have a timeline we have to stick to." When he would have issued another protest, she held up her hand and shook her head.

Obviously not happy about her decision, Flynn led the way to the narrow rutted road. It split through the forest like a dusty brown snake. Sadie shuddered. She was extremely thankful they hadn't run into any creepy creatures. At least not the kind without legs.

When the silence had dragged on about as long as she could tolerate, she said, "You know, I thought you left me this morning." Might as well make conversation while they walked toward their doom.

He glanced at her. "You still don't trust me?"

"It wasn't about trust." In fact, she hadn't considered the idea of trust in a while now. She had instinctively trusted him. "I assumed you weren't given a choice. Then they took me for a bath, gave me clean clothes and fed me. The next thing I knew I was in Aikman's office with you."

His gaze traveled down the length of her, pausing on her bare legs before shifting back up to her face. "I noticed."

His attention swung back to the road. She smiled. Funny how such a simple, offhanded compliment could give her a moment's pleasure even at a time like this. But then, when you might not live beyond the next few hours it didn't take much.

As cold as she'd gotten in that cave last night, it was already hot enough to make her sweat this morning. The humidity was off the charts. Made the uphill journey even more of a slog.

Since Flynn had given her a sort of compliment, maybe she would give him one. "Thanks for keeping me warm last night." She flashed him a smile. "That was very gentlemanly of you."

"I thought you were keeping me warm."

Her jaw dropped, then he grinned. "You're a real

comedian." She laughed. "Seriously, though, I appreciate it. I woke up shivering after you were gone but I remembered you keeping me warm through the night."

"You're welcome, but it was a mutual exchange."

Combined body heat. "What's going to happen when we get there?" As much as she would like to pretend they wouldn't really have to return to that damned compound, she knew there was no way around it outside the cavalry showing up out of the blue to take over the situation.

No one even knew their exact location. They were on their own and the chances of either one of them surviving were about nil. If they walked away, Levi, her target, would die. No matter that they would likely all three die anyway, she couldn't just walk away and leave him without attempting to do something. She glanced at the man beside her. She couldn't just walk away and leave Flynn to deal with this on his own, either.

"I have one sibling, a sister, and my parents." Sadie wasn't sure why she made this abrupt announcement. Just seemed like the thing to do. They might as well enjoy each other's company until they were taken prisoner again.

He said nothing for a while, just kept walking. She did the same.

"No siblings. Parents are long gone. It's just me."

So he was completely alone. "No wife or kids or best buds?"

He shook his head. "The job fills those slots."

This she understood all too well.

"Same here. Although my parents aren't going to be happy if I don't come back."

Another span of silence.

"I guess I'll have to make sure that doesn't happen."

She glanced at him again and this time he was looking back. They smiled simultaneously. It was foolish, she knew, but the shared smile had butterflies taking flight in her stomach. "I'm sure they would appreciate that. I know I would."

The conversation waned from there. What was there to say? They both had at least a couple of choices. If they chose not to go through with this, Levi would die. If she walked away and left Flynn to go on his own and he and Levi didn't make it out, she would have to live with that decision. Levi was not Flynn's problem but he was choosing to take that responsibility. No way was she leaving him to do her job. Walking away wasn't an option.

An hour later, the road was scarcely more than a path now. They were close. Sadie remembered the terrain. The memories sent a chill over her skin. Whether it was self-preservation or utter desperation, she suddenly stopped.

"There has to be something else we can do." She surveyed the endless woods. "Someone who lives out here who has a phone or a vehicle."

There was no one. She was aware of this. Not anywhere close by at any rate. Still, she couldn't *not* ask the question again. Being ambushed was one thing but walking into a death trap was just plain crazy. Of course, that was exactly what she'd done to get into the compound in the first place.

What did that say about the two of them? Maybe they both had death wishes that they explained away with their careers.

"There's no one for miles." He stopped walking and turned to face her. "I understood the risk when I started this. There's no way out."

Sadie moved in on him, taking the three steps between them. "Are you doing this for you or for your father?"

He looked away from her but not before she saw emotions cloud his eyes. "Does it matter?"

She folded her arms over her chest to prevent reaching out to him. One of her instructors had warned her about a place exactly like this. The place you find yourself when you've lost all sight of the difference between your life and your work. When work becomes more important than anything else—even surviving.

"This is the job, Flynn. This isn't about you or your father. This is the job. Justice. Doing the right thing. Taking down the bad guys for the greater good, not for your own personal reasons. Like maybe revenge."

He laughed, shook his head. "Did you spend the last hour thinking up that speech or did you suddenly remember it from your agent-in-training handbook?"

She had definitely hit a nerve. "Don't be a smart-ass. I'm only trying to help. To make you see that we've both lost sight of what we were trained to do. What we swore to do when we started this journey."

"I don't need a lecture, and the only way you can

help is to walk down that mountain to safety while I do what I have to do."

Now he was just being arrogant. "Levi Winters is my target. He's my responsibility. I have just as much right to walk into this trap as you do."

He stared at her long and hard. "It's only a trap if you don't see it coming."

"We need a plan, Flynn. We shouldn't just walk into this, whatever you want to call it, without a plan."

"I have a plan."

That was the moment she remembered what Aikman said. The memory had rocks forming in her gut. "What did your friend mean when he said he would wait for your signal?"

"Let's go."

When he would have turned to start walking again, she grabbed him by the arm. "We're in too deep for you to blow me off at this stage of the game."

He stared at her, his own anger blazing in his eyes.

"It means just what he said, I give the signal, he and his people invade. I've given them the access codes along with the guard locations. Now let's get moving."

Did he really think she was going to let it go? "What's the signal?"

Since they didn't have a cell phone, beacon, flare gun, air horn or any damned thing else, just how the hell did he expect to give anyone outside the compound a signal?

The stare-off continued. Ten seconds, fifteen, twenty.

Enough. She made up her mind then and there. She grabbed him by the shirtfront and jerked his face down to hers. Then she kissed him. Kissed him hard on the mouth. Kept her lips pressed to his until he reacted. His fingers plowed into her hair and pulled her more firmly into him, deepening the kiss, taking control.

She poured herself into the kiss, into the feel of his mouth, his lips and his palms against her face. When the need for air forced them apart, he looked her straight in the eye and said, "I'm still not telling you."

The answer to the question was suddenly as clear as shiny new glass. He had no way of sending a signal.

"They have someone inside, don't they? That's the person who'll give the signal when you've done whatever it is Aikman has asked of you."

He looked away.

She shook her head. "All this time they've had someone inside. Why the hell do they need you?"

"We're running out of time. Let's go."

She grabbed him by the forearm, kept him from turning away. "No. Not until you tell me the truth."

Fury tightened the lips she had only moments ago kissed. Wanted to kiss again, damn her.

"You don't have a need to know, Agent Buchanan."

A sharp laugh burst out of her. "Don't even try playing that game with me." She held his gaze, silently demanding an answer. She saw the answer without him having to say a word. The determination as well as the resignation. Her heart stumbled. "You're going to kill Prentiss, aren't you? That's the signal Aikman will be waiting for."

He snapped his gaze away from hers and started to

walk once more, but not before she saw the defeat in his eyes.

Prentiss's bodyguards would kill Flynn.

There was no way he would survive.

She had to figure out a way to turn this around.

Chapter Thirteen

Smith started walking. He could not allow her to sway his decision. She didn't understand. Aikman would have killed her after doing other unspeakable things if Smith hadn't agreed to his terms.

There was no other choice. No way out.

It was true that at this moment there was some measure of leeway. Quite possibly they could take off and maybe get down this damned mountain before they were caught. But that would be like putting a gun to Levi Winters's head and pulling the trigger. If that wasn't bad enough, Prentiss would no doubt disappear.

This—right now—was the one chance Smith had of stopping him.

"You're a fool."

He ignored her, which wasn't easy to do. She had surprised him when she kissed him. He'd felt the mutual attraction almost from the beginning, couldn't have missed it if he'd tried. The intensity of it was his own fault. It had been way too long since he'd allowed himself basic human pleasures. She made him want to indulge those ignored needs. It was difficult for a starving man to ignore a buffet right in front of him.

"This goes against your training. We both understand what needs to happen. This is a textbook example of a no-win situation. We need backup."

"You feel strongly about following the rules, is that it, Buchanan?" She was as bad as him. She'd walked into a deadly situation without so much as a blink and damned sure without any backup. She had no right to judge his actions.

"It's not the same," she argued.

"It's exactly the same."

She stopped and turned to him. He bumped into her shoulder.

"I didn't walk into that compound prepared to kill a man."

Anger clenched his jaw. He struggled to utter an answer. She couldn't possibly understand. "He deserves to die."

She nodded. "Maybe so but not because you want to put a bullet in his brain. What you're talking about is premeditated murder. Are you a murderer, Flynn?"

He bit his lips together to prevent denying the charge. Maybe he was a murderer. He had never wanted to kill another man the way he wanted to kill Prentiss.

"If you are, what makes you any better than him?"

A part of him wanted to refute her words. To explain his reasoning. But did any of it really matter? He wanted to watch Rayford Prentiss die. He couldn't wait to see him take his last breath. Equally important, he wanted the bastard to know that he—Smith Flynn, the son of

Avery Flynn—had been the one to bring his ruthless reign and his life to an end.

"Nothing," he admitted.

He walked on. They were close to the compound. The watchers would spot them and send out a team to bring them in. It wouldn't be long now.

The answer he'd given to her last question kept her quiet for a few minutes. She was searching for some other rationalization for why he couldn't do what Aikman had ordered him to do. He could practically hear the wheels in her head turning. She wanted to help him.

But she couldn't.

No one could. Not at this point. It was too late.

As much as he regretted what he had become and all the things he'd had to do, if necessary he would do it all again to stop Prentiss.

"Once we're inside, give me some time," she suddenly said, her voice low as if she feared the trees had ears. Most likely they did.

"Time for what?" He asked this without looking at her. He didn't want to look at her. Not simply because she was attractive and alluring and made him want things he shouldn't. But because she reminded him of all that was good—of the reason he became an agent in the first place. She made him want the career he'd had before this journey started. She made him wish things had been different.

Could he be that man again? Did the good part of him even still exist? He had worked for two long years to erase that guy. To make him immune to the emotions that would only get in his way.

Buchanan had made a valid point. He was a murderer. He'd killed the man he used to be. What he was now was no better than Prentiss.

He doubted there was any going back.

She stopped again, moved in close to him, making his body yearn to pull her close. "Once we're inside, give me time to create a distraction. We can turn this around, Flynn, make it work for us."

The hope in her eyes made him want to believe her. Made him want to grab on to the life raft she offered and hang on for the ride.

But what if she was wrong?

"He won't be fooled so easily this time. He knows he can't trust either of us. How do you expect to manipulate him in any way to buy time or anything else?"

She was an optimist. A woman who wanted to stand by the goodness and justice she believed in. She needed him to believe, too, but he'd lost the ability to blindly believe in anything.

"Trust me, Flynn. You would be surprised at the tricks I have up my sleeve."

He shouldn't agree to the idea. He should do what he had to do and be grateful for the opportunity.

But she made him want to do the right thing.

"I'll give you as much time as I can."

She grinned. "That's all I can ask for, partner."

Despite the worry and uncertainty nagging at him, he smiled back at her. Maybe they could turn this around.

He just hoped she lived through it. He had never expected to survive this assignment, but he didn't want to be the reason she lost her life.

As they ascended the next ridge, troops came out of the trees. Seven, no eight. The group swarmed out and surrounded their position, weapons leveled on his and Buchanan's heads.

Smith held perfectly still. "I need to see Prentiss."

"He doesn't want to see you."

Smith knew this soldier. He was an ambitious man. He would want to prove he was somehow responsible for Smith's capture.

"Take me to him," he said to the younger man, daring him to argue. Smith was now listed as an enemy but there would be those who had their doubts. Those who feared turning their backs on him since it was not out of the question that he could be restored to his former position. After all, he was Avery Flynn's only son.

The soldier gave a nod to one of his minions. "Search them both."

When he and Buchanan had been patted down to the man's satisfaction, he ordered his team to move out. The soldiers stayed in a tight ring around Smith and Buchanan as they continued on to the compound.

The compound was only a mile or so away at this point. He glanced at Buchanan. Somehow he had to find a way to keep her from ending up dead no matter that she refused to cooperate.

She'd asked for time, which likely meant she had a plan. Maybe he should listen to her reasoning. She wasn't emotionally tangled up with this situation and he was. Her reasoning might be clearer than his own. He'd been guilty of a lot of mistakes over the years but he didn't have to make one today.

PRENTISS WAITED ALONE in the meeting room.

Of course he wouldn't want any of the other members of the Council present when he said what he had to say. The secrets and lies he had kept over all these years were not the sort he wanted anyone to know, particularly those who looked to him to lead them. There was not a bigger con artist alive. The man was capable of anything if it gained him what he wanted. But the other members of the Council, the followers, none of them would ever believe he was anything other than a selfless leader who protected their way of life.

Smith had barely resisted the urge to take a swing at one of the guards when he prepared to separate Buchanan from him. As two guards dragged her away she had shouted for him to remember what she said.

He did remember.

For what it was worth, he would try his best to give her some time.

Smith was shackled and escorted to a chair, where he was forced to sit before the shackles around his ankles were anchored to the floor. Prentiss didn't speak until the guards had left the room. Only the two of them would ever know the whole story if Prentiss had his way.

"Is it true?" the old man asked as if he could hardly believe the reality of what had occurred.

"What would you know about the truth?" Looking at him sickened Smith. How had he managed these past two years?

"I know enough," Prentiss warned. "I know a mole

when I see one. A traitor. A man whose entire existence is a betrayal to his own people."

"Doesn't matter now," Smith mused, deciding on a delay tactic that might just work. "You're finished."

The old man's gaze narrowed. "I don't believe you. If the feds had anything on me, they would be here now arresting me and pinning medals on you." He glanced around the room. "I don't see or hear anyone coming to your rescue. Perhaps you should pray about this dilemma in which you find yourself."

Smith chuckled. "I don't need to pray, old man. I've spent two years feeding information to those feds. They have what they need, they're only waiting for the perfect moment. Believe me when I say that moment is close at hand."

"If that's true, then why were you and your friend still wandering about on this mountain? Why haven't your comrades rescued you? Or have they forsaken you as you have forsaken me?"

"I refused a rescue. I want to watch from right here." He smiled. "I want to witness them dragging you away in shackles." He shook his head. "Too bad the other members of the Council are going down with you. They are only guilty of following your orders. How fast do you think one or more of them will roll over and start spilling his guts about the executions and the shipments?"

Prentiss stood and moved toward him. He looked even older and more than a little frail in those overalls and worn boots. But there was nothing frail about this bastard. He was dangerous. Ruthless. Cunning as hell.

"I will know what you've told them," he warned as he braced his hands on the arms of the chair and leaned in close to Smith. "I will know every secret and every name you've shared. And then you will die a slow, agonizing death."

Smith allowed a wide smile to slide across his lips once more. "I shared them all. Every single name, every single secret. They know about your partners in South America. They know your next incoming shipment and the distribution channels you intend to use. They know *everything.*"

"I want names," Prentiss demanded. "Who are your contacts?"

"You can't stop this, old man. They're coming and you and all this will fall."

Prentiss drew back sharply as if he feared catching some contagious disease. "Your father would be sickened by your actions. He would kill you himself."

Smith leaned forward as far as his shackles would allow. "My father was not like you. He would be grateful to me for stopping you."

Prentiss held his ground. "Maybe you're right. Avery had grown weak in his old age. He failed to see what was best for the security of our people. Progress is necessary. As is extending our reach. He was blind to those needs."

"But they followed him. Looked up to him. Not you," Smith reminded him. "You were always in his shadow."

Prentiss was the one smiling then. "And yet I'm still here and he is gone."

"How much longer do you think you can hang on

when your people learn you failed to see the traitor in their midst? Or maybe they'll see you as the traitor."

"They already know what you are. You're just like your father. Weak. Shortsighted. A stumbling block to survival."

Anger ignited deep inside Smith. "My father was not weak. His vision was far greater than yours. You will never be half the leader he was."

"Before I order your public execution perhaps it's time you were told what really happened."

Smith stilled. His father suffered a heart attack. "I'm well aware of how he died."

On some level he would always believe that his decision to leave had been part of the burden that weighed upon his father, making him a prime candidate for a sudden heart attack. He couldn't help wondering if he'd secretly discovered what Smith had become, a traitor to all his father believed.

"His heart stopped true enough." Prentiss reared back, his thumbs hooked into the side splits of his overalls. "It was the only way to protect what we had achieved. He would have ruined everything."

Something cold and dark swelled inside Smith. "What does that mean?"

"It means," the bastard said, obviously enjoying the moment, "that he wanted to pull back. When he found out about my deal with the cartel, he demanded I leave. He intended to put me out after I had dedicated my life to the cause." Prentiss shrugged. "It was him or me. He was too sick to understand what he was saying and doing. So, as you can see, it wasn't me."

Shock radiated through Smith. "You killed him?"

"I did," Prentiss confessed. "Just like I'm going to kill you."

SADIE DIDN'T BOTHER STRUGGLING. Prentiss had ordered her to the tunnels. Her friend Levi, Prentiss had warned, was already there, unless he'd ended up as dinner earlier than expected.

No wonder Flynn wanted to kill the man. He was a ruthless degenerate. Every minute he drew breath, someone else suffered.

The dome was pulled back by one of her guards, revealing the ladder that led deep under the ground. Sadie went along, feigning uncertainty. She had a plan and having it start in the tunnels would work to her advantage.

When she reached the bottom of the ladder, George was waiting. He still wore those flimsy flip-flops he'd bartered out of her.

"Wasn't expecting you back," he said. "I heard you ran off."

"I missed you and decided to drop by for a visit."

He stared at her a long moment, her light sarcasm seemingly lost on him. Finally, he nodded. "Anyway, your friend is down here, too. He ain't faring so well."

"What's wrong with him?"

"I guess he don't like the idea that if an emergency happens and we run out of food, he'll be the backup."

Levi was supplies. Prentiss had enjoyed telling her that, as well. Before George could turn and start walking away, she said, "We should probably talk before joining the others."

He frowned. "You know the drill down here. What do we have to talk about?"

Sadie looked around as if to make sure no one else was nearby. "They're coming today. If all of you are still here, you'll end up in jail, too."

Confusion flashed in his eyes. "Who's coming?"

"The feds, local law enforcement. They're coming to take Prentiss and the Council to jail. They know everything about this place."

He shrugged. "They've boasted about taking Prentiss down before and it never happens. He's way too careful."

"Trust me, George. I'm with the FBI. They know everything. You were nice to me so I'd like to help you and the others down here. But there isn't a lot of time. We should get out of here while we still can."

"What?" He drew back as if her words had attacked him.

"You know how to get out. You've dug egress routes. You know where they are and how to use them. Don't pretend you don't, George."

"I think we should get to work." He started walking deeper into the tunnel.

Sadie didn't move. She stayed next to the ladder. She wasn't going anywhere until she got George thinking about how easy it would be to escape this tunnel and flee to someplace well beyond the reach of the Resurrection. Not that the group would have any power left when this was done. She decided on a new tactic.

"Prentiss and the rest of the Council are leaving. You think they're going to let you guys out of here before they evacuate?" She shook her head. "They'll leave you to die. The authorities can't question the dead."

He stalled, shook his head at her. "You're lying."

"I'm not lying, George. I have no reason to lie. I just don't want to die and that's what will happen if we don't get out of here."

He started walking again. She followed.

"The feds are coming to take Prentiss and his Council down. They'll be here before nightfall. We don't have time to waste. Prentiss and his cronies are going to get away clean and all of us down here won't."

He stopped and glanced back at her again. "If what you're saying is true, what do you expect us to do?"

"You told me about the egresses you've prepared. Let's go to the closest one and get out of here before it's too late. Before Prentiss orders any and all loose ends cleaned up."

"There will be guards waiting at the egresses," he argued. "They'll shoot us."

She shook her head. "They'll be gone. They're afraid. They're not going to hang around once word about what's coming gets around."

George kept moving until he reached the work area. Sadie trudged along behind him. Levi was there and he looked in reasonably good condition. No visible injuries. Relief rushed through her. Maybe this would be a second chance to get him safely out of here. This time she wasn't allowing him out of her sight. She fully intended to deliver him to his sister.

With his shovel in his hand, George joined the others. Sadie wanted to shake him. Why the hell wasn't he listening? She needed something to happen soon if she was going to help Smith.

"Hey," she shouted at him. "Didn't you hear what I said? We have to get out of here or we're all going to die. Why aren't you telling these people?"

Several of the men glanced at her and then at George but made no move to stop what they were doing.

"Levi!" She waited for him to look at her. "Come on. We're getting out of here."

He looked around at the other men. Just when Sadie was certain he would keep working, he threw down his shovel and walked toward her.

Another wave of relief swept through her. "Who else is with us?"

She scanned the dirty faces. All stared at her, their expressions weary, defeated.

"Tell them, George," she urged. "Tell them what's about to happen up there. We have to run while we still can."

George stared at her for a long moment, then he threw down his pickax and stalked toward her. She held her breath, not certain whether he intended to yank her over to take his place or if he intended to join her.

When he reached her, he turned back to the others. "We'll need shovels and axes. It'll take us at least twenty minutes and if they see us on the cameras, they'll come down here and make us wish we hadn't listened to her."

"We can do this," Sadie urged, not wanting his warning to dissuade them. "We'll work faster than we ever have before."

George surveyed the men now watching him. "Grab your shovels and the axes. We're out of here."

Much to her immense gratitude, George led the way. Sadie and Levi followed. At least twelve more hustled along the corridor behind them. She glanced at the cameras placed overhead approximately every fifteen yards along the seemingly endless corridor. They wouldn't have a lot of time.

The alarm was sounding by the time they reached the closest egress. Six of the men climbed the ladders and started to dig. Six more formed a wall across the tunnel in anticipation of the guards who would no doubt come.

The sound of boots pounding on the ground echoed through the tunnel. George and his friends were shouting at each other to hurry. Sadie dragged Levi closer.

"As soon as that egress is cleared," she murmured close to his ear, "we have to get out of here and go for help."

He nodded his understanding.

Shouting in the tunnel echoed some ten yards away.

Hurry. Sadie looked from the wall of bodies standing between the coming guards and their position to the men jabbing and poking overhead.

"Go!"

Sadie jerked her attention toward George. Sunlight suddenly poured into the tunnel. Three of the men were already scrambling out.

"Let's go." Sadie nudged Levi forward.

They rushed up the ladders and climbed out. Two

guards who had been taking a smoke break suddenly turned toward them. George and the others were on top of them before they could get their weapons into position.

Others were clambering out behind Sadie and Levi.

Sadie didn't look back. She held on to Levi's hand and ran through the woods as fast as she could.

She had no idea how far they were from help but she had to get to wherever that was as quickly as possible.

Smith's life depended upon it.

Chapter Fourteen

Sadie kept a firm grasp on Levi's hand as they ran through the woods, branches and undergrowth slapping at her bare legs.

The crack of gunfire behind them forced Sadie's heart into a faster cadence.

She charged forward with a new burst of adrenaline-inspired speed. Levi managed to keep up though he was barefoot and stumbling with exhaustion. He would pay for the lack of shoes or boots later. She imagined he had blisters on his hands just as she'd had after her time in the tunnel, though hers were partially healed now.

If the guards got off a good shot, the two of them would have far more than blisters to worry about.

"This way." Levi tugged at the hand she had clenched around his.

He knew the area and she didn't. She might as well trust him. He had as much reason to want to escape this mountain as she did. Staying alive was always a strong motivator no matter which side of the equation one was on.

Levi deviated into a different direction. Plowed through the jungle of trees.

By the time they slowed Sadie could barely get her breath.

"Hold on a minute." Levi leaned against a tree and struggled to catch his breath, as well.

Sadie propped against the nearest tree and took slow, deep breaths. When she could string words together, she asked, "How far to civilization?"

"If we keep going this way—" he hitched a thumb in the direction they'd been headed, south Sadie thought "—we'll hit the valley in about a mile and a half. There are a few houses in that area. We can probably use a phone there."

Sadie nodded. Worked for her.

When they headed out again they moved considerably slower. Sadie's muscles burned from the hard run and the abuse they'd suffered the past several days. She would need weeks to recover from the way she'd mistreated her body on this mission.

Assuming she survived. She glanced over her shoulder to ensure no one was coming. Clear for now.

As they moved downward the underbrush grew less dense. Even the trees weren't so thick. Up ahead beyond the tree line an open pasture came into view. She and Levi hesitated at the edge of the woods to have a look at what lay beyond.

Sadie spotted a house and barn in the distance. Judging by the cows in the field and the farm equipment scattered about, someone lived there. There were other houses beyond that one. Acres of open pasture rolled out between the houses. She glanced behind her once more. Moving through those open areas would be risky if the enemy on their trail caught up with them.

Sadie turned to the man at her side. "Do you know any of the people who live on this stretch of road?"

Levi shook his head. "All we need is to use the phone, right? Surely one of them will let us do that whether they know us or not."

Sadie nodded. "We'll tell them our car broke down. If we mention the trouble on our heels, they may not let us in the house. Some people don't like to get involved."

"Yeah." He surveyed the expanse of green space in front of them. "You're right. We can't tell them what's really going on."

Sadie scanned the woods behind them. She listened for several seconds. "Maybe we lost those guards."

More than a dozen people had escaped the tunnel. Most went in different directions. Hopefully, the two guards she had spotted as well as those who had come up from the tunnel had followed some of the others. Not that she wished that unlucky break on anyone, but she was only human.

"Let's try that first house," she suggested. "The sooner we get to town the sooner we can send help for Flynn." Her stomach twisted at the idea that he could be dead already. She had urged him to buy some time. To do his best to drag out the inevitable. She hoped he was successful. As long as he didn't allow his emotions to take over, he would be okay. He was a well-trained agent. Hopefully that training would kick in and keep him thinking smart.

With one last backward glance, she and Levi dashed across the pasture. Part of her braced for the crack of a weapon firing at them but it didn't come. As they neared the house a cow raised its head and stared at them.

They bounded up onto the front porch. Levi reached the door first. He knocked. Sadie kept a watch on the tree line to ensure no one came rushing out after them. All they needed was a phone. One call.

Her pulse pounded as Levi knocked again. No television sound, no footsteps moving about. The house sounded empty. Worried that was indeed the case, Sadie peered through the nearest window. *Kitchen.* There were drying dishes on a towel on the counter. If no one was home now, they had been earlier.

"Somebody lives here." She checked the tree line and pasture again.

A loud thump drew her attention to the door. Levi backed up and body-slammed it again, using his right shoulder.

Sadie winced as he slammed it a third time before it gave way and burst inward.

She exhaled a big breath and followed him across the threshold. Breaking and entering wasn't such a bad thing considering they were running for their lives.

"Phone's over here," Levi said.

Sadie went to the side table beneath the big front window. "Have a look around and make sure no one's in the shower or something. We don't need an armed homeowner thinking we mean harm to him or his property."

She sure as hell didn't want to escape armed killers only to end up shot by a terrified farmer or his wife.

Levi nodded and headed into the hall. The house was a brick rancher, not so large. It wouldn't take him long to have a look.

Sadie entered 911 into the handset. As soon as the dispatcher finished her spiel, she identified herself and asked to be connected to Sheriff Tanner.

Tanner was on the line in under twenty seconds.

Sadie sagged with relief. "Tanner, we're…" Hearing footsteps, she turned to ask Levi exactly where they were.

Gun.

She froze.

Levi stood in the cased opening between the living room and the hall, his hands high in the air. An older man wearing a cap had the business end of a rifle jammed into the side of his head. Levi's eyes were round with fear.

"I tried to tell him we need help," Levi explained.

"Put the phone down," the man demanded.

Damn. "Sir, I'm on the phone with Sheriff Tanner." She thrust the phone at the man. "We're unarmed. Speak to the sheriff and he'll explain everything."

The man backed away from Levi but kept a bead on his head. He took the cordless phone receiver from Sadie and backed a few steps farther away in order to keep them both in his line of vision.

"Sheriff Tanner, this is Cord Hawkins." Hawkins gave the address and then listened as Tanner spoke.

Sadie couldn't make out what he was saying but she heard the rumble of his voice. Judging by the way the man lowered the barrel of his weapon, he understood Sadie and Levi were no threat to him.

"I'll do it," Hawkins said. He offered the receiver to Sadie. "Sheriff wants to talk to you again."

"Thank you." Sadie took the phone and pressed it to her ear. "Tell me you're on your way. We don't have much time."

As Tanner passed along orders via another phone line, Sadie was vaguely aware that Hawkins had brought cans of cola from the kitchen. He passed one to Levi and offered one to her.

Sadie summoned a smile and murmured a thank-you. She popped the top and downed half the can before Tanner turned his attention back to the conversation with her.

"Sit tight, Agent Buchanan, we're on our way to you. We'll have that mountain covered within the hour."

Sadie ended the call and drank more of the cola. Levi leaned against the wall and slid to the floor as he guzzled his cola. Sadie closed her eyes against the weariness dragging at her. She had never been so tired in her life.

"Are those friends of yours?"

Sadie jerked her attention back to the here and now and rushed across the room to the big window. Hawkins pointed at three men running across the same pasture she and Levi had sprinted across. She peered across the distance to make out their faces. One was George, she decided. She didn't need to recognize the faces of the other two. All wore the dirty sweats and sported the greasy hair and dirty faces of tunnel workers.

"They were prisoners just like us." She turned to Hawkins. "They're not the bad guys."

His fingers tightened around his rifle. "You sure about that, ma'am?"

She nodded. "I'll go out and talk to them."

"I'll be watching," Hawkins assured her.

"Thank you."

Sadie stepped out the front door as the three men bounded up the porch steps. "Did they follow you?" She hadn't seen anyone else coming out of that tree line.

George shook his head. "We lost them."

"Hurry." Sadie opened the door. "Let's get inside. The sheriff is on the way with help."

Hawkins passed out colas to the three and dug up a couple of big bags of chips. The men ate as if they hadn't eaten in days. Probably hadn't. She kept her attention on the tree line and said a prayer for Flynn.

He was still at that compound. On his own.

"The sheriff's here," Hawkins announced.

A whole parade of official vehicles arrived. Uniformed deputies and officers poured into the house. Paramedics insisted on giving Sadie, Levi and the other three a quick check while she and George provided information about the compound, the people there and the precarious position in which they'd left Agent Smith Flynn.

Winchester's chief of police, William Brannigan, was already on the phone with the ATF. The state police and the Bureau had been notified en route. Through the window Sadie spotted Agent Ross and Cece Winters, coming up the porch steps.

"Levi." Sadie turned to the young man who had resumed his seat on the floor. "Someone's here for you."

He pushed to his feet at the same time that his sister and Ross entered the house. The reunion of brother and sister was the one good thing that had happened this day. Sadie was grateful to be a part of it.

Cece Winters hugged Sadie next. "Thank you for rescuing my brother."

Sadie glanced at Levi. "I think it was a mutual rescue."

He smiled. "Maybe."

Special Agent Deacon Ross shook Sadie's hand. "I appreciate what you must have gone through to make this happen."

"We're not finished yet," she warned. "There's a war about to happen on that mountain. The Resurrection and the *others* are going head-to-head. Agent Flynn is caught in the middle of it. He could be dead already. We have to hurry."

George suddenly stepped forward. "I know the one access road to get to that compound. Know the codes, too. I'll take you there."

The other two who had come with George echoed his offer.

They all wanted to see Prentiss go down.

No one wanted that more than Sadie.

"Ms. Winters will take you back to my office," Tanner said to Sadie.

She shook her head. "No way. I'm going with you."

Tanner started to argue but he must have seen the

absolute determination in Sadie's eyes. He nodded. "All right, then, let's move out."

SMITH STRUGGLED TO FOCUS.

He hung from a hook attached to the ceiling, his feet dangling several inches off the floor. He'd been stripped to the waist and tortured for hours. He'd lost track of the time.

The beating he rode out without much more than a flinch. The shock torture had become tedious the last half hour or so. This was nothing he hadn't endured before. But it was the burns that were about to be inflicted with a branding iron he would just as soon skip.

Prentiss, the son of a bitch, watched from a safe distance across the room as the irons turned red amid the fiery coals. Smith knew the soldier tasked with the job of inflicting the torture. The man didn't appear to feel bad about having to torture an old friend. Maybe Smith had made more enemies than he'd realized during his time here. Or maybe the guy was just glad to be the one inflicting the torture and not the one receiving it.

Who could blame him?

The one thing Smith knew with absolute certainty was that providing he survived long enough he would kill Rayford Prentiss if it was the last thing he ever did.

The bastard had admitted to murdering his father.

Prentiss was responsible for the deaths of countless other people with his gunrunning and drug trade. And that was only the beginning.

As if his thoughts had summoned him, Prentiss dared to venture closer. He surveyed Smith, enjoying the blood dribbling from his mouth and nose, the swelling of his face and eyes as well as the bruises forming on his torso. All these things gave him pleasure. This bastard had tortured and murdered many. But Smith would be his last, one way or another.

Whether Smith survived this day or not, Buchanan would ensure the bastard got what he deserved.

If she had survived.

Smith closed his eyes against any other possibility. She was too smart and too determined to fail. Prentiss had been called out of the room once, a couple of hours ago. Smith hadn't been able to hear all that was said but he'd picked up on the gist of the conversation. There had been an escape. Ten or twelve people had dug out of the tunnel and evaded the posted guards.

She would be one of them, Smith felt certain.

Go, Sadie.

A smile tugged at his damaged lips. He liked her name. *Sadie.* He liked her sassiness and her courage.

He hoped he had the chance to get to know her better.

"What on God's green earth do you have to smile about, boy?"

Smith opened his swollen eyes as best he could. "I was just thinking how you'll rot in prison with all your friends. Oh wait." He managed a rusty laugh. "You don't have any friends. That should be interesting."

He'd expected Aikman to show up even though he didn't get a signal indicating Smith had taken care of Prentiss. With all the access codes and information Smith had provided him, he'd figured the man would make a move either way.

"I thought maybe you were worried about your own friend, or enemy as the case might be," Prentiss said. "Aikman, I believe his name is."

Smith clenched his aching jaw to prevent showing a reaction to the name.

"You see, I found out about his man inside. He was watching, nosing around in places he didn't belong today, so I guessed something was up. Unlike you, he sang like a bird with very little prodding. My people are on high alert. No one is getting into this compound today or any other. Strange." He rubbed at his beard. "I understand you were going to kill me. Whatever changed your mind?"

Smith smiled again, his split lip burning like fire. "I decided I'd rather know that you're rotting in a prison cell than give you an easy way out. I want you to live, old man. A very long time so you can enjoy what the future holds for you when justice is served."

Prentiss picked up one of the knives lying on the table with all the other torture instruments. He turned it over in his hand, pretending to inspect the stainless steel blade and handle.

Tension slid through Smith. He braced to lift his legs and kick him across the room. He'd been waiting for time alone with the guy administering the torture in hopes of using that move as a means to escape, but so far that moment hadn't come. Once he attempted any sort of maneuver, if he was unsuccessful steps would be taken to ensure he was unable to repeat the effort. So he had waited. Unfortunately, his strength was waning far too quickly. He'd have to make a move soon or find himself unable to do so.

The door on the other side of the room opened and one of Prentiss's private bodyguards rushed in. He whispered something in the old man's ear. Prentiss set the knife aside. His gaze settled on Smith as he listened to the rest of what the man had to say.

It was happening. Smith didn't have to hear the words. He saw the abrupt fear in the old man's eyes.

Prentiss looked to the other man in the room. "Finish him and clear out."

Oh yeah. Either Aikman and his people were descending on the compound or the backup Sadie had gone after was close.

Either option suited Smith.

Prentiss hurried out with his bodyguard.

Smith held very still as the man who'd beat and tortured him walked toward him for the last time. Mentally preparing himself to expend the last of his physical strength, Smith waited until the man was close enough to pick up that big-ass knife from the table. His fingers wrapped around the handle and he weighed it, hoping to add a layer of tension, to build the dread.

Smith made his move.

He wrapped his legs around the man's neck and squeezed. Struggling to free himself, the bastard lifted his right hand, aiming the knife at Smith.

Smith used his whole body to jerk to the right, snapping the bastard's neck. His eyes bulged. The knife fell from his slack fingers and clanged on the floor. Smith loosened his hold and the now-lifeless body followed that route, dropping like a rock.

Swinging his legs to the left, Smith grabbed hold of the table with his bare feet. He hung that way for a moment to catch his breath and to give his muscles a moment to recover. Slowly, he used his feet to drag the table closer. When he could kneel on it, he rested another moment. Finally, he pushed upward, lifting his bound hands from the meat hook that had held him suspended in the air. He collapsed into a kneeling position on the table. A few minutes were required for his arms to stop stinging.

He scooted off the table and found his footing on the floor. Where the hell was the key to these wrist shackles? He checked the table and the items that had been flung to the floor when he'd dragged it close. No key. Then he checked the dead guy who'd wielded the hours of torture. The key was in his right front pocket. Smith pulled the key free.

Collapsing into a cross-legged position, he focused on getting the key into the lock that held an iron bracelet around his left wrist. He dropped the key, once, twice before he managed to get it into the lock. He had to twist his right hand in an awkward position to turn the key but he finally managed. The lock on his left wrist fell open. Relief surged through him. He picked up the key and unlocked the bracelet on his right wrist. When the final shackle fell free, he rubbed his wrists and dragged in a deep breath. His damaged ribs ached with the move.

Pushing to his feet, he surveyed the room for a weapon. Depending on who had arrived, he could be in for another battle for his life. He turned over the dead guy, snatched the gun from his waistband. He checked the ammo cartridge. Full. He shoved the gun into his waistband and went in search of his shoes. He finally found them in a pile with the shirt that had been cut from his body. The shirt he could live without but the shoes would be useful.

Now to find Prentiss before the bastard managed to slip away.

Smith stalled halfway to the door and went back to the dead guy for his cell phone. It was possible Prentiss would call to ensure Smith was dead. He no doubt wanted Smith dead as badly as Smith wanted him caught. A vehicle fob fell out of the guy's pocket. Smith took that, as well.

Running footsteps in the corridor outside the door snapped Smith's attention in that direction. He started toward the door. Halfway across the room it opened.

Smith leveled the weapon on the potential threat.

Aikman.

Chapter Fifteen

"Well, well, if it isn't the man who failed his mission." Aikman shook his head. "*Tsk, tsk*, Flynn, I had you pegged for better than that."

Apparently the idea that Smith was the one holding the gun aimed at him didn't faze the guy. Aikman's weapon was in his hand but not aimed at anything other than the floor. Whoever else had been in that corridor with him had moved on to the next door. A bad decision any way you looked at it.

"I was working on it and the bastard found out you had invaded the compound. So he took off while I was still a little tied up."

Aikman glanced at the meat hook beyond Smith. "Ouch."

Smith wasn't sure whether the guy was trying to put him off-balance or if he really wasn't worried about the weapon aimed at his head just now.

"You might want to put that weapon away," Smith suggested. "I don't want to get nervous and do something we'll both regret."

Aikman smiled, made a laugh/grunt sound. "Of

course." He tucked the weapon into his waistband. "We've decided we prefer these accommodations over our own. So we'll be taking over the compound."

"You planning on killing everyone here?" Smith hoped like hell backup was close.

Aikman shrugged. "There are some I'd rather have join my team." He made a questioning face. "You interested, Flynn?"

He lowered his weapon and wiped his bleeding mouth. "Why not? As long as the terms are agreeable."

Aikman glanced around the room. "Where's your little friend? I was looking forward to seeing her again."

"I'd like to know the answer to that one myself." He started toward the door that Aikman currently blocked. "I'm hoping Prentiss didn't take her with him." Smith knew that wasn't the case but Aikman couldn't know.

Aikman turned his back to Smith and exited the room first. The guy continued to surprise Smith.

"We've rounded up all the Council members." Aikman glanced at him as they moved along the corridor. "Except Prentiss and you, of course."

Dread thickened in Smith's gut. "Did you kill them?"

Aikman shook his head. "Not yet. They no doubt have information I'll need going forward. Unless you have everything you think we'll need. In that case we can be rid of them right away."

"Prentiss was careful never to give all the power to one person. Each of us had our domain. We'll need them all."

This was a lie but if it kept Aikman from performing a mass execution, that was all that mattered.

There was just one problem as far as Smith could see. He couldn't be sure which of the Council members would be smart enough to keep his mouth shut about him being an undercover agent. If any of those who knew warned Aikman, this situation would do a one-eighty in a heartbeat.

He needed that backup to arrive now.

"I have them gathered in the conference room." Aikman glanced at him. "We'll join them and start the downloading of information, so to speak."

"I'll meet you there in fifteen. I need to wash the blood off my face and change clothes. We don't want them to see any sign of weakness. We need to present strength and unity so they'll understand the shift in power."

"Smart move. Fifteen minutes." Aikman suddenly stopped and turned back. "Ollie!"

One of his followers hustled up to join them. "Escort our friend Mr. Flynn to his personal lodging. Ensure he's in the conference room in fifteen minutes."

"Yes, sir." The man named Ollie turned his shaggy head to glare at Smith. "Let's go, Flynn."

Aikman didn't trust him as much as he'd let on. That made them even because Smith didn't trust him at all.

Outside was quiet. "Where is everyone?"

"They're in the detection center."

Smith was surprised the other man, Ollie, gave him an answer but he was glad he had. As much as Smith despised Prentiss, he did not want this day to turn into a mass killing of people whose only mistake was believing in the wrong man.

Walking across the quad was eerie. No sound. No movement. Nothing. The faces in the guard towers were unfamiliar to Smith. Aikman's people, no doubt. When they reached his cabin, Ollie went in, looked around and then waited outside, leaving the door open.

"If you go in the bathroom," he said to Smith, "don't close the door."

"Got it."

Smith grabbed fresh clothes and went into the tiny bathroom. He pulled the cell phone from his pocket, placed it on the sink, then did the same with the gun. When he'd dragged on the clean clothes, he looked to see that Ollie was still outside the door. He held the phone where it couldn't be seen from the door and sent a text message to 911. He had no idea if the 911 service in the area was able to receive text messages but, at the moment, it was his only available option. He couldn't risk making a call with Aikman's man right outside.

Once he'd sent the text, he deleted it. He set the phone to silent just in case the dispatcher tried to call him back, then slid it into his hip pocket. He shoved the weapon into his waistband at the small of his back, then washed his face.

His eyes and jaw were swollen, and he was reasonably sure he had a couple of cracked ribs, but things could be far worse.

He joined Ollie outside. "I'm ready."

The walk across the quad was the same as before, too quiet. Too still. They reached the headquarters and entered. Two guards were posted outside the door to the conference room. Ollie walked right up and opened the door and entered. Smith followed him.

The scene in the room brought him up short. The members of the Council lay on the floor in a neat line. All were dead, all had been shot once in the head.

His gaze swung to Aikman, who stood in the center of the room. Behind him someone was seated in a chair but Smith couldn't see who it was since Aikman blocked his view.

"I thought we were going to interrogate them." He glared at Aikman, his fingers itching to reach for the weapon in his waistband.

As if Ollie had sensed his thought, he plucked the weapon from Smith.

"That was far too much trouble," Aikman said. "It seemed far easier to simply go to the head and learn everything straight from the source."

He stepped aside, revealing the person in the chair. *Rayford Prentiss.*

"You weren't expecting to see me, were you, *Agent* Flynn?" Prentiss laughed. "Looks like this game of double-cross is going to turn out just fine for me." He glanced up at Aikman. "New blood is always a good thing."

SADIE DROPPED TO her haunches next to Sheriff Tanner. "Aikman and his people have taken over," she said, worry gnawing at her. "We can't wait, we have to move fast. The killing won't stop until we stop it."

The text message relayed to Tanner from the 911 dispatcher mentioned heavily armed men and numerous prisoners. Dozens were dead already.

Sadie's chest squeezed. The text had to be from Flynn, which meant, for now, he was still alive. She hoped he stayed that way until they could get in there and stop the killing.

The good news was, inside those walls were the leaders of the Resurrection and those of the *others*. This operation was going to stop two of the worst kind of extremist organizations in one fell swoop.

As much as she wanted to be grateful for that possibility, she couldn't help worrying about Flynn. She didn't want him to end up a casualty. She wanted to spend time with him. Time that didn't involve a mission or a race to stay alive.

Tanner nodded. "We're almost ready."

Sadie had been able to warn them about the scouts around the compound. Strangely they hadn't spotted any outside the walls. Had to have something to do with the takeover. Several bodies had been discovered.

Tanner put a hand on her arm. "We're moving." His gaze locked with hers. "But you're staying right here until we have the situation under control."

She drew her arm away from his touch. "No way, Sheriff. I'm going in with you."

He nodded to someone behind her and she shot to her feet only to come face-to-face with two female deputies.

"Ma'am," the dark-haired one said, "we'll go in as soon as we receive the all-clear signal from the sheriff."

Anger swirled through Sadie as she watched Tanner sprint forward. He'd double-crossed her. Dwelling on the reality would only distract her so she shrugged it off and focused on the events unfolding only yards away.

The two deputies moved in close next to her. One wore earbuds to listen in to the ongoing operation. The other watched through binoculars. Tanner hadn't left these two women with her because he didn't think women were as strong as men. Sadie had noticed seven female deputies. The other five had obviously gone in with Tanner. One of the women, she noticed, was very pregnant. She would have needed to stay away from live fire anyway.

Obviously she was fearless or she wouldn't be in these woods right now.

The echo of gunfire jerked her attention forward. The exchange was happening outside the entrance to the compound that had been built into the mountainside. Aikman no doubt had the entrance heavily guarded.

The sudden silence was more unnerving than the bursts of gunfire had been.

One minute turned into two and Sadie couldn't take it a second longer.

"Sorry, ladies, but I can't do this."

Sadie took off in a sprint. The deputy who wasn't pregnant rushed after her. Sadie ran harder. She disappeared into the thick trees and underbrush that camouflaged the entrance. The entrance stood open, dead followers lying on the ground.

Inside, Tanner's deputies had fanned out and were entering buildings.

Sadie palmed her weapon and headed for the headquarters building. As she neared the entrance, Tanner and the female caught up with her.

He pulled her next to a vehicle that had been parked there.

"What the hell are you trying to do, Buchanan?"

"They'll be in there." She jerked her head toward the building that was the headquarters. "This is where all the decisions are made. Where the Council meets."

"And you're certain Flynn will be in there."

His words hit like a blow to her midsection. She wasn't certain. She was guessing. Speculating. Concluding the most likely scenario.

"It makes the most sense." Sadie suddenly felt completely unsure.

Tanner used his radio to divert resources to their position. Sadie's heart thundered in her chest. What if she was wrong?

A single shot exploded beyond the walls of the headquarters building. Sadie might not have heard it if one of those moments of absolute silence hadn't settled around them beforehand. And the entry door stood open.

Tanner was the first to move. He burst through the open entrance.

Sadie was right behind him. The other deputy behind her.

With Tanner's glance at her, Sadie moved ahead of him and led the way to the conference room where she had been questioned by the Resurrection Council.

At the door Tanner gave her the signal to wait.

His next signal had Sadie and the deputy dropping into a crouch. Tanner banged on the closed door.

The door opened and a guard walked out.

Tanner rammed the muzzle of his weapon into his temple and pulled him aside.

Another guard rushed out. Sadie handled him.

"Well, well, it appears we have the proverbial stand-off."

Sadie recognized the voice. Aikman.

"Do come in," he said. "Agent Flynn and I were just discussing our next move."

Leaving the two guards under the careful watch of the female deputy, Tanner and Sadie entered the conference room.

"Drop the weapon," Tanner ordered.

Sadie moved to one side of Tanner, who had a bead on his target. When her brain absorbed the image before her, her heart sank to the floor.

Aikman had Flynn on his knees. His weapon was pressed against Flynn's forehead. Nearby Prentiss sat in a chair, the bullet hole between his eyes leaking blood.

On the floor to her left was a line of dead bodies.

The Council members.

"I'll drop the weapon when I'm safely on my way out of here," Aikman argued. "I'll turn Agent Flynn loose at that time, as well. Otherwise, I'm going to do the same thing to him that I did to Prentiss and the members of his esteemed Council."

As Tanner negotiated with the man who wasn't going to change his mind, Sadie made a decision. She lowered her weapon. "Take me instead. The Bureau is far more flexible in these negotiations than the ATF. Did we mention that both are here?"

Something flashed ever so briefly across Aikman's face. Flynn's was far easier to read: he was not happy with her offer.

"Back off," Tanner muttered to her.

Aikman grinned, obviously enjoying the dissention. "Well, aren't you the brave one? Come on over here and I'll let your friend go."

Sadie stepped forward.

"Don't do it, Buchanan," Tanner warned, his attention zeroed in on Aikman.

"It won't be my first bait and switch, Sheriff." She looked directly at Smith as she said this but quickly shifted her gaze to Aikman. "I'm not afraid of this guy."

Aikman smirked. "That's an astounding statement considering the dead bodies lining the room."

It was in that moment—that fraction of a second when Aikman thought he had to prove how scary he was—that Flynn made his move.

He twisted and dove into Aikman's knees.

Sadie dropped to the floor.

As if he'd been in on the plan from the beginning, Tanner fired one shot straight into Aikman's right shoulder. The fool's weapon fell from his suddenly limp fingers as he was propelled backward by Flynn.

Flynn grabbed Aikman's weapon and pushed to his feet. Aikman clutched at his shoulder, right where that major nerve center would be, and howled.

"Good shot," Flynn said to Tanner.

Sadie pushed to her feet but her knees had gone so weak she had no idea how she would remain upright.

Tanner took over the prisoner and Flynn walked toward her.

Her breath caught at the injuries to his face or maybe just at the sight of him moving toward her.

He was alive.

She was alive.

And they were getting out of here.

Flynn wrapped his arms around her and hugged her. The weapon in her right hand slipped to the floor. Her arms went around him.

"Thanks for coming back to rescue me," he murmured against her hair.

She turned her face up to him. "It's what I do."

He smiled then grimaced.

"Your face looks like hell," she pointed out.

"Feels like it, too."

THE NEXT SEVERAL hours were filled with rounding up prisoners and getting medical attention to those injured, as well as identifying the dead.

Flynn refused to bother with being checked out until the work was done. By the time they were off that mountain, Sadie was ready to drop.

George was in the DA's office making a deal. Sadie was glad. He'd paid in that tunnel for whatever he'd done wrong. Aikman was trying to work out a deal, as well. As it turned out the remains in that rock hole at Aikman's compound were those of Jack Kemp. The FBI had waited a long time to learn this information but both Ross and Tanner assured Sadie that Aikman wouldn't be getting any sort of deal beyond the possible setting aside of the death penalty.

Aikman was like Prentiss; he didn't deserve a deal. He deserved a long life behind bars where he'd have plenty of time to reflect on his bad judgment.

Deacon Ross had accompanied Levi Winters for his statement.

The place was crawling with federal agents.

Sadie's SAIC had called and made sure she was okay. Flynn had been sequestered to one of the interview rooms for his debrief. She had called her parents just to hear their voices. There was really no reason at this point for her to stay. She had done what she came here to do. She could go home. Maybe even call her sister.

Maybe if she told herself a couple more times there was no reason to stay she would talk herself into walking away without waiting for a chance to say goodbye to Flynn. He'd already thanked her for rescuing him. Goodbye wasn't actually necessary.

Except it felt necessary.

"Agent Buchanan."

Sadie looked up at the sound of her name. Cece Winters smiled as she walked through the door of the sheriff's office where Sadie had taken refuge. It was about the only room in the building that wasn't filled with agents and deputies. Tanner had told Sadie to make herself at home.

"Hey." Sadie returned the smile. "I'm sure they'll allow Levi to go home soon. This part takes a while sometimes."

Cece nodded as she sat down in the chair next to

Sadie. "I wanted to thank you again for saving my brother not once but twice."

"He did his part," Sadie told her. "He's a good guy. A little confused maybe, but a good guy."

"Deacon and I plan on seeing that he gets back on the right track."

Sounded like the two were definitely a couple. Sadie had gotten that impression.

"Ladies."

Sadie's attention swung to the door once more. Flynn stood there, still looking a little worse for the wear.

Cece got to her feet. "I should see how Levi's doing."

She slipped out of the office and Flynn walked in. He closed the door behind him. Sadie looked from the closed door to him, her pulse starting to pound.

"I was afraid you'd left already."

"I was just getting ready to go." She tried to think what to say next. "It'll be good to get home."

He nodded. "I don't want to keep you." He exhaled a big breath. "But I was hoping we could get a bite to eat first. I don't know about you, but I'm starved."

As if her belly had just realized how empty it was, she nodded. "I could eat. Sure."

"Good."

They stood there for a moment without saying more. Sadie suspected he felt as awkward as she did. Neither of them was the kind of person who did this well.

"We both live in the Nashville area."

"Home sweet home." She felt heat rush to her cheeks. What a totally dumb thing to say.

He smiled, grimaced. "Yeah. Anyway, I hoped we

might spend some time together. You know, get to know each other better."

She felt certain the grin that spread across her face said way too much about how happy his words made her. "I would like that very much."

"It's been a long time," he admitted, "since I've met anyone who understood this life...who made me want to get to know them better."

She was certain it would be entirely dorky for her to say the same thing. Instead, she put her hand in his. "I'm ready."

"I could take you home," he offered. "I heard you lost your car."

She laughed. "I would love for you to take me home."

That was all she needed to say. The rest would take care of itself.

* * * * *

MURDERED IN
CONARD COUNTY

RACHEL LEE

Prologue

Three years earlier

"Have either of you ever heard of Leopold and Loeb? They thought they could commit the perfect murder."

A large fire burned in the huge stone fireplace, casting dancing tongues of orange light and inky shadows around the cabin's sitting room. The wood sizzled and crackled, adding its dry music to the light and occasionally loud pops that sounded almost like gunshots.

The log walls, burnished by the years, added weight to the entire scene. Trophy heads of bighorn sheep, elk and deer hung everywhere, beneath each a plaque memorializing a past hunter.

Clearly this was a hunting lodge, one of generous size, able to house a fairly large party. But its heyday was in the past and now only three men occupied it.

It seemed like the last place on earth three men would plot murders.

Dressed in camouflage, their orange caps and vests tossed onto a nearby chest, they sat in a semicircle of comfortable lounge chairs in front of the fire, sipping brandy from snifters. Two of them enjoyed fat cigars with a surprisingly pleasant aroma.

"It was really cold out there," remarked one of them,

a man with dark hair and a luxuriant mustache who appeared to be about thirty, maybe a couple of years older. He'd been the one who had asked the question about Leopold and Loeb, but having received no response, he dropped it. For now.

"Good for the deer, Will," said the man nearest him. His name was Karl, and he looked like his Nordic ancestors, with pale hair and skin and frigid blue eyes. The deer he referred to had been field dressed and was hanging in a shed outside, protected from scavengers.

"Yeah," said Jeff, the third of them. He had the kind of good looks that could have gotten him cast on a TV drama, but he also had a kink in his spine from a military injury and he didn't quite sit or stand straight. He often endured pain but seldom showed it. "It's probably already frozen stiff."

"Like a board," Karl agreed. "Thank goodness we have a sling on our side-by-sides."

"And tomorrow maybe we'll get an elk," Jeff added. They'd won the drawing for a coveted license for an elk, and since they'd been hoping for one for years, this was no small deal.

Silence fell for a while, except for the crackling of the fire. Three men, looking very content, enjoying their hunting lodge after a successful day. Except one of them was not quite content.

Will spoke. "Do you two ever get tired of this hunting trip? Every year since we were boys, coming up here with our dads. Now just the three of us."

"Something wrong with the company?" Karl drawled.

"Of course not," Will answered. "It's just that I was thinking we've been doing this so many years, and we've never gone home empty-handed. Not much of a challenge, is it?"

Jeff nearly gaped. They'd spent the better part of three days tracking the buck that was now hanging in the shed. "We almost missed that mature eight-pointer. He was smart."

"We still got him," Will pointed out.

Karl spoke. "The elk will be even more of a challenge. What do you want, Will? To stop making these trips? I thought we were doing it more for the time away together. Three guys, brandy and cigars, traipsing around in the woods on the cusp of winter… A lot of guys would envy us."

"We aren't a lot of guys. In fact, I believe we're smarter than the average bear. All of us."

"So?"

"So, how about we hunt a different kind of prey? Not to kill but for the challenge."

"What are you talking about?" Jeff asked.

"You ever hear of Leopold and Loeb?" This time Will spoke more emphatically.

Both Karl and Jeff shook their heads. "Who were they?" Karl asked.

"Two guys who thought they were smart enough to commit the perfect murder. Back in the 1920s. But they got caught in twenty-four hours."

The other two men froze into silence.

"We're smarter," said Will presently. "Think of all the planning we'd have to do, a lot more than hunting deer or elk. And even without the murder it would be a helluva challenging game."

Silence, except for the fire, reigned for a while. Then Jeff said, "You *are* talking about a game, not a real murder, right?"

Will waved the hand holding his cigar. "The game would be the planning and stalking. Just like when we hunt deer. The kill hardly matters at that point. We only follow through because we want the meat and the rack. You can't hang a man's head on the wall."

That elicited a laugh from Karl. "True that." Even Jeff smiled after a moment.

"The most challenging game of all," Will continued. "How do we do it without leaving any evidence? How do we creep up on our prey?"

Karl snorted. "Men aren't as smart as deer, Will."

"But they're almost never alone."

After a bit, Jeff said, "Sorta like playing D&D when we were younger?"

"Like that," Will agreed. "Plotting and planning and stalking. That's all."

Presently all the men were sitting easily in their chairs and began to toss ideas around. If nothing else, it was an entertaining way to spend an icy evening.

Chapter One

Blaire Afton slept with the window cracked because she liked the cool night breeze, and the sounds of animals in the woods. As park ranger for the state of Wyoming, she supervised a forested area with a dozen scattered campgrounds and quite a few hiking trails, most all the camps and trails farther up the mountain.

Her cabin was also the main office, the entry point to the park, and her bedroom was upstairs in a loft. The breeze, chilly as it got at night, even in July, kept her from feeling closed in. The fresh air seemed to make her sleep deeper and more relaxed, as well.

It also seemed to keep away the nightmares that still occasionally plagued her. Ten months in Afghanistan had left their mark.

But tonight she was edgy as all get-out, and sleep stubbornly evaded her. Maybe just as well, she thought irritably. Nights when she felt like this often produced bad dreams, which in turn elicited worse memories.

Sitting up at last, she flipped on the fluorescent lantern beside her bed and dressed in her park ranger's uniform and laced up her boots. If sleep caught up with her finally, she could crash on the sofa downstairs. Right now, however, early coffee was sounding delicious.

There was absolutely no way she could make her boots

silent on the open wooden staircase, but it didn't matter. All her staff were home for the night and she could bother only herself. Right now, bothering herself seemed like a fairly good idea.

The electric lines reached the cabin, having been run up the side of this mountain by the state, along with a phone landline that extended out to all the campgrounds in case of emergencies. Neither was perfectly reliable, but when they worked, they were a boon. Especially the electricity. Phone calls about vacant campsites didn't light up her life, nor did some of the stupid ones she received. Want a weather report? Then turn on the weather.

"Ha," she said aloud. The good news was that she had electric power this night. She walked over to her precious espresso machine and turned it on. A few shots over ice with milk and artificial sweetener...oh, yeah.

And since she was wide awake and had the power, maybe she should check her computer and see if she had internet, as well. Monthly reports were due soon, and if she had to be awake, she might as well deal with them. Reports weren't her favorite part of this job, and sometimes she wondered if some of them had been created by a higher-up who just wanted to be important.

When her coffee was ready and filling her insulated mug, she decided to step outside and enjoy some of the night's unique quiet. It wasn't silent, but it was so different from the busier daylight hours. Tilting her head back, she could see stars overhead, bright and distant this nearly moonless night. The silvery glow was just enough to see by, but not enough to wash out the stars.

Sipping her coffee, she allowed herself to enjoy being out in the dark without fear. It might come back at any moment, but as Afghanistan faded further into her past, it happened much less often. She was grateful for the incremental improvement.

Grateful, too, that the head forester at the national forest abutting her state land was also a veteran, someone she could talk to. Gus Maddox guarded a longer past in combat than she did, and there was still a lot he wouldn't, or couldn't, talk about. But he'd been in special operations, and much of what they did remained secret for years.

In her case, her service had been more ordinary. Guarding supply convoys sounded tame until you learned they were a desirable target. She and her team had more than once found themselves in intense firefights, or the object of roadside bombs.

She shook herself, refusing to let memory intrude on this night. It was lovely and deserved its due. An owl hooted from deep within the woods, a lonely yet beautiful sound. All kinds of small critters would be scurrying around, trying to evade notice by running from hiding place to hiding place while they searched for food. Nature had a balance and it wasn't always pretty, but unlike war it served a necessary purpose.

Dawn would be here soon, and she decided to wait in hope she might see a cloud of bats returning to their cave three miles north. They didn't often fly overhead here, but occasionally she enjoyed the treat.

Currently there was a great deal of worry among biologists about a fungus that was attacking the little brown bat. She hoped they managed to save the species.

A loud report unexpectedly shattered the night. The entire world seemed to freeze. Only the gentle sigh of the night breeze remained as wildlife paused in recognition of a threat.

Blaire froze, too. She knew the sound of a gunshot.

She also knew that no one was supposed to be hunting during the night or during this season.

What the hell? She couldn't even tell exactly where it came from. The sound had echoed off the rocks and slopes of the mountain. As quiet as the night was, it might have come from miles away.

Fifteen minutes later, the phone in her cabin started to ring.

Her heart sank.

TEN MILES SOUTH in his cabin in the national forest, August Maddox, Gus to everyone, was also enduring a restless night. Darkness had two sides to it, one favorable and one threatening, depending. In spec ops, he'd favored it when he was on a stealthy mission and didn't want to be detected. At other times, when he and his men were the prey, he hated it. The protection it sometimes afforded his troops could transform into deadliness in an instant.

As a result, he endured an ongoing battle with night. Time was improving it, but on nights like this when sleep eluded him, he sometimes forced himself to step outside, allowing the inkiness to swallow him, standing fast against urges to take cover. He hated this in himself, felt it as an ugly, inexcusable weakness, but hating it didn't make it go away.

The fingernail moon provided a little light, and he used it to go around the side of the building to visit the three horses in the corral there. His own gelding, Scrappy, immediately stirred from whatever sleep he'd been enjoying and came to the rail to accept a few pats and nuzzle Gus in return.

Sometimes Gus thought the horse was the only living being who understood him. *Probably because Scrappy couldn't talk*, he often added in attempted lightness.

But Scrappy did talk in his own way. He could communicate quite a bit with a toss of his head or a flick of his tail, not to mention the pawing of his feet. Tonight the horse seemed peaceful, though, and leaned into his hand as if trying to share the comfort.

He should have brought a carrot, Gus thought. Stroking the horse's neck, he asked, "Who gave you that silly name, Scrappy?"

Of course the horse couldn't answer, and Gus had never met anyone who could. The name had come attached to the animal, and no one had ever changed it. Which was okay, because Gus kind of liked it. Unusual. He was quite sure the word hadn't been attached to another horse anywhere. It also made him wonder about the horse's coltish days five or six years ago.

Scrappy was a gorgeous, large pinto whose lines suggested Arabian somewhere in the past. He was surefooted in these mountains, though, which was far more important than speed. And he was evidently an animal who attached himself firmly, because Gus had found that when Scrappy was out of the corral, he'd follow Gus around more like a puppy than anything.

Right then, though, as Scrappy nudged his arm repeatedly, he realized the horse wanted to take a walk. It was dark, but not too dark, and there was a good trail leading north toward the state park lands.

And Blaire Afton.

Gus half smiled at himself as he ran his fingers through Scrappy's mane. Blaire. She'd assumed her ranger position over there about two years ago, and they'd become friends. Well, as much as two wary vets could. Coffee, conversation, even some good laughs. Occasional confidences about so-called reentry problems. After two years, Scrappy probably knew the path by heart.

But it was odd for the horse to want to walk in the middle of the night. Horses *did* sleep. But maybe Gus's restlessness had reached him and made him restless, as well. Or maybe he sensed something in the night. Prickles of apprehension, never far away in the dark, ran up Gus's spine.

"Okay, a short ride," he told Scrappy. "Just enough to work out a kink or two."

An internal kink. Or a thousand. Gus had given up wondering just how many kinks he'd brought home with him after nearly twenty years in the Army, most of it in covert missions. The grenade that had messed him up with shrapnel hadn't left as many scars as memory. Or so he thought.

He was tempted to ride bareback, given that he didn't intend to go far, but he knew better. As steady as Scrappy was, if he startled or stumbled Gus could wind up on the ground. Better to have the security of a saddle than risk an injury.

Entering the corral, he saw happiness in Scrappy's sudden prance. The other two horses roused enough to glance over, then went back to snoozing. They never let the night rambles disturb them. The other two horses apparently considered them to be a matter between Scrappy and Gus.

Shortly he led the freshly saddled Scrappy out of the corral. Not that he needed leading. He followed him over to the door of his cabin where a whiteboard for messages was tacked and he scrawled that he'd gone for a ride on the Forked Rivers Trail. A safety precaution in case he wasn't back by the time his staff started wandering in from their various posts. Hard-and-fast rule: never go into the forest without letting the rangers know where you were headed and when you expected to return. It applied to him as well as their guests.

Then he swung up into the saddle, listening to Scrappy's happy nicker, enjoying his brief sideways prance of pleasure. And just like the song, the horse knew the way.

Funny thing to drift through his mind at that moment. A memory from childhood that seemed so far away now he wasn't sure it had really happened. Sitting in the car with his parents on the way to Grandmother's house. Seriously. Two kids in the back seat singing "Over the River" until his mother begged for mercy. His folks were gone now, taken by the flu of all things, and his sister who had followed him into the Army had been brought home in a box from Iraq.

Given his feelings about the darkness, it struck him as weird that the song and the attendant memories had popped up. But he ought to know by now how oddly the brain could work.

Scrappy's hooves were nearly silent on the pine needles that coated the trail. The duff under the trees was deep in these parts, and he'd suggested to HQ that they might need to clean up some of it. Fire hazard, and it hadn't rained in a while, although they were due for some soon to judge by the forecast. Good. They needed it.

The slow ride through the night woods was nearly magical. The creak of leather and the jingle of the rings on the bridle were quiet, but part of the feeling of the night. When he'd been in Germany he'd learned the story of the Christmas tree. The idea had begun with early and long winter nights, as travelers between villages had needed illumination to see their way. At some point people had started putting candles on tree branches.

Damn, he'd moved from Thanksgiving to Christmas in a matter of minutes and it was July. What the hell was going on inside his mind?

He shook his head a bit, then noticed that Scrappy was

starting to get edgy himself. He was tossing his head an awful lot. What had he sensed on the night breeze? Some odor that bothered him. That could be almost anything out of the ordinary.

But the horse's reaction put him on high alert, too. Something was wrong with the woods tonight. Scrappy felt it and he wasn't one to question an animal's instincts and senses.

Worry began to niggle at him. They were getting ever closer to Blaire Afton's cabin. Could she be sick or in trouble?

Maybe it was an annoying guy thing, but he often didn't like the idea that she was alone there at night. In the national forest there were people around whom he could radio if he needed to, who'd be there soon if he wanted them. Blaire had no such thing going for her. Her employees were all on daylight hours, gone in the evening, not returning until morning. Budget, he supposed. Money was tight for damn near everything now.

Blaire would probably laugh in his face if she ever guessed he sometimes worried about her being alone out here. She had some of the best training in the world. If asked he'd say that he felt sorry for anyone who tangled with her.

But she was still alone there in that cabin, and worse, she was alone with her nightmares. Like him. He knew all about that.

Scrappy tossed his head more emphatically and Gus loosened the reins. "Okay, man, do your thing."

Scrappy needed no other encouragement. His pace quickened dramatically.

Well, maybe Blaire would be restless tonight, too, and they could share morning coffee and conversation. It was gradually becoming his favorite way to start a day.

Then he heard the unmistakable sound of a gunshot, ringing through the forest. At a distance, but he still shouldn't be hearing it. Not at this time of year. Not in the dark.

"Scrappy, let's go." He touched the horse lightly with his heels, not wanting him to break into a gallop that could bring him to harm, but just to hurry a bit.

Scrappy needed no further urging.

"WE THINK SOMEONE'S been shot."

The words that had come across the telephone seemed to shriek in Blaire's ears as she hurried to grab a light jacket and her pistol belt as well as a shotgun out of the locked cabinet. On the way out the door she grabbed the first-aid kit. The sheriff would be sending a car or two, but she had the edge in time and distance. She would definitely arrive first.

The call had come from the most remote campground, and she'd be able to get only partway there in the truck. The last mile or so would have to be covered on the all-terrain side-by-side lashed to the bed of the truck.

If someone was injured, why had it had to happen at the most out-of-the-way campground? A campground limited to people who seriously wanted to rough it, who didn't mind carrying in supplies and tents. After the road ended up there, at the place she'd leave her truck, no vehicles of any kind were allowed. She was the only one permitted to head in there on any motorized vehicle. She had one equipped for emergency transport.

She was just loading the last items into her vehicle when Gus appeared, astride Scrappy, a welcome sight.

"I heard the shot. What happened?"

"Up at the Twin Rocks Campground. I just got a call. They think someone's been shot."

"Think?"

"That's the word. You want to follow me on horseback, or ride with me?" It never once entered her head that he wouldn't want to come along to help.

IT NEVER ENTERED his head, either. "I'm not armed," he warned her as he slipped off the saddle.

"We can share."

He loosely draped Scrappy's reins around the porch railing in front of the cabin, knowing they wouldn't hold him. He didn't want them to. It was a signal to Scrappy to hang around, not remain frozen in place. A few seconds later, he climbed into the pickup with Blaire and they started up the less-than-ideal road. He was glad his teeth weren't loose because Blaire wasted no time avoiding the ruts.

He spoke, raising his voice a bit to be heard over the roaring engine. "Have you thought yet about what you're doing for Christmas and Thanksgiving?"

She didn't answer for a moment as she shifted into a lower gear for the steepening road. "It's July. What brought that on?"

"Danged if I know," he admitted. "I was riding Scrappy in your direction because I'm restless tonight and it all started with a line from 'Over the River' popping into my head. Then as I was coming down the path I remembered how in the Middle Ages people put candles on tree branches on long winter nights so the pathways would be lit for travelers. Which led to…"

"Christmas," she said. "Got it. Still weird."

He laughed. "That's what I thought, too. My head apparently plays by its own rules."

It was her turn to laugh, a short mirthless sound. "No kidding. I don't have to tell you about mine."

No, she didn't, and he was damned sorry that she carried those burdens, too. "So, holidays," he repeated. No point in thinking about what lay ahead of them. If someone had been shot, they both knew it wasn't going to be pretty. And both of them had seen it before.

"I'll probably stay right here," she answered. "I love it when the forest is buried in snow, and someone has to be around if the snowshoe hikers and the cross-country skiers get into trouble."

"Always," he agreed. "And doesn't someone always get into trouble?"

"From what I understand, it hasn't failed yet."

He drummed his fingers on his thigh, then asked, "You called the sheriff?"

"Yeah, but discharge of a weapon is in my bailiwick. They have a couple of cars heading this way. If I find out someone *has* been shot, I'll warn them. Otherwise I'll tell them to stand down."

Made sense. This wasn't a war zone after all. Most likely someone had brought a gun along for protection and had fired it into the night for no good reason. Scared? A big shadow hovering in the trees?

And in the dead of night, wakened from a sound sleep by a gunshot, a camper could be forgiven for calling to say that someone *had* been shot even without seeing it. The more isolated a person felt, the more he or she was apt to expect the worst. Those guys up there at Twin Rocks were about as isolated as anyone could get without hiking off alone.

He hoped that was all it was. An accident that had been misinterpreted. His stomach, though, gave one huge twist, preparing him for the worst.

"You hanging around for the holidays?" she asked. Her voice bobbled as the road became rougher.

"Last year my assistant did," he reminded her. "This year it's me. What did you do last year?"

"Went to visit my mother in the nursing home. I told you she has Alzheimer's."

"Yeah. That's sad."

"Pointless to visit. She doesn't even recognize my voice on the phone anymore. Regardless, I don't think she feels lonely."

"Why's that?"

"She spends a lot of time talking to friends and relatives who died back when. Her own little party."

"I hope it comforts her."

"Me, too." Swinging a hard left, she turned onto a narrower leg of road that led directly to a dirt and gravel parking lot of sorts. It was where the campers left their vehicles before hiking in.

"You ever been to this campground?" she asked as she set the brake and switched off the ignition.

"Not on purpose," he admitted. "I may have. Scrappy and I sometimes wander a bit when we're out for a day-off ride."

"Everything has to be lugged in," she replied, as if that would explain all he needed to know.

It actually did. *Rustic* was the popular word for it. "They have a phone, though?"

"Yeah, a direct line to me. The state splurged. I would guess lawyers had something to do with that."

He gave a short laugh. "Wouldn't surprise me."

Even though Blaire was clearly experienced at getting the side-by-side off the back of her truck, he helped. It was heavy, it needed to roll down a ramp, and it might decide to just keep going.

Once it was safely parked, he helped reload the ramp and close the tailgate. Then there was loading the first-aid supplies and guns. She knew where everything went, so he took directions.

With a pause as he saw the roll of crime scene tape and box of latex gloves. And shoe covers. God. A couple of flashlights that would turn night into day. He hoped they didn't need any of it. Not any of it.

At least the state hadn't stinted on the side-by-side. It had a roof for rainy weather, and a roll bar he could easily grab for stability. There were four-point harnesses as well, no guarantee against every danger but far better than being flung from the vehicle.

These side-by-side UTVs weren't as stable as three-wheelers, either. It might be necessary for her job, but if he were out for joyriding, he'd vastly prefer a standard ATV.

She drove but tempered urgency with decent caution. The headlights were good enough, but this classified more as a migratory path than a road. Even knowing a ranger might have to get out here in an emergency, no one had wanted to make this campground easily accessible by vehicle. There were lots of places like that in his part of the forest. Places where he needed to drag teams on foot when someone got injured.

Soon, however, he saw the occasional glint of light through the trees. A lot of very-awake campers, he imagined. Frightened by the gunshot. He hoped they weren't frightened by more.

The forest thinned out almost abruptly as they reached the campground. He could make out scattered tents, well separated in the trees. Impossible in the dark to tell how many there might be.

But a group of people, all of whom looked as if they'd dragged on jeans, shirts and boots in a hurry, huddled together, a couple of the women hugging themselves.

Blaire brought the ATV to a halt, parked it and jumped

off. He followed more slowly, not wanting to reduce her authority in any way. She was the boss here. He was just a visitor. And he wasn't so stupid that he hadn't noticed how people tended to turn to the man who was present first.

He waited by the vehicle as Blaire covered the twenty or so feet to the huddle. Soon excited voices reached him, all of them talking at the same time about the single gunshot that had torn the silence of the night. From the gestures, he guessed they were pointing to where they thought the shot came from, and, of course, there were at least as many directions as people.

They'd been in tents, though, and that would muffle the sound. Plus there were enough rocks around her to cause confusing echoes.

But then one man silenced them all.

"Mark Jasper didn't come out of his tent. His kid was crying just a few minutes ago, but then he quieted."

He saw Blaire grow absolutely still. "His kid?"

"He brought his four-year-old with him. I guess the shot may have scared him. But… Why didn't Mark come out?"

Good question, thought Gus. Excellent question.

"Maybe he didn't want to take a chance and expose his boy. They might have gone back to sleep," said one of the women. Her voice trembled. She didn't believe that, Gus realized.

Blaire turned slowly toward the tent that the man had pointed out. She didn't want to look. He didn't, either. But as she took her first step toward the shelter, he stepped over and joined her. To hell with jurisdiction. His gorge was rising. A kid had been in that tent? No dad joining the others? By now this Jasper guy could have heard enough of the voices to know it was safe.

He glanced at Blaire and saw that her face had set into lines of stone. She knew, too. When they reached the door of the tent, she stopped and pointed. Leaning over, he saw it, too. The tent was unzipped by about six or seven inches.

"Gloves," he said immediately.

"Yes."

Protect the evidence. The opening might have been left by this Jasper guy, or it might have been created by someone else. Either way…

He brought her a pair of latex gloves, then snapped his own set on. Their eyes met, and hers reflected the trepidation he was feeling.

Then he heard a sound from behind him and swung around. The guy who had announced that Jasper hadn't come out had followed them. "Back up, sir." His tone was one of command, honed by years of military practice.

"Now," Blaire added, the same steely note in her voice. "You might be trampling evidence."

The guy's eyes widened and he started to back up.

Now Blaire turned her head. "Carefully," she said sharply. "Don't scuff. You might bury something."

The view of the guy raising his legs carefully with each step might have been amusing under other circumstances. There was no amusement now.

"Ready?" Blaire asked.

"Yup."

She leaned toward the tent and called, "Mr. Jasper? I'm the ranger. We're coming in. We need to check on you." No sound answered her.

"Like anyone can be ready for this," she muttered under her breath as she reached up for the zipper tab. The metal teeth seemed loud as the world held its breath.

When she had the zipper halfway down, she parted the canvas and shone her flashlight inside.

"Oh, my God," she breathed.

Chapter Two

Blaire had seen a lot of truly horrible things during her time in Afghanistan. There had even been times when she'd been nearly frozen by a desire not to do what she needed to do. She'd survived, she'd acted and on a couple of occasions, she'd even saved lives.

This was different. In the glare of the flashlight she saw a man in a sleeping bag, his head near the front opening. Or rather what was left of his head. Worse, she saw a small child clinging desperately to the man's waist, eyes wide with shock and terror. That kid couldn't possibly understand this horror but had still entered the icy pit of not being able to move, of hanging on to his daddy for comfort and finding no response.

She squeezed her eyes shut for just a moment, then said quietly to Gus, "The father's been shot in the head. Dead. The kid is clinging to him and terrified out of his mind. I need the boy's name."

Gus slipped away, and soon she heard him murmuring to the gathered campers.

Not knowing if she would ever get the boy's name, she said quietly, "Wanna come outside? I'm sort of like police, you know. You probably saw me working when you were on your way up here."

No response.

Then Gus's voice in her ear. "Jimmy. He's Jimmy."

"Okay." She lowered the zipper more. When Gus squatted, she let him continue pulling it down so she didn't have to take eyes off the frightened and confused little boy. "Jimmy? Would you like to go home to Mommy? We can get Mommy to come for you."

His eyes flickered a bit. He'd heard her.

"My friend Gus here has a horse, too. You want to ride a horse? His name is Scrappy and he's neat. All different colors."

She had his attention now and stepped carefully through the flap, totally avoiding the father. She wondered how much evidence she was destroying but didn't much care. The priority was getting that child out of there.

The floor of the tent was small and not easy to cross. A small sleeping bag lay bunched up, a trap for the unwary foot. Toys were scattered about, too, plastic horses, some metal and plastic cars and a huge metal tractor. She bet Jimmy had had fun making roads in the pine needles and duff outside.

As soon as she got near, she squatted. His gaze was focusing on her more and more, coming out of the shock and into the moment. "I think we need to go find your mommy, don't you?"

"Daddy?"

"We'll take care of Daddy for you, okay? Mommy is going to need you, Jimmy. She probably misses you so bad right now. Let's go and I'll put you on my ATV. You like ATVs?"

"Zoom." The smallest of smiles cracked his frozen face.

"Well, this is a big one, and it definitely zooms. It's also a little like riding a roller coaster. Come on, let's go check it out."

At last Jimmy uncoiled and stood. But there was no way Blaire was going to let him see any more of his father. She scooped him up in her arms and turned so that he'd have to look through her.

"Gus?"

"Yo."

"Could you hold the flap open, please?"

Who knew a skinny four-year-old could feel at once so heavy and light? The flashlight she carried wasn't helping, either. She wished she had a third arm.

"Are you cold, Jimmy?" she asked as she moved toward the opening and bent a little to ease them through.

"A little bit," he admitted.

"Well, I've got a nice warm blanket on my ATV. You can curl up with it while I call your mommy, okay?" Lying. How was she going to call this kid's mother? Not immediately, for sure. She couldn't touch the corpse or look for ID until after the crime techs were done.

"Gus? The sheriff?"

"I radioed. There's a lot more than two cars on the way. Crime scene people, too."

"We've got to get this cordoned off."

"I'll ask Mr. Curious to help me. He'll love it. The kid?"

"Jimmy is going to get my favorite blanket and a place to curl up in the back of the ATV, right, Jimmy?"

Jimmy gave a small nod. His fingers dug into her, crumpling cloth and maybe even bruising a bit. She didn't care.

Walking carefully and slowly with the boy, almost unconsciously she began to hum a tune from her early childhood, "All Through the Night."

To her surprise, Jimmy knew the words and began to sing them with her. His voice was thin, frail from the shock, but he was clinging desperately to something familiar. After a moment, she began to sing softly with him. Before she reached the ATV, Jimmy's head was resting against her shoulder.

When the song ended, he said, "Mommy sings that." Then he started to sing it again.

And Blaire blinked hard, fighting back the first tears she'd felt in years.

GUS WATCHED BLAIRE carry the small child to the ATV. He'd already recovered the crime scene tape and there were plenty of trees to wind it around, but he hesitated for a moment, watching woman and child. He could imagine how hard this was for her, dealing with a freshly fatherless child. War did that too often. Now here, in a peaceful forest. Or one that should have been peaceful.

His radio crackled, and he answered it. "Maddox."

"We're about a mile out from the parking area," came the familiar voice of the sheriff, Gage Dalton. "Anything else we need to know?"

"I'm about to rope the scene right now. The vic has a small child. We're going to need some help with that and with finding a way to get in touch with family as soon as possible."

"We'll do what we can as fast as we can. The witnesses?"

"Some are trying to pack up. I'm going to stop that."

He was as good as his word, too. When he clicked off the radio, he turned toward the people who had dispersed from the remaining knot and started to fold up tents.

"You all can stop right there. The sheriff will be here soon and you might be material witnesses. None of you can leave the scene until he tells you."

Some grumbles answered him, but poles and other

items clattered to the ground. One woman, with her arms wrapped around herself, said, "I feel like a sitting duck."

"If you were," Gus said, "you'd already know it." That at least took some of the tension out of the small crowd. Then he signaled to the guy who'd tried to follow them to the tent and said, "You get to help me rope off the area."

The guy nodded. "I can do that. Sorry I got too close. Instinct."

"Instinct?"

"Yeah. Iraq. Know all the parameters of the situation."

Gus was familiar with that. He decided the guy wasn't a ghoul after all. He also proved to be very useful. In less than ten minutes, they had a large area around the victim's tent cordoned off. Part of him was disturbed that a gunshot had been heard but no one had approached the tent of the one person who hadn't joined them, not even the veteran. The tent in which a child had apparently been crying.

But it was the middle of the night, people had probably been wakened from a sound sleep and were experiencing some difficulty in putting the pieces together in any useful way. Camping was supposed to be a peaceful experience unless you ran into a bear. And, of course, the sound of the child crying might have persuaded them everything was okay in that tent. After all, it looked untouched from the outside.

Scared as some of these people were that there might be additional gunfire, they all might reasonably have assumed that Jasper and his son were staying cautiously out of sight.

Once he and Wes, the veteran, had roped off the area, there wasn't another thing they could do before the cops arrived. Preserve the scene, then stand back. And keep witnesses from leaving before they were dismissed by proper authority. He could understand, though, why some of them just wanted to get the hell out of here.

The fact remained, any one of that group of twelve to fourteen people could be the shooter. He wondered if any one of them had even considered that possibility.

Blaire settled Jimmy in the back of the ATV after moving a few items to the side. She had a thick wool blanket she carried in case she got stranded outside overnight without warning, and she did her best to turn it into a nest.

Then she pulled out a shiny survival blanket and Jimmy's world seemed to settle once again. "Space blanket!" The excitement was clear in his voice.

"You bet," she said, summoning a smile. "Now just stay here while we try to get your mommy. If you do that for me, you can keep the space blanket."

That seemed to make him utterly happy. He snuggled into the gray wool blanket and hugged the silvery Mylar to his chin. "I'll sleep," he announced.

"Great idea," she said. She couldn't resist brushing his hair gently back from his forehead. "Pleasant dreams, Jimmy."

He was already falling asleep, though. Exhausted from his fear and his crying, the tyke was nodding off. "Mommy says that, too," he murmured. And then his thumb found its way into his mouth and his eyes stayed closed.

Blaire waited for a minute, hoping the child could sleep for a while but imagining the sheriff's arrival with all the people and the work they needed to do would probably wake him. She could hope not.

HE HADN'T KNOWN the kid was there. God in heaven, he hadn't known. Jeff scrambled as quietly as he could over rough ground, putting as much distance between him and the vic as he could.

He'd been shocked by the sight of the kid. He almost couldn't bring himself to do it. If he hadn't, though, he'd be the next one The Hunt Club would take out. They'd warned him.

His damn fault for getting too curious. Now he was on the hook with them for a murder he didn't want to commit, and he was never going to forget that little boy. Those eyes, those cries, would haunt him forever.

Cussing viciously under his breath, he grabbed rocks and slipped on scree. He couldn't even turn on his flashlight yet, he was still too close. But the moon had nose-dived behind the mountain and he didn't even have its thin, watery light to help him in his escape.

His heart was hammering and not just because of his efforts at climbing. He'd just killed a man and probably traumatized a kid for life. That kid wasn't supposed to be there. He'd been watching the guy for the last two weeks and he'd been camping solo. What had he done? Brought his son up for the weekend? Must have.

Giving Jeff the shock of his life. He should have backed off, should have told the others he couldn't do it because the target wasn't alone. Off-season. No tag. Whatever. Surely he could have come up with an excuse so they'd have given him another chance.

Maybe. Now that he knew what the others had been up to, he couldn't even rely on their friendship anymore. Look what they'd put him up to, even when he'd sworn he'd never rat them out.

And he wouldn't have. Man alive, he was in it up to his neck even if he hadn't known they were acting out some of the plans they'd made. An accomplice. He'd aided them. The noose would have tightened around his throat, too.

God, why hadn't he been able to make them see that? He wasn't an innocent who could just walk into a police station and say, "You know what my friends have been doing the last few years?"

Yeah. Right.

He swore again as a sharp rock bit right through his jeans and made him want to cry out from the unexpected pain. He shouldn't be struggling up the side of a mountain in the dark. He shouldn't be doing this at all.

He had believed it was all a game. A fun thing to talk about when they gathered at the lodge in the fall for their usual hunting trip. Planning early summer get-togethers to eyeball various campgrounds, looking for the places a shooter could escape without being seen.

The victim didn't much matter. Whoever was convenient and easy. The important thing was not to leave anything behind. To know the habits of the prey the same way they would know the habits of a deer.

Did the vic go hiking? If so, along what trails and how often and for how long? Was he or she alone very often or at all? Then Will had gotten the idea that they should get them in their tents. When there were other people in the campground, making it so much more challenging. Yeah.

He had believed it was just talk. He'd accompanied the others on the scouting expeditions, enjoying being in the woods while there were still patches of snow under the trees. He liked scoping out the campgrounds as the first hardy outdoorsy types began to arrive. And that, he had believed, was where it ended.

Planning. Scouting. A game.

But he'd been so wrong he could hardly believe his own delusion. He'd known these guys all his life. How was it possible he'd never noticed the psychopathy in either of them? Because that's what he now believed it was.

They didn't give a damn about anyone or anything except their own pleasure.

He paused to catch his breath and looked back over his shoulder. Far away, glimpsed through the thick forest, he caught sight of flashing red, blue and white lights. The police were there.

He'd known it wouldn't be long. That was part of the plan. Once he fired his gun, he had to clear out before the other campers emerged, and not long after them the cops.

Well, he'd accomplished that part of his task. He was well away by the time the campers dared to start coming out. But the little kid's wails had followed him into the night.

Damn it!

So he'd managed to back out of the place without scuffing up the ground in a way that would mark his trail. No one would be able to follow him. But now he was mostly on rocky terrain and that gave him added invisibility.

The damn duff down there had been hard to clear without leaving a visible trail. It had helped that so many campers had been messing it around this summer, but still, if he'd dragged his foot or... Well, it didn't matter. He hadn't.

But then there had been the farther distances. Like where he had kept watch. His movements. Too far out for anyone to notice, of course. He'd made sure of that.

So he'd done everything right. They'd never catch him and the guys would leave him alone. That's all he wanted.

But he hated himself, too, and wished he'd been made of sterner stuff, the kind that would have gone to the cops rather than knuckle under to threats and the fear that he would be counted an accomplice to acts he hadn't committed.

Now there was no hope of escape for him or his soul.

He'd done it. He'd killed a man. He was one of them, owned by them completely. Sold to the devil because of a threat to his life.

He feared, too, that if they were identified they would succeed in convincing the police that he was the killer in the other cases, that they were just his friends and he was pointing the finger at them to save his own hide.

Yeah, he had no trouble imagining them doing that, and doing it successfully. They'd plotted and planned so well that there was nothing to link *them* to the murders except him.

At last he made it over the ridge that would hide him from anyone below, not that the campground wasn't now concealed from view by thick woods.

But even if they decided to look around, they'd never find him now. All he had to do was crawl into the small cave below and await daylight. Then he would have a clear run to his car to get out of the forest.

All carefully planned. He'd be gone before any searcher could get up here.

Damn, he wanted a cigarette. But that had been part of their planning, too. No smoking. The tobacco smell would be distinctive, so they avoided it unless campfires were burning.

Who had come up with that idea?

He couldn't remember. He was past caring. He slid into the dark embrace of the cave at last, with only a short time before dawn.

Past caring. That was a good place to be. He envied the others. Instead he kept company with the remembered cries of a young boy.

BLAIRE WISHED SHE could do more. She was the kind of person who always wanted to take action, to be useful, but right now the police were in charge, using skills she didn't have to look for evidence, so she kept an eye on the little boy in the bed of her ATV and on the scene where some officers were busy questioning other campers and the rest were busy photographing the scene and hunting for evidence. Pacing back and forth between the two locations, she imagined she was creating a rut.

At least Jimmy slept. She hoped he slept right through when they removed his father in a body bag. She hated the thought that such a scene might be stamped in his mind forever.

She knew all about indelible images. She wished sometimes for a version of brain bleach. Just rinse your head in it and the dark, ugly stuff would be washed away.

Nice wish. She was old enough, however, to realize how unrealistic such a wish was. Life was the accumulation of experiences, and you could only hope that you'd learn from all of them, good or bad.

Gus stayed close to the line, attentive as the officers questioned the witnesses. Dropping by from time to time, she heard the same story repeated by everyone. They'd been asleep. Awakened suddenly by the loud, sharp clap. At first they hadn't even been sure they'd heard it.

Some had sat up, waiting to see if it came again. Others considered rolling over and going back to sleep.

Then came the sound of Jimmy's crying. Yes, he sounded scared but that might be a reaction to the sudden, loud noise. He was with his father, so he'd be okay.

Only slowly had some come to the realization that perhaps they'd better look outside to see what had happened. By then there was nothing to see, and the night had been silent except for the little boy's sobbing.

Which again they ignored because he was with his father. Except for Wes.

"I was in Iraq. I'll never mistake a gunshot for anything else. When the boy kept crying, I knew. I just knew someone had been shot. Maybe suicide, I thought. I was the first one out of my tent. The others took another couple of minutes. Regardless, I'm the one who ran to the emergency phone and called the ranger. No, I didn't touch a thing."

Wes paused, looking down, saying quietly, "It was hell listening to that kid and not acting. But his dad might have been okay. My appearance might have just scared the boy more." His mouth twisted. "They don't make rules of engagement for this."

"I hear you," Gus said. Several deputies who were also vets murmured agreement.

The sheriff spoke. "You did the best thing."

Except, thought Blaire, she'd moved in, opened the tent, stepped inside and took the boy out. She'd interfered with the scene. Next would be her turn to be grilled.

By the time they came to her, however, they were allowing the others to pack up as long as they were willing to leave contact information with the deputies. The early morning sun cast enough light on the world that details had emerged from the night, giving everything more depth. Making the trees look aged and old and maybe even weary. But that might be her own state of mind. Usually the forest gave her a sense of peace, and the trees offered her a stately temple.

The sheriff, Gage Dalton, and one of his deputies, Cadell Marcus, she thought, joined her just outside the roped area.

"Yes," she said before they even asked, "I touched the front of the tent. I was wearing gloves. I pulled the zipper down partway, poked my flashlight in and saw the scene. I had to get the little boy out of there."

Dalton nodded. "Of course you did. So what did you first see as you approached?"

"The zipper was pulled down from the top. I don't know how familiar you are with camping gear, but these days you can get tents with zippers that open both ways. A top opening allows in air while keeping protection down low from small critters. Anyway, it was open six or seven inches. Then I opened it more."

She paused, closing her eyes, remembering. "I didn't think about it at the time, but the inner screen wasn't closed. Doesn't necessarily mean anything because we don't have much of a flying insect problem up here."

Gage nodded. "Okay."

Cadell was making notes.

"Anyway, almost as soon as I poked the flashlight in, I saw the victim and I saw his son clinging to him. My only thought at that point was to get the child out of there as fast as I could. I asked Gus to pull the zipper down the rest of the way. I entered, trying not to disturb anything, and picked the boy up. I carried him to my ATV, where he's sleeping now."

"Did you notice anything else?"

She shook her head and opened her eyes. "Frankly, once I saw that man's head, I was aware of nothing else but the little boy. I seem to recall some toys being scattered around, the boy was out of his sleeping bag which, if I remember correctly, was pretty balled up, and that's it. I was completely focused on removing the child while trying not to step on anything." She paused. "Oh. I turned so Jimmy wouldn't be able to see his father."

Gage surprised her by reaching out to pat her upper arm. "You did the right things. We just needed to know where any contamination might have come from."

"What about Jimmy?" she asked. Concern for the

child, kept on simmer for the last couple of hours, now bubbled up like a pot boiling over.

"Sarah Ironheart has called child services. They're contacting the mother." He paused. "Do you think Jimmy trusts you?"

"Insofar as he can. He let me put him in my ATV to sleep." She smiled without humor. "I think the space blanket did it."

"Probably. I'm wondering, if I put you and him in the back of my car, we can take him to town to the social worker. His mom should be on the way."

She hesitated, hating to walk away from what was clearly her job. This campground was her responsibility, and once the cops left...

"Go ahead," said Gus. "I'll meet your staff when they arrive in the next hour and explain. I'm sure they can fill in for you."

The sheriff spoke. "And after the techs are done I'm leaving a couple of deputies up here so the scene won't be disturbed. You're covered."

He gave her a half smile as he said it.

"Yeah, CYA," she responded. "Okay." She couldn't bear the thought of waking Jimmy only to turn him over to a stranger without explanation. The car ride to town would give her plenty of opportunity to reassure him, and maybe by the time they reached Conard City his mom will have arrived.

She looked at Gus. "I promised him a horse ride."

"We might be able to work in a couple of minutes when we get to your HQ. If that's okay with Gage."

"Fine by me. That little boy needs everything good he can get right now."

Chapter Three

Jimmy woke quickly. At first he looked frightened but he recognized Blaire and when she told him they were going to take a ride in a police car, he seemed delighted. Not once, not yet, did he ask the dreaded question, "Where's my daddy?"

They sat in the back of Gage's official SUV and Gage obliged him by turning on the rack of lights but explained people in the woods were still sleeping so he couldn't turn on the siren.

Jimmy appeared satisfied with that. Then Blaire began the onerous task of explaining to him that they were taking him to his mom and finally he asked, "Where's my daddy?"

Her heart sank like a stone. How the hell did you explain this to a four-year-old? It wasn't her place. He'd need his mom and a social worker for this.

She cleared her throat. "He can't come with us right now."

After a moment, Jimmy nodded. "He's helping the police, right?"

She couldn't bring herself to answer and was grateful when he didn't press the issue, apparently satisfied with his own answer.

Which gave her plenty of time to contemplate the kind

of monster who would shoot a man while his young son was nearby. Only in battle when her comrades were in danger had she ever felt a need to kill, but she felt it right then and memories surged in her, the past burst into the present and she wanted to vomit.

But Jimmy fell asleep and they sailed right past her headquarters building without offering him the promised horse ride. Gus, who had been following them down, pulled over and gave a hands-up signal as they drove past. Letting her know he'd figured it out.

It was good of him to offer to stay and inform her staff what was going on. She could hardly stop to call and radio, and she couldn't wait for them herself, not with this trusting, precious little boy cuddled up against her.

Just as well. She wasn't sure what world she was inhabiting. Afghanistan? Conard County? The state park? Images, like mixed-up slides, kept flashing in her mind and she had to make a huge effort to focus on the back of Gage's head, on the fact she was in his vehicle. On the boy curled against her so trustingly.

That trust was killing her. Nobody should trust her like that. Not him most especially. He was just a kid and when he found out and finally understood what had happened, he might never trust another soul in his life.

Almost without realizing it, as the town grew closer and the day grew brighter, she was making a silent promise to herself. Somehow she was going to find the SOB who'd done this. If the cops didn't get him first, she wasn't going to give up the hunt.

Because someone deserved to pay for this. Someone deserved to die.

MILES AWAY, THE killer was hotfooting it down a mountainside to his vehicle. The cries of the child rang loud in his head and he thought bitterly that he should have just kidnapped the kid and carried him along.

He'd been angry at his friends. He'd been scared of them, maybe even terrified. But now he loathed them. He wished he could find a way to get even that wouldn't involve putting himself in prison for life.

Thoughts of revenge fueled him as he raced toward safety.

GUS HAD LOADED the ATV onto Blaire's truck and brought everything down to her HQ, where he waited patiently. As staff members reported for their day's work, he explained what had happened and told them to avoid the upper campground, so they wouldn't get in the way of the police.

While he was telling them, an ambulance brought the body down. Silence fell among the six men and women who were about to fan out to their various jobs. They stood, watching it pass, and for several long minutes, no one spoke.

Then Gus's radio crackled. It was one of his own staff. "You coming back today, Gus, or you want me to stand in?"

"I'm not sure." He was thinking of Blaire. She might need more than a cup of coffee after this. "You take over, Josh. I'll let you know what's up."

"Terrible thing," Josh said. "You can bet we're going to be on high alert today."

"Good. We don't know which direction the perp took off when he left. Or whether he'll shoot again."

That made the local crew shift nervously and eye him. *Oh, hell,* he thought. He'd just messed up everything. What could he say? He couldn't very well send them out to patrol the other campgrounds. Not after this. They were seasonal workers, not trained for this kind of thing. And he was still more used to talking to other soldiers than civilians. He needed to guard his tongue.

"You got stuff you can do nearby?" he asked, scanning them.

One spoke. "Blaire's been talking about replacing the fire rings at the Cottonwood Campground."

"Nearby?"

"Yeah."

"Then do that."

"We'll need the truck to cart the concrete and the rings."

Gus nodded. "Okay. Good idea. Stick together. I'm almost positive the threat is gone, though."

"I'll feel better tomorrow," one said sarcastically.

He helped them unload the ATV, then fill the truck bed with bags of concrete and steel fire rings. Finally, he turned over the keys and watched them drive away. East. Away from the campground where the shooting had occurred. Not that he could blame them.

Then he went inside and made a fresh pot of coffee. He eyed the espresso machine because he loved Blaire's espresso, but he didn't know how to use it. Maybe he'd remedy that when she got back, ask for instructions.

While he waited for the coffee he went outside and whistled for Scrappy. Five minutes later, the gelding emerged from the woods to the north, looking quite perky. He must have picked up some sleep during all the uproar.

When the horse reached him, he patted his neck, then was astonished—he was always astonished when it happened—when Scrappy wrapped his neck around him, giving him a hug.

The horse was a mind reader? No, a mood reader. He

patted and stroked Scrappy until the horse needed to move and pranced away.

"You getting hungry?"

Scrappy bobbed his head emphatically. If that horse could talk…

He had some feed in one of the saddlebags and put it on the edge of the porch, making sure Scrappy's reins wouldn't get in his way. Water. He needed water, too.

He went back inside and looked around until he found a big bucket in a supply closet. That would do.

A little while later, cup of coffee in his hand, he perched on the step of the small porch and shared breakfast with Scrappy. Maybe his best friend, he thought.

But his mind was wandering elsewhere, to Blaire, to the murder, to the little guy who'd lost his father.

It had been a while, thank God, since he'd felt murderous, but today was shaking him back into that old unwanted feeling.

A sleeping man. His child nearby. What kind of person would take that shot without a threat driving him? And how offensive could a sleeping man be? Kid aside, the killer had to be the worst kind of coward.

Afraid of where his thoughts might take him, because he'd spent a lot of time getting himself past the war, he forced himself to notice other things. The play of the light on the trees as the sun rose ever higher. The bird calls. Even more entertaining were the squirrels darting around, jumping from branch to branch and walking out on slender twigs, looking like high-wire daredevils. Even at times hanging upside down while they gnawed a branch. Weird, they usually did that only in the spring and fall.

BLAIRE RETURNED IN the late morning, looking absolutely wrung out. A police vehicle dropped her off, then turned around and headed back down the mountain. Gus rose as she approached, but she lowered herself to the porch step, eyeing Scrappy, who'd found a clump of grass to investigate.

"You must want to get back," she said.

"I most likely want to get you a cup of coffee. Regular because I don't know how your espresso machine works." He lowered himself beside her and asked, "Awful?"

"Awful," she agreed. "That poor little boy. At least his mother was already there when we arrived. But then he asked the question he didn't ask before."

"What's that?"

"Where's Daddy?"

"Oh. My. God." Gus didn't even want to imagine it, but his mind threw it up in full view, inescapable.

"Yeah." She sighed, leaned against the porch stanchion and closed her eyes.

"Your crew is out working on fire rings at Cottonwood. They didn't seem too eager to split up."

Her eyes opened to half-mast. "I don't imagine they would. I'm not too eager myself. God, what a monster, and it's too soon to hope he's made his way to the far ends of the Earth. He could be hanging around out there."

He couldn't deny it. "Look, we've both been up most of the night. If you want to sleep, I'll stand guard here until your people are done for the day. If not, let me get you some coffee."

"Coffee sounds good," she admitted. "I may be over-tired, but I'm too wound up to sleep. What I really want is to wrap my hands around someone's throat. A specific someone."

He could identify with that. He'd just finished brewing a second pot of coffee so he was able to bring her a piping mug that smelled rich and fresh. He brought one for himself and sat beside her once again.

"I'm still trying to wrap my mind around the kind of person who would do something like that," she said. "It had to be in cold blood. Nothing had happened as far as anyone knows."

"His wife?"

"She's already been gently questioned. Nobody who'd want to kill him, nobody who'd had a fight with him recently, Gage told me."

"Well, great. The trail is awfully lean."

"If it's there at all." She sighed and sipped her coffee. "You must need to get back."

"My assistant is filling in. Unless you want to get rid of me, I'm here for now."

She turned her head, looking straight at him for the first time, and he noted how hollow her eyes looked. "Thanks. I'm not keen on being alone right now."

"Then there's no need." He paused. "We've shared a whole lot over cups of joe."

"That we have." She tilted her head back and drew several deep breaths as if drinking in the fresh woodland scents. "I'll share something with you right now. If the police don't have much success quickly, I'm going to start a search of my own. I know these woods like the back of my hand. He can't have come in and out without leaving some trace."

He turned his mug in his hands, thinking about it. "You're right. If it comes to that, I'll help you. But we can't wait too long. One rain and everything will be lost."

"Yeah." Again she raised her coffee to her lips, and this time she nearly drained the mug. Rising, she put her foot on the step. "I need more caffeine. If you want, I'll make espresso."

"Only if I can watch and learn. Then you'll never get rid of me."

That at least drew a weak laugh from her. Once inside, he leaned against the narrow counter with his arms folded and watched her make the beverage. From time to time she told him things that wouldn't be immediately obvious, like turning the handled filter to one side to create the pressure.

"Espresso has to be brewed under pressure."

But her mind was obviously elsewhere, and to be frank, so was his.

"People get murdered," she remarked as she finished and handed him a tall cup holding three shots. "Doctor as you like. Ice in the freezer, thank God, milk in the fridge, sweetener in these little packets."

"Ice will water it down," he remarked.

"Yeah, but I like mine cold unless it's winter. Your choice."

He went for the ice, saying, "People get murdered… But what? You didn't finish that thought."

"No, I didn't." Her own cup in hand, she scooped ice into it and topped it with milk. "People get murdered, but not often by strangers while sleeping in a tent with their little son."

"Agreed."

"Outside?" she asked.

"I hate being stuck indoors." Another leftover from years in the military. He never felt all that safe when four walls held him and cut off his view.

They returned to the front steps. Scrappy looked almost as if he were sleeping standing up. Usually, he curled up on the ground, but not today. The tension the two of them were feeling must be reaching him, as well.

"I like your horse," she remarked. "Wish I could have one."

"Then get one."

"It's not in my nonexistent budget. And I don't get paid enough to afford one. Besides, I'm so shackled by things I need to do he might not get enough exercise."

"You're even more understaffed than I am."

"No kidding."

It was easier to talk about budgets and staffing than what had happened during the wee hours this morning. He sipped his espresso, loving the caffeine kick because he was tired, too, from lack of sleep, and waited. There'd be more. They were both vets. Memories had been stirred up, especially for her because she'd had to see it all.

Yeah, there'd be more. Because she'd had to help the kid.

But as noon began to approach, she said nothing more, and he had nothing to say. He was cramming the memories back into the dark pit where they belonged and he decided she must be doing the same.

Unfortunately, burying them wasn't a permanent solution. Like zombies, they kept rising anew and they were never welcome. And sometimes, like zombies, they'd devour you whole and all you could do was hang on. Or give in because there was no fighting it.

He glanced down into his cup and realized he'd finished his espresso. He'd have liked some more but decided not to ask.

At long last she turned to look at him, for the first time that day her blue eyes looking almost as brilliant as the sunny western sky. "That kid is going to have problems. He may not have seen the mess, he may not understand what happened, but he would remember that he left his dad behind in a tent on a mountainside. His mom will tell him about it later, but he's going to remember leaving his dad."

Gus nodded. "Yeah, he will." Of that he was certain. "The question will be whether he believes he abandoned his father."

She nodded and looked down at the mug she held. "More espresso?"

"I'd like that."

Those blue eyes lifted again. "You sure you don't have to get back?"

"Not today. I have a good staff. But even so, I'm in no rush to face the inevitable questions about what happened over here."

"Me neither." Her eyes shuttered briefly. "So my crew are out replacing fire rings?"

He'd told her that but under the circumstances didn't feel she'd slipped a memory cog. Overload. She must be experiencing it. "Yeah, it was the first thing they thought to do when I explained what had happened. Besides, I exceeded my authority."

Her head snapped around to look at him again. "Meaning?"

"I suggested today would be a good day to stick together."

After a few beats, she nodded. "You're right. I didn't even think of that. The creep could still be out there."

"I don't think there's any question that he's still out there. The only question is, did he leave the forest or is he hanging out somewhere?"

Her charming, crooked smile peeked out. "Correcting my precision now?"

He flashed a smile back at her. "You know why."

Of course she knew why. With a sigh, she rose. "Let's go make some more coffee. If I tried to sleep I wouldn't rest anyway, so I might as well be wired."

Inside the cabin was dim. Because of the harsh, cold winters, the builders hadn't been generous with windows except at the very front where visitors would enter. Consequently, the rear room that housed the small kitchen and dining area was dim and needed the lights turned on. Blaire flipped the switch, then turned on the espresso maker.

"How many shots?" she asked Gus.

"It's funny, but I'm not used to thinking of coffee in terms of shots."

That drew a faint laugh from her. She picked up and wagged a double shot glass at him. "How many of these?"

He laughed outright. "Okay, two."

She nodded and turned back to the machine.

"You gonna be okay?" he asked as the pump began pushing water through the coffee grounds. Noisy thing.

"Sure," she said, leaning against the counter and watching the espresso pour into the double shot glass. "I'm always okay. It's not necessarily pleasant, but I'm okay."

Yeah, *okay* was a long way from being happy, content or otherwise good. He shook his head a little and pulled out one of the two chairs at the small table, sitting while he watched her. "This day is endless."

"What brought you this way this morning?"

"I was restless and couldn't sleep. Scrappy was agitating for a ride so I decided to saddle up. I think he was feeling my mood."

"That wouldn't surprise me. Animals are very sensitive to energy, at least in my experience." She placed his mug in front of him again. "You know where the fixins are."

Making himself at home in her kitchen felt right. At

least at the moment. He dressed up his espresso and waited for her to make her own. "Plans for today, since you can't sleep?"

"I'm probably going to run this morning like a broken record in my head." She finished pouring milk into her mug, added a few ice cubes, then turned. "Outside, if you don't mind. The walls are closing in."

He knew the feeling well. He held open the front door for her and resumed his perch on the step. She paced for a bit on the bare ground that probably served as a parking lot when people checked in and were directed to their campgrounds.

"I keep thinking," she said, "that the crime scene guys aren't going to find much that's useful. The ground was a mess, did you notice? People had obviously scuffed it up pretty good last night even if they didn't this morning."

"I saw," he said in agreement. "What are you thinking?"

"That this guy knew what he was doing. That he didn't just walk into a random campsite and shoot someone through an opening in their tent."

He sat up a little straighter. He must have been more tired than he realized not to have thought of this himself. "You're saying stalking."

"I'm suggesting it, yes. No bumbling around in the dark as far as anyone knows. Certainly some of the people in the other tents must be light enough sleepers that they'd have heard activity."

"Maybe so." He was chewing the idea in his head.

"So, if he planned in advance he had to watch in advance. He'd have done that from a distance, right?"

He nodded. He'd done enough recon to know the drill. "Say he did."

"Then the cops might not find anything useful at the scene."

He nodded, sucking some air between his front teeth as his mouth tightened. "What are your plans for tomorrow? Got any time for reconnaissance?"

"I can make it."

"Can you ride?"

"Sure."

"So shall I borrow an extra mount or do you want to walk a perimeter first?"

She thought about it. "Walk," she decided. "We don't want to miss something."

"This assumes the cops don't find something today."

"Of course."

Their eyes met and the agreement was sealed. They'd do a little searching of their own.

That made him feel a bit better. He hoped it did for her, too.

THAT EVENING, JEFF pulled his car into the lodge's small parking area and went to face the music. He'd made a mistake and wished he could figure out a way of not telling Will and Karl. Desperately wished. Because things were going to get worse now.

But Jeff was acutely aware that he was a lousy liar. He could see them when they arrived tomorrow and pretend that everything had gone off without a hitch, but it wouldn't take them long to realize he was being untruthful.

The bane of his existence.

He let himself in and began to build a fire on the big stone hearth. That task was expected of the first to arrive, and given that the nights were chilly at this altitude, even in the summer when it had been known to snow occasionally, a small fire burning all the time was welcome.

The heavy log construction of the lodge acted like an insulator, too. Once it had caught the chill, it hung on to it until it was driven out.

The others weren't expected until late tomorrow, though. Fine by him. There was plenty to eat and drink and maybe he could find a way to omit mentioning his oversight. His major oversight.

Besides, it might amount to nothing. One shell casing? How much could that tell anyone? That he'd used a hollow-point bullet in a .45? Lots of folks bought hollow points and even more owned .45s. Hollow points were less likely to pass through the target and cause collateral damage, while still inflicting far more damage on the target than a full metal jacket.

He couldn't have been sure what he'd be facing when he opened that tent a few inches, but he knew he wanted to kill his target without killing anything else.

They'd find the remains of the bullet at autopsy anyway. A popular brand that could be purchased in an awful lot of places. No, that wouldn't lead to him.

But the shell casing automatically ejected by his pistol? He should have scooped that up, but in his panic to get away, he'd clean forgotten it was lying on the ground. What if it had retained his fingerprints?

Not likely, he assured himself. The way he'd handled those bullets, any fingerprints should be just smears. The heat of the powder burning before it ejected the round from the shell should have wiped out any DNA evidence.

So yeah, he'd made a mistake. It wasn't a god-awful mistake, though. Hell, they couldn't necessarily even link it to the shooting, regardless of bullet fragments they might find at autopsy. No, because *anyone* could have been shooting out there at any time. That brass casing might be months old.

So no, it wasn't a catastrophe.

He spent a great deal of time that evening sipping beer and bucking himself up, dreading the moment tomorrow when his friends would come through the door.

Friends? He wasn't very sure of that any longer. Friends would have taken his word for it that he wouldn't squeal on them. Friends should have trusted him rather than threatening him.

Thinking about those threats put him in the blackest of moods. He wasn't a killer. He *wasn't*. He'd killed, though. In self-defense, he reminded himself. Because failing to take that guy out would have been signing his own death sentence. Yeah, self-defense, not murder.

That proved to be a small sop to his conscience, but he needed one. While the cries of the child had begun to fade to the background, the memory of them still made him supremely uncomfortable.

He'd caused that. Did self-defense justify that? He hoped the kid was too young to understand what had happened.

Because he hated to think of the nightmares he'd caused if the kid wasn't.

Chapter Four

The morning was still dewy when Blaire awoke from troubled, uneasy dreams. At least she'd finally been able to crash after a day that had seemed like a nightmare that would never end, a day during which she'd become so exhausted she had often felt as if she were only slightly attached to her own body.

She'd had the feeling before, in combat and the aftermath, but not since then. Not until yesterday.

It hadn't just been lack of sleep that had gotten to her. Jimmy had gotten to her. He had caused her an emotional turmoil unlike any she had felt since one of her comrades had been hit in a firefight. Or blasted by a roadside bomb.

All she could remember was how he'd been crying and clinging to his dead father. Yeah, he'd perked up well enough after she'd carried him away, singing to him, and he loved the silvery blanket, but how much trauma had he endured? How much had he understood and how much of that would stay with him forever?

She had no idea how good a four-year-old's long-term memory might be, but she suspected those memories were stronger if they carried a huge emotional impact. Heck, that was true for most people. Some events just got etched into your brain as if by acid.

Her staff showed up, trickling in around 8:00 a.m. The

first thing they wanted to know was news about the shooting. She had none. Then they asked if they could keep working on the fire rings as they had yesterday.

Of course they could. It wasn't like the job hadn't been done, and from what she'd seen yesterday afternoon, she figured there was hardly a camper left in the park. When she climbed into her truck to check out all the sites, she found she was right: only one hardy camper remained, a guy who always spent nearly the entire summer here. He was friendly enough, but clearly didn't want to strike up any lengthy conversations. Most days he sat beside a small fire drinking coffee. Beans seemed to be his preferred meal. Sometimes he went fishing in the tumbling stream a couple of hundred yards behind his campsite, and she'd occasionally seen a couple of freshly cleaned fish on a frying pan over his small fire.

"Nothing better than fresh fish," she inevitably said.

"Nothing," he always agreed before they went their separate ways.

Finally, because she couldn't ignore it any longer, she drove up to the site of yesterday's horror. She left her truck in the small parking lot next to a sheriff's vehicle but eschewed her ATV. She needed the walk back to the site, needed to stretch her legs and try to clear the air. When she got there, she felt a whole lot better.

The deputies Gage had promised stood guard. Seeing them, she wished she'd thought to bring a thermos of soup or something with her. Their only seat was a fallen log outside the taped-off area, and neither of them looked as if they were having a good time.

"Boring duty, huh?" she asked as she approached. Her uniform identified her as theirs identified them. She couldn't remember having met either of them before. They looked almost brand spanking new. Together they formed a sea of khaki, hers interrupted with dark pants and a dark green quilted vest over her shirt. Both of the deputies looked as if they wished they'd brought a vest or jacket with them.

"I suppose you can't light a fire?" she said. "The firepit is outside the crime scene area and you guys look cold."

"We ran out of coffee," one admitted frankly. His chest plate said his name was Carson. "We'll be relieved soon, though, Ranger. Only four hours at a stretch. If they need us up here tomorrow, we'll both be better prepared."

"You're not from around here, huh?" That seemed apparent. Anyone who lived in these parts knew how chilly it could get up here even at the height of summer.

"That's obvious, I guess," said the other guy. His last name was Bolling and his face was so fresh looking he could have passed for eighteen. Which she guessed was possible, however unlikely. "I'm from a small town in Nevada and I got sick of being hot."

Blaire had to laugh, and the two men joined her. She looked at Carson. "You, too?"

"Different town, more Midwestern. I wanted mountains. Visions of hiking and skiing. That kind of thing."

"I'll bet you never thought you'd be standing guard like this in the middle of nowhere."

"Not high on my list," Bolling said. "So is the skiing good?"

"We still don't have a downhill slope right around here. Something goes wrong with every attempt. But if you want to off-trail cross-country, that's great. So is snowshoeing. Just check in with me or with the national forest before you go. I need to know you're out here and you need to know if we have avalanche conditions. Mind if I walk around a bit?"

Carson chuckled. "I think you're in charge of this place except for the roped-off area."

"Yeah, that's yours."

She circled the campground, eyeing the signs of the hurried departures yesterday. And they had been hurried. Sure, it was unlikely the shooter was around or they'd have known it for certain, but she couldn't blame them for wanting to get the hell away from here.

Death had visited a few tents over. And it was not a natural death. Uneasiness would cause almost anyone to want to get as far away as possible.

She knew she and Gus had planned to check out the area together, but he also had responsibilities at the national forest. Her load was a lot lighter, for the most part. She could afford to set her staff to replacing fire rings, especially now that they were empty of campers.

She had no idea what she expected to find that the scene techs hadn't. They'd probably applied their version of a fine-tooth comb to most of the area, even beyond the circle of yellow tape.

But she kept walking slowly anyway. A campground was an unlikely place to pick up a trail, though. People were in constant motion at their sites and places in between. All of them had to traipse to one of the two outdoor chemical toilets, which meant they either walked around tents or passed between them. Kids, especially, scuffed the ground and kicked up needles and duff.

She paused at one spot where she had to smile. It seemed some kids had been laying out roads, probably to use to play with miniature cars. There were even a couple of twigs broken off trees and firmly planted to make the road look tree-lined. Clever.

How many kids had she seen last night? Not many, but

that didn't mean they weren't there. Their parents might have insisted they stay inside tents.

Then she spied something red that was half-buried in earth and squatted. A small metal car, she realized as she brushed the debris away. She hoped it wasn't someone's favorite.

Just in case she got a letter in a week or so from some youngster, she slipped it into her vest pocket. It wouldn't be the first time she'd heard from a kid who'd left something behind and who couldn't come back to retrieve it. Usually it was an inexpensive, small item that the parents didn't consider worth the time and effort to return for. She could understand both sides of that issue, but she didn't mind sending a toy back if it made a boy or girl happy. In fact, just doing it always made her smile.

Since Afghanistan, her smiles had become rarer and far more precious to her when she could summon a genuine one. Gone were the days when laughter came easily. She hoped both would return eventually. She had to believe they would. A battlefield was a helluva place to lose all your illusions, and while humor had carried most of them through, it had become an increasingly dark humor. Something that no one on the outside would ever understand.

Swallowing her memories yet again, she forced herself to move slowly and sweep the ground with her eyes. The guy had to have come from somewhere. He wasn't a ghost.

There was a basic rule to investigation: whoever took something from a scene also left something behind. She'd first learned that in Afghanistan when they'd been tracking the people who had attacked them or one of their other convoys. Nobody could move over even the rockiest ground without leaving traces, however minor.

But this damn forest floor was a challenge unto itself.

So much loose debris, easily scuffed and stirred. Even the wind could move it around. Moreover, under the trees it was soft, softer than a carpet, and footprints would disappear quickly unless boots scraped. Weight alone didn't make a lasting impression, not unless it rained, and rain here at this time of year was rare enough. They certainly hadn't had any in the several days leading up to the murder.

Eventually she called it a day. A wider perimeter would need the help that Gus promised and it might be a wild-goose chase anyway.

The killer was obviously skilled, had clearly taken great care not to leave a trail behind him.

Which left the question: Why Jasper? And why when his kid was there? Was Jimmy an unexpected complication for him? Too late to back out?

She seemed to remember one of the campers saying Jasper had brought his son up here just for the weekend. Yeah, if someone had been stalking him, Jimmy was probably a complete surprise.

She found herself once again hoping Jimmy could forget that night. If he retained any memory of it at all, she hoped it was of a space blanket and a ride in a police car. Not what had happened inside that tent.

Heading back, she passed the two cold deputies again. They no longer sat, but were moving from foot to foot. Too bad she hadn't picked up another survival blanket to offer them. "Much longer?" she asked.

Bolling looked at his watch. "A little less than an hour."

She nodded. "Keep warm." As if they could do much about it without lighting a small fire, which they didn't seem inclined to do. Maybe they didn't know how.

Shaking her head, knowing their relief was already on

the way, she headed back to her truck, walking among the tall trees and the occasional brush that looked parched.

The peace she usually found in these woods had been shattered, she realized. The niggling uneasiness she'd been trying to ignore hit her full force during her walk back to her truck. A killer had stalked these woods. He might still be out there. He might be watching even now. And he could always return to repeat his crime.

She told herself not to be fanciful, but she'd spent time in a place where such threats were as real as the air she breathed and the ground she walked on.

The guy could be out there right now, savoring his kill, enjoying his apparent success, wanting to see everything that happened. Hadn't she read somewhere that criminals often came back to the scene, especially to watch the cops?

Or it could be another kind of killer. The kind who got a kick out of reliving his actions. Who enjoyed the sense of power the killing gave him. Or the secret power of being so close to the very cops who were supposed to find him. Cat and mouse, maybe.

His motivation scarcely mattered at this point, though it might become useful eventually. No, all that mattered right now was that these woods were haunted by the ghost of a dead man and the evil of a murderer. That a little boy's cries might have soaked into the very trees and earth, leaving a psychic stain.

God, was she losing it?

But her step quickened anyway. Back to HQ. Back to check on her team. To call the sheriff and ask if they'd learned anything at all.

Despite every effort to ignore the feeling, she paused

and looked back twice. The sense of being watched persisted, even though she could detect nothing.

An icy trickle ran down her spine.

A THOUSAND YARDS away in a small hide left by some hunter in a past season, Will and Karl peered through high-powered binoculars. They'd happened on this point during reconnaissance during their spring planning and were delighted with it.

Here, below the tree line, there were few spots where one could see any great distance through the grid work of tree trunks and the laciness of tree branches. Not much brush under these trees, but not much open space for any appreciable distance.

This was a natural forest, not one neatly replanted by a lumber company, which would have given them corridors to peer along. No, here nature did her best to scatter the trees everywhere, giving each a better chance at a long life.

Some saplings added to the screening effect, huddled around the base of mother trees that, science had learned, actually provided nutrients to their offspring. On occasion, an older tree would sacrifice its life to ensure the growth of the new ones. Roots underground were carriers of messages and food.

Will had read about it. It tickled him to think of how much a forest was invisibly intertwined. When he was in a fanciful mood, he'd sometimes close his eyes and imagine a brightly lit neural-type network running beneath his feet, messages passing among the sheltering trees.

Then there was that massive fungus scientists had discovered under the ground that turned out to be a single organism covering square miles. As he started thinking about that, however, Karl spoke, shattering the moment.

"Jeff did it."

Yes, he'd done it. The solitary tent surrounded by crime scene tape and the two deputies wandering around as if they wished they were anywhere else… It was all the diagram he needed. But he remained anyway, peering through the binoculars, both enjoying the success and wanting to annoy Karl, who felt no appreciation of the miracle under them, buried in the ground.

Once he'd tried to tell Karl about it. Once was enough. It didn't even matter to him that it was actual science. Not Karl. He prided himself on being hardheaded. Will could tell him about it, and Karl would absorb the information factually and move on, finding nothing entrancing about it.

That was the only thing he didn't like about Karl. Had never liked, even though they were good friends in every other way. Karl had a distinct lack of imagination. A trait that proved helpful in this endeavor, were Will to be honest about it.

While he himself might see a network of patterns and possibilities and race down various avenues of attack, Karl remained firmly grounded in their scouting expeditions and what they knew and didn't know. He wasn't one to make even a small assumption.

Although sending Jeff on this expedition had left them both wondering if he'd just walk into the nearest police station.

They had that covered. Two against one, if Jeff tried to nail them, the two of them would nail him. They were each the other's alibi.

Not that they'd need one. This was their fifth kill in the last two summers, and neither he nor Karl had ever left a shred of evidence. Hell, the murders hadn't even been linked to one another.

They'd vastly overshadowed careless Leopold and Loeb. Funny, though, Will thought while watching the campground, seeing the ranger stray around out farther looking for something. He and Karl hadn't been content to prove the point and stop at one.

No. He and Karl had discovered a real taste for this kind of hunting. Deer could be slipperier, of course, but hunting a human? They weren't nearly as evasive, but they were so much more dangerous to take down.

It was always possible to leave traces, and cops would be looking, unlike when you took a deer during season with a license. They'd be paying attention to anything out of line. And if you weren't cautious enough, your victim might get wind that he was being stalked.

It wasn't the top thing on most people's minds, which had aided them, but one of their vics had had an almost preternatural sense that he was being followed. When they realized he seemed to be taking evasive action, they'd nearly salivated over the prospect of taking him out. A *real* challenge.

He studied the campground below once again, satisfying himself that no one seemed to be acting as if there was something significant to find.

Karl spoke, lowering his own binoculars. "Jeff's a wimp. I still can't believe he managed this."

"We kind of put him on the spot," Will reminded him.

Karl turned his head a bit to look at him. He shifted as if he were getting tired of lying on his stomach on the hard rock. "Would you have killed him?"

"I said I would."

"But he's one of us."

Will put down his own binoculars, lifting a brow. "He's one of us until he screws us. How far do you trust him?"

"More than I did a few days ago."

"Exactly. He's in it all the way now. But if he'd backed off, neither of us would have had a choice."

Karl nodded. "I know. I wish to hell he hadn't found out. Been jumpy since I learned he knew what we're doing. He's always been a bit of a coward. I like the guy, always have. We grew up together, went to college together. Joined the same fraternity, screwed the same girls…"

"Hey, that's almost as much of a crime these days as shooting someone."

Karl afforded one of his cold smiles. "Guess so, but I seem to remember those sorority gals fighting to get an invitation to our parties. And it wasn't a secret we were looking to get laid."

"Usually that was true. I remember a few who didn't seem to be clued in, though."

Karl nodded and lifted his binoculars again.

There *were* a few, Will recalled. Girls who were taken by surprise and had to be silenced before they got someone in trouble. Silencing them had been pathetically easy, though. All they'd had to do was tell them the stories they'd make up about the girls. How they'd come off looking like two-bit hookers. The strength of the fraternity, its numbers.

In a smaller way, he and Karl had that strength now, more so with Jeff actively involved.

God, how had that man pieced it all together from a few snips of conversation he'd overheard between Will and Karl? Why had he even believed it? What had been the clue that had made Jeff realize it was no longer a game?

Someday he was going to make Jeff spill the beans. But not yet. Jeff was entirely too nervous. He didn't want to do anything that might make Jeff take flight.

"I don't like that ranger," Karl remarked.

Will picked up his binoculars, focused them again and found the woman. "Why not?"

"She just picked up something from the ground and put it in her pocket. She's actively searching outside the crime scene area."

"She won't find anything useful," Will said, although sudden uncertainty made his stomach sink.

"She shouldn't if Jeff did what we said. But she just found something and picked it up. I couldn't tell what it was."

"Hell."

He zeroed in on the woman more closely, but she scanned the ground for a little while longer before waving to the deputies and heading for the parking lot. She didn't seem to be in a hurry, which could well be the best news for them.

At least until she started down the rutty walking path to the parking lot. Her step quickened, then quickened again and he saw her looking over her shoulder.

"What the hell?" he muttered.

She paused again and looked back.

"She senses we're watching," Karl said abruptly. "Look at something else."

"But…" Will started.

"No *buts*. If she'd found something she'd have showed it to the deputies. Instead she just stuck it in her pocket. Let it go."

Will, who'd been letting a lot go without much trouble for the last few years, suddenly found himself unable to do that. What had she picked up? It had been important enough to tuck in her pocket. Why hadn't she given it to the deputies?

Karl was probably right, he assured himself. But the way she'd looked back, twice… His stomach flipped again.

"Let it go," Karl said again. "People can often tell when they're being watched. It's some kind of instinct. But since she couldn't see anyone, she's probably convinced she imagined it."

"It would be easy enough," Will remarked. His literal-minded Karl might not get it, but Will himself had no desire to be any closer to that campsite. Something might be lurking down there, although he didn't want to put a name to it. He often told himself he didn't believe in ghosts or all that crap.

But the truth was, he feared they might exist.

That was one thing he hadn't considered when he'd embarked on this venture with his friends: that he might be collecting ghosts that could haunt him. Where was it written that they had to stay where they were killed?

He swore under his breath and rolled onto his back, looking up at the graying sky. "It's going to rain. Maybe we should go."

"It rarely rains up here."

"Don't you smell it?" He had to get out of here. Now. Because he honestly felt as if *something* were watching him.

"Well, we're supposed to meet Jeff at the lodge this evening," Karl said grudgingly. He pulled out a cigar from an inner pocket on his jacket. "Just a few puffs, first."

They were far enough away that the tobacco smell should waft away to the west, away from the campground and the deputies if it could even reach that far.

Giving in, Will pulled out a cigar of his own and clipped the end with his pocket tool before lighting it from a butane lighter. Then he held the flame to Karl, who did the same. The cellophane wrappers got shoved deep into their pockets.

It *was* relaxing, Will admitted to himself. Staring up

at the graying sky that didn't look all that threatening yet. Lying still, refusing to think about all the worrisome problems that had been stalking *him* since they embarked on this venture.

Would he undo it? No way. He'd gotten thrills for a lifetime the last couple of years.

"What's eating you?" Karl asked after a few minutes. "You're edgy."

Well, there was no way Will would tell him that he didn't like being within range of the scenes where any of the victims had died. He stayed away once the deed was done. It was always Karl, whether it had been his kill or not, who wanted to go back and look the site over. Some quirk or odd fascination.

"Coming back could be dangerous," he said finally, although he didn't say how. No need for that.

"They would never look up here. You know that. We can look down on them, but when we checked it out two months ago, we realized this position was well shielded from below. Different sight lines. You know that. Besides, those deputies look bored out of their minds."

"Yeah." He puffed on his cigar, liking the way it tasted and gave him a mild buzz. "That ranger was acting weird."

"She probably just wants the campground back. Funny, though," Karl added.

"Yeah?"

"Every campground in the park emptied out. Talk about having an impact."

"Kind of a broad-brush response," Will agreed. That hadn't happened before. He pondered that reaction for the next ten minutes while drawing occasionally on his cigar. Maybe it was because this park was so small. While they'd chosen the most rustic of the campsites, farthest from the ranger's cabin and the entrance, the distance wasn't huge.

If people thought a killer was hanging out in these woods, yeah, they'd get the hell out.

Abruptly, he returned to the moment as a huge drop of rain hit the tip of his nose. While he wandered in his thoughts, the sky had darkened considerably, and for the first time, he heard the rumble of thunder.

He spared a thought for those deputies standing guard below, not that he cared about them. The rain would mess up the scene even more, covering any inadvertent tracks Jeff might have left. Not that he thought any had been left. They'd picked a time when the campground would be full and well scuffed up by the campers. Probably covered with bits of their trash, as well.

He looked at his cigar, hating to put it out. He bought only expensive ones and felt guiltier about wasting them than he felt about wasting food.

He sat up and Karl did, too, after some raindrops splattered his face.

"We've seen enough for now," he told Karl.

"Yeah. Jeff did the job. If he followed all his instructions, we're clear."

Will looked at him. "Of course we're clear. Why wouldn't we be? He's been doing the stalking part with us since the beginning. He practiced the approaches. He's as good as either of us."

"Maybe."

Will sometimes thoroughly disliked Karl. Not for long, but there were moments. This was one of them. "No *maybe* about it," he said firmly.

The sky opened up, settling the question of what to do with the cigar as sheets of rain fell. He cussed, ground out his cigar and tossed the stogie to the ground, kicking leaves and pine needles over it. The rain would take care of it. Karl followed suit.

Together they rose, gave one last look back down the mountain, then started heading over the crest and back to their vehicle. Another successful hunt.

Irritated as he'd begun to feel, Will smiled as the rain hid them in its gray veils. Jeff had graduated. Maybe they ought to throw him a small party.

Chapter Five

Gus spent a lot of time thinking about Blaire the next two days. He'd hated leaving her at night, knowing she was going to be all alone in the park. But he didn't want to hover and make her feel that he was doubtful of her ability to care for herself.

Dang, those campers from the other campgrounds had bailed even before the cops had released the folks at the crime scene. Word had traveled on the wind, apparently, and nobody wanted to be camping out here when there'd been a murder.

An unusual murder. It wasn't as if Jasper had been killed by his wife after an argument, or as if he'd gotten into a fight with someone else at the campground.

No, to all appearances this shooter had been a stranger. That might change once the cops dug into Jasper's background more deeply, but the people at the surrounding campgrounds weren't going to take a chance that it wasn't a grudge killing.

Even a few of the national forest campgrounds had cleared out. The farther they were from the state park, the less likely people had been to leave, but there was still a marked quiet.

Weird, especially since people booked sites months in advance to make sure they'd have a place to pitch a tent

or park an RV. Weirder still when you considered how
hard it was to find a place to camp anymore. Gone were
the days he remembered from childhood where you could
drop in almost any place and find a site.

Anyway, once he got things sorted out with his staff,
leaving Holly Booker in charge of the front office and the
rest of his people out doing their regular jobs with guns
on their hips and in their saddle holsters, he headed for
Blaire's place again. The need to check on her had been
growing more powerful all day.

Once upon a time being a ranger had been a relatively safe job. Well, except for problems with wildlife,
of course. But that had changed over the last decade or
so. Rangers were getting shot. Not many, but enough that
anyone who worked in the forest needed to be alert to
strange activity.

Now they'd had this killing, and he wasn't convinced
the shooter had left the woods. What better place to hide
out than in the huge forests on the side of the mountain?
And what if he hadn't settled whatever problem had
caused him to do this in the first place?

Lack of knowledge about the victim frustrated him,
but since he wasn't a member of the sheriff's department
he thought it very unlikely they'd give him any useful information. Investigations were always kept close to the
vest, and for good reasons.

Reasons that didn't keep him from feeling frustrated
nor ease his concern about what might be going on over
in the state park. Most of his staff were certified as law
officers for the US Forest Service and carried weapons.
Things were different on the other side of the line. Blaire
was the only park ranger over there who was an autho-
rized law officer. The rest were civilian seasonal hires.
Given this was Wyoming, he figured any of them could

come armed to work, but he had no idea what training they might have.

He was confident of Blaire's training, especially with her Army background, but come sunset she'd be all alone in that deserted park. The last two nights hadn't worried him so much with cops crawling all over the crime scene, but tonight?

He was worried.

He'd gone on a few solo missions when he'd been in spec ops, but he always had backup at the other end of his radio: a helicopter that could swoop in quickly if he got in trouble. Only once had that failed him, and he'd had to travel for three days as surreptitiously as he possibly could before he got a radio connection and found a reasonably safe place for the chopper to come in. But there was only that once.

Blaire was over there with no one nearby. He was the closest thing to a backup she had, and training combined with the recent murder made him feel he could back her up a whole lot better over there.

Holly was happy to take over for him. She seemed to like the office work almost as much as she enjoyed taking small groups on tours of the wildflowers and wildlife. She said she just liked meeting the people, and she had a natural way of making everyone feel like a friend.

He kind of lacked that ability. Too much had closed up inside him over the years. Trust didn't come easily, and chitchat was largely beyond him. Holly had a gift, and he didn't mind taking advantage of it when she enjoyed it.

For himself, he preferred to be out in the woods riding Scrappy, occasionally stopping by campgrounds for a few words with people, and if he chatted much it was with hikers. Loners like himself.

Scrappy seemed in no particular hurry this evening. He

ambled along and Gus swayed in his saddle, enjoying the soothing sound of creaking leather. During a number of missions in Afghanistan, he'd ridden horseback on saddles provided by the Army, but this was somehow different. Hell, he'd never be able to put his finger on the triggers that could send him into rage or cause him to get so lost in memory he didn't know where he was.

Edginess was a constant companion. He lived with it as he lived with bouts of anxiety. Mostly he controlled it. Sometimes he thought that Scrappy was his personal comfort animal.

They reached the end of the trail and Scrappy turned toward the ranger's cabin and Blaire without any direction from him. He guessed he was getting predictable.

Blaire was sitting on her porch step as the twilight began to deepen. She waved when she saw him and stood.

"Coffee?" she called.

"When have I ever said no?"

He swung down from the saddle as Blaire went inside, presumably to bring him some coffee. He'd just reached her step when she reemerged carrying two insulated mugs. Even in midsummer, when the sun disappeared behind the mountains, the thin air began to take on a noticeable chill. She was wearing a blue sweater and jeans, and he pulled a flannel shirt out of his saddlebag to wear.

Scrappy eyed him from the side with one warm brown eye, then began to explore his surroundings. He'd tossed the reins loosely over his neck so they didn't get caught on something. Probably wouldn't be long before he shook them off anyway.

Blaire sat, and he sat beside her, resting his elbows on his knees, taking care to keep space between them. He didn't ever want her to feel as if he were encroaching.

"You hear anything?" she asked.

"Not a peep. You?"

"Nada. I did wander around up there at the outer edge of the campground. I found where some kids had been making roads in the duff and picked up a miniature red car in case someone calls me or writes about it."

"Really? For a miniature car?"

She looked at him, a crooked smile tipping her mouth. "You had a deprived childhood, Gus. Small things can be the most important stuff in the world to a kid. This is a little tow truck. Even has a hook on the boom."

He felt a smile grow on his own face. "Really cool, then."

"Clearly." She laughed quietly. "You know, this place is this deserted only at the height of winter. An awful lot of people have canceled reservations and most haven't even asked for their deposits back."

"Really? I know we're quiet, too, at least on your side of the forest, but I didn't check cancellations."

"Ah," she said. "Holly is taking over."

Something in the way she said that made him uncomfortable. He decided to take the possible bull by the potential horns. "*Not* because she's a woman. She happens to like it."

"Did I say anything?"

"Your voice was hinting."

She laughed, a delightful sound. Like him, she seemed to have trouble laughing at times, but when she relaxed enough he enjoyed hearing the sound emerge from her. He was glad the laughter hadn't been totally wiped out of her. Sometimes he wondered if *he* had much left.

He glanced up the road that led to the higher campgrounds, especially the one where the murder had happened. "It seems so out of the blue," he remarked.

"I know. Especially with the kid there. I keep wondering who would do a thing like that. Had the boy's presence been unexpected? Did the shooter even see Jimmy before he pulled the trigger?"

"Questions without answers right now," he remarked unhelpfully, then hated the way that sounded. "Sorry, I didn't mean anything by that." He took a long swallow of hot coffee.

"I didn't think you did. It's true, though. I have all these questions rolling around in my head, and the answers are beyond my knowing. I wonder if the sheriff will even share anything with us. Probably not."

"Not unless he thinks it would be useful, is my guess." Gus shifted, watching Scrappy knock the end of a branch with his nose, as if he found it entertaining to watch it bounce. It was probably easier to understand that horse's mind than the killer's mind.

After a few minutes, she spoke again. "One of my seasonals gave me chills earlier. Dave Carr. You've met him, I think?"

"Yeah, doesn't he lead backcountry ski expeditions in the winter?"

"That's him."

"So how'd he give you chills?" Turning until he leaned back against the porch stanchion, Gus sipped more coffee and waited to hear.

"Apparently there was a buzz going around town yesterday and early this morning. Some people are claiming there's a serial killer running around the mountains all the way up to Yellowstone and over to Idaho."

Gus stiffened. "Why in the hell?"

"Five murders in two years. Of course, that doesn't mean much. They were all in different places, and you can't even say all of them were killed in tents. They were all asleep when they got shot, but one guy was in the bed of his pickup, pulled over at a turnout on an access road up near Yellowstone. Sleeping, yeah, but out in plain sight." She shook her head a little. "From what Dave said, there's really nothing to link the killings."

"Other than that they all happened in the mountains and the victims were all sleeping."

"*Presumed* to be sleeping. That's talk. I'd have to ask Gage if he can check on the murders, and right now he's probably too busy to be worrying about what happened hundreds of miles away."

"True." He settled again but turned the idea around in his head. Linking murders was a chancy thing at best, especially if widely spread apart. The killer would have to leave some kind of "calling card." And if he had, wouldn't someone have picked up on it by now?

Blaire put her mug down on the porch, linked her hands as she leaned forward to rest her arms on her thighs and stared into the deepening night. "I was up at the scene. Oh, I already told you that. Sheesh, I'm losing my wits."

"I doubt it. Little car, roads in the duff."

She flashed a smile his way. "Yeah, and they were making little trees out of the ends of branches. I bet those kids were having a blast."

"I would have," he admitted. "I was really into making roads and hills to drive my cars and trucks over. My dad told me once I ought to get into model railroading, build my own scenery."

"Why didn't you?"

"I didn't have a place to do it, or the money, even though I was working at a sandwich shop, and then the Army."

Her crooked smile returned. "The Army would do it."

"Didn't leave me a whole lot of time for anything else.

So, you were up at the scene? Why do I feel you have more to say about that?"

"Probably because you're perceptive and I do. Yeah, I was up there yesterday, about midday. Two miserable deputies standing watch, neither of them prepared for how chilly it can get in the thin air up there. I felt sorry for them. Anyway, I felt as if I was being watched."

That definitely snagged his attention. He'd learned the hard way never to dismiss that feeling. "But you didn't see anyone?"

"Not a soul, other than the deputies. It felt as if the woods were still trying to get back to normal after all that happened. Not quite the same, if you know what I mean."

"Disturbed. Yeah. I've felt it."

"So anyway, maybe it was my own reaction to events and the feeling that some animals have moved away for a while. I couldn't blame them."

"Me neither." He drained his mug and was about to set it down when Blaire asked, "You want some more? I have to admit I'm feeling reluctant to go to sleep tonight."

He eyed her closely. "Did you sleep last night?"

"Mostly. I guess it hadn't sunk in yet. Tonight it's sinking in." Rising, she took his mug and her own. "If you want to come inside?"

"I'm kind of enjoying the night. Unless you'd rather be indoors."

"Not especially."

He stared out into the woods, noting that Scrappy had wandered closer to the cabin again. The horse seemed calm and content, which was a good sign. Nothing going on out there to put him on edge.

Now he, himself, was a different story. Almost always on edge. He wished he could contain it some way so that he could help Blaire relax because despite her outward demeanor, he sensed she was wound up tight inside.

She returned with more coffee and the surprising addition of a small package of cinnamon rolls. "Sugar's good for whatever ails you."

He summoned a smile. "Until you're diabetic."

"I'm not. My kingdom for a chocolate bar. I'm a chocoholic."

"A common affliction." He opened the package of rolls, which sat on a silvery tray, and helped himself to one, waiting for the next development. Because there would be one. They'd spent enough time chatting over the last two years for him to have learned the rhythms of their revelations. She had more to say. She was troubled.

"There's something wrong with this situation," she said eventually.

"No kidding."

She shook her head a little. "I don't just mean the murder. But think about it. The shooter knew to walk up to a tent. I'm betting a specific tent. You?"

He thought about it. "There were plenty to choose from. Okay, let's assume he had a specific target in mind."

"But if it wasn't some guy he knew…" She paused. "Jimmy's presence is bothering me. A lot. If the shooter knew Jasper, he'd know about Jasper's kid. If he knew Jasper well, he'd probably know the guy liked to bring his kid camping with him. So… This is an awful place to take out a man you're mad at if you know he might have a child with him. It'd make more sense to get him near work or home."

"Maybe so." He was listening to her spin a theory and wouldn't interject anything unless he saw a glaring flaw. So far, he didn't. People who were mad at someone didn't usually follow them to an out-of-the-way campground to off them. Unnecessary effort, no special benefit. Bigger chance of getting caught, actually.

As if she were reading his thoughts, she said virtually the same thing. "You want to get rid of someone you hate, do it in a heavily populated area without witnesses. Not out here where you might stand out like a sore thumb. Someone's got to know the shooter was in this area, and I seriously doubt he's a local."

He made a sound of agreement.

"I'm not used to thinking this way," she said slowly. "If I go off the rails, let me know."

"Like I'm used to thinking this way?"

That drew a fleeting smile from her, but it didn't reach her eyes. Damn, he wanted to see her blue eyes smile again.

"Anyway," Gus continued, "what I'm getting at is that the victim may have been selected at random. And that our killer must have done some scouting beforehand. How else would he know how to get in and get out so quickly and easily? He couldn't have just been wandering in the woods in the middle of the night."

He was slipping into tactical ways of thinking, and wasn't at all certain that was the right direction to take with this. It wasn't a military operation. No reason to think the killer had been thinking of…

The thought halted midstream. His mind swerved onto a slightly different track without much of a hitch. "Planned operation," he said. He felt her gaze settle on him, almost as warm as a touch. Damn, he needed to ignore the attraction he felt for her. It wouldn't be good for either of them. Besides, right now it seemed to be important to her to puzzle out this murder. Like they had any real information.

"Planned operation?" she repeated.

"Yeah. It crossed my mind for some reason." The only

reason possibly being that occasionally he was distractible. He never used to be that way, but since coming home for good, he had his moments of wandering. To escape unpleasant thoughts mostly, he imagined. "I'm starting to think tactically."

She turned toward him, attentive. "Yeah," she said quietly. Same wavelength.

"So, say this was planned. How long was Jasper at the campground?"

"Two and a half weeks. I checked."

"Long enough to figure out his habits, to get a sense of the area and people around him. Long enough to plan an approach and egress."

She nodded and turned more, pulling up one leg until it was folded sideways on the porch in front of her, half a cross-legged posture. Nodding again, she sipped her coffee, evidently thinking about what he'd said.

Which, frankly, sounded like a load of crap to him now that he'd said it out loud. Was he proposing some kind of mastermind killer? To what end? Even a soldier like him wouldn't be thinking of such things if he wanted to get rid of somebody. Hell no. Get 'em in a dark alley late at night, shiv 'em in the middle of a crowd... Escape routes were easier to come by than on a nearly unpopulated mountain. Any one of those campers might have responded immediately to the gunshot. No killer had any way to know no one would.

"Doesn't make sense," he said before she could raise a list of objections that would probably mirror his own. "No reason for anyone to treat the murder tactically. Habitual thinking on my part."

"But not necessarily wrong." She looked down into her mug, remaining quiet again.

He turned his head to find Scrappy meandering around

the gravel parking lot at the edge of the woods. He loved that gelding. Probably the only living thing he allowed himself to love anymore.

"Love," he said, for no particular reason, "is a helluva scary proposition. Friendship, too, for that matter."

"Where'd that come from?"

He turned his head, meeting her eyes. "The horse, believe it or not. He's got a long life expectancy. Iraq and Afghanistan taught me to be stingy with my feelings."

"Yeah, it sure did." She closed her eyes briefly. "Maybe too stingy. I don't know. That little boy really upset me, his terror and knowing he is going to grow up without his father. But I've seen it before. Half the world seems to live in that condition."

He nodded. Nothing to say to that. It wasn't only lost comrades who haunted his nightmares, though. Plenty of civilians did, too.

"Well," she said, "if you think there's any possibility that this guy was stalking the victim, then we owe it to ourselves and everyone else to take a look-see."

"For a distant sight line."

She nodded. "A place someone could watch from and not be noticed."

He looked up the mountain. "We'll have to cover a lot of territory." No denying it. Hundreds if not thousands of acres.

"Let's start with some parameters. How far out would the guy have to hide? Would he choose upslope or down? Whatever we decide, we can expand the area later if we need to."

"We could be wasting our time."

"It's better than doing nothing at all."

With that he felt complete agreement.

THEY'D THROWN A party for him. Even a bottle of champagne, decent champagne. Jeff felt pretty good and kept his lone slipup from Karl and Will. He figured that one shell casing couldn't give him away. Like he'd already thought, the heat of the exploding powder it had contained probably would have burned away any oils his fingers might have left behind. No reason to mention it.

At best they might find a partial, and fat lot of good it would do the cops even though he'd been fingerprinted when he joined the Army. A partial wouldn't create a match strong enough to stand up on its own. He knew because he'd looked it up.

But once they parted ways, he began to gnaw worriedly on the idea of that shell casing anyway. Useless, he kept telling himself, but part of him couldn't believe it.

So, without telling the others, he decided to go back and scout around a bit. If they hadn't found the casing, he'd remove it. Simple. Make sure there was nothing there. And he'd drive up just like any other tourist so there'd be no risk.

But that shell casing was haunting him, causing him so much anxiety that he was having trouble sleeping.

Worse, it was probably too soon to go back. He had to be sure the local authorities felt the site had nothing left to offer them, that they were totally ready to release it and forget about it.

And he'd need a cover story in case anyone wondered about him being up there. Time. He had to make himself wait a little longer.

He had a couple of weeks before he started teaching again. If he wanted to. He'd considered applying for a sabbatical for the fall term, and his department chair was agreeable, asking only that he give the department a couple of weeks warning so they could arrange for a stand-in.

But the idea of the sabbatical no longer enticed him. Sitting in his comfy little house on the edge of Laramie was proving to tax him psychologically.

Because of what they'd made him do. Because of what he'd done. Because the cries of a young child still echoed in the corridors of his mind.

Hell, if he were to be honest, the shell casing was the least of his worries. The biggest worry was how he would live with himself now. And an equally big worry was that they would insist he do this again. That they wouldn't buy that he now was so deeply involved he couldn't talk.

Damn, this was supposed to have been a *game*. Not real killings, merely the planning of them. How had Will and Karl moved past that? He'd never guessed they were so warped.

How could he have known them for so long and failed to realize they were probably both psychopaths? No real feeling for anyone else.

And how could they have known him for so long and not believe him when he said he'd never tell. Loyalty would have stopped him. But they didn't believe him, they didn't trust him, and that told him even more about them.

Friends? He'd have been better off with enemies.

Finally, anxiety pushed him to look up the state park's website. He needed to make a plan for going back there, maybe with a metal detector. After all, people still sometimes panned for gold in the streams in these mountains. It wouldn't be weird for someone to want to wander around with a metal detector hoping to find a nugget.

So he could get a metal detector and look around until he found the shell casing and then get the hell out. Easy plan. No reason to tell the others because he still didn't want them to know he'd left that casing behind.

Slow down, he told himself. *Take it easy.* Don't make a mistake that could get him into serious trouble.

He hadn't really looked at the park's website before. They'd taken a brief drive up the road to do recon and that didn't require a website. All he had needed to find was that rustic campground that vehicles couldn't. It had been easier than anticipated, too. GPS was a wonderful thing, as was a satellite receiver to track where he was. No need for a nearby cell repeater.

Thus he really didn't know anything about Twin Rocks Campground. The web page had the usual scenery pictures, one of an RV campsite, another of a rustic site and some general information for day hikes. Clearly nobody had spent a whole lot of time or money on this page.

He was about to move on to something else when he saw a name at the bottom of the page:

Blaire Afton, Chief Ranger.

Everything inside him felt as if it congealed. He had seen her from a distance on their one recon, but had thought he was mistaken.

Blaire Afton. That couldn't be the Blaire Afton he'd met in the Army and asked to go out with him. She'd declined, then he'd been injured in that training accident and mustered out. Turning to her brief bio page, he looked at her photo. It was the same Blaire Afton.

He hadn't really known her.

But what if she remembered him? What if his name came up somehow and she recalled him, either from the Army or from him passing her on his way up the road?

Suddenly a partial fingerprint on a shell casing seemed like a bigger deal. If the cops mentioned that it seemed to belong to a Jeffery Walston, would she remember the name after all this time? What if she saw him at the park and remembered his face?

He closed his laptop swiftly as if it could hide him from danger. Bad. Bad indeed. He knew the ranger, however slightly. She might be able to identify him if they somehow came up with his name. But Jeffery Walston wasn't an unusual name. It could be lots of guys.

Unless she saw him at the campground running around with a metal detector. Unless she connected him to the location of the murder.

God, he'd better stay away from her. Far away. But that shell casing was practically burning a hole in his mind.

If he'd had the guts, he might have killed himself right then. Instead he sat in a cold sweat and faced the fact that he'd probably have to fess up about the shell casing…and God knew what else.

He'd smoked, hadn't he? Thank heaven it had rained. He couldn't have left any DNA behind, could he? Surely that casing wouldn't still hold enough skin oil to identify him, either by partial print or DNA.

Surely.

But he stared blankly as his heart skipped beats, and he didn't believe it one bit. He'd broken the rule. He'd left enough behind to identify him.

God help him when the others found out.

Whatever the risk, he had to go back and make sure he found that casing and picked up any cigarette butts, rain or no rain.

And try to avoid Blaire Afton.

But he knew what the guys would tell him. He knew it with leaden certainty. Jeffery Walston might be a common name, but if Blaire Afton could link it to a face, well…

They'd tell him to kill her. To get rid of her so she couldn't identify him. Or they'd get rid of him. Squeezing his eyes closed, he faced what would happen if he ran into the ranger. He had to avoid her at all costs while cleaning up the evidence. If she saw him…

He quivered, thinking about having to kill another person, this time one he knew, however slightly.

God, he still couldn't believe the mess he'd gotten into, so innocently. Just playing a game with friends.

Until he learned the game was no game.

Terror grew in him like a tangled vine, reaching every cell in his body and mind. He had to go back and remove any evidence. No, he hadn't been able to go back for the casing while the cops were poring over the site, but they had to be gone by now. So he had to hunt for the casing and remove it if it was still there. Then he needed to go to the observation point and remove anything that remained of his presence there. Then he'd be safe. Even if Karl and Will got mad at him, he'd be safe, and so would they.

It didn't help that the kid had screamed and cried until he couldn't erase the sound from his own head. It chased him, the way fear was chasing him. He was well and truly stuck and he could see only one way out that didn't involve his dying.

He needed to calm down, think clearly, make sure he knew exactly what to do so he didn't make things worse. Reaching for a pill bottle in his pocket, he pulled out a small white pill. For anxiety. To find calm.

He had a lot of thinking to do.

Chapter Six

"I'm off the next two days," Gus said to Blaire two nights later. "I've got time to do some poking around if you can manage it."

She nodded. As the night thickened around them, the hoot of an owl filled the air. A lonely sound, although that wasn't why the owl hooted.

She murmured, "The owl calls my name."

"Don't say that," Gus said sharply. "I don't take those things lightly and you shouldn't, either. We've both seen how easily and senselessly death can come."

Little light reached them. The moon had shrunk until it was barely a sliver, and clouds kept scudding over it. Still, he thought he saw a hint of wryness in her expression.

"Superstitious much?" she asked with a lightness that surprised him, mainly because it meant her mood was improving. "I was thinking of the book."

"Oh." He'd reacted too quickly. "Some indigenous peoples consider the owl's hoot to be a bad omen. I was thinking of that."

"That's okay. And really, any of us who've gone where we've been probably pick up some superstitions. Heck, my mother even handed me a few when I was a kid. The *knock-on-wood* kind. And she hated it if anyone spilled salt."

He gave a brief laugh. "Yeah, I learned a few of those, too. You got any Irish in the family? My mom was Irish and I think she picked up a tote bag full of stuff like, *never leave an umbrella open upside down in the house*. More than once I saw her leap up, telling me not to do that."

"I never heard that one."

"It's a belief if the umbrella is open upside down it'll catch troubles for the house and family. There were others, but I left most of them behind." He paused. "Except this." Reaching inside his shirt, he pulled out a chain necklace. "My Saint Christopher medal. Apparently, he's not really a saint after all, but plenty of us still carry him around."

"Belief is what matters." She stood, stretching. "Are you heading back or do you want to use the couch? I think it's comfortable enough."

He rose, too. "That'd be great. Let me see to Scrappy and give Holly a call. And what about you? Can you get some time off tomorrow?"

"I can take two days whenever I want. Given that we're deserted right now, nobody really needs to be here. But Dave's my assistant. He'll stand in for me. I was thinking of going to town, too. I need some staples and a few fresh bits for my fridge."

INSIDE, BLAIRE SCANNED her small refrigerator in the back kitchen to see what else she might need to add to the list she'd been building since she last went grocery shopping. She didn't consume much herself, but she kept extra on hand for Dave, in case he worked late and for when he filled in for her on her days off.

Come winter she'd have to keep the fridge full to the brim because getting out of the park could sometimes be uncertain. Right now, however, when she was able to take a day or two every week, it wasn't as big a concern.

She called Dave on the radio, and he said he'd be glad to fill in for her tomorrow. *Good guy, Dave.*

Much as she tried to distract herself, however, her thoughts kept coming back to the murder. And to Gus. She'd learned to trust him over the two years since they'd met. They had a lot in common, of course, but it was more than that. At some point they'd crossed a bridge and for her part she knew she had shared memories with him that she would have found nearly impossible to share with anyone else.

Now, like her, he wanted to do some investigating up at the campground. Being in the Army had given them a very different mind-set in some ways, and when you looked at the murder as if it were a campaign, a mission, things popped to mind that might not if you thought of it as merely a random crime.

She was having trouble with the whole idea of random. Especially since Dave had told her that people were starting to talk about other murders, as well, and that they might be linked somehow.

Tomorrow she was going to make time to talk to the sheriff. She didn't know how much he'd tell her, but it was sure worth a try. She needed something, some kind of information to settle her about this ugly incident. She'd never be comfortable with the idea that that man had been murdered, never feel quite easy when she recalled little Jimmy's fear and sobbing, but she had a need to...

Well, pigeonhole, she guessed. Although that wasn't right, either. But even in war you had ways of dealing with matters so you could shove them in a mental rucksack out of the way.

This murder wasn't amenable to that because there were too damn many questions. War was itself an answer to a lot of things she'd had to deal with. Yeah, it was random, it was hideous, it was unthinkable. Life in a land of nightmares. But it had a name and a way to look at it.

Jasper's murder had nothing to define it except "murder."

So she needed a reason of almost any kind. An old enemy. Someone who bore a grudge. His wife's lover. Damn near anything would do because just *murder* wasn't enough for her.

She was pondering this newly discovered quirk in herself when the door opened and Gus entered, carrying his saddle with tack thrown over his shoulder. "Where can I set this?"

"Anywhere you want to."

For the first time she thought about his horse. "Is Scrappy going to be all right? I mean, I don't have a covered area for the corral here."

"I used some buckets from your lean-to. He's got food and water. And he's used to this." Gus lowered the saddle to the floor near the sidewall where there was some space. "I often go camping when I can get away, and he's happy to hang around and amuse himself, or just sleep."

"Oh." She felt oddly foolish. "I didn't know."

"Why should you? And, of course, being the nice person you are, you want to know he's okay."

She shook her head a little. "I think I care more about animals than people these days. Sorry, I was lost in thought. I just realized I have a driving need to make pigeonholes."

"Pigeonholes?"

"Yeah." She turned to go to the back and the kitchen. "Beer?"

"Thanks."

She retrieved two longnecks from the fridge and brought them out front. He accepted one bottle, then sat on the edge of the couch that filled one side of the public office space. Her living room, such as it was.

"I always liked this sofa," he remarked. "You lucked out. All I have are some institutional-type chairs."

"The last ranger left it. It doesn't suffer from overuse." She smiled. "In fact, you're the only person who uses it regularly."

"Yeah, I come visit a lot. Do you mind?"

"Of course not. If I did, I'd have told you a long time ago."

He twisted the top off his beer, flipped it into the wastebasket that sat in front of the long business desk that separated the public area from her office and raised it in salute. "Back to pigeonholes."

She didn't answer immediately, but went instead to get the office chair from behind the long bar and bring it around. She sat on it facing him, as she had so many past evenings. "Maybe not pigeonholes," she said finally, then took a sip of her beer. Icy cold, her throat welcomed it. The air was so dry up here.

"Then what?"

"Maybe what I'm trying to say is that I need some context. This murder is so random."

"That it is." He leaned back, crossing his legs loosely at the ankles. "So what do you need to know?"

At that she had to laugh. "Motive. Identity. All that stuff nobody probably knows yet. Nice as that would be, I realize I won't be told until the case is closed. But I still need something. Who was the victim? What did he do? Why was he here with his son and not the rest of his family?"

"Did he have any enemies?" he added.

She nodded, feeling rueful. "Context. I guess I don't

want to believe he was chosen randomly by someone with an itch to kill. That makes me crazy."

"It'd make anyone crazy. Anyone who cares, that is." He sighed and tipped his head back as he swallowed some more beer. "I guess we have to wait for our answers."

She leaned forward on her chair, cradling her frigid beer in both hands. "I need to deal with this. It's unreasonable to be uneasy simply because I don't have all the answers. I had few enough of them in Afghanistan."

"It wasn't answers we had over there. It was one big reason. If any of us had stopped to ask *why*, we might have had a bigger problem. But the reason was baked in from the moment we arrived. It was a war. This isn't a war. I don't blame you for being uneasy. Hell, the whole reason I rode over here tonight was because I couldn't stop feeling uneasy about you being alone over here. I'd have been over here last night but I know how damn independent you are."

"Gus…"

He held up a hand and she fell silent. "Let me finish. This is no criticism of you, or an expression of doubt in your abilities to look after yourself. No, I was uneasy because we've got a big question mark with a gun running around out there and that's a lot more difficult to protect yourself against than some known."

"Known? How so?"

"How many sandbag walls did you sit behind in Kandahar? How much armor did you wear every time you poked your nose out? Can we turn this cabin into a fortress? Not likely. It's a whole different situation, and being alone out here isn't the safest place to be, not until we can be sure the killer has moved on."

She nodded slowly, accepting his arguments. And though she could be fiercely independent and resented any implication that she was somehow less capable than a man, fact was, she was touched by his concern for her.

She stared down at her hands, cradling the beer she had hardly tasted, and remembered her early days here. She'd been on maybe her third or fourth night, feeling a mixture of pride at her recent promotion and a bit of discomfort about whether she was ready for the responsibility. Being alone out here, though, had always felt soothing. Comfortable. A long way away from ugly thoughts, pain and anguish.

Then Gus had come riding out of the spring mist that clung close to the ground that day. Wisps of it parted before him and Scrappy. Except for his green jacket, the brass badge and the Forest Service hat, she'd have wondered who the hell was riding in when the park hadn't officially opened for the season.

Iconic, she'd thought then. Even for a girl raised in the West, he looked iconic.

He'd raised a hand to wave, calling, "I'm Gus Maddox, the head ranger at the national forest next door." He and his horse had come closer. "You must be Blaire Afton?"

Thus had begun a relationship that had started as two strangers with similar jobs, then had been welded by sharing that they were both vets and sometimes had some difficulties dealing with the past. The revelations had come slowly, carefully. Trust was hard won in some areas. But now she trusted him completely.

In all that time, they had remained friends who treated each other as colleagues and occasionally as comrades. When they met up, either at one of their cabins or in town for coffee, they had the kinds of conversations she'd had with the guys in her unit in the Army.

As if there was a line that couldn't be crossed. Had they still been in the service, that line would definitely be there. But that was in the past, and now was now, and she felt ever increasing urges to know him in other ways.

A striking man, he'd have made almost any woman drool. She was a little astonished to realize she was getting to the drooling stage with him.

For some reason, the thought cheered her up, drawing her out of the uneasy darkness that had been haunting her since the murder. It was like a permission slip to get out of the serious stuff for a little while.

She looked at the bottle in her hand and noticed she'd hardly made a dent in that beer. Good. This was no alcohol-fueled mood.

Rising from her chair, she went to sit on the couch, not too close, but not exactly tucked into the far end, either. Even from more than a foot away, she could detect his aromas, wonderful aromas, the faint scent of man mixed with the outdoors, a bit of horse and a bit of beer. Very masculine.

Very sexy.

Oh, God, was she about to do something stupid? His gray eyes, eyes the color of a late afternoon storm rolling in over the mountains, had fixed on her and settled. It was a frank stare.

She was crossing the invisible line. He sensed it. All of a sudden she was nervous and afraid to move. She didn't want to make him uncomfortable. She didn't want to risk the precious friendship they'd built, and in her experience taking a relationship beyond that eventually led to a parting of ways.

And what if they *did* have sex? Would they become uncomfortable with one another afterward? It might prove to be a major sacrifice.

But his eyes held hers, drew her as if they were magnetic. "Blaire?"

Frank words emerged. There was little she hadn't told him about the bad things in the past, and dissembling with Gus seemed impossible now. "I'm telling myself not to go where I'm thinking about going."

That made him smile. Man, she loved the way the corners of his eyes crinkled when the smile reached them. "You are, huh? Afraid of repercussions?"

"Aren't there always repercussions?"

"Depends." Leaning to one side, he put his beer bottle on the battered end table. Then he took hers from her hands and put it beside his.

"You," he said, "are the most attractive woman I've known in a long time. Like you, I've been trying not to risk our friendship. But a lot of good things can begin between friends."

She nodded as her mouth went dry. A tremor passed through her.

"I get your reluctance. I share it. But I want you."

Oh, boy. Magic words. They lit her up like a thousand sparklers, tingling in every cell. She felt almost as if she couldn't catch her breath.

He reached out and took her hands. His touch was warm, his fingers and palms a bit calloused from hard work. He looked down at her smaller hands, then squeezed her fingers and drew her over until she sat beside him.

"I don't want to mess things up, either," he said. "But a hug ought to be safe, shouldn't it?"

He was quite a perceptive man, she thought as she nodded and let him gently pull her closer. He'd sensed what she was thinking and had turned out to be thinking along the same lines. As his arm wrapped around her, cuddling her to his side, she felt as if a spring-tight tension in her released. She relaxed, more completely than she had in a long time. She softened.

In the hollow of his shoulder, she found a firm pillow, and she could hear the beating of his heart, strong and steady. The arm he had wrapped around her gave her a gentle squeeze, then his hand began to stroke her arm.

Apparently trying to make sure matters didn't progress further until and unless they were both ready, he began to talk about tomorrow. "Do you have good topographic maps for the area we're going to explore?"

"Yeah. Down to a meter or so. Some geology students did it as a class project a while back. There may be some differences, though. The mountain moves."

"That it does. Rocks fall, landslides happen… But whatever you have, let's mark out a plan of action tomorrow."

"Sounds good."

"But first you want to go to town, right?"

"I need a few things, but that could wait. What I really want is to talk to the sheriff."

"I've had cause to talk to Dalton quite a few times when we've had problems. He's a good man."

She nodded, loving the way the soft flannel of his shirt felt beneath her cheek. "He used to head up the crime scene unit before he was elected sheriff."

"And before that, undercover DEA." He gave a muted laugh. "That guy has a lot of experience under his belt. Even if he can't share details with us, maybe he can offer a few opinions or speculations."

"A sense of what might have been going on," she agreed. "He doesn't strike me as a man who likes the idea of a random killing, either."

"Stranger killings are the hardest to solve." A slight sigh escaped him. "More beer?"

"I misjudged my mood."

She felt, rather than saw, his nod, then his movements

as he reached for his own bottle and took a few swallows. Tentatively she let her hand come to rest on one of his denim-clad thighs. She felt the muscles jump a bit at the touch, then relax. God, he was as hard as steel. Must be all that riding.

But he didn't reject her touch, nor did he do anything to encourage it. Her hand began to absorb his warmth, and she felt an even deeper relaxation filling her. Like a cat finding sunlight, she thought with some amusement at herself.

"I'm making too much of this," she remarked. "Too much. These things happen."

"Sure, they happen all the time in the desolate woods at a campground. If I thought you were making too much of this, I wouldn't have ridden over tonight. I'm concerned, too. You're right about needing a reason. Without it, we have no idea what this killer might be planning. Not a good time to be hanging out alone."

"But Jasper wasn't alone. He was in a campground with at least eight other camping groups. A really strange place to pull this."

"Which may be the biggest clue we have. Only problem is what to do with it."

Absently her fingers had begun to stroke the taut denim on his thigh. She'd always loved the feel of worn denim, but it never occurred to her that she was self-comforting. Well, possibly in the depths of her mind, but she wasn't ready to face that.

Her self-image was one of toughness. She'd survived Afghanistan and all that went with that. She'd helped lead convoys through hell, and for all she was supposed to be a noncombatant, being female, she'd seen plenty of combat. She could handle a lot, and getting in a tizzy over a random murder struck her as an extreme overreaction.

Until she remembered Jimmy.

"It's the kid," she said presently, her voice evincing the slightest tremor. She hated the sound of weakness. "I should be able to just let this go, Gus. Let the sheriff handle it. But I can't and it's because of that little boy. Sure, maybe the guy had a ton of enemies. Maybe he was a drug dealer or a mob type, or whatever. But what kind of sick twist would have him shot when he was in a tent with his little boy?"

"That's troubling, isn't it?" Surprising her, he put his beer down then laid his hand over hers, clasping it lightly. "It bothers me, too. When it happened, I could see it might tear you apart."

"It was awful, Gus! That poor little kid! He didn't understand what had happened, thank God. And I'm fairly sure he didn't see how badly his father was wounded. I tried to keep my back to all that. But my God! What kind of sicko would do that?"

Gus didn't answer immediately. "Maybe he didn't know the child was there. But a sicko any way you look at it, kid or no kid. The man was sound asleep in a tent. No chance to defend himself."

"And no chance to protect Jimmy. That shooter could have hit the boy, too. Accidentally or not. Everything about it makes me furious."

"I feel pretty angry myself," he agreed.

But as her thoughts roamed even further backward in time, Blaire remembered her days in the Army. "Too many kids get traumatized," she said after a minute. "Too many. I just hope Jimmy has no clear memories of that night."

"Me, too." He squeezed her hand. "You did what you could to protect him, Blaire. You took good care of him, from what I could see."

"Little enough." She lowered her head, closing her eyes. "It's killing me," she admitted. "I want to get that guy. And I'm sure the impulse has mostly to do with Jimmy."

"Hardly surprising." He turned a little, drawing her into a closer embrace. "We can only do what we can," he reminded her. "Tomorrow we'll check with the sheriff to make sure we won't get in the way. Then we'll build our strategy."

"I don't recall any ops planning that happened like this." Meaning the way he held her. She felt the laugh begin in his belly and roll upward until it emerged, a warm, amused sound.

"Nope," he agreed. "I remember always standing, or if we could sit, it was on miserable folding chairs around a table that was always gritty with dust. Hell, *we* were almost always gritty. We rigged a shower at our forward operating base and you'd barely switch into a clean set of camos before you'd be dusty again."

"It seemed like it. This is way more comfortable."

"By far."

She realized she was smiling into his shoulder. She wanted to wrap an arm around his waist but stopped herself. Lines that shouldn't be crossed. She never wanted to lose Gus's friendship.

She spoke. "I appreciate you not coming over last night to watch over me."

"I don't think I'm watching over you now. I've got a higher respect for your abilities, and it's not my place, anyway. I just kept getting this sense that it might be easier for you not to be alone at night."

"Given what happened, you're right." In Afghanistan she'd almost never been alone. That was the whole idea of a unit. But she didn't have a unit here to watch her back and there might still be a deranged killer out there running around in the woods. With everyone fleeing the camp-ground, that didn't leave many targets for him.

"This brings me back to the random thing," she re-marked. "If he's still hanging around out there, looking for someone else to shoot, the target population just shrank to next to nothing."

"I thought about that," he agreed. "My end of the for-est isn't quite as deserted as yours, but I'm not sure that should make me feel complacent."

"Then there's what Dave said this morning. People have started talking about scattered killings in the woods over the last few years. Some are calling for all of them to be investigated as one case."

"I'm sure Gage would do it if he had some proof."

"Exactly. When my computer is being reliable, I've spent hours today looking up news articles." She fell si-lent, wishing she could let go of all of it and just enjoy this rare opportunity to be so close to Gus.

"And?" he prompted her.

"I think I found the murders that concern some peo-ple." She sensed him grow more alert, a bit stiff.

"And?" he asked again.

"And people might be right. There are similarities but also differences."

"The gang-working-together idea?"

"Makes you wonder." Her heart grew heavy at the thought. "Gang. It sounds so much worse in a way."

"Also maybe easier to solve. More people, more chances for a slipup."

She tilted her head and he obligingly tilted his so they could look at one another from a distance of about three inches.

"You're a glass-half-full kinda guy."

"I try. Wish I could say I always succeed."

She smiled, lifted her hand a bit and lightly touched his cheek. "You're a good influence."

"When I'm not in a dark pit." But he didn't seem to want to discuss that. "So, would it feel more like operational planning if I brought over a folding camp table and sprinkled a little dirt on it?"

The laugh escaped her. She hadn't even realized she was trembling on the cusp of one, but there it came. He had such a good effect on her, Gus did. He could steer a course through the difficult things and eventually bring back a happier mood. At least in her.

She was well aware he carried his own troubled memories, and he'd shared them with her. At least some of them. But like a cork, he always managed to bob back up. She could use a touch of that.

"Sure. I could even cut up the map."

He laughed again, his gray eyes dancing. "Absolutely. After all, every battle occurs at the juncture between four map sections…"

"In the dark and in the rain," she completed for him. An old saying, truer than she would have believed until she faced it.

"We do so much on computers now," she remarked, remembering scrolling through maps that were downloaded from a satellite.

"When the connection worked. I didn't like the limited view on the computer, though. Call me old-fashioned, but I always wanted a big paper map."

"Well, that's what I've got. Better yet, they're rolled, not folded, so no tears, and no corners at a point where we want to be."

He chuckled again. "There we go. I couldn't ask for

better. Do you have any idea how the terrain may have changed since the mapping?"

"Some, but I've never done a complete survey. Basically, I'm here to make sure campers are safe and that no one commits vandalism or annoys anyone else. I know the ground I routinely cover pretty well. Then comes winter and it all changes anyway."

"Yeah. And we're out there with an eye on possible avalanche risks after a heavy snow." She knew he had pretty much the same winter tasks.

"I'm not exactly looking for boulders that might have moved a few feet." Closing a park didn't mean no one would use it. A surprising number of people showed up to cross-country ski on fresh unpacked snow, or to hike around on snowshoes. Hardy types, but they weren't always aware of winter dangers.

Yes, there was a sign out front, and in several other locations, warning people they entered at their own risk. But that didn't mean Blaire didn't keep an eye out. She lived here year-round, including the deep winter months, so if someone needed something and could get to her, they'd find help.

The hard part was keeping out the snowmobilers. The amount of damage they could do, even in the dead of winter, was appalling. It was a constant battle, even though there weren't that many places where the woods opened up to give them a path.

She closed her eyes, though, and thought about what it was like up here in the winter. Beautiful. Quiet. Serene. Almost magical. She found peace here. It filled her and mostly drove away the ghosts that followed her so restlessly.

"I wish it were winter," she heard herself murmur.

"Yeah. Me, too."

She realized he'd helped ease her tension to the point that she was getting sleepy. Much as she hated to do it, she eased away from him. "Let me get you some blankets."

"Tired?"

"I guess I've been more wound up since the murder than I realized."

He smiled and stood, offering his hand to help her up. "Sleep is always good. I think we both learned that the hard way. Where are the blankets? I can get them."

She pointed up to the loft. "My bedroom."

"Then just toss them down to me."

"Okay. You know where the half bath is?" Of course he did. This wasn't his first visit to this cabin. She must be even more worn out than she had thought.

After she tossed pillows and blankets down to him and said good-night, she pulled her boots off and flopped back on the bed. God, how had she grown so tired?

Then she faced it. She hadn't been sleeping well since the murder. She'd been on edge, wound up, and tossing and turning.

But right now, calm seemed to have descended. Gus was downstairs. She could let go of everything and let relaxation seep through her every cell.

Problems could wait for morning.

And almost before she finished the thought, she fell soundly asleep, still dressed, her legs hanging over the edge of the bed.

DOWNSTAIRS, GUS MADE his bed on the sofa, glad he'd decided to stay tonight. He got the feeling that Blaire seriously needed company. He could understand that.

Being locked inside your own head with your own worries and thoughts could be crazy-making. He'd been there and now tried to avoid it as much as possible.

Sometimes it was okay. Like her mentioning the winter woods. Like her, he loved that peaceful beauty. Or when he was out taking a lazy ride with Scrappy. But maybe being with Scrappy wasn't really being alone, he thought wryly.

He stepped outside to make sure his horse was okay and found that Scrappy had settled onto the ground, having evidently found himself a soft enough spot to curl up in. Scrappy plainly thought the world was safe tonight.

Back inside he reacquainted himself with the fact that a six-foot couch wasn't quite long enough for his six-foot-two length, but it wasn't impossible. Prop his head up a bit on the pillow and he just about made it.

Judging by the quiet from above, he guessed Blaire had fallen out quickly. Good. He suspected she might not have been sleeping well. Well, why should she? This murder had been bound to reawaken old wounds, even if only to a small degree. He felt some mental twinges himself. But like her, he wondered who could have committed an act like that.

A very sick man.

Which didn't comfort him even a little. It only made the perp more unpredictable.

Then, with nothing else he could do, he scooched onto his side and sought sleep. As with most soldiers, it wasn't hard to find.

Chapter Seven

Morning brought the dread visit to Jeff. The champagne they'd toasted him with the first night had worn off. Now they wanted to discuss their next move.

He wanted no part of it, and as they began to talk in the most general terms over coffee and sweet rolls, his mind ran around frantically trying to find a way to step out of this. To get away. To have no further part in their sick game.

Because he finally had to admit it wasn't just shocking, it was sick. He hardly recognized his friends anymore. They weren't the men he'd believed them to be.

Sociopaths. Psychopaths. Whatever. It didn't matter. They were strangers to him now, as if they'd been possessed by demons.

How could he get away from this? He couldn't commit another murder. He didn't want to know anything about what they intended to do next. No way.

But fear held him silent. Maybe too silent because Karl finally said to him, "What the hell is wrong with you, Jeff? You're as silent as a tomb."

That made Will laugh. Maybe in the past a phrase like that would have amused Jeff. Now it only made him feel ill.

Karl dropped his joking manner. "What's going on,

Jeff?" This time it sounded like an inquisition, barely veiling a threat.

Jeff's mind, already skittering around like a cornered rat trying to find an escape, was now joined by a wildly hammering heart. He had to say something, preferably something that would get him out of this mess. He'd done his killing. They knew he couldn't squeal. He'd implicate himself as a murderer, not as an accomplice.

But what could he say that wouldn't make things worse?

He had to clear his throat to make sound emerge. "You didn't tell me there was a kid there."

"Kid?"

"Little one. In the tent with his father."

"Did he see you?" Will's immediate concern, Jeff thought bitterly. For his own safety.

"No. Too dark. Hell, I could barely see him. But I had to listen to his screams all the way up the mountain."

The two of them exchanged looks. Jeff was rapidly reaching the point where he didn't care. If they killed him, at least he'd be out of this.

"We didn't know there was a kid," Karl said.

"Great planning," Jeff answered bitterly. "What if I'd hit him, too? You wanna talk about a manhunt?"

The other two were silent for a minute or so. Then Karl remarked, "They wouldn't be able to find us anyway. You didn't leave a trail."

Didn't leave a trail. Well, that was the big problem, wasn't it? A missing shell casing. And he was rapidly getting to the point where he didn't care if they knew.

"I left one thing," he blurted out.

Two heads swiveled to look at him, and neither looked very friendly. "What?" Karl demanded.

"A shell casing."

Will swore. "We warned you."

"Warn all you want. I forgot it. Do you know how many people were in that campground?" He was winding up now and didn't care where it took him. "Lots, and as soon as I fired my pistol, the kid started shrieking and the whole place woke up. I didn't have time to pull out my penlight and look for a casing. I had to get the hell out."

Although the truth of it was, he hadn't even remembered the casing. He might well have been able to find it and remove it. The chance the police hadn't found it was slim, but he was going to have to go back and look for it anyway, because he couldn't take the chance that he'd left evidence that could identify him and that it was still lying out there waiting to be found.

Bad enough he'd had to commit the murder. He sure as hell didn't want to *pay* for it.

"It's probably no big deal," Karl said a few minutes later. "The heat of the exploding powder probably would have burned it clean."

"And if it didn't?" Will demanded.

Karl shrugged. "Say it's got a fingerprint or two. Partials at best. And Jeff's never been fingerprinted, have you?"

Jeff couldn't force the lie past his throat. It was as if a vise clamped it and wouldn't let him speak.

"Jeff?" Will's voice had tightened and lowered until it almost sounded like a growled threat. "Fingerprints?"

Jeff wished he were already dead. He'd like to be out of body, watching this all from the ceiling. He wasn't going to get out of this, though. His silence was already an answer.

"When I enlisted in the Army. They took everyone's prints."

Karl swore and jumped up from his chair.

Will looked at him. "You said there'd be nothing left," Jeff said.

"There shouldn't be. That doesn't mean there won't be."

Jeff cringed instinctively as Will raised his hand. He expected to be struck, and having experienced that once before years ago, he knew it would be painful. The man was religious about staying in shape, and part of that was bodybuilding.

But Will didn't strike him. He lowered his hand and said, "We ought to bury you out back right now."

Jeff felt a flare of anger, a welcome relief from the terror he'd been living with. These men were supposed to be his friends? What alternate universe had he been living in?

He leaped up and glared at both of them. "I never wanted to do this, and you know it. I only killed that guy because you threatened to kill me if I didn't. I'm not happy about it. And if I made a freaking mistake, I'm the only one who'll go down for it, and you know it!"

"How are we supposed to know that?" Will asked.

"Simple, you jackass. No matter what I might tell the cops, you could tell them I'm nuts. There's nothing to implicate *you*. Why would I even bother? I told you months ago I'm not a rat."

"And we warned you about leaving behind any evidence," Karl growled. "Damn it, Jeff, are you missing some screws?"

"No." Jeff was getting fed up beyond containment. "You're clear. What do you care if I get picked up?"

"You need to go back and find it," Karl said. "Because the crime scene people might not have. You need to look for the shell casing, Jeff."

"How could they have missed it?"

"They're not big-city cops. A bunch of rubes. They'd miss their own noses if they didn't have mirrors."

"I can't go back there," Jeff said finally, and sagged into his chair.

"Why not?"

"Because the time we went on recon, I saw the ranger."

Will waved a hand. "Wait a minute. Why were you walking up the road? We told you to avoid that!"

"Remember, you took me on the recon. And the night of the killing. I came in from the back just like you said."

"Then why…" Karl trailed off as if he couldn't find words.

"It's simple," Jeff admitted. "I knew the ranger when we were in the Army. Just briefly. If she saw me when we drove up there, she never recognized me. As far as she was concerned, I was a total stranger."

Karl and Will exchanged long looks, then Karl said, "You're a jerk, Jeff. A total jerk. What if she remembered you afterward? What if she wonders what the hell you were doing there? You should have told us. We'd have found another place."

"I'm telling you…"

"You don't get to tell me anything. There's only one solution for this. You go back and kill her."

GUS AND BLAIRE decided to make a small social occasion out of the morning. Gus took Scrappy back to his corral just as the first morning light was dusting the eastern sky with pink. A half hour later, as the rim of the sun just started to lift above the mountains, he picked up Blaire in his green Forest Service truck. Some of the large tools rattled in the back but that was par.

She climbed in beside him, a smile on her face. For now they were out to banish the ugly things and reach for the good ones. One of the best was breakfast at Maude's diner. For a little while she could allow her concern about what had happened to that man, Jasper, and by extension his little boy, move into the background.

She used to be better at putting things aside. She'd quickly learned when she was overseas that you just couldn't let things weigh on you constantly or you'd wear yourself out, or worse, become useless. Compartmentalizing, she thought it was called. Well, for the duration of breakfast she was going to compartmentalize the murder.

Maybe in a way what made it so hard for her was the protectiveness she felt for all the people camping in the park. As if she were their caretaker or something, which was ridiculous. Still, she handed out bandages, topical antiseptics, advice on a whole bunch of things, like starting a fire in a firepit, and even, at times, how to assemble a tent.

Mothering adults. Did she have an overinflated sense of her own importance? Or did inexperienced people just decide to go camping?

Only some of Maude's morning regulars had arrived at the café, so they had no trouble finding a seat. Blaire had loved Maude's—or the City Diner as it was properly named—since the first time she had visited it. It was vintage in every respect, right down to the matching tape covering cracks in the upholstery of chairs and booths. The tabletops, some kind of plastic laminate, had been wiped so many times that they showed white spots. And the aromas…ah, the aromas. At this hour, they were mostly of coffee and frying bacon or ham, and enough to create an appetite even on a full stomach.

Her stomach was far from full.

They both ordered omelets filled with cheese and ham. Blaire chose rye toast on the side, but Gus asked for a double helping of home fries with his meal. And, of course, coffee, but this time Blaire ordered one of the lattes Maude had started making a few years ago, from what she understood. One concession to modernity.

It would have been nice to get through the meal without a reminder, but an older man rose from a nearby table and came over to speak to them with little preamble.

"So what's with that murder? You got any leads yet?"

Blaire weighed a response. This would be a bad time to shoot from the hip. Gus was looking at her, probably deciding that since the murder had happened in *her* park, she should answer. "The police are looking into it. Right now, you probably know as much as I do."

The man nodded, rubbing his chin. Calloused skin rasped on beard stubble. "Folks are talking about some other murders, too. Been five of them in the mountains."

"I wouldn't know about them."

He shook his head. "I think people are inclined to make up stories because it's more interesting, if you know what I mean. Well, I thought maybe you could give me some ammo to stop some of that talk."

"Sorry, I know as much as you do."

He glanced at her name tag. "Thanks, Ranger Afton." Then he returned to his table.

"So much for forgetting for half an hour," she mumbled as she lifted the latte to her lips.

"I guess once you poked your nose out, someone was going to ask about it."

"He could have been a bigger nuisance," she admitted and pulled a smile from somewhere. "So much for our little social hour."

"We can try it again around a campfire tonight."

Her smile broadened. "I like the sound of that." And she did. It had been a while since she'd done that, and never with Gus. Sometimes she held campfires with storytelling for guests at the camp, especially when there were quite a few children of appropriate age.

She enjoyed those times, times when all the bad stuff at the back of her mind went into dark corners and stayed there.

After breakfast, they walked over to the sheriff's office. Blaire didn't spend a whole lot of time with the police, but she knew a few of the officers and greeted them. Gus seemed to know everyone there who was getting ready to go out on patrol or settling into a desk. He was, after all, law enforcement himself.

She still found it hard to get to know people. Brief conversations with campers, or informative campfires, were different somehow. Odd, but she hadn't always been that way. Something had happened to her in her time in the Army. It was almost as if she were afraid to commit any real emotion, as if she feared the person would just leave. As so many of her friends had during that year in the 'Stan.

She gave herself an internal shake, telling herself not to go there. It was over except inside her own head. Ghosts. Just ghosts.

Velma, the eternal dispatcher, waved them back to Gage's office with a cigarette in her hand. Over her head on the wall a huge no-smoking sign hung.

Blaire stifled a giggle.

"Skip the coffee," Gus whispered as they entered the back hallway. "Some of the deputies say it tastes like embalming fluid."

Another reason to laugh. Was she ready for that? She guessed she was. But everything changed the instant they stepped into Gage Dalton's office.

The sheriff, one side of his face scarred by an old burn, motioned them to sit in the chairs facing his desk. If she sat just right, Blaire could see around the tippy stacks of paper and the old-fashioned cathode-ray tube monitor on the computer. That thing needed to be put out to pasture, she thought.

"Need a bigger desk?" she heard herself ask.

Gage chuckled. "I need not to have to keep every report on paper as well as on the computer. Don't ask me why. I keep thinking I should make an executive decision to put a halt to the duplication, but then a clerk over at the courthouse reminds me we'll always need a paper trail. What if the computers go down or get hacked? I still need an answer for that one. So, what's up?"

Gus looked at Blaire, so she spoke first. "We want to do a perimeter check, but we don't want to get in your way. And if there's anything you've discovered about the murder that you can share, it'd be really helpful."

Gage looked at both of them. "Don't you have your own park to watch?" he asked Gus.

"Right now I want to help catch this guy so Blaire isn't out there all alone at night wondering if he's still in the woods."

Gage nodded. "I hadn't thought of that. We've been presuming he's long gone. No reason to hang around. And as near as we can tell so far, he picked Jasper at random. He worked as an accountant for an oil company. No reason to have any enemies. God-fearing, churchgoing and nobody so far has a harsh word to say. Although that could change."

She couldn't help herself. "How is Jimmy? The little boy?"

"His mom says he doesn't seem to be aware of what happened, but she's taking him to therapy anyway. He's going to need help, at the very least, with dealing with his dad being gone for good."

"I should say so." She shook her head, remembering that sobbing little boy in her arms on a cold, cold night.

"His mom says she can't separate him from the rescue blanket, so you made a hit with that one."

"Space blanket," she said. "That's what I told him. Maybe he'll dream of being an astronaut." She sighed. "But back to the big questions. I'm hearing from one of my team members that people are talking about this murder being related to others."

"I'm hearing that, too. I have some investigators looking into it and consulting with other police departments. We'll see if we can find any links. God knows we need something more than a spent shell casing."

Gus leaned forward. "He left a shell casing behind? That's amateurish."

"Yeah, it is," Gage agreed. "Very. So the likelihood that he's responsible for other murders that left no evidence behind is pretty slim."

"Blaire had an idea," Gus said. He looked at her.

"It's probably silly," she said, ready to dismiss it.

"Nothing's silly," Gus replied, "and certainly not from you with where you've been. Spit it out."

She shrugged one shoulder. "It seems random. But when you add in the other murders people have mentioned, maybe… Maybe it's not one guy acting alone. Especially since I'm hearing that they're all different, but you say they left no evidence behind."

Gage nodded thoughtfully. "I'm not ready to agree, but it's an interesting notion. Let me see what I get back from other agencies. Then there's the question of what you mean by a perimeter search."

Gus spoke. "We were talking about how this guy had to have somewhere to watch the campground. To make sure when it was safe to go in, to choose his target, whatever. A staging location. We thought we might find something."

"Point is," Blaire admitted almost ruefully, "I'm not good at sitting on my hands. This might turn up evidence."

"You're thinking in bigger terms," Gage remarked. "Tactical terms."

Blaire nodded. "It's our training."

"It's good training. It's also a great idea. The likelihood that he just hung around until everyone went to sleep bugs me. But with kids running around the place, he'd probably be seen."

"Probably," they agreed as one.

"Go for it. At this point the likelihood we'll get anything useful off that shell casing is slim. I'll be able to match it to a weapon if we ever find it, but right now…" Gage shook his head. "Find me a pistol while you're at it."

A few minutes later, they were heading out with Gage's promise to share any information he received on the other murders. Not this investigation, of course. He couldn't breach that confidentiality. But the others? Most were probably cold cases by now. Few secrets he couldn't share.

Before they got out the door, however, Connie Parish and Beau Beauregard, both deputies, suggested coffee at Maude's. Blaire exchanged looks with Gus and got the impression that he felt that might be significant. He nodded to her and she smiled.

"Sure," she said.

Maude's had quieted some after the breakfast hour, and they had no trouble finding a relatively private booth. Coffee arrived automatically, and it seemed Maude had decided Blaire was a latte drinker, because that's what she received in a tall cup. Not that she was about to complain.

"Primarily," Connie said, speaking first, "I'm worried about you being out at the campground all alone, Blaire, especially at night. So is Beau. This was such a random killing, and the guy could still be out there. Wouldn't be the first weirdo we've had playing hermit in those mountains."

"Nor the last," Beau remarked. "The *he always kept to himself* kind don't always limit that to the apartment next door."

Despite herself, Blaire was amused. "What do you think we're dealing with here?"

"Damned if I know. The vic was an accountant. For an oil company," Connie said. "Now, how likely is that to get you shot on a camping trip? Oh, I suppose there could be reasons, but I can't imagine any. If he'd angered someone at the company, why follow him out here? This feels so random."

"At least it appears to be," Gus agreed. "But if you really think about it, a lot of life is random. Even so, maybe he had some debts he couldn't meet. Gambling, drugs."

"That's so cliché," Blaire murmured, unexpectedly drawing a laugh from the other three. "Well, it is," she protested. "Easy fallback position. Blame it on the vic."

He shrugged. "You're right. But we have so little to go on, at least as far as I know."

Turning her latte in her hands, Blaire studied it as if it might have answers. Afghanistan had been nothing like this, she thought. Nothing. It struck her as odd that one murder was bothering her so much after all that she'd lived through. Yet somehow this one murder seemed scarier. Maybe because it was so far inexplicable.

Beau spoke. "We were thinking we'd feel better if you had a dog, Blaire."

Her head snapped up. "A dog?"

"A trained police dog," Beau clarified. "I spoke to Cadell Marcus yesterday. I don't know if you've met him, but he trains our K-9s. He's got a Malinois almost ready to go, and he said he'd be willing to pass her to you, or just let you keep her for a while, whichever you prefer."

This was so unexpected, Blaire had to think about it. She liked dogs. Hell, they'd had a few bomb sniffers with them in Afghanistan. She felt great respect for a dog's abilities. But she'd never thought of wanting or needing her own K-9.

"That isn't extreme?" she said finally.

"Hardly," Gus said drily. "I slept on your sofa last night because I didn't like the idea of you being alone out there. I know you can take care of yourself, but that didn't keep me from worrying one bit. Some things seem to be engraved on my DNA."

She might have laughed except right now she felt far from laughter. A man was dead, they didn't know why and some creep might be haunting the woods.

Before she could make up her mind, Gus spoke. "I was also thinking about getting her a horse. At least for now. We want to ride around up there looking for evidence of a staging area or an isolated camp. Gideon Ironheart's the man for that, right?"

Connie nodded. "My uncle-in-law," she explained to Blaire. "In case you don't know."

"I thought everyone in the county knew how all the Parishes are related," Gus said. "It's one of the first things I heard about."

Connie flashed a grin. "For a while we just kept expanding. Anyway, if you want, I'll call Gideon. I'm sure he'll be glad to bring a mount to the park for Blaire. How well do you ride?"

"I'm pretty much a novice," Blaire warned her, but she had to admit she liked the idea of being able to ride around the mountain instead of hiking for a few days while they hunted for any kind of evidence. "I did some riding while I was in Afghanistan but I haven't done much since."

"Gideon will have a gentle, patient horse. He'll take care of everything."

"And the dog?" Beau prompted.

Blaire had to hesitate. Much as she liked dogs, she wasn't sure she wanted one living with her. She'd become attached, for one thing. For another, animals weren't allowed in the park. "You know we don't allow pets in the park. Mainly because people don't keep them leashed. They chase deer and other animals. Then, most people don't scoop up after them. So how can I have a dog and tell campers they can't?"

"Get him a K-9 vest," Beau said. "That should do all your explaining for you."

He had a point, but she still hesitated. "Let me think about it," she said finally. "Right now the place is completely empty, but give it a few days. Fears will subside and there'll be plenty of people around. Then none of you will have to worry about me being alone."

She was touched by their concern. Inwardly she was aware of her own uneasiness because of the incomprehensibility of this murder, but she didn't want to display it. She'd been to war. If she could survive that, even with some emotional damage, she could certainly survive this. And she had a reasonable, tested belief in her ability to look out for herself. Not that she was a superhero or anything, but she could handle quite a bit.

Everything except someone creeping up on her in her sleep. But she had locks and a sturdy building. She wasn't sleeping in a tent like Jasper.

But something else was going on with the idea of getting a dog. "We had bomb-sniffing dogs in Afghanistan."

"Yup," Gus agreed, then waited.

"We lost a few." She closed her eyes. "Getting attached... I'm not ready to do that again, okay?"

"Okay," said Connie. "Let me call Gideon. We'll get you a horse on loan so you can roam around with Gus and check out the area faster. I bet he can get one up there by late this afternoon. Will you be around?"

Gus spoke. "It's my understanding that Blaire wants to lay in some supplies. Then?"

The question was directed at her. "Just some supplies. Gage said he'll let us know what he learns. Beyond that, I have no business." She turned her head toward Gus. "You?"

"The same." He looked at Connie and Beau. "Figure we'll be back in place at the park by two or a little after."

Connie nodded. "I'll call Gideon now."

THE TRIP TO the grocery felt almost like emerging from night into day. It was so damn normal, she thought as she and Gus wended their way through the aisles, sharing a cart. She even decided to splurge a little on a box of frozen clam strips and a bag of frozen North Atlantic cod. Her freezer wasn't large, so she had to resist a whole lot more than that and stick to staples like boneless, skinless chicken breasts that provided a good protein base for almost anything, some frozen veggies and canned goods that would keep for a while.

When she was done, she realized she'd bought more than she usually did, and looked at the sacks she piled into the back of Gus's truck.

"I overdid it," she remarked.

He laughed. "You, too?"

She shook her head a little. "I share with my staff once in a while, but you can't eat everything out of a box or a can. It gets boring."

"Jars," he said. "I depend on jars. Tomato sauce, Alfredo sauce, things like that."

She nodded. "I'm stocked with enough soup cans to feed an army, I believe."

"I love soup."

They were both pretty cheerful as they pulled out of town and began rolling toward the mountains and the park.

Gus brought up the problem of storage. It seemed a safe enough topic, she supposed, because with each passing mile the shadow of the murder seemed to be looming larger.

"Can't you get the state to give you a bigger refrigerator and freezer? It seems awfully small if you can't get out of the park for some reason."

"Mostly I only have to worry about myself," she answered. "I always have some backup in the cupboards during the summer, and come winter I've got the world's biggest freezer."

He laughed. "True that."

The road into the park began to rise before them, and way up above the mountain peak storm clouds seemed to be brewing. But something else was brewing inside Blaire, and finally she decided to address it directly.

"I must be crazy."

"Why?" He turned the wheel a bit trying to avoid a pothole. The truck bumped only a little.

"Because it's ridiculous to think the murderer might still be up there hiding out in the woods. And that even if he is, that he might kill someone else."

"I don't think that's crazy." Surprising her, he freed one hand from the wheel to reach over and squeeze hers. Just a quick squeeze because as the road grew rougher, he needed both hands to control the truck. "It would be easier to dismiss the idea if we knew why Jasper was killed. A reason for it. But as it stands, the whole damn thing is an ugly mystery, and now the possibility that five other murders might be linked makes it even worse."

"Serial killer," she said. The truck engine strained a little as the climb became steeper. A short distance with a steep grade that the park system kept talking about leveling out.

"Well, we don't know that, either. But as long as it's a possibility, there's no reason to feel crazy for worrying."

"I guess not. I didn't used to be so easy to creep out."

He snorted. "You're not used to this situation. Overseas we knew we were always at risk and the threat could come from anywhere. Here, we don't expect those things. It's so out of place in the park that it's downright jarring."

"So is this road," she remarked, trying to change the subject. She didn't want to give in to the morbid maundering of her imagination, especially since her experience in Afghanistan had given her enough vivid images and memories to fill in the imaginings. The important thing was to keep control of her mind.

Yeah. She'd been working on that for years. It ought to be a perfected skill by now, but occasionally the wrong stuff still popped up and disturbed her.

"We've been talking about resurfacing this road," she remarked as the truck jolted yet again. "I don't think we're high on the state's priority list, though. We're a small campground, comparatively speaking."

"With the national forest right next door, what do you expect?" he asked lightly. "We get the roads. If people want to drive a huge RV in, they come to us. On the other hand, your campgrounds offer a lot more privacy."

"Yeah. We get a lot of tent campers. Pop-up trailer

types. Not so many big RVs, but quite a few smaller ones at lower altitudes where we have hookups."

Covering familiar ground, talking about stuff he already knew, probably because she was trying to cover up her crawling sense of unease. Like when she'd been on missions. Knowing the enemy was out there, never knowing when he might strike.

"You looking forward to having a horse for a few days?" he asked, bringing them around a hairpin bend where the road went from pavement to gravel.

"Yeah, except it occurred to me, too late, I know next to nothing about caring for one. Heck, those saddles we used in Afghanistan were nothing like the one you have."

"Well, I'll share a secret with you."

"What's that?"

He flashed a smile her way. "I'll help you take care of the horse. In fact, I'll bring Scrappy over and the two can share your corral for a few days. Make a party of it."

Her discomfort subsided a bit. "A party? Seriously? When we're looking for evidence to lead us to a killer?"

He laughed. "Thought you'd like that one."

At last they pulled through the official entrance to the campground and into the small parking lot in front of her cabin. Dave was sitting on the front porch on a battered lawn chair with his feet on the railing. He waved as they pulled up. A man of about forty, mostly bald, with a friendly face and a personal uniform of plaid shirts and jeans, he made people feel welcome. Blaire sometimes wondered if *she* did.

"Didn't expect you back so soon," Dave remarked. "I thought when you said you wanted a couple of days you planned to be scarce around here."

Blaire smiled. "I do. Someone's lending me a horse and Gus and I are going to take some rides in the mountains."

Why did she feel as if she couldn't share the truth with Dave? He wasn't one for gossip, and what did it matter anyway? It wasn't as if she were embarking on a top secret mission where a little talk could cost lives.

She was slipping back into the military mind-set. Whether that was good or bad, it was too soon to say. She guessed she'd find out.

"So you want me to hang around?" Dave asked. "Or come back tomorrow? I don't see two horses and it's getting kind of late in the day to take much of a ride anyway."

Blaire chewed her lip momentarily. "Would filling in for me tomorrow be a problem?"

"I'd planned to anyway. And an extra day if you want. My wife and kids went to Buffalo to visit her family, so it's not like anyone's going to miss me."

Gus spoke. "I need to go over to my place to get my horse and some supplies. If you could hang out here, I'll take Blaire with me and she can drive my truck back over while I bring Scrappy." He eyed Blaire. "If that's okay with you?"

"That's fine," she agreed. She liked the idea that Gus was evidently planning to stay another night, and that he'd help her learn how to take care of the horse that Gideon should be bringing.

"Just one thing," Gus said. "Gideon Ironheart is bringing a horse for Blaire to ride for a few days, so if it arrives while we're gone?"

Dave nodded. "That I can handle. The corral out back is still good, mainly because I fixed it up last spring. You never know when the state might decide it would help to get us mounts. On the other hand, the way the road paving argument is going, I figure I'll be walking or using the ATVs for years to come."

"They work," Blaire pointed out with humor.

"Sure, but they don't go everywhere a horse could."

She half smiled. "And they tear up the terrain."

"Exactly." Dave pretended to be struck by the thought. "I never thought of that. Sheesh, Blaire, you ought to pass that along to the powers that be. Hey, guys, the ATVs damage the environment."

"Probably no more than the campers," she retorted. "Okay, that's how we'll do it, then." She looked at Gus. "How long should we be?"

"An hour at most. By truck my cabin isn't that far away if you take the wood trail."

She knew what he meant. There was a road between the two cabins, basically two ruts that ran between the trees, but it shaved off a lot of travel time. Gus's truck had high suspension for dealing with the rugged terrain around the forest. It could probably handle it better than most ATVs.

Thanking Dave yet again, she climbed back into the truck with Gus, and they headed along the wood trail toward his headquarters.

Chapter Eight

Gus loaded the back of his truck with all kinds of horse needs, like bags of feed, currycombs and so on. He believed in taking care of any animal in his care, and some that simply needed help. When it came to Scrappy, however, it felt as if he were taking care of family.

Instead of taking the trail back to Blaire's place, he took the wood road. He led the way on Scrappy with her following behind in his truck. The day was beginning to wane. The sun had disappeared behind the mountain he was traveling over, and the light had become flat. It was still daytime, the sky above a brilliant blue, but the shadows beneath the trees seemed to have deepened anyway.

The forest didn't feel right, he thought. He supposed that was something left over from the war, but it was a feeling he couldn't dismiss anyway. As if a threat could lurk behind any tree.

Maybe it could. Some lunatic had killed a man inoffensively sleeping in his tent. Killed him with his young son beside him. What kind of person did that? The question had been bugging him since the outset.

The kind of person who would do that was exactly the reason he couldn't bring himself to leave Blaire alone again. He'd fought his instincts the first nights after the murder, but finally he couldn't continue an internal war that clearly wasn't going to sign a cease-fire.

He was worried for Blaire. She was out there alone at night, and if the campground had been full to the rafters, he'd have felt he was extraneous. But everyone had fled after the murder, and there was still no sign of a return.

People had become spooked. Unless they caught the bad guy, Blaire's campground might remain mostly empty for the rest of the season. That meant she'd be all alone out there in the woods at night after her seasonal staff went home for the day. Ordinarily that wasn't something she, or he, would worry about.

Now he was worrying. The woods didn't feel right, and instinct was crawling up and down his spine telling him this wasn't over. How he could be sure of that, he didn't know, but he remained on high alert for anything that didn't seem normal. Anything that might indicate an important change of some kind.

For certain, he was in agreement with Blaire that something about the murder seemed more like a planned operation. An assassination. Which made him truly eager to learn anything he could about the victim, but no one was going to feed that information to him. Police stuff. Civilians not wanted.

Yeah, he was a law enforcement officer, but only in the national forest. If the murder had happened over there, he'd be part of the investigation. This was different. He didn't have a clear idea of Blaire's role vis-à-vis this kind of thing. But wasn't she, too, law enforcement in the park? But maybe not for major crimes. Maybe she was expected to rely on local authorities. It wasn't as if she had the manpower to do much else.

But still… Maybe she could press Gage a little more. Maybe, given her position, he might be willing to share

more with her than information about the other murders
that were now worrying people.

And man, hadn't that seemed to come out of nowhere?
All of a sudden people worrying about other murders that
had happened in the woods over the last couple of years.
Linked? How likely was that? He had no idea.

He just knew that his gut was screaming this wasn't
over, and he couldn't stop worrying about Blaire.

Tomorrow they'd pack up some supplies and do a survey of the surrounding area. The killing had been planned.
Of that he was certain. And that meant someone had spent
at least a little time surveying the campground and the
victim. Which also meant a greater likelihood the guy
had left some kind of evidence behind.

He just hoped his need to protect Blaire wasn't offend-
ing her. She had experience in combat, in military operations, and while she hadn't been in special ops the way
he had, it remained she was no greenhorn. He'd often felt
kinship with the way her mind worked.

So maybe he should ask her if she resented his hovering. He couldn't blame her if she did. Yeah, he should
ask. He should do her that courtesy.

He also needed to be wary of his attraction to her. He'd
felt it when they first met, and it hadn't lessened any with
time, but he honestly still didn't feel emotionally fit to en-
gage in a meaningful relationship deeper than friendship.
And from things she'd said occasionally, he believed she
felt much the same way: wary.

A misstep could kill their friendship, and he treasured
that too much to risk it. Still, sometimes his body ached
with yearning when he thought of her or was around her.

Careful, dude. Just be careful.

The radio on his hip crackled and he lifted it to his ear.
A satellite transceiver, it usually worked, but occasion-

ally dense woods could interfere a bit. No real interference right now, though.

"Maddox," he said into the receiver.

"Hey, boss," came the voice of Tony Eschevarria.

"What's up?" Gus asked.

"You said you'd be out of pocket the next two days?"

"At least. Over at the state campground."

"Weird, that killing," Tony remarked, his voice crackling a bit. "Listen, a deputy is here. He's looking for you and I can send him over that way if you want."

"Sure thing. I should be there in about twenty minutes."

"I hope he's got good news, Gus."

"Me, too," Gus answered. "Me, too."

He clipped the brick back in its belt holder, then leaned forward to pat Scrappy's neck. The saddle creaked a bit, a sound he'd always loved, and nearly vanished in the shivering of deciduous tree leaves in the gentle breeze. The storm that had appeared to be building over the mountains hadn't materialized, but he swore he could smell it. Tonight, maybe.

The wood road, as they called it, little more than a cart track, had once been used by lumberers gathering wood to build the old mining town on Thunder Mountain, abandoned more than a century ago. Still, the cart tracks had been convenient enough that they'd been kept clear by usage over those years.

At last the track emerged onto a portion of paved roadway just above Blaire's cabin. A truck and horse trailer now filled part of the gravel lot, and Dave was standing out front talking to Gideon Ironheart. Gus smiled. He'd always liked Gideon.

The man had once been an ironworker who'd walked the high beams, but when he came here to visit his estranged brother, Micah Parish, he'd fallen in love with one of Micah's colleagues in the sheriff's office. At least that was the story. Anyway, these days Gideon raised horses, trained them for their owners and rescued mustangs. His two teenage children often led trail rides for tourists, sometimes at the national forest.

While Blaire parked the truck, he dismounted Scrappy and called a greeting to Gideon, who walked over with an extended hand. "I hear you're planning to do a little exploring with Blaire Afton."

"That's the plan. Thanks for the help."

Gideon grinned. "It's good for the horses to have a little adventure every now and then. I might have some big paddocks but they offer little new to explore. Lita will enjoy herself a whole bunch."

"Lita's the horse?" He heard Blaire's footfalls behind him as she approached.

"Most well-behaved mare a body could ask for." Gideon turned, smiling and offering his hand. "You must be Blaire Afton."

"I am," she answered, shaking his hand. "And you're Gideon Ironheart, right?"

"So I've heard."

Gus was glad to hear her laugh. "Your reputation precedes you," she said. "I heard someone call you a horse whisperer. So, you whisper to them?"

Gideon shook his head. "Most of so-called whispering is knowing horses. They communicate quite well if you pay attention and, if you listen, they decide to please you. Sort of like cats."

Another laugh emerged from Blaire. Gus felt like a grinning fool, just to hear her so happy.

"Let me introduce you," Gideon said. "Then I'm going to ride her up the road a ways to work out the kinks from being in the trailer. After that, she's yours as long as you need her."

"Somebody say that to me." Dave pretended to groan. "We need horses up here so badly I even took a wild hair and repaired the corral for them. Sell that to the state."

"I would if I could," Gideon answered. "I've got some fine mounts that would love working up here."

Gus and Dave helped him open the trailer and lower the ramp, then Gideon stepped inside and led an absolutely gorgeous chestnut out of the trailer.

"Oh, wow," Blaire breathed.

Gideon walked her slowly in a circle, leading her by a rein, then brought her toward Blaire. "Get to know her. Pat her neck first, don't approach her from the front until she gets to know you. Remember, she's got a big blind spot in front of her nose. And talk to her so she'll recognize your voice."

Blaire apparently didn't feel any reluctance to make friends with the horse. She wasn't quite as big as Scrappy, but still large. But then, Blaire had ridden in Afghanistan so this wasn't exactly utterly new to her.

It wasn't long before it became evident that Lita liked Blaire. Five minutes later, the horse wound her neck around and over Blaire's neck and shoulder, a horse hug.

"There you go," said Gideon. "She's yours now. Need anything in the way of supplies?"

Gus recited the list of items he'd brought with him, from bags of feed to grooming supplies.

"You'll do," Gideon agreed. "Call me if you need anything at all."

"You could send another horse," Dave laughed. "As long as you're lending them."

NOT TEN MINUTES after Gideon drove off, Dave helped carry the groceries inside, then left to spend the evening at home. He once again promised to take over for Blaire the next day if needed.

Blaire swiftly put away the groceries with an obliging Gus's help. Then the Conard County deputy arrived.

A big man, appearing to be in his sixties, he unfolded from the SUV. He had long inky hair streaked with gray, and his Native American ancestry was obvious in his face. He looked at them from dark eyes and smiled.

"Micah Parish," he said, shaking their hands. "I saw my brother headed on out." He pointed with his chin toward Lita. "New acquisition?"

"A loaner," Blaire answered. "You're storied in these parts, and I don't even spend that much time in town so I don't get all the gossip."

Micah chuckled, a deep rumbling sound. "I'm storied because I broke some barriers around here."

Gus doubted that was the only reason.

"You talked to my daughter-in-law, Connie," he said. "And, of course, she talked to me. Then Gage talked to me. Seems like folks are worried this murder might be linked to others in the mountains. So, I'm here to share information. Thing is, Gus, I was sent first to you. Somebody's nervous about the national forest."

"The killer, you mean?" Gus frowned. "Has there been a threat?"

"No." Micah looked at Blaire. "You got maps of the whole area?"

"How much do you want?"

"Most of the mountain range on up to Yellowstone."

"On my wall. Come in. Do you want some coffee?"

"My wife, Faith, tells me the day I turn down coffee I'll be at the Pearly Gates."

She pointed him to the large map hanging on the wall and went to start a pot of coffee. For a minute or so, there was silence from the front room, then Micah and Gus began to talk.

"The thing here is this," Micah said. "Can't imagine why no one noticed it before. Hey, Blaire?"

"Yes?" She punched the button to start the pot, then came round into the front room.

"Okay to use the pushpins to mark the map?"

"Go ahead." She didn't usually do that, but the map wasn't inviolate. There was a corkboard beside it, and other than an announcement of a campfire group every Friday evening, it was simply covered with colored push-pins.

Micah pulled a pad out of his jacket pocket and flipped it open. Then he read from it and began sticking red push-pins into the map along the mountain range. "Nobody's perfect," he remarked as he stuck the last pin in place. "I can only approximate the GPS readings on this map."

He stepped back a bit. "These are in order, marking those five murders that everyone is worried about." He pointed to the highest pin. "Number one."

Then as his finger trailed down along the pins to the one in the state campground, he called the order. There was no mistaking it. The murders had moved southward through the mountains.

"As you can see, it's not anywhere near a perfect line, but it's too close to ignore. All of the victims were isolated, but *not* alone. Like the one in your campground, Blaire. It's as if the killer wanted the body to be found immediately."

She nodded, feeling her skin crawl.

"Anyway," Micah continued, "Gage sent me to warn you, Gus, because the forest might be next in line. Although what you can do about it, I don't know. That's a whole lot of territory. But judging by the previous timing, the threat won't be too soon. You'll have time to figure out what you can do."

"What I can do?" Gus repeated. "Right now I must have thirty hikers out in the woods, plus about sixty families camping mostly at the southern side. I can't just empty the park indefinitely. Not even for this. Damn, I can hear HQ hit the roof."

Micah smiled faintly. "So can I. All you can do is have your people remain alert. These instances might not even be linked. There sure hasn't been anything like the Jasper murder with a kid in the tent."

Blaire had been studying the map closely and eventually spoke. "It looks as if someone is trying to make these events appear random."

The men looked again, and both nodded.

"Not doing very well," Gus remarked.

"Actually, take a closer look. Every one of these killings occurred in a different jurisdiction, including two that happened across the state line. That would make linking them very difficult because the different jurisdictions operate independently. That's clever."

"If it's one killer," agreed Micah.

"It looks," said Gus, "like a carefully planned operation."

Silence fell among the three of them. Blaire's skin tightened the way it often had before going on a transport mission, knowing that danger lay ahead, but having no idea what kind, or from where.

Micah muttered, "Well, hell," as he stared at the map. "That would explain a lot." He faced them. "Gage was going to send you some of the reports, the ones he can get. I'm not sure who'll bring them up or when. Most of these cases are cold and getting colder. And from what he said, none of them have any evidence except bodies. Very useful."

"But there are two murders every summer, right?" Blaire asked. "That's what I heard."

"So it appears, not that you can be sure of much with a sample set of five. All right, I'll head back on down and pass this information to Gage. Good thinking, Blaire. You may have hit on something important."

"Important but probably useless," she responded. "Somebody with brains is behind this but finding that brain isn't going to get any easier."

"Maybe that'll change," Gus offered. "We might find something useful in our survey over the next few days. Or just thinking about all the murders from the perspective you provided might generate some ideas."

"Criminal masterminds," Micah rumbled, and half snorted. "Word is they don't exist."

Blaire couldn't suppress a smile. "That's what they say. They also say that every perp brings something to the scene and leaves something behind. Nobody's apparently found anything left behind except bodies and the bullets in them. Oh, and one shell casing."

"Yeah. The reports will verify it when Gage gets them, but from what he mentioned this morning to me, all the weapons were different, too. God help us."

Micah stayed just long enough to finish a mug of coffee, then headed back down the mountain toward town. Gus helped Blaire with grooming Lita and feeding her, along with taking care of Scrappy, and she had to admit a certain excitement at the prospect of riding around the mountains with him in the morning.

It had been a long time since she'd been in the saddle, and she'd realized during those days in Afghanistan that she really loved to ride, that she enjoyed the companionship of a horse, and that a horse could be as much of an early warning system as a trained dog. They reacted to strangers by getting nervous, for one thing.

When the horses were taken care of, they headed back inside. "I need a shower," Blaire remarked. "I smell like horse. And since you were here last night, you probably are starting to feel truly grungy."

"I'm used to grungy," he reminded her. "But I'll never turn down a hot shower. You go first."

"It's a luxury, isn't it?"

She'd never realized just how much of one it was until those long missions in the 'Stan. Sometimes she'd felt as if dust and dirt had filled her pores and could never be scrubbed out. She ran upstairs to get clean clothes.

She would have liked to luxuriate in the shower, but she needed to save hot water for Gus. Making it quick, she toweled off swiftly and climbed into fresh jeans and a long-sleeved polo with the state park logo on the shoulder. From the tiny linen cupboard, she pulled out fresh towels for him and placed them on a low stool she kept in the corner for holding her clothes.

In the front room, she found Gus unpacking fresh clothes from a saddlebag.

"Always ready?" she asked lightly.

"That's the Coast Guard, but yeah. A change of clothes is always a handy thing to have around. I'll hurry."

"I'm done. If you want to use up all the hot water, be my guest."

He laughed, disappearing down the short, narrow hallway from the kitchen into her bathroom. A short while later she heard the shower running.

Now to think of dinner. Fortunately that had been at the back of her mind while she'd been shopping, and it was easy enough to choose a frozen lasagna and preheat the oven. She'd gotten lazy. She could have cooked for two, but in the summers she avoided cooking even for herself, except when her freezer gave her fits. She had plastic containers full of things like pea soup and stew on her refrigerator shelf, but none of them held enough for two. The lasagna did.

Gus apparently believed in conserving water, because he emerged from the bathroom, his hair still wet and scented like her bar soap, before the oven beeped that it was preheated.

He looked over her shoulder, giving her the full force of his delightful aromas. "Oh, yum," he said. "I assume you're making dinner?"

"I wouldn't make this much just for me."

He laughed. "So you were thinking about me when we were at the store."

She was thinking about him a lot, she admitted to herself. Maybe too much. But she could deal with that later once things settled down around here.

She put the lasagna in the oven, still covered by its plastic sheeting per directions, then filled their mugs with more coffee. "Front room?" she asked.

"Let me go hang up this towel." He pulled it from around his neck. "Be right there."

She carried the coffee out to the front room, placing his cup on the rustic end table and hers on the counter that separated the room from the workspace. Everything here was rustic, which she liked, but it also felt empty without the usual comings and goings of campers.

She settled behind the counter on her swiveling stool, feeling it might be a safer move than sitting beside him on the sofa. She didn't know why she needed to feel safe as he posed no threat to anything except possibly her peace of mind.

Afraid of damaging their friendship, she didn't want him to even guess how sexually attractive she found him. The pull hadn't worn off with familiarity, either. It seemed to be growing, and in the last couple of days it had grown by leaps and bounds.

He joined her just a few minutes later and dropped onto the couch. "Okay," he said. "There's one thing I want to know, and I want complete truth."

Her heart skipped a beat and discomfort made her stomach flutter. "That sounds ominous."

"It's not." He waved a hand before picking up his coffee mug and toasting her with it in a silent *thank-you*. "I just want to know if I'm driving you nuts by hovering. You're a very capable woman. You don't need a man for much."

She nearly gaped at him, then laughed. "Sexist much?"

"I don't want you to think I'm *being* sexist," he answered. "That's all."

"Ah." She bit her lower lip, but she felt like smiling. "I don't. I just thought you were being a concerned friend."

"Okay, then. It's just that you've taken care of yourself in some pretty sketchy places and situations. I *know* that, and I don't underrate it."

She nodded, liking him even more, if that was possible. "Thank you, but I'm glad you've decided to help. How much ground can I cover alone? And to be quite honest, I feel uneasy. *Really* uneasy. This whole situation stinks, and I don't care how many pins have marked that map, how do we know the killer has moved on? He might hang out in the woods. And if I were to go start poking around by myself, I might make him nervous enough to act, but he might hesitate if I'm not alone. Heck, despite what Micah Parish pointed out with those pins, how can I know I don't make an attractive target out here if I'm by myself?"

"That's my fear," he admitted. "My main fear. This guy obviously likes killing. You might look like a pear ready to pluck."

"I hear most serial killers escalate, too. Speed up." She leaned forward, her elbows on the polished pine counter, and wrapped her hands around her mug. "I've always hated being blind and I was on too many missions where we were just that—blind and waiting for something to happen. That's what this feels like."

"I hear you." Leaning back on the sofa, he crossed his legs, one ankle on the other knee. "I don't like this whole thing. One bit. I could be completely off track, though. Comparing this to anything we went through overseas on missions might really be stretching it. Those instincts could be completely wrong."

"But what are they telling you?"

"Probably the same thing yours are. There's something more than a single murder going on, and I don't mean five of them." He drummed his fingers on his thigh. "That was a really interesting point you made about the murders all being in different jurisdictions. It's not like there's a free flow of crime information between them. Not unless someone has reason to believe the crimes are linked, or they know the perp has crossed jurisdictional lines."

She nodded. "That was my understanding."

"Cops are like anyone else, they're protective of their turf."

"They don't even like the FBI, from what I hear."

"And if this really does cross state lines, the Bureau could get involved. Another reason not to open their eyes."

"Gage has."

"Gage was a Fed once himself," Gus replied. "I suspect he's less turf conscious than many."

Shaking her head, she tried to ease the tension that was

growing in her neck. "There are moments when I feel as if I'm overreacting. I have no more evidence that this killer might act around here again than we have evidence period. And it's driving me nuts not to know a damn thing about why or how this happened."

He put his coffee aside and rose. "Neck tight?"

"Like a spring."

He came around behind her and began to massage her shoulders and neck. "Tell me if I press too hard or it hurts."

At that all she could do was groan with the pleasure of it. "Don't stop."

"I won't. You're tight as a drum."

She could well believe it. Part of her couldn't let this go, couldn't just brush it off. The police were dealing with it. The other part of her wouldn't just leave it alone. They needed more than a spent shell casing. A whole lot more, and if some guy had watched the campsite long enough to know how to approach and when, then he must have left something behind. *Something.* She knew optics, knew how far it was possible to see with a good scope or binoculars. He could have been more than a hundred yards away. All he needed was a sight line.

Her neck was finally letting go. Her head dropped forward and she felt the release. "Thank you."

"Okay now?"

"Yup. For now."

Dinner was ready. The oven timer beeped, letting her know. "Hungry?" she asked.

"Famished. And I suggest an early night. We should start at first light."

FROM THE WOODS farther up the road, in the trees, Jeff watched in frustration. Wasn't that ranger ever going to go back to his own park? He was all over Blaire like white on rice.

He'd been told he needed to take Blaire out, but he wasn't at all sure she'd even remember their brief encounter or connect him to any of this. Why should she?

But he knew why he was here. This was his punishment for having lost that shell casing. This was his punishment because he'd known Blaire long ago. He shouldn't have told the guys that he'd passed her on his first recon out here. Hell, she hadn't recognized him then. He was probably just another face among hundreds she saw every summer, and he hadn't really noticed her. Why would she remember him any better than he'd remembered her?

But he had his marching orders. Kill or be killed. Damn, damn, damn, how had he walked into this mess? How had he honestly believed his friends were just playing a game? He should have known Will better. Should have recognized the cold streak in him.

Should have? Psychopaths were notorious for being able to hide their missing empathy, for seeming like people you really wanted to know. So many were successful con men because they appeared so warm and likable. Hard for a mere friend to begin to suspect such a thing.

But that was Jeff's conclusion now, too late. And Karl was probably no better, or else how could they have turned this "game" so deadly? He'd been wrestling with that since he had first realized what was going on, but almost immediately they'd snared him right into this mess. His life or someone else's.

He wished he had more guts. Evidently, for him anyway, it took less guts to shoot someone else.

So now here he was, under orders to kill Blaire Afton, which he *really* didn't want to do, and she might as well have a bodyguard. What was he supposed to do? Take them both out?

He ground his teeth together and leaned his head back against a tree trunk, wishing himself anywhere else on the planet. He couldn't shoot both of them. There was enough of an uproar over the first murder.

And he still had the cries of that child hammering inside his head. He didn't lack feeling the way the other two guys did. He wished he could have shot anyone except a guy with a little kid. Why those two had picked that man...

He'd assumed it was because he was camping alone. And at first he had been, or so it had seemed. Somewhere between the time the details had become fixed and when he'd crept into that campground to shoot the man, a child had arrived. How could he have missed that?

But he knew. In his reluctance to carry out the killing, he hadn't been as attentive as he should have been. No, he'd sat up there higher in the forest, just like this, with his eyes closed, wishing he was in Tahiti, or even the depths of Antarctica.

Reluctantly, he looked again and saw the national forest truck was still parked alongside the state truck. He wondered about the chestnut horse that had been delivered that day and was now out in the corral with the forest ranger's horse.

Maybe the two were lovebirds. Maybe they planned a nice ride in the forest and up the mountainside. Why else would there be another horse in the corral? And if that was the case, how would he ever get Blaire alone so he could shoot her? He sure as hell didn't want another body to add to his conscience.

He ached somewhere deep inside over all this and was beginning to feel that he'd be hurting over this murder until the day he died. Crap, the Jasper guy had been bad. His kid had made it worse. And now he was supposed to kill someone he had actually known however long ago and however briefly?

This time he carried a rifle so he could shoot from a distance, but he also had his pistol. He pulled it out of his holster and stared at it. All he had to do was take himself out and all of this would be over.

He turned it slowly in his hand and thought about how easy it would be. The victim had died instantly. He never moved a muscle, and while Jeff wasn't terribly educated in such things, he had expected at least some twitching or even moaning, shot to the head notwithstanding.

But the kill had apparently been instantaneous. No muscle twitching, no moan, then the kid had started screaming and Jeff had hurried away as fast as he could without pounding the ground with his feet.

As his more experienced "friends" had told him, no one would dare come out to check what had happened for a minute or two, giving him time to slip away. They'd been right. Except for the kid's squalling, the campground had remained silent and still. Confusion and self-protection had reared long enough for Jeff to vanish into the shadows of the night. All without so much as scuffing his feet on the pine needles, dirt and leaves.

No trail. No sound, certainly not with the boy screaming. No evidence other than losing a shell casing.

And now all because of that casing, and the possibility that Blaire might remember his face or name after all these years, he was back here facing another nightmare.

The night was deepening. Lights came on in her cabin. Smoke began to rise from a chimney. It was getting cold out here, so maybe it was cooling down inside.

Maybe, he thought, he ought to try popping her through

the window. Sure, and that ranger would come barreling after him instantly.

Nope.

A sound of disgust escaped him, and he brought his weary body to its feet. He had to find a protected spot for the night. He hadn't bothered to locate one while there was still daylight, and through his distress he felt some annoyance with himself.

He grabbed his backpack with one hand and turned to head deeper into the woods, away from any chance encounter with someone coming up that road. He'd spend another day watching. What choice did he have?

Well, said a little voice in his head, he *could* go back to Will and Karl and confess that he was a complete failure and leave it to them to shoot him.

Except he had a very bad feeling about that. Their little game of not getting caught meant that however they chose to remove him they'd have to make it look like an accident. Which meant he could die in all sorts of ways, from a fire, to a car accident, to a rockfall. Ways that might make him suffer for quite a while.

He wouldn't go out as easily as his own victim had. No way. They'd come up with something diabolical that would keep them in the clear.

It finally was dawning on him that he had plenty of good reason to hate the two men he had always thought were his closest friends. Plenty of reason.

Clouds raced over the moon, occasionally dimming the already darkened woods even more. Each time he had to pause and wait for the light to return. All so he could find a sheltered place where the wind wouldn't beat on him all night and he could bundle up in a sleeping bag.

Maybe his mind would work better in the morning.

Maybe he'd find a solution one way or another. A good solution. Hell, maybe he'd find a way out of this altogether.

Vain hope, he supposed. It was hard to hide completely anymore. Very hard. And he had no idea how to stay off the grid.

Damn it all to hell! There had to be a way. And if that way was killing Blaire Afton, what was she to him? Nothing. Not as important as his own life.

Because that's what it really came down to. Who mattered more.

He was almost positive that despite what he'd done, he mattered more. Blaire had gone to war. She probably had a body count that far exceeded anything he could do.

Hell, maybe she even *deserved* to die.

He turned that one around in his head as he finally spread out his sleeping bag against the windbreak of a couple of large boulders.

Yeah. She deserved it.

Now he just had to figure out the best way to do it.

Feeling far better than he had in a couple of days, he curled up in his sleeping bag with some moss for a pillow, and finally, for the first time since he'd killed that guy, he slept well.

Chapter Nine

Dawn was just barely breaking, the first rosy light appearing to the east, as Blaire and Gus made a breakfast of eggs, bacon and toast. They ate quickly, cleaned up quickly, then with a couple of insulated bottles full of coffee, they went out back to the corral and found two horses that looked ready for some action.

Gus helped Blaire saddle Lita, carefully instructing her on the important points of the western saddle. They weren't so very different from the saddle she had used a few times in Afghanistan.

He saddled Scrappy with practiced ease, and soon they were trotting up the road toward the rustic campsite where a man had been killed. They hadn't talked much, but Gus wasn't naturally chatty in the morning, and Blaire didn't seem to be, either.

The horses seemed to be enjoying the climb, prancing a bit, tossing their heads and whinnying once in a while as if talking to one another.

"I hope you slept well," Blaire said, breaking the prolonged silence. "That couch is barely long enough for you. Oh, heck, it's not long enough at all."

"It was fine. And yeah, I slept well. You?"

"Nightmares." She shook her head as if she could shake loose of them.

"About anything in particular?"

"I wish I knew. No, just woke up with the sensation of having spent a frightening night. I probably ought to be glad I can't remember. For too long, I could."

He knew exactly what she meant. Long after coming home, long after returning to civilian life, he'd relived some of his worst experiences in his dreams. "This situation hasn't been good for the mental health."

"No," she admitted. "I'm beginning to feel as if I'm teetering on a seesaw between the past and present." She paused. "Hey, that's exactly the thing I've been describing as being uneasy. I just realized it. Yeah, there was a murder, it was heinous, but that alone can't explain why tension is gripping me nearly every single minute."

"Maybe it could." But he didn't believe it.

Another silence fell, and he would have bet that she was considering her post-traumatic stress and how this event might have heightened it.

Everyone had it to some degree. Some were luckier, having it in smaller bits they could more easily ignore. Some couldn't get past it at all. He figured he was somewhere in the middle, and after all this time he had a better handle on it. Hell, he and Blaire had spent hours over coffee discussing it, as if talking about it would make those memories and feelings less powerful.

Maybe it had. The last few months he'd thought the two of them were moving to a better place. Now this. Not a better place at all.

When they reached the turn to the rustic campground, they paused. "Want to look over the scene again?" he asked her.

"I'm thinking. How much could the crime scene techs have missed? They certainly found the shell casing."

"True. So let's start circling farther out."

But she chose to circle the evident edge of the camping area, with all the sites in clear view. She drew rein at one point and looked down.

Gus followed her gaze and saw the small metal cars in the dirt, roadways still evident. Kids playing. Kids whose parents had been stricken enough by events that they'd left without getting these toys. Maybe the youngsters had been upset enough not to care about them, or had even forgotten them in the ugliness of what had occurred.

"Sad," Blaire remarked.

"Yeah."

They continued on their way, and through the trees he could see the tent where the man had been killed, and the crime scene tape that still surrounded the area. He wondered if anyone would clean that up or if it would be left to Blaire and her staff.

He asked, "Are they done with the scene?"

"I don't know. I need to ask. Then I guess we get to do the cleanup."

That answered his question. "I'll help."

She tossed him a quizzical look. "I thought you had your own responsibilities."

"I do, but Holly's in her element. She always enjoys standing in for me. One of these days, I bet she replaces me."

That drew a smile from Blaire and he was relieved to see it. She'd been awfully somber this morning.

After the first circuit, during which they'd noted nothing of interest, they moved out another fifty yards. The woods grew thicker but when he looked uphill, he saw more than one potential sight line. Not far enough, maybe, before they were blocked by the growth, but they were still there. He felt, however, that a watcher would have stationed himself a much longer way out if he could. Away from chance discovery.

"Kids like to run in the woods," Blaire remarked. "Several times a year we have to go looking for them. You?"

"No different for us."

"They're usually farther out than this. Far enough that they completely lose sight of the camp. Too much of a chance that someone would stumble over our killer here."

"The same thought crossed my mind."

Another smile from her. "Well, we're on the same wavelength quite a bit."

"So it seems." Mental echoes of one another at times. When he wasn't appreciating it, he could become amused by it. Right now he knew exactly what she was doing when she moved her reins to the left and headed them uphill.

"Hundred yards next?" he asked.

"Yes, if you agree."

"Why wouldn't I?" He was enjoying her taking charge and doing this her way. He'd never minded women being in charge, even though he hadn't come across it often in spec ops, and he had no trouble seeing Blaire as a complete equal. They'd walked the same roads, to some extent, and shared a lot of experience. Now they even had similar civilian jobs.

The only thing that troubled him was the attraction that kept goading him. Boy, that could blow things up fast. Then there was the protectiveness he was feeling. Even though she had said she didn't mind him hanging around, he had to hope she wasn't beginning to feel like he didn't trust her to take care of herself.

That would be demeaning. Not at all what he wanted her to feel.

They reached a point on the second circle where she

drew rein sharply. He paused, just behind her, and strained his senses when she said nothing. Waiting, wondering if she had heard or seen something.

Then he noticed it, too. At first the jingle and creak of harness and saddle had made him inattentive to sound, but now that it was gone, he could hear it. Or not hear it as the case was.

She turned Lita carefully until she could look at him sideways. "The birds."

He nodded. They had fallen silent.

"Could be a hiker," she said quietly. "I don't have any registered at the moment, but simple things like letting someone know where you're going up here don't always seem important to people."

"I know," he answered just as quietly. "Not until we have to send out huge search parties to hunt for someone with a sprained ankle who can barely tell us which quadrant he's in. Don't you just love it?" Then he fell silent, too, listening.

A breeze ruffled the treetops, but that was nothing new. The air was seldom still at that height, although here at ground level it could often become nearly motionless because of the tree trunks and brush.

None of that explained the silence of the birds, however. No, that indicated major disturbance, and he doubted he and Blaire were causing it, or they'd have noticed it earlier.

Problem was, he couldn't imagine what could be causing the unusual silence. The birds were used to ordinary animals and threats in the woods, and if the two of them on horseback hadn't silenced them, what had?

Another glance at Blaire told him the silence was concerning her. The birds had to feel threatened.

Then, almost in answer to the thought, a boom of thunder rolled down the mountainside.

"Great time for Thunder Mountain to live up to its reputation," Blaire said.

They both looked up and realized the sky just to the west had grown threateningly inky. It was going to be bad.

"Better head back," he said.

She nodded reluctantly.

He understood. This search of theirs had only just begun, and now they were having to cut it short. Who could guess how much evidence might be wiped away by a downpour. Probably anything that there might be.

She started to turn Lita, then paused.

He eased Scrappy up beside her, trying to ignore the electric tingle as their legs brushed briefly. "What?" he asked.

"I just felt…something. The back of my neck prickled. Probably the coming storm." She shrugged and started her mount back toward the road.

Gus followed. Her neck had prickled? He knew that feeling and he seriously doubted it was the storm.

Growing even more alert, he scanned the woods around them. He didn't see a damn thing.

HELL'S BELLS, JEFF THOUGHT. He saw the growing storm, although he doubted it would hit that quickly. What annoyed the dickens out of him was that the two were headed away, probably back to the cabin. He couldn't keep up with those horses unless he tried to run, and he figured he'd either make too much noise and be heard, or he'd break an ankle and die out here.

Regardless, any chance he might have found to take out Blaire was lost for now. Instead he had to figure out how to weather this storm without freezing to death. Nobody needed to draw him a map about how dangerous it was to get wet up here. He'd done enough hunting to know.

Having to hunker under a survival blanket while trying to keep his gear dry and hoping he hadn't chosen a place where he'd quickly be sitting in runoff didn't please him one bit.

Thunder boomed again, hollow but louder. Time to take cover, and quickly. He found himself a huge boulder that looked as if it sank into the ground enough to prevent a river from running under it and began to set up his basic camp. Only as he was spreading his survival blanket, however, did he realize it had a metallic coating.

Damn! Would it be enough to attract lightning? Or would he be safe because of the high trees and the boulder? Except he knew you shouldn't shelter under trees during a storm. So where the hell was he supposed to go?

The first big raindrop that hit his head told him he was out of time. He'd just have to set up here, and if he was worried about the survival blanket maybe he shouldn't use it. Just sit here and get drenched and hope the rain didn't penetrate his backpack. Out of it, he pulled a waterproof jacket that was too warm for the day, but it might be all he had to prevent hypothermia in a downpour.

Or use the damn blanket, he argued with himself. Getting struck by lightning would at least get him out of this mess. It would probably be a much better end than going back to his so-called friends without having completed this task.

Task. Murder. *Might as well face it head-on, Jeff,* he said to himself, then spoke aloud. "You're a killer now. You killed a man you didn't even know for no good reason at all except to save your own damn neck."

The woods had lost their ability to echo anything back at him. Maybe it was the growing thickness of the air, or the rain that had begun to fall more steadily. The only good thing he could say about it was that any evidence he'd left behind would be washed away.

He pulled the survival blanket out of his backpack and unfolded it, tucking it around himself and his gun and gear. A bolt of lightning would be a good thing right now.

And he didn't give a damn that this blanket must stick out like a sore thumb. Somebody finding him and taking him in for any reason at all would be almost as good as a lightning strike.

Miserable, hating himself, hating the weather, he hunkered inside the blanket.

BLAIRE HELPED GUS as much as she could with the horses. The saddles went under the lean-to to be covered with a tarp that was folded in there. The horses… Well, horses had withstood far worse for millennia, but Gus left the wool saddle blanket on their backs and gently guided them under the lean-to.

Blaire patted Lita on the neck and murmured to her. Her flanks quivered a bit as the thunder boomed, but she remained still.

"If they were free, they'd run," Gus said. "Unfortunately, I can't let them do that. They could get hurt on this ground."

She nodded, stroking Lita's side. "They'll be okay?"

"Sure. I'm positive Lita has been through storms at Gideon's ranch, and I know for a fact Scrappy's been through a bunch of them. I just want them to feel comfortable under the lean-to."

She nodded. "And if they get wet…"

"The wool saddle blankets will help keep them warm. They'll be fine, Blaire. Scrappy's never been pampered and I'm sure Gideon doesn't have enough barn space to bring his animals inside. Nope, they'll withstand it. Unlike us. Can we make some coffee?"

She laughed and led the way inside, but she honestly wasn't feeling very good. This storm threatened to kill any possibility of finding some evidence to help locate the killer. Maybe they'd been asking for too much. "Gus? Espresso or regular?"

"I could use espresso for the caffeine, but on the other hand regular might give me an excuse to drink more hot liquid, and I feel like I'm getting a little chilled."

"You, too? I think the temperature must have dropped twenty degrees while we were riding back. Maybe we'll need a fire." Then she put her hands on her hips and tipped her head quizzically. "So, coffee? Espresso or regular?"

He grinned. "That was an evasion. I can't make up my mind. Whichever you want."

"Some help."

He followed her around to the kitchen. "Want me to bring in some wood? And do you want the fire in the fireplace or in the woodstove?"

The cabin had both. Blaire didn't know the history, but there was a nice stone fireplace next to a Franklin stove that could really put out the heat. She preferred the stove in the winter, but right now it wasn't that cold.

"Let's start with the fireplace, if that's okay."

"More romantic."

She froze as that comment dropped, but he was already on his way out to get wood. What had he meant by that? Anything? Nothing?

Dang. Her heart started beating a little faster as she wondered if he'd been joking. Since first meeting him, she'd been quashing the attraction she felt toward him, but it was very much alive and well. Those simple words had nearly set off a firestorm in her.

More romantic?

Oh, she wished.

With effort, she focused her attention on making a pot of fresh regular coffee. If he still wanted more caffeine later, it wasn't hard to make espresso.

GUS GAVE HIMSELF quite a few mental kicks in the butt as he gathered logs and kindling into a large tote clearly made for the task. Hadn't he seen a wood box inside? In a corner on the front side of the room? Serving as an extra seat beneath a tattered cushion? Maybe he should have checked that out first.

But after what had slipped out of his mouth, he was glad to be out here under the small lean-to alongside the cabin. The corral was out back with another lean-to, but this was the woodshed, capable of holding enough fuel for an entire winter. Right now he looked at nearly six cords of dry wood. Good enough.

He took more time than necessary because if he'd walked out on a mess of his own making with his casual comment, he needed a way to deal with it. Problem was, that would all depend on how she had reacted to it. Maybe she'd taken it as a joke. He half hoped so, even though truth had escaped his lips.

A fire in the fireplace *would* be more romantic. The question was whether this was the time or place. Or even the right relationship. She might be no more eager than he to risk their friendship.

And romance could tear it asunder if it didn't work out. Funny thing about that, how a relationship that could be so close could also be a god-awful mess if it went awry.

He ought to know. He hadn't spent his entire life living like a monk. He'd had girlfriends. He'd considered asking one of them to marry him, too. He thought he'd found true love at last. Just like a soap opera.

And just like a soap opera it had turned out that when he was away on assignment, she liked to fool around. Being alone wasn't her cup of tea at all.

That one had hurt like hell. Mostly the betrayal, he'd decided later. He couldn't even be sure afterward that he'd really loved her. Maybe he'd been more in love with the idea of having a wife, and maybe a kid or two, and coming home after a mission to a family.

It was possible. He might well have deluded himself.

Or possibly he'd been every bit as scorched as he'd felt.

Inside he found Blaire heating up canned clam chowder as if nothing had happened.

"If you're allergic to shellfish, tell me now," she said. "I can make you something else."

"Not allergic, thank God. Life without shellfish would suck."

She laughed lightly as he went out to the fireplace and built a nice fire on the hearth. When he finished, he had a nice blaze going and she'd placed bowls of soup, a plate of crackers and some beer on the kitchenette table, where he was able to join her.

"If the bowls weren't so hot, I'd suggest eating in front of the fire," she said. "You did a nice job."

"You do a nice job of heating up canned soup," he retorted, drawing another laugh out of her. Man, he loved that sound.

"Yeah. I'm not much of a cook. Mom tried to teach me, but I felt no urge to put on an apron."

Which might be what led her to the military. No standard role for this woman. He liked it.

After dinner he insisted on taking care of washing up. When he'd dried his hands and came out to the front room, he found her staring at the map Micah Parish had stuck with pins.

"It's a definite plan," she murmured.

"I agree," he said, coming up beside her.

"But the killings are so far apart in time as well as location, there's no reason to expect him to act again anytime soon."

"You wouldn't think."

"So he's atypical for a serial murderer. Not escalating."

"Not yet anyway."

She turned her head to look at him. "This is so stupid, feeling uneasy that he might be hanging around. He's probably gone home to think about his next move."

"Maybe."

She arched a brow. "Maybe?"

He shook his head a little. "This guy appears to be smart, unless this is all chance," he said, pointing at the map.

"But if he *is* smart?"

"Then what better way to throw us off than by breaking the pattern?"

She caught her breath. "So I'm not crazy."

"Did I say you were?"

She shook her head and faced him. "You feel it, too."

"Call it combat sense. I don't know. I've got this itch at the base of my skull that won't leave me alone. I tried to act like the murder was over, the guy had gone away. That's why it took me two days to start hovering around you. Because I can't escape the feeling that this isn't over. Don't ask me why. It's just there, an itch. A sting like a pinprick in my brain. Anyway, there's no one else here for him to go after, so I started worrying about you."

She dropped her head, looking down at the wooden floor. "Yeah. From the outset I haven't been able to shake it. Something about that murder… My God, Gus, I can't get over it. What kind of monster shoots a sleeping man when his small son is right beside him? He's got no limit, evidently. So what next? My seasonal staff?"

"Or you," he said quietly.

She whipped around and faced the fire, placing her hands on her hips. It was a defiant pose, he thought.

"Let him try," she said. "Besides, this is all speculation."

But neither of them believed it. Not completely. Finely honed senses were pinging and couldn't be ignored.

WILL WAS FED UP with Jeff. He didn't bother to discuss it with Karl. He didn't want any kind of debate, even though he and Karl were very much on the same wavelength.

Jeff must be dealt with. Not necessarily killed but hamstrung enough that he'd never murmur a word about any of this. And while Karl might think that being responsible for one murder would be enough to shut him up, Will didn't.

Damn, he hated overdeveloped consciences.

He, Jeff and Karl had been friends since early childhood. Their fathers had been hunting buddies and when the boys were old enough, they'd joined the hunts with them. Always spending a few weeks here at this lodge, sharing plenty of laughter, talk and beer. It had never occurred to him that friendship with Jeff could become an Achilles' heel.

Of course, when he'd started this damn game, he'd never intended to start killing, so it had never struck him it might be best not to mention it to Jeff.

So he'd sat here in this very chair shooting off his mouth about a game. All because he'd recently come across the story of Leopold and Loeb and had wondered if the three of them could prove they were smarter. Actually, it wasn't really a question, because Leopold and Loeb had been nowhere near as smart as they had believed.

Still, it had been intended to be a game, just as he had said that night. For a while, the stalking and planning had been enough, but then one night Karl had said, "The thrill is going away."

Fateful words. The first few times, they'd simply shot to miss, to cause a bad scare. And they'd been careful not to let Jeff know what was up, because they'd learned long ago that Jeff's conscience was probably bigger than Jeff himself. Besides, they knew him for a weakling. He hated confrontation, and when they were kids he'd been inclined to run away rather than stand up for himself.

Wimp.

So now here they were. They'd managed to pressure Jeff into killing one man just to make it impossible for him to run to the cops. But had they *really* made it impossible?

He had sensed Jeff's fear. Not that Jeff's being afraid was anything new, but the guy was afraid that he and Karl would kill *him*. They would if it became necessary. Regardless, he and Karl were certain they'd left no traces behind so even if Jeff went running to the cops, they could claim they knew nothing at all and Jeff must have gone nuts.

After all, they were, every one of them, respectable people without police records. He and Karl were pillars of their community. Jeff was…well, an underachiever. Not a man to like taking risks even to get ahead.

Now this. Jeff had been in the Army with that ranger woman. She'd glimpsed him on their first survey trip when they'd gone to pick the campground for the hit. He said he was sure she hadn't recognized him.

But Jeff had recognized *her* and that stuck in Will's craw like a fish bone. Not good.

Karl didn't like it, either. There was a link now, and Jeff was that link. They either had to get rid of Jeff or get rid of the ranger. Neither of them especially wanted to kill Jeff. He'd been part of their entire lives, and his father had been like a beloved uncle to them.

But one or the other had to go. If that woman ranger remembered Jeff being there, and found just one thing, anything, that made her draw a connection, there was going to be hell to pay.

Jeff had called just an hour ago on the sat phone, telling Will that a thunderstorm had him pinned down and he couldn't act tonight, especially with another ranger there. Will figured he just needed some goading.

For Pete's sake, pinned down by a freaking thunderstorm? Jeff needed to grow some cojones. If there were two rangers there, so what? Take them both out, then get the hell out of there. At the least, it would make this case stand out from the others in case the growing talk made the authorities think about the murders being linked.

Frustration with Jeff was nothing new these days. Will growled to himself, then pulled his tablet out of its case and looked at the map on which he'd been following Jeff's every move. Jeff had no idea that Will and Karl could track him, not that it probably mattered to him.

But it mattered to Will and Karl. If the man took a hike anywhere near a cop, they wanted to be able to step in. So far Jeff hadn't entertained any such thoughts, at least none that he'd evinced.

But that didn't ease Will's frustration any. He and Karl had agreed that after this murder they needed to take some time off. Maybe a couple of years. Find another way to amuse themselves. If they did that, any links someone might perceive would go up in smoke.

He settled back in his chair, puffing on his cigar, staring at the red blinking dot on his map. It came and went, but he was fairly certain that was because the wimp was huddling under a survival blanket, hiding from the rain. Each time the dot returned, it assured him that Jeff hadn't moved.

But damn it, Jeff, he thought. The rain would make a perfect cover to just get the job done. No one would hear a thing. It was likely any evidence would just wash away if the downpour was as heavy as Jeff had said.

He was also fairly certain that Jeff wouldn't leave another shell casing behind. So, use the high power rifle and take out the rangers and get out of the rain.

Sometimes Jeff didn't think too well.

Hell, maybe most of the time.

Will set the tablet aside and sat smoking his cigar with one hand and drumming his fingers with the other. He needed a way to motivate Jeff. Soon. This couldn't continue as long as there was a whisper of a chance that that ranger might remember him somehow, especially if his name came up. If the cops had found some kind of evidence.

Will sat forward suddenly, unpleasant feelings running down his spine. If Jeff had left behind a shell casing, maybe he'd left even more behind. He clearly hadn't been cautious enough.

Well, of course not. The wimp had been afraid. He'd scurried away leaving that casing behind and who knew what else. One of his cigarette butts? God knew how the police might be able to use something like that.

He picked up the sat phone and called Jeff. "Still raining?" he asked. He hoped so.

God, maybe he should just go out there, kill Jeff himself, then take out the ranger to be extra careful. Yeah, somehow make Jeff nearly impossible to identify because he *could* be linked to Karl and Will.

Hell! He was beginning to think more like a movie or television show. What was he going to do? Murder Jeff, cut off his fingers and face, then murder a ranger so she wouldn't suddenly remember Jeff's name?

No, Jeff was supposed to kill the ranger, tie up the last important loose end, and it was the least he could do considering he'd left that damn shell casing behind. First rule in this game: leave nothing behind. Nothing.

Jeff answered, his voice shaking.

"Why are you shaking?" Will demanded.

"Cold," came the abbreviated answer.

"Man up," Will said shortly. "Take advantage of the rain and just take the woman out. Then you can get inside again and warm your delicate toesies."

"Shut up," Jeff said. It sounded as if he'd gritted the words out between his teeth.

"I will not shut up. I might, however, come out there and kill you myself to close this out."

Complete silence answered him. Then, suddenly, he clearly heard the sound of rain beating on the survival blanket for just a few seconds before the line went empty. He glanced at the tablet and saw that Jeff had disappeared again. The son of a gun had cut him off. Probably deliberately.

But no, a few seconds later he heard Jeff's voice again and saw the dot reappear on the map.

"I'll get her tomorrow," he said. "And you know what, Will?"

God it was almost impossible to understand Jeff with his voice shaking like that. "What?"

"She saw me, all right. I don't think she recognized my face but she might have. Anyway, she knows we went up there five days before I killed that guy, and at some point she's going to put that together."

Will felt stunned. Ice water trickled down his spine. "You lie."

"No, I lied the first time. I don't trust you, and I didn't want to kill *her*, and now that's exactly where I am because you and Karl are goddamn psychopaths who don't give a flying fig about anyone else on this planet. I have half a mind to come to the lodge and kill the two of you for getting me into this."

"You don't have the stones."

"Are you sure of that? But to cover my own butt I have to make sure that woman can't put me together with this mess. That's all on you, jerk. All of it. When this is done, I want nothing to do with the two of you ever again. Buy out my share of the lodge, then stay out of my life."

Yeah, like they'd pay him a dime. But now was not the time to get into that, or even think about it.

"Has it occurred to you," Jeff asked, his voice quavering, "that she may have recognized me, but she also saw the two of you?"

"All the more reason to erase her," Will said sharply.

"No, you're not getting it, you ass. If I turn up dead, she may remember you two and give your descriptions."

That silenced Will. For once he hadn't thought of something.

"And if you think killing me will save you, think again. I turn up dead, everyone knows we're friends... Nah, you'll be under the microscope."

Dang, thought Will, maybe the guy had some stones after all.

Several seconds passed before he spoke again. "Then you'd better take her out and tie off the loose end. We told you that you could be our next target, and we're not stupid. We can make it look like an accident." Will felt his own bravado covering his sudden uncertainty.

"Yeah. Sure."

"Just do it, Jeff."

"I will, damn it. But just leave me alone. I'm not sitting out here in this miserable rain and cold because I enjoy it."

Then he disconnected, leaving Will to listen to the static of a disturbed signal.

After a minute or two, Will put down the phone and picked up his tablet. Jeff was still there. Will looked across the room to the gun rack, which held seven rifles, some good for hunting, but a couple for much longer-range shooting. Damn near sniper rifles. His dad and Karl's had often liked to practice target shooting over a thousand yards.

Jeff had one of those rifles with him right now. He didn't even have to get close to the woman.

But Will thought about going out there and using one of them on Jeff. He studied the map on his tablet, bringing up the terrain. No roads nearby. He'd have to hike through the night, a dangerous thing to do even without a storm.

Hell! He almost hurled the tablet in frustration. If Jeff didn't take that damn woman out by tomorrow night, he and Karl were going to have to do something about Jeff.

No escaping it. Especially since Jeff had pointed out that she'd seen all three of them. They'd have to get rid of him in a way that wouldn't jog her memory so they could stay clear of her.

Or they'd have to kill them both along with that nosy federal ranger.

Either way, if Jeff failed, they'd have to mop up. They should have gotten rid of him as soon as they learned he'd figured out what they were doing. Honoring an old friendship this way had proved to be the biggest head-ache they'd had so far.

He was coming to hate Jeff.

THE WIND HAD picked up considerably and was blowing rain so hard against the window glass that it sounded like small pebbles.

"Will the horses be okay?" Blaire asked.

"Yeah," Gus said. "They know how to hunker together and they've got pretty thick hides. If they didn't there wouldn't be any horses."

"I guess you're right. I know I wouldn't want to be out there in this."

"Not if I can avoid it," he agreed.

She rubbed her arms as they sat on the couch sepa-rated by a couple of feet. "This place doesn't usually feel drafty." She paused. "Let me take that back. It can in the winter because of the temperature differential between the glass and the log walls. That's when I put up the shut-ters. No shutters tonight."

She had already pulled on a cardigan, but now she rose and went to sit on the rug in front of the fire. Closer to the heat and warmth.

"Is that a wood box over there?" Gus asked.

She twisted and followed his pointing finger. "Yes, it is. I think it's full. I should have mentioned it rather than you going outside to get wood."

"I think by the time I got to the door you were in the kitchen starting soup. It's okay." Rising, he went to the box, lifted the long seat pillow off it and looked inside. "I certainly won't have to go out for more wood tonight."

She pulled her knees up under her chin and wrapped her arms around them. "This fire feels so good. But there went all hope of finding any evidence out there. This rain is heavy enough to wash it all away. And the wind will probably knock down the tent and the crime scene tape. Of course, that'll make the area fresh and clean again."

"There are advantages." He joined her on the floor, sitting cross-legged. "There had to be some place he was hanging out to observe from. I doubt the rain will wash that away. And if we find it, we might find something useful."

She glanced at him. "So you still want to go on the hunt tomorrow?"

"If this weather improves. But absolutely. If you're like me, you want to feel like you're actually accomplishing something, not sitting on your hands. I mean, I'd settle back if the police had the guy."

"So would I. But until then…" She turned her attention back to the fire. "I can't stop hearing that little boy cry. It makes me so mad. Furious. Someone needs to pay."

"Yeah. I'm with you."

Watching the flames leap, she thought about what she'd just revealed to him and herself. It *was* about the boy, she admitted. As much as anything, she wanted that boy to grow up with the satisfaction of knowing his father's killer had been caught and sent to prison. Yeah, she was worried he might still be hanging around, and she couldn't blame Gus for being concerned about her safety. Every night, with the campers all gone, she was out here all alone. It wasn't as if she never needed to emerge from this cabin during the hours when her staff weren't here.

Nope. And if this guy was in it just for the thrill, she'd make a great target. Maybe he even thought she might have found some evidence. After all, she'd been the first person to approach the tent.

"Oh, heck," she said in a burst of frustration. She reclined on the rug, staring up at the dancing shadows on the ceiling. "I hate feeling like everything is messed up and I can't do anything to sort it out. Things were a lot clearer in the Army."

"*Some* things were," he agreed. "But that kind of thinking is what makes it so hard to adjust to the return to civilian life."

"I'm sure. I've been guilty of it more than once." She rolled on her side and propped her chin in her hand. "I don't remember my life before the Army being so messy, but maybe that's not true. No way to tell now. And I'm probably misremembering a lot of things from my military days. Nothing is all that clear-cut."

"Except lines of authority, and even those can get muddy."

He unfolded his legs and stretched out beside her, also propping his chin in his hand. "What I'm trying to think about now is how I'm in a warm cabin with a full belly and a good friend instead of stuck in a frigid cave hoping the paraffin flame will actually make the instant coffee hot."

"Good thoughts," she said after a moment. Then a heavy sigh escaped her. "This is a form of PTSD, isn't it?"

"What is?"

She closed her eyes a moment. "I need to face it. A gun report. A man shot in the head, in vivid Technicolor for me, a crying kid and now I've been paranoid since it happened. The paranoia isn't based in any evidence, merely in my past experience."

She opened her eyes and found him staring at her, appearing concerned, his eyes as gray as the storm outside. He spoke. "Then we're both having PTSD. I feel the paranoia. You might be right. It might be a leftover reaction. But what if it isn't? I'm not prepared to stake everything on dismissing this. It's not like I was walking down a street and heard a backfire. This is a whole different level."

He had a point, but she hated not being able to trust her own judgment. "It's awful," she said frankly. "Not being able to trust myself. It's a new thing."

"You didn't feel this way in Afghanistan?"

"Not often. That's what I meant about everything being so clear. There were bad guys, there were good guys, and if there was any doubt, it didn't last long. But this is different. I'm worrying about the stupidest possible thing. That a killer, who has most likely already moved on so he won't be found, might be stalking *me*. I have absolutely no evidence for that. It's just a feeling. A phantasm."

He reached out to grip her shoulder firmly but gently. "Given how many times a *feeling* has saved my life, I'm not going to dismiss this one, and neither should you. When the guy is locked up, then we can kick our own butts for our reactions. But on the off chance…" He didn't complete the sentence. He just gave her shoulder a squeeze, then let go.

"We're hot messes, Gus," she remarked after a few minutes.

"Sometimes. Not always. We're luckier than a lot of people. Holding steady jobs. Having friends."

"One *real* friend," she said honestly.

He shook his head a little but let it pass. She figured he didn't see any point arguing with the plain truth. She knew a lot of people, but as for counting friends of the kind she could truly share her mind and heart with, Gus was it. He'd been there. He understood. Considering she wasn't a hop away from a support group, Gus was priceless in that regard.

But it was more than his understanding. Gus had been there any time she needed someone. Like now. Running around with this paranoid fear clawing at her, he'd been right beside her, his mere presence making her feel safer.

"Thanks for being you," she said quietly. "Your friendship means the world."

His expression softened from concern. "I could say the same to you. Two slightly bent vets who've spent the last two years sharing things we couldn't share with most people. Then we're pretty much on our own in separate parks, tied up too much to go seeking the company of other vets. There's a support group in town, but how often could we get there? Honestly."

"Not frequently," she admitted. Her days off were generally jam-packed with things she needed to do, and come winter there was often no getting out of here at all. But Gus always managed to find his way over here on Scrappy.

She shifted her position so she could look at the fire again. Staring at him was awakening feelings in her that had absolutely nothing to do with paranoia. She was afraid she might simply leap into his arms.

No time for this, she warned herself. Not now. No way did she want to do something that would make him feel it was necessary to get out of here. He'd never evinced any sexual interest in her that she could be sure of, and she'd been careful to avoid the same.

Sometimes it seemed as if their shared experience was a wall between them. Maybe it was. Who knew what might happen if they knocked down that wall and moved past friendship.

"You ever dated much?" he suddenly asked, surprising her.

She turned to see him. "Yeah. A bit."

"Never found the right one?"

Forgetting her concerns for a moment, she smiled. "Apparently not. You?"

"I got really serious once. It turned out to be a big mistake. When I left town, she found someone else to fill in until I returned."

"Ouch!" She winced. "I don't know that I ever had that going on. Of course, I never got serious. Nobody inspired that in me."

"A tough nut, huh?" But his eyes danced a little.

"Maybe. Or maybe I'm just too damn picky."

"Picky is a good thing to be."

Taking her by surprise, he rolled onto his back, then drew her toward him until her head rested on his shoulder and his arm wrapped her back.

"Gus?" Her heart leaped with delight.

"A little comfort for us both," he answered. "Not that it's going to last long because the soles of my boots are starting to get too warm. You?"

"Yeah." She gave a quiet little laugh. "At least I'm not cold now."

"Always a good thing. Except those summers when we wished we were on an iceberg."

"Yeah. Huge extremes." Unable to resist, she snuggled a little closer and inhaled his scent. Wonderful. And the way her boots were getting warmer, she figured they'd both be safe. Another couple of minutes and they'd have to back away from the fire or completely change position.

But right now she wanted to revel in the rare experience of physical closeness with another human being. With a man. Since coming home she'd avoided it, feeling that she was too messed up to get involved without hurting someone.

Yeah, she was adapting pretty well, but if her paranoia

of the past few days didn't make it clear that she wasn't completely recovered, nothing would.

And if she couldn't trust her own mind and feelings, she wasn't fit to be anyone's companion.

Then she felt her feet. "Aw, damn," she said, pulling away from his delicious embrace and sitting up. If the heat from the fire had penetrated the thick soles of her work boots, it would steadily get hotter for a while, and those soles wouldn't cool down quickly. *Been there, done that,* she thought as she tugged at laces. *Bad timing, though.*

Gus half laughed and sat up, reaching for his own boots. "You're right. I just wasn't ready to let you go."

The words warmed her heart the way the fire had warmed her boots. She tossed him a sideways smile, as she pulled her boots off and set them to one side. Stockinged feet were always comfortable in here unless the floor got really cold. That seldom happened so her feet were generally warm enough.

She realized she was growing thirsty. Beer with dinner had been great, but the soup had been salty as had the crackers. "Something to drink?" she asked.

"Sure." He rose with her and they walked around to the kitchen. "This is sort of like a shotgun house," he remarked.

"I think it was built piecemeal by adding at the back, but I'm not sure. At least I have the loft for a bedroom."

"I bet it's toasty on winter nights."

"Oh, yeah." She opened the refrigerator, revealing a couple of bottles of juice, a few more beers and soft drinks. "Or do you want coffee or tea?"

"I told you I never refuse coffee, but if it's too late for you…"

It wasn't. In fact, it wasn't that late at all, she thought

as she glanced at the digital clock on the wall. She turned on the espresso machine, then said, "Latte?"

"Perfect."

Outside, the wind howled and rain beat on the windows, but inside all was warm and dry. Blaire was really glad not to be out there tonight.

Chapter Ten

Jeff had just about had it. After his reaming out over the satellite phone from Will, the person he most wanted to shoot was Will. Followed, probably, by himself.

But neither of those things was going to happen. Nope. Instead he sat there shivering under a survival blanket that, while it was keeping him dry, was too open to keep him warm. The storm had dropped the temperature fast, and at this higher altitude it never got exactly hot to begin with. His fingers, even inside gloves, felt so cold he wondered if he'd get frostbite. Being reduced to eating energy bars didn't help much, either.

But he had to keep the blanket spread to protect his backpack full of essential items, like food and survival equipment, and even though it *shouldn't* make any difference, he didn't want to expose either his rifle or his pistol to the rain. They should still fire, but... What about the scope he might need? It wouldn't help to have it full of water or steamed up when he found his opportunity.

If he ever found his opportunity.

Don't leave a trail or evidence behind. The first rule, one they had repeated until his brain felt like it was being cudgeled. So maybe Blaire had recognized him. It didn't mean she'd connect him to the murder.

But since he'd admitted to knowing her, other thoughts

had danced unprompted through his head. Maybe she had recognized him. Maybe she would wonder why he never registered for a campsite or signed in as a hiker. What if, by chance, she put him together mentally with the murder, or simply mentioned it to the law because it started to nag at her.

The way he'd begun to be nagged by the moment of recognition.

Or what if they found a fingerprint on that damn shell casing. She'd recognize his name if they mentioned it to her. Oh, she'd probably be able to tell them more than the Army could after all these years. It hadn't been for long, but they'd trained side by side for a few weeks. How much had he shared with her?

He couldn't recall now. Too long ago, and he hadn't placed any undue emphasis on avoiding chitchat about personal things like families and high schools and other friends. Hell, for all he knew he'd mentioned Will and Karl to her. What if she remembered *that*?

Oh man, maybe he should just risk his neck and slide down this sodden mountain through slippery dirt and duff, banging into rocks. And once he got there, he could burst into that damn cabin and take out two people before they could react. They wouldn't be expecting him at all.

And he had been a pretty good marksman even before the Army and he'd kept it up with all the hunting trips and target practice.

He *liked* shooting. A target range was one of his favorite places to spend time.

Or it had been before he'd killed a man.

His alternatives had become so narrow since Will and Karl had told him to kill a man or be killed himself. He could go to the police, turn himself in.

Yeah. And if he pointed a finger at those two, which he

increasingly wanted to do, they'd have each other for alibis. Friends? Friends? Really? He couldn't think of them that way anymore. He'd told them he'd keep his mouth shut, but they'd threatened him anyway.

Psychopaths.

After the way Will had talked to him tonight, he was beginning to wonder if they wouldn't kill him anyway even if he got rid of Blaire Afton.

He swore loudly. There was no one to hear, so why not? He needed to vent the horrible stew of overwhelming anger, hatred, fear and self-loathing he was now living in. Thanks to Will and Karl.

His friends. Lifelong friends. Why had he never before noticed they were missing something essential? That thing that made most people humane: compassion.

How could he have missed that they were basically ice inside and only pretended to be like everyone else?

Well, he'd missed it until just recently, and now he was paying for his blindness. Kinda astonishing that he could know someone for so long and not see the rot at their core.

Now there was rot at his, as well. When this was over, he swore to himself, he would never again speak to either of them. Never. He would banish them from his life and try to find some way to make up for the ugliness that had planted inside him.

But first he had to get through this, and if he was going to get through this, he needed to act soon or there'd never be any atonement.

He shook his head sharply, trying to get rid of the thought. Atonement? Later. Because right now he wasn't sure there could ever be any, even if he spent the rest of his life trying.

He was a wimp. Will had called him that and he was

right. If he weren't such a wimp, he'd have put the gun to his own head.

But then, unbidden, came thoughts of his wife and soon-to-be-born child. He'd managed not to think of them once through this whole mess, managed to keep them separate and clean, and prevent their memories from making him feel any uglier than he already did.

Now they surged to the forefront, and one question froze even his shivering from the cold. How in the hell could he ever touch Dinah again with these soiled hands?

IN THE CABIN, the lattes were almost drained from their tall cups. Gus had drawn Blaire close to his side and kept an arm around her while they sipped and watched the fire dance.

"We'll go out again tomorrow," he told her. "If there's anything left to be found, we'll find it."

She wanted to believe him, but she knew she had to look, unlikely though it was. She wouldn't rest unless she tried. That was how she was built.

"Promise you won't hate me?" he said a few minutes later.

"I don't think I could do that," she said honestly. He'd been there every time she'd needed him for an emotional crisis in the last couple of years. Every time she'd needed him for anything.

"Oh," he answered, "it's always possible."

She shook her head a little. "Why are you afraid I'd hate you?"

"Because I want to cross a line."

She caught her breath as her heart slammed into a faster rhythm. "Gus?" she nearly whispered.

"I want to kiss you," he said quietly but bluntly. "I'm

going out of my mind wanting you. I realize you probably don't feel the same but…"

"Hush," she said, hardly able to keep her breath.

He hushed instantly and started to draw his arm away. That was not at all what she wanted. She twisted around until she was pressed into him and able to look straight at his face.

"Kiss me. Just do it. And don't stop there."

She watched his expression change radically. It went from a little intense to soft warmth. "Blaire, I wasn't…"

"No, but I am. I know I've been trying to hide my attraction to you because I didn't want to damage our friendship, but—" She stopped, all of a sudden afraid that she'd gone way too far, that he might want to get out of here without even that kiss he'd asked for.

Then he spoke, hardly more than a murmur. "I was worried about the same thing. What we have is already irreplaceable."

She nodded, her mouth going dry, her throat threatening to close off and her heart hammering hard enough to leap out of her breast. She'd blown it, and she hadn't been this frightened since her first exposure to hostile fire. "We can keep it," she said hoarsely and hopefully. "We're grown-ups."

"I want a lot more than a kiss from you," he said. "A lot. But if you change your mind…"

"I know how to say no. I'm not saying it."

He started to smile, but before the expression completed, he clamped his mouth over hers in the most commanding, demanding kiss she'd ever felt. Her heart soared as his tongue slipped past her lips and began to plunder her mouth in a timeless rhythm.

Electric sparkles joined the mayhem he'd already set

loose in her, filling her with heat and desire and a longing so strong it almost made her ache.

She'd waited forever, and now the wait was over. He was claiming her in the only way she'd ever wanted to be claimed.

She raised a hand, clutching at his shirt, hanging on to him for dear life. This felt so right, so good. So perfect. *Never let it end.* Then she felt his hand begin to caress her, first down her side, then slipping around front until he cradled her breast.

His touch was gentle, almost respectful, as he began to knead sensitive flesh through layers of sweater, shirt and bra. Those layers might as well have not been there. The thrill from his touch raced through her body all the way to her center until she had to clamp her thighs together. She felt her nipple harden, and when he drew back slightly from the kiss she had to gasp for air.

"You're so beautiful," he whispered, releasing her breast just long enough to brush her hair back from her cheek. "Beautiful. I've had to fight to keep my hands off you."

Music to her soul. When he released her she almost cried out, but he stood and drew her up with him. Then she looked down as he pushed the cardigan off her shoulders and reached for the buttons of her work shirt. She wished she were wearing lace and satin, fancy lingerie, instead of simple cotton, but the wish vanished swiftly as he pushed the shirt off her shoulders and let it fall to the floor.

His gaze drank her in, noting her in a way that made her feel as if he truly never wanted to forget a single line of her. Then with a twist, he released the back clasp of her bra and it, too, drifted to the floor as she spilled free of her confinement.

"Perfect," he muttered, bending his head to suck one of her nipples.

She gasped again as the electric charge ran through her and set off an ache at her center that could be answered only one way. Helplessly she grabbed his head, holding him close, never wanting the sensation to end.

She felt his fingers working the button of her jeans, then his hands pushing them down along with her undies. Then, taking his mouth from her breast, causing her to groan a protest, he urged her back onto the couch.

Her eyes, which had closed at some point she couldn't remember, opened a bit to see him tug her pants off and toss them away. Then without a moment's hesitation he began to strip himself, baring to her hungry gaze the hard lines of a male body at its peak of perfection.

"You're gorgeous," she croaked as he unwrapped himself.

"Not as gorgeous as you," he said huskily.

Man, he was ready for her, and her insides quivered and clenched in recognition. All of him was big, and right now all of him was hard, too.

He reached for her hands and pulled her up until she was pressed against him, front to front, and his powerful arms wrapped around her. As he bent his head to drop kisses on her neck, she shivered with delight and with being naked against his heated nakedness.

There was no feeling in the world, she thought, like skin on skin, like having his hard, satiny member pressed against the flat of her belly, an incitement and a promise.

"Want to go up to the loft or make a pallet down here?" he asked her between kisses.

She sighed, hanging on to her mind with difficulty while he busily tried to strip her to basic instincts. "Climbing that ladder isn't sexy."

"Unless you're the one climbing behind."

Her sleepy eyes popped all the way open as she felt as if she were drowning in the gray pools of his. They wrapped around her like his arms, the color of the stormy sky outside, but bringing a storm of a very different kind. And with them came a sleepy smile.

Teasing her. At a time like this. She loved it as warmth continued to spread into her and turn into heat like lava. Her legs began to quiver, and all she wanted was to feel his weight atop her and his member hard inside her.

He must have felt her starting to slip, because suddenly his hands cupped her rump, such an exquisite and intimate experience, and lifted her. Then he put her carefully on the couch.

"Before one of us falls down," he said thickly, "I'll make that pallet."

Damn, she hated that he'd let her go, but there was nothing she could do except press her legs together in anticipation, waiting for the moment he would satisfy the burgeoning ache inside her.

He grabbed the folded blankets she had given him the night before and spread them on the rug before the hearth, folding them in half for extra padding. The pillow soon joined it. Then before she could stir much at all, he once again lifted her and laid her down on the bed he'd made for the two of them.

Softness below, hardness above, heat from one side and a chill from the other. Sensations overwhelmed her, each seeming to join and augment the hunger he had awakened in her. "Gus…" she whispered, at once feeling weak and yet so strong. Her hands found his powerful shoulders, clinging. Her legs parted, inviting his possession.

Nobody in her life had ever made her feel this hot so swiftly. No one. It was as if he possessed a magic connection to all the nerve endings in her body, so that his least touch made every single one of them tingle with awareness and need.

He kissed her mouth again, deeply but more gently. His hands wandered her shoulders, her neck, and then her breasts. After a few minutes of driving her nearly crazy with longing, his mouth latched onto her nipple, sucking strongly until she arched with each pull of his mouth, feeling devoured but hungrier still. Her hips bucked in response, finding her rhythm, and then, depriving her of breath, he entered her.

Filled, stretched and finding the answer she had so needed, she stilled for just a moment, needing to savor him, needing the moment to last forever.

He must have felt nearly the same, because he, too, stilled, then caught her face between his hands. Her eyelids fluttered and she looked into his eyes, feeling as if she could see all the way to his soul.

Never had any moment felt so exquisite.

HUNGER WASHED THROUGH Gus in powerful waves. He'd had good sex before, but this was beyond any previous experience. Something about Blaire had lit rockets in him, driving him in ways that stole his self-control.

Part of his mind wanted to make this flawless, to give her every possible sensation he could before completion. Most of him refused to listen. There'd be another time for slow exploration, gentle touches and caresses. Time to learn all that delighted her.

Right now he could not ignore the one goal his body drove toward. After those moments of stillness that had seemed to come from somewhere out among the stars, his body took over again, leaving his brain far behind.

A rocket to the moon. A journey beyond the solar

system. A careening sense of falling into the center of the universe.

Everything that mattered was here and now. All of it. Blaire and he became the sole occupants in a special world beyond which nothing else existed.

He pumped into her, hearing her gasps, moans and cries, goaded by them and by the way her hips rose to meet his. Her nails dug into his shoulders, the pain so much a part of the pleasure that they were indistinguishable.

He felt culmination overtake her, felt it in the stiffening of her body and the keening cry that escaped her. He held on to the last shred of his self-control until he heard her reach the peak once more.

Then he jetted into her, into the cosmos. Into a place out of time and mind, feeling as if his entire soul spilled into her.

EVENTUALLY HE CAME BACK to their place in time, aware that he had collapsed on her, that his weight might be uncomfortable. But she was still clinging to his shoulders, and when he tried to roll off she made a small sound of protest, trying to hang on, then let him go.

"My God," he whispered.

"Yeah," she murmured in reply.

Perspiration dried quickly in the heat from the fire. He rolled over and draped an arm around her waist. "You okay?"

"Okay? I don't think I've ever been better."

He saw her smile dawn on her puffy lips. He'd kissed her too hard, but at least she wasn't wincing. That kiss had come from deep within him, expressing a desire he'd been trying to bury since he'd first met her.

But since she wasn't complaining, he wasn't going to apologize. She wiggled around a bit until she faced him and placed her hand on his chest. "We can do this again, right?"

If he hadn't spent every ounce of energy he had on her, he'd have laughed and proved it. Instead he returned her smile and said, "Believe it."

She closed her eyes, still smiling, and ran her palm over his smooth skin. "All this time and I never dreamed how perfect you are without clothing."

"Perfect? You're missing the scars."

"Battle scars," she retorted. "I have a few, too. You didn't point them out and I'm blind to yours. Just take the heartfelt compliment. I knew you were in great shape, I just never imagined such a striking package."

"I can say the same. I've been pining for you since day one."

A quiet little laugh escaped her. "We were behaving."

"We wanted to take care of our friendship."

Her eyes opened wider. "I know. Have we blown it?"

He shook his head slowly. "I don't think so."

"Me, either. This feels incredibly right."

He thought so, too. Holding her close was no longer ruled by the passion between them. He felt a different kind of warmth growing in him, the sense that an emptiness had been filled, that places perennially cold in his heart were thawing. He gave himself up to the gift that felt perilously close to a peace he had forgotten existed.

He was not the kind of man who wished for the impossible, but at that moment he wished he could stay in this place forever, with Blaire in his arms, with the warmth in his heart and soul. To cling to feelings he'd lost so long ago, that had become the detritus of war.

He spent a lot of time *not* thinking about the war. Sometimes it was like trying to avoid the elephant in the room, but he tried to focus on the present day and the needs of the forest he protected and the people he served. Just taking care of Mother Nature and offering a bandage to a kid who'd cut his finger on a sharp piece of wood, those things made him feel good about himself.

So he tried not to remember. Still, the demons roared up out of the depths from time to time. They did for Blaire, too, and when it happened they got together whether in town for a trip to the diner or at one of their headquarters. Sometimes they hardly had to speak at all. A simple word or two would convey everything that was necessary.

They'd been balm for each other for a long time. He actually depended on her and she seemed to depend on him. But this was so very different. This wasn't dependence of any kind. This was a meeting of two souls with a hunger for something greater.

She ran her hand over his back, not paying any special attention to the burn scar that wrinkled his back on one side. "Your skin feels so good," she murmured.

He stroked her side in return. "So does yours. Plus your curves. Enough to drive a guy crazy. Did that give you any trouble on duty?" He'd seen more than enough men crossing the line with women in their units.

"Some. Funny thing, though. After infantry training I wasn't an easy target anymore. Most of them wisely didn't press the issue."

He liked the thought of her scaring the bejesus out of some young fool who thought he was entitled to take what he wanted, to expect some woman to be grateful for his attentions.

"I was also luckier than some because my superiors weren't into sexual harassment at all."

"Fortunate. I saw some of that stuff. I'm glad it overlooked you."

And there they were, returning to the safe—safe?—

ground of their military experience. He could have sighed, and it was all his fault.

Then he found the escape hatch before he totally destroyed the mood. His stomach growled. A giggle escaped Blaire.

"Yeah," he said. "I guess the soup didn't stick. Want me to wander into the kitchen and find something for both of us?"

IN THE END, they slipped into jeans and shirts and went barefoot into the kitchen together. She did have a few things handy, things she didn't usually buy in any kind of quantity because they were too tempting. But tucked into her freezer, lying flat beneath a load of other food, was a frozen pizza.

"I can doctor it with canned mushrooms and some fresh bell peppers," she offered. She'd splurged on a couple of peppers at the store. In fact, as she looked inside her fridge, she saw a whole bunch of splurges she'd hardly been aware of making. Her mood? Or because she had hoped that Gus would stay the night again? The latter, she suspected. Regardless, her usually bare refrigerator was stuffed to the gills tonight.

"Mind if I look around?"

She waved him toward the fridge. "Help yourself. And if you like to cook, so much the better."

But cooking never became involved. He found her brick of white Vermont cheddar cheese, an unopened package of pepperoni slices that she'd almost forgotten she had and a box of wheat crackers in the cupboard. He wielded her chef's knife like a pro and soon had a large plate full of sliced, crumbly cheese with crackers and pepperoni. It looked like a professional job.

"I suppose I should have saved the pepperoni for the

pizza," he said as he carried the plate into the living room and pulled the end table around to hold it. She followed with two cans of cola.

"That pizza is a desperation measure," she answered. "I can always get more pepperoni."

They curled up on the couch together. She tucked her legs beneath herself.

These moments were heavenly, she thought as she nibbled on crackers and cheese. Everything felt so right. She only wished it could last. And it might, for the rest of the night.

But her PTSD was still gnawing at the edges of her mind, trying to warn her of the threat outside, a threat held at bay only by the violent storm.

Except she couldn't be certain there was any threat at all. Just leftover tatters of her mind from some seriously bad experience.

She tried to shake it off and let her head lean against Gus's shoulder. He didn't seem to mind at all. Every so often he passed her a cracker holding a bit of cheese or pepperoni. Taking care of her.

A sudden loud crack of thunder, sounding as if it were right in the room, caused her to start. The bolt of lightning flashed even through the curtains that were closed against the night.

"Wow," she murmured. It awoke memories she didn't want, causing her to leave the comfort of being close to Gus. She rose and began to pace rapidly, wishing the room were a lot bigger.

"Blaire?"

She glanced at him, taking in his frown, but she suspected he knew exactly what was going on. That crack of thunder had sounded like weapons fire. Too loud, too close. Her hands suddenly itched to be holding her rifle, her body to be ducking down behind something until she could locate the threat.

At least she didn't try to hide. She hadn't lost her sense of where she *really* was, but the sound had awakened deeply ingrained impulses. At least there'd been only one crack of thunder. The grumbling continued, but that's all it was, grumbling.

"It was just thunder," Gus said.

But she could tell he was reminding himself as much as her. Some things, she thought, would never be normal again. She hated the fireworks displays the town put on, so she stayed out here rather than joining the celebration. At least fireworks were forbidden in the state park and in the national forest.

Which, of course, didn't mean she never had to put a stop to them and threaten people with arrest if they didn't listen. But walking up to a campsite where people were setting off bottle rockets, reminiscent of the sound of mortars, and firecrackers that sounded like gunshots... That was an effort of will on her part.

"Yeah," she answered Gus.

"I'd pace along with you but I think we'd collide."

"I'm sorry."

"Don't be. It jolted me, too. I'd been out about six months when a kid lit a string of fireworks right behind me. Firecrackers, probably. I swung around instantly into a crouch and I really didn't see him. Didn't see the fireworks. I hate to think what might have happened if my buddy hadn't been there to call me back."

She nodded, understanding completely. Gradually the tension the bolt had set off in her was easing, and after a couple of more minutes she was able to return to the couch. She sat near him, but not right beside him. She didn't think she was ready to be touched yet.

He still held the plate of crackers and cheese that they'd made only a moderate dent on. "Have some more," he said, holding it toward her. "Eating something usually brings me back to the present. Especially something I never had overseas."

The fire had begun to burn down and she considered whether to put another log on it. Mundane thoughts. Safe thoughts. Her taste buds were indeed bringing her back from the cliff edge. Tart cheese, crunchy, slightly bitter wheat crackers. An anchor to the present moment.

At last she was able to look at Gus and smile. The magic of the evening was beginning to return.

JEFF GAVE UP. He didn't care if someone spotted him. He popped open a can of paraffin used to heat foods on the trail and lit the flame with his lighter. Then he set it in front of him, holding his freezing hands over it. Within minutes the survival blanket caught some of the flame's heat and began to reflect it back toward his face.

Thank God. He'd begun to think his nose would fall off from frostbite, although he was sure it wasn't *that* cold. Having to sit out here like this was pure misery, and he wondered that he hadn't started shivering. Although his insulated rain jacket was probably capturing his body heat as effectively as it kept the rain out.

As soon as his fingers felt a little better, he reached inside his jacket and pulled out a pack of cigarettes from his breast pocket. They were a little crushed, but still smokable, and damn he needed a smoke.

The misery of the night was beginning to drive him past moral considerations. He hated his friends even more now, but step by step he made up his mind to get Blaire Afton out of the way so he never needed to do this again.

One shot. He was pretty good at several hundred yards.

Maybe more. That other ranger wouldn't be able to find him fast enough if he picked his spot and knew all the places for concealment or quick escape. First thing in the morning, he promised himself. Then he was going to shoot Blaire in the same way he would shoot a game animal.

After that, having bought a few days, he was going to move to Timbuktu or some other faraway place so that Will and Karl would leave him alone. Forever. He just wanted to be left alone forever. Dinah and his baby would be better off without him. Yeah, he could run as far as he wanted.

And he didn't care if it was called running because, damn it, he needed to run for his life. He no longer trusted those guys not to kill him anyway. They weren't going to let him go simply because he'd done what he'd been told to do.

Then another thought crept into his brain. Why shoot Blaire if it wasn't going to save his own life?

Double damn, he thought. Why had he needed to think of that? Because, he reminded himself, killing her would give him time to make plans and extricate himself. He couldn't just march out of here tomorrow and be on a plane by midnight. Nothing was that easy, even without thinking of his family.

He started making a mental list as he continued to warm his hands. Passport. Cash. Arranging for his bank and credit cards to accept charges from overseas. Clothes. He needed to take at least some clothing with him. He wasn't rich like the other two and couldn't be needlessly wasteful.

But he *did* have enough to get away to some cheaper place, and enough to sustain him until he could find some kind of work. He didn't mind getting his hands dirty, he was strong and healthy, and educated. He ought to be able to find something somewhere.

Regardless, he figured if he left the country, Will and Karl would lose all interest in him. He wouldn't be around to make them nervous, or to annoy them. Out of sight, out of mind would most likely apply because he didn't think either one of them would want to waste time tracking him down in some other country.

Yeah. Kill the woman and hightail it. The plan would work. He just needed to take care the other ranger couldn't find him first. Hell, he ought to shoot the man, as well. Will had suggested it. It would certainly buy him time to leave this park behind, to get out of the mountains.

Another thing to hash over in his mind as he sat there in misery. He hardly even noticed that the storm rolled out after midnight. All *that* did was make the night colder.

Damn, his life sucked.

Chapter Eleven

Blaire and Gus made their way up to her loft bedroom instead of feeding the fire on the stone hearth. Heat rose and it had filled the loft, which captured it. Blaire's predecessor had used the room farthest back in this cabin for a bedroom, but it hadn't taken long for Blaire to figure out the loft stayed warmer on frigid winter nights. She burned less fuel and didn't need to use space heaters. She now used the back room for storage.

Her successor would probably change everything around, a thought that occasionally amused her. As it was, she had a tidy space, big enough for a queen bed, a small chest of drawers, a night table, a chair and a lamp. Inconvenient as far as needing a bathroom, but it was a small price to pay.

She had to warn Gus to watch out for his head, though. The loft ceiling nearly scraped her head.

"This is cozy," he remarked. The light had several settings and she had turned it on low so he was cast in a golden glow.

"*Cozy* is a pleasant word for *tiny*," she answered. "But I like it."

"I can see why. Nice and warm, too."

Three or four minutes later they were both tucked under her comforter, naked and locked in tight embrace.

This time Gus used his mouth and tongue to explore her, at one point disappearing beneath the covers to kiss and lick her sweet center until she thought she was going to lose her mind. When she was sure she couldn't stand it anymore, she turned the tables, rising over him to discover his defined muscles, the hollows between them and finally the silky skin of his erection. It jumped at her first touch, and she felt an incredible sense of power and pleasure, unlike anything she'd ever felt.

But he was doing a lot of that to her, giving her new sensations and a new appreciation of sex. This was in no way the mundane experience she'd had in the past. This was waking her to an entirely new view of being a woman.

She enjoyed his every moan and shudder as her tongue tried to give him the same pleasures he had shared with her earlier. Finally his hands caught her shoulders and pulled her up. Straddling his hips, she took him inside her, then rested on him, feeling as if they truly became one.

Their hips, welded together, moved together, and the rising tide of passion swept her up until it carried her away almost violently. They reached the peak together, both of them crying out simultaneously.

Then, feeling as if she floated on the softest cloud, Blaire closed her eyes and drifted away.

LYING LIKE SPOONS beneath the covers, Gus cradled her from behind, holding her intimately. She felt his warm breath against the back of her ear, and even as sleep tried to tug at her, she spoke.

"That was heaven."

"If that was heaven, sign me up." Then he gave a whispery laugh. "I'm sure it was better."

She smiled into the dark in response. "I don't think I've ever felt this good."

"Me, either." He pressed a kiss to her cheek, then settled back again. Their heads shared the same pillow and she could feel his every move. "I hate to be the practical one, but the storm has passed and if you want to ride out in the morning…"

She sighed. "We need to sleep. I know. I've been fighting it off because I don't want to miss a minute of this."

"This won't be the last minute," he answered. "Unless you tell me to take a hike, I plan on being right here with you tomorrow night."

She hesitated. "What about Holly?"

"She always wanted to replace me."

Blaire gasped. "Seriously?"

He chuckled. "Not really. But she enjoys ruling the roost sometimes. Which is the only reason I can ever take a vacation or get to town. Holly is the best, but she's told me more than once that she likes being able to point at me when someone's unhappy."

"Ooh, not so nice." She was teasing and she could tell he knew it when he laughed.

"She has her moments, all right." She felt him pull her a little closer. "Sleep," he said. "It's going to be a long day in the saddle."

IN THE EARLY MORNING, before the sun had risen when the light was still gray, Gus went to the corral out back to check on the horses. They regarded him almost sleepily and stood close together because the chill had deepened overnight. Remembering summers elsewhere, he sometimes wondered how folks could ever really think of this climate as having a summer. A few hot days, but up here in the forest on the mountain little of that heat reached them. Eighty degrees was a heat wave.

The lean-to over one part of the corral, against the

cabin, seemed to have done its job. The wind must have been blowing from a different direction because the feed was dry and if the horses had gotten wet at all, he couldn't tell. Even their blankets seemed mostly dry.

They nickered at him, apparently glad to see a human face. He could well imagine. The night's rain had left a lot of mud behind, and that wasn't good for them to stand in. He needed to move them out of here soon.

He loved the morning scents of the woods after a storm, though. The loamy scent of the forest floor, the pines seeming to exhale their aroma with delight…all of it. Fresh, clean and unsullied by anything else.

Well, except horse poop, he corrected himself with amusement. Grabbing a shovel that leaned against the cabin wall, he scooped up as much as he could find and dumped it into the compost pile on the other side of the fence. He wondered if the compost ever got put to use. He knew some folks came up to grab a load or two of his in the spring for their backyard gardens. Maybe they came here, too. He turned some of it and felt the heat rise. Good. It was aging.

Smelly, though, he thought with amusement. So much for that fresh morning aroma.

The sky had lightened a little more as he returned inside, wondering if he should start breakfast or let Blaire sleep. He was used to running on only a couple of hours of sleep in the field. Today wouldn't be a problem for him. He didn't know about her.

As he stepped inside, he smelled bacon. Well, that answered the question. He passed the kitchen area to the bathroom, where he washed his hands, then returned to Blaire.

"Morning," he said. "I hope I didn't wake you when I got up."

"Not really. I was starting to stir. How are the horses?"

"Champs. They're fine, but they really need a ride today. At the moment they're standing in mud."

She turned from the stove to look at him and he thought he saw a slight pinkening of her cheeks. "Bad for them?"

"Bad for their hooves if they stand too long. A few hours won't cause a problem, I'm sure, but I know they'd feel better if they could dry off their feet."

"Who wouldn't?" She turned back to the stove and flipped some strips of bacon.

"Can I help?"

"Make some toast if you want it. We've got power this morning, amazingly enough. I was sure that storm would have left us blacked out. Anyway, the toaster's over there. We don't have to use the flame on the stove."

He found a loaf of wheat bread next to the toaster and a butter dish with a full stick. He dug out a knife and began by popping two slices of bread into the toaster. "Did you ever see those four-sided metal tents you could use to make toast over a gas flame?"

She thought a moment. "Those things with the little wooden handles so you could pull down the piece that held the bread in place against the grill? My great-grandmother had one, but I never saw her use it."

"I've sometimes thought I'd like to find one somewhere. Power goes out over at my place, too, and I like my toast."

"Then we ought to look for one. Now that you mention it, that would probably help me out a lot in the winter."

He watched her fork bacon onto a plate with a paper

towel on it. She immediately placed more strips in the pan. "I stuck my nose outside," she said. "It's cold, isn't it?"

"Relatively. We'll need jackets and gloves for certain."

"Then we should eat hearty. Stoke the internal heater."

He absolutely didn't have any problem with that.

THEY RODE OUT after the sun crested the mountains far to the east. It hung red and hazy for a while, then brightened to orange. Soon it became too brilliant to look at.

The cold clung beneath the trees, however. At Gus's suggestion they started circling the murder scene about two hundred yards out.

"He had to watch for a while before moving in," Gus said needlessly as they had already discussed this. "So he'd have some kind of hide. Maybe use one left by another hunter."

She was riding beside him as their path through the trees allowed it. A slight shudder escaped her. "I don't like the way you phrased that. *Another* hunter. Like this guy was after deer or elk."

She had a point. "I hope you know I didn't mean it that way."

"I do," she acknowledged.

"You okay?"

"Hell, no," she answered frankly. "Ants of bad memories are crawling up and down my spine, and occasionally all over me. If you mowed this forest to the ground, maybe then I'd be able to believe there isn't an ambush out here waiting for us."

"I read you." Yeah, he did. It might all be PTSD from their time in war, but whether it was didn't matter. They couldn't afford to ignore it until they were *sure* the shooter wasn't out here.

A little farther along, she spoke again. "We started this whole idea to find evidence."

"True."

"How much could be left after that storm last night? Seriously."

He shook his head but refused to give in to the despair that sometimes accompanied the memories. His brain had a kink in it since Afghanistan and all he could do was make the best use of it he might. Ignoring it never won the day.

They used both GPS and a regular compass to navigate their way around a wide arc. The GPS didn't always catch a weak satellite signal through the trees, but as soon as another satellite was in place it would strengthen. In the interim, when the signal failed, they used the old-fashioned method.

About an hour later, Blaire made a sound of disgust. "I haven't yet been able to see the Jasper tent through the trees. If someone was going to observe, he'd need the sight line or he'd have to be a lot closer. What's the smart money?"

Gus reined in Scrappy and waited until Blaire came fully beside him, their legs almost touching.

"Here." He reached into his saddlebag and pulled out a huge pair of binoculars that would have served a sniper's crew well. "Look upslope and see what catches your attention."

"Why up?"

"Because if there's a high spot up there, or even along this arc, those trees aren't necessarily going to matter. We don't have to see *through* them."

She gave him a crooked smile. "Which is why you were special ops and I wasn't." She looked upslope again. "You're right, I'm probably looking in the wrong direction."

"We should look both ways. In case he might have found an open sight line here, too."

"I hope we're not on a fool's errand," she remarked as they moved forward.

"We've got to look. Neither of us is the type to sit on our hands." Nor did he want to tell her that he could swear he felt eyes boring into the back of his neck. Those sensations had never let him down in the 'Stan, but they hadn't always been right, either.

Even so... "You know, Blaire, we're both concerned he's still hanging around, but I can't understand why he would."

"I can't understand why he killed that poor man in the first place. Besides, I've heard criminals like to come back to the scene. To relive their big moment. To see what the cops are doing. We're looking. Maybe he's interested in that. Maybe it makes him feel important."

"Possibly." He tilted his head a little, looking at his display and seeing the GPS was down again. He pulled the compass out of his breast pocket to make sure they were still following their planned route. So far so good. He looked downslope again but saw only trees. A lot of trees. He could have sighed. "That was good reasoning, you know."

She had been looking upslope with the binoculars. "What was?"

He smiled. "Your rationale for why he still might be here. Maybe our senses are completely off-kilter."

She lowered her head for a moment, then said something that made his heart hurt. "I hope not. I'm still learning to trust my perceptions again."

THEY WERE GETTING too close, Jeff thought. He'd made his way back to the hide atop a big boulder from which he'd watched the campground. It would give some hunter a panorama for tracking game. For him it gave a view of the killing field.

He caught himself. That was too dramatic. That called to mind the most god-awful massacre, and he didn't want to associate with that, even in a private moment of thought.

But putting his binoculars to his eyes, he watched the two of them. If he took Blaire out now, the guy might dismount to take care of her. Would he have time to get away before the man came looking for him?

He looked up the slope and recalled the night of the shooting. He'd had to go into the campground that night, right to the tent. This time he could keep a much safer distance and just hightail it. It wasn't as far, and he knew the way. He ought to since he'd covered the path so many times.

Shooting Blaire might spook the horses, too. The guy—Gus, he thought—might get thrown. That would be helpful. Of course, a man could probably run faster over this terrain than a horse could. But would he leave Blaire if she was bleeding?

Yeah, if she was already dead.

Crap.

He rolled over again and watched the two of them. If they came up any higher, he was going to have to retreat from this spot. He had little doubt they'd find it. It worked as a deer blind, not a human blind. The guy who'd built this nest hadn't wanted it to be impossible to find in subsequent years. Too much work had gone into it, such as moving heavy rocks for a base.

Damn, he wanted a cigarette. The thought made him look down and he realized he'd left a heap of butts already. Damn! He scooped them up and began to stuff them into a pocket. Not enough to leave a shell casing behind. No, now he'd leave DNA for sure. Maybe Will was right to scorn him.

No, Will wasn't right. Will wasn't right about a damn thing except he needed to make sure Blaire didn't have a sudden memory of him and make a connection.

Then Jeff was going to clear his butt out of this country.

His thoughts stuttered a bit and he wondered if his thinking was getting screwed up. Energy bars barely staved off the cold and he was almost out of them. Maybe his brain was skipping important things.

But he knew one thing for sure. If he went back without killing that woman, Will and Karl were going to kill *him*. So he had to do it. Just to buy time.

He needed those two to split up a little more. More space between them, more distance. He didn't want to add *two* people to a body count that shouldn't even exist.

He closed his eyes briefly, wishing himself on another planet. Or even dead and buried. Anything but lying here watching a woman he had nothing against, waiting for an opportunity to shoot her as if she were a game animal.

It was self-defense, he told himself. Indirectly, perhaps, but he needed to defend himself and this was the only way. Self-defense. He kept repeating it like a mantra.

GUS DREW REIN and Scrappy slowed, then stopped. Realizing it, Blaire slowed Lita down and looked over at him. "Something wrong?"

"Scrappy just started to limp. Maybe he's got a loose shoe or something. I need to check. Give me a minute?"

"Of course." She watched him dismount, then turned her attention to the woods around them. She just didn't see any place yet that would have given the shooter a clear view of the campground. They needed to get higher, unless Scrappy was truly lame, in which case they'd have to head back.

Because she was busy telling herself this was a fool's errand, they'd never find anything useful and it was simply born of their military training that required them to act against a threat… Well, she wouldn't necessarily mind if they had to call this off. She loved being out here on horseback, and Lita was a great mount, but the sense of danger lurking around every tree was ruining it and probably ridiculous besides.

Since she'd left the combat zone for the last time, she'd been forced to realize how powerful post-traumatic stress could be. She hadn't been inflicted with it as badly as some of her former comrades, but she had it. Enough to make her uneasy for no damn good reason, like the last few days.

A random murder had occurred. It might not even be random at all. They wouldn't know that until the police collected more evidence. But right now, riding through the woods, hoping to find the place from which the shooter could have observed the campground, had its footing more in her memories than in the present.

Yeah, it was creepy, but *this* creepy? She needed to talk herself down. Needed to accept that the killer was long gone and every bit of the uneasiness she couldn't shake was being internally generated by a heap of bad memories that couldn't quite be buried.

Then maybe she could get back to doing her job, and Gus could get back to doing his. Holly and Dave might not mind standing in for them for a while, but it wasn't fair. They both had jobs to do and they were letting them slide because neither of them could quite believe in the safety of the woods.

That thought caused her to sit back in the saddle.

Couldn't believe in the safety of the woods? Seriously? This retreat she had come to in order to escape the bustle of the busy, populated world because it somehow grated on her and kept her on alert too much? It no longer felt safe?

God, this was bad. Maybe she needed to get some counseling. Never had the detritus of her military experience gotten this far out of hand. Nightmares, yeah. Disliking crowds, yeah. But the woods? The safe haven she'd found here?

"It seems he got a stone in his hoof," Gus said, dropping Scrappy's right foreleg to the ground.

"Do we need to go back?"

"Nah. I've got a tool in my saddlebag. I'll get it out in a minute and then we can move on."

She watched him come around Scrappy's left side and unbuckle the saddlebag. "Is he bruised?"

"I don't know yet. He didn't limp for long, so I hope not."

"Well…if he needs a rest…" She trailed off as it hit her how far away they were now from everything. Miles from her cabin. Probably miles from the dirt road. Could they shortcut it through the woods? Maybe. It all depended on how many ravines were lurking between here and there. So far they'd been lucky. At any moment the mountain could throw up a huge stop sign.

"It'll be fine," Gus said as he pulled out the tool. "We can always walk them, but I don't think it'll be necessary."

Blaire felt the punch before she heard the report. She started to fall sideways and grabbed the saddle horn only to feel it slip from her fingers. She felt another blow, this one to her head as she wondered with confusion why she was on the ground. Then everything went black.

JEFF HAD A clear escape route. He could run up to the cave like a mountain goat, nothing in his way from here. When the guy dismounted his horse and started to check its hoof, it seemed like a fateful opportunity. He had a clear shot at Blaire, and from over two hundred yards he had no doubt he could make it.

If he was one thing, he was a superb marksman with this rifle. One shot was all he'd need.

He looked downslope and liked what he saw. Damn fool ranger wouldn't be able to reach this spot fast. Too many rocks, a ravine that looked deep enough to swallow him and his horse. It made great protection for Jeff.

Okay, then.

Lifting his rifle to his shoulder, he pulled the bolt to put a shell in the chamber. Then, with his elbows resting on a rock, he looked through the scope. Suddenly Blaire was big, a huge target.

Holding his breath, steadying his hands until the view from the scope grew perfectly still, he fired. He waited just long enough to see Blaire fall from her horse.

Then he grabbed his pack and gun and started to run uphill. He didn't wait to see the result. He didn't need to. He was a damn fine shot.

What he hadn't seen was that the man was looking right in his direction when he fired.

GUS REMOVED THE STONE from Scrappy's foot and tossed it away. Bending, he looked closely and saw nothing worrisome. He straightened and looked up at Blaire, who was still straddling Lita. "He might be a bit tender later, but he's fine to continue."

"Good," she said.

Then the entire world shifted to slow motion. He saw

a flash from up in the woods some distance away. His mind registered it as a muzzle flash. Only then did he hear the familiar *crack*.

Before he could act, he saw red spread across Blaire's sleeve and begin to drip on her hand. He had to get her down. *Now.*

She reached for the saddle horn, but before he could get there, she tipped sideways and fell off Lita. He heard the thud as her head hit the ground.

Everything inside him froze. The clearheaded state of battle washed over him, curling its ice around everything within him, focusing him as nothing else could.

He left Scrappy standing and dealt with Lita, who was disturbed enough by the sound and Blaire's tumble to be dancing nervously. He feared she might inadvertently trample Blaire as she lay on the ground, so he grabbed her by the bridle, then grabbed Scrappy with his other hand.

He knew horses well enough to know that Scrappy might react to Lita's nervousness and begin to behave the same way. While it wasn't usually necessary, he used the reins to tie Scrappy to a tree trunk along with Lita.

They nickered and huffed, an equine announcement of *let's get out of here*, but he was sure they weren't going anywhere.

Only then, what seemed like years later but couldn't have been more than a half minute, he knelt next to Blaire. She had the rag doll limpness he recognized as unconsciousness, and he feared how badly she might have hit her head.

But there was a sequence, and the first thing he needed to do was stanch the blood from her wound. Time slowed down until it dragged its heels. Only experience had taught him that was adrenaline speeding up his mind, that time still moved at its regular pace.

With adrenaline-powered strength, he ripped the sleeve of her jacket open and kept tearing until he could see where the blood was heaviest. Then he tore her shirt and revealed her shoulder, turning her partly over to see her back as well as her front.

A through-and-through wound, bleeding from both sides, but not through the artery, thank God. Bad enough, but no spurts. Grabbing the sleeve he had just torn, he ripped it in half and pushed it against the two holes, front and back, as hard as he could.

He could use her jacket sleeve for a tourniquet, he thought, but his mind was only partly on first aid. "Blaire. Blaire?"

Her unconsciousness worried him as much as anything. How hard had she hit her head? Head wounds could be the absolute worst, even though he was sure he could stop the bleeding from her shoulder.

He kept calling her name as he wound the jacket sleeve around her shoulder, making it tight. Stop the bleeding. Find a way to wake her up.

Only then could he search out the shooter, and he damn well knew where he was going to start.

BLAIRE CAME TO with a throbbing head and a shoulder that was throbbing even harder. She cussed and suddenly saw Gus's face above hers.

"Thank God," he said. "You hit your head."

"How long was I out and who shot me?"

"You were out for about two minutes and I don't know yet who shot you. But I saw the muzzle flash."

"Then go get him, Gus."

"No. I REALLY WANT to but I'm worried about you. I need to get you help."

She tried to sit up, wincing a bit, so he helped her, propping her against a tree.

"I don't think you lost a lot of blood," he said, "but if you start to get light-headed, you know what to do."

"Not my first rodeo," she said between her teeth. "The blow to my head wasn't that bad. I'm not seeing double or anything. The headache is already lessening. The shoulder... Well, it hurts like hell but I can't feel any serious damage." She moved her arm.

"The shooter messed up," she said after a few moments. "Just a flesh wound. He must have used a full metal jacket." Meaning that the bullet hadn't entered her shattering and spinning, causing a lot of internal damage.

"Blaire..."

She managed a faint smile. "I always wanted to say that."

He flashed a grin in response. "Your head is okay."

"My shoulder's not too bad, either."

He rested his hand on her uninjured shoulder, aware that time was ticking, both for her and for the escaping shooter. "I'm going to radio for help for you. Then, if you think you're okay by yourself for a bit, I'm going after that bastard."

With her good arm, she pushed herself up. "I'm coming with you."

"Stop. Don't be difficult, Blaire. You've been shot."

She caught his gaze with hers. "I've also been in combat. So have you. Trust me, I can judge my own fitness. There's a ravine up there and I know the way around it. What's more, he obviously has a long-range weapon. Do you? Do you really want to go after him alone? He could be perched anywhere."

He frowned at her, a frown that seemed to sink all the way to his soul. "You might start bleeding again."

"If I do, I'll tell you. This feels like you've got me bandaged pretty well. Quit frowning at me. I won't be stupid."

"Riding up there is stupid," he said flatly. But looking at her, he realized he was fighting a losing battle. If she could find a way to get herself back on Lita, she'd follow him. Never had he seen such a stubborn set to a woman's jaw. He wanted to throw up his hands in frustration. "I'm trained for this," he reminded her. "Solo missions."

"I'm trained, too," she retorted. With a shove, she reached her feet and remained steady. "See, I'm not even weak from blood loss. I'm *fine*."

Well, there were different definitions of that word, but he gave up arguing even though he had an urge to tie her to that tree. But, he understood, if that shooter realized she was still alive, he might be circling around right now. He could get in another shot without being seen.

"Hell and damnation," he growled. But he gave in. Better to keep her close.

He had to help her mount Lita since she had only one workable arm, but once she was astride the horse, feet in the stirrups, she looked fine. No paleness to her face, no sagging. Maybe the wound wasn't that awful.

It was her left shoulder that was injured and she was right-handed. Like many of the rangers out here who needed to go into the woods, she carried a shotgun as well as a pistol. The shotgun was settled into a holster in front of her right thigh, and before he would allow her to move, he asked her to prove she could pull it out and use it with one arm. She obliged while giving him an annoyed look.

"It's a shotgun," she said. "I hardly have to be accurate."

If he weren't getting hopping mad, he might have

smiled. "I just need to be sure you can use it. And I'm radioing this in, like it or not. We aren't going to play solitary superheroes out here."

Damn! He'd gone from violent fear that she was dead into relief that she was reasonably okay and now he was so mad he was ready to kill.

Someone had shot her. Why? Hell, he didn't care why. Whoever it was, needed to be grabbed by the short and curlies, tied up in handcuffs and marched to jail.

As they moved farther upslope, his radio found an area with clear satellite transmission, and he gave the sheriff's office a rundown as they rode, including that Blaire had been wounded but was riding at his side. He asked they be tracked, and dispatch promised they would.

Insofar as possible, he thought as he hooked the radio onto his belt again. He kept glancing at Blaire to be sure she was still all right and wondered if she had any idea how distracting she was. This wasn't helping the search much. His concern for her wasn't making him a better hunter.

He would have liked to be able to shield her with his body, but since there was no way to know if the guy might circle around and take another shot, there was no safe place for her to ride. He suggested she lead the way because she knew how to get around the ravine, and all he had to do was point out where he had seen the muzzle flash. Plus, he could see if she started to weaken.

She was a born navigator with a lot of experience. She guided with surety, part of the trip taking them away from the area from which he'd seen the flash, much more of it angling toward it and up as they left the ravine behind.

He glanced down into that ravine as they crossed a narrow ledge of rock and realized there'd have been no way to cross it directly. None. The shooter was probably counting on it to slow them down.

But their horses moved swiftly when the terrain allowed. Soon they found a trampled muddy place that he'd probably been using. From there his trail was clear for about twenty feet or so, giving them direction, then it disappeared in the sopping duff and loam beneath the trees.

She drew rein and waited for him to catch up to her. "He probably followed as straight a path uphill as he could. For speed?"

He nodded. "I agree."

"And there's a road on the other side of that ridge," she said, pointing. "Not much of one, little more than a cart track used by hunters, but he could have left a vehicle there."

"I bet." He paused. "Let's speed up. This is a rough climb. He had to get winded. To slow down."

But the horses wouldn't, he thought. They'd just keep climbing steadily and as quickly as they could, as if they sensed the urgency. They probably did. Horses were sensitive animals.

He kept one eye on Blaire while he scanned the area around them. The guy might have angled away from a straight path. It all depended on how scared he was and how much time he thought he'd have. If the shooter thought Blaire was down, he might think he had a lot of time.

He hoped so. The fury in him had grown cold, a feeling he remembered from other conflicts. He was riding its wave, heedless of danger to himself, focused on the mission, focused on Blaire's safety. Nothing else mattered.

She, too, was scanning around them, but he had little hope they'd see much. The shooter probably had the sense to wear woodland camouflage, although the higher they climbed the thinner the trees grew. They were nowhere near the tree line, but for some reason the growth here was thinner. He tried to remember if there'd been a fire here at some point. The ground was plenty brushy, but the trees didn't seem as big or as stout as they had farther below.

Then he saw it. A flash of movement above them.

"Blaire."

She halted and looked back at him.

"I think I saw him. We're sitting ducks right now. We'd better split up." He hated to suggest it, given that she was wounded, probably suffering a great deal of pain and maybe even weakening. But together they made a great target.

"Where?" she asked quietly.

"Eleven o'clock. About three hundred yards upslope."

"Got it."

Then with a brief nod she turned Lita a bit, angling away from where he'd seen the movement. Misleading as if she were going to look elsewhere.

He did the same heading the other direction, but not too much, teeth clenched until his jaw screamed, hoping that their split wouldn't tell the guy they'd seen him.

Then Blaire called, "I think I saw something over here."

Did she want him to come her way? Or was she sending their intended misdirection up to the shooter?

"I'll be there in a minute," he called back. "Need room to turn around."

"Yo," she answered, her voice sounding a little fainter.

The brief conversation gave him the chance to look up again to the spot where he'd seen movement. There was more movement now. Rapid. Then something happened and he heard rocks falling. A man's shape, suddenly visible, lost its upward momentum and instead he seemed to be scrambling frantically.

Gotcha, he thought with burning satisfaction. "Now, Scrappy." He touched the horse with his heels, speeding him up. If ever he had needed this horse to be sure-footed, he needed it now. Scrappy didn't disappoint.

With amazing speed, the horse covered the ground toward the man, who was still struggling as more rocks tumbled on him from above. The guy had evidently made a serious misstep and gotten into a patch of very loose scree.

Taking it as a warning, Gus halted Scrappy about two hundred feet back, then dismounted, carrying his shotgun with him. He approached cautiously, aware that the guy was armed and desperate.

Then he swore as he saw Blaire emerge from the trees on the other side. He was hoping to have dealt with this before she entered the danger zone. He was, however, glad to see she'd unholstered her shotgun and angled Lita so she could use it.

"Keep a bead on him," Gus called to her as he hurried carefully toward the man.

The guy turned over, his rifle in his hands, looking as if he were ready to shoot. Gus instantly squatted and prepared to take aim, but the man evidently realized he was outnumbered. If he shot in any direction, one of two shotguns would fire at him.

"Put the rifle away," Gus demanded, rising and making it clear that he was ready to shoot. "Now."

He could see the guy's face clearly, reflecting panic. He looked around wildly, his feet pushing at the scree beneath him but gaining no purchase.

"Give up," Blaire called. "You wouldn't be the first man I've shot."

Well, that was blunt, Gus thought, easing closer to their quarry. Vets didn't like to say things like that. He hoped to hell that wasn't the blow to her head talking.

"I've got him," Gus called when he was ten feet away. Resignation had replaced panic on the guy's face. He took one hand from his rifle, and with the other tossed the weapon to the side.

Then he said the strangest thing: "I'm so glad I didn't kill her."

Chapter Twelve

A half hour later, with Jeff Walston securely bound in zip ties, Gus heard the sound of helicopter rotors from overhead. Medevac was on the way, and as he'd been told over the radio, a couple of cops were riding along.

Good. He needed to be away from the source of his anger. He had enough experience to know he wouldn't take it out on his prisoner, but he had never liked the uncomfortable, conflicting emotions the situation brought out in him. The guy could have killed Blaire. Maybe had wanted to. It would have been easy for Gus to treat him like a soccer ball.

But he didn't. Instead he sat beside Blaire, whom he'd helped to dismount and sit against a tree. For all she had claimed it was just a flesh wound, it was taking a toll on her. He was amazed at the strength and determination that had brought her this far.

"I wouldn't have minded having you on my team over there," he told her.

"That's quite a compliment," she murmured. "Thanks, Gus."

"You're remarkable."

"I'm a soldier." That seemed to be all she needed to say. From his perspective, it was quite enough.

Because of the chaotic winds aloft so near the peak of

the mountain, the helicopter couldn't come very close or low. Through the trees he caught glimpses of three people sliding down ropes to the ground, and after them came a Stokes basket.

Then another wait.

"I wish I could go to the hospital with you," Gus said. "But the horses…"

"I know. Take care of the horses. They were good comrades today, weren't they?" She smiled wanly. "Gus?"

"Yeah?"

"I think I was running on adrenaline."

That didn't surprise him at all, but before he could respond, three men burst out of the trees in tan overalls. He instantly recognized Seth Hardin, a retired Navy SEAL who'd helped build the local rescue operations into a finely honed operation.

They shook hands briefly as the other two put Blaire on the basket and strapped her in. Gus repeated her injuries to the two EMTs, then watched them race back through the woods to get Blaire onto the helicopter.

Seth remained with him. "I'll keep watch over the prisoner if you want to head back."

Gus nodded. "I need to take care of two horses. But FYI, I didn't touch the guy's weapon or much of anything except to put the zip ties on him."

Seth arched a brow. "That must have required some restraint."

"Exactly." They shared a look of understanding, then Gus rose. "You armed?"

Seth patted his side, pointing out the rather obvious pistol attached to his belt. "Of course."

"You want one of our shotguns? He said he's alone but…"

"Hey, you know what we're capable of. I'll be fine. I'm

just going to make sure this creep can't move an inch, then I'll stand back and pay attention. It won't be for long. The second chopper is supposed to be following with some more cops. You just get out of here. You don't need to wear a neon sign to tell me how worried you are about Blaire."

JEFF WALSTON WANTED to spill his guts. He started talking in the helicopter and by the time Gus was able to reach town, they had a pretty clear picture of the so-called Hunt Club.

It was an ugly one. Micah Parish filled him in as Gus drove to the hospital. Gus listened with only one ear. He could get the nitty-gritty later, but right now he was badly worried about Blaire. Blood on the outside of the body didn't necessarily mean there wasn't internal bleeding. She'd held on, probably longer than she would have without a flood of adrenaline coursing through her, but now the question was how much damage had she worsened with her stubbornness.

At the hospital they wouldn't tell him much except that she was now in recovery. He could see her when she woke up.

The wait was endless. His pacing could have worn a path in the waiting room floor. Still, pieces began to fall together in his mind. He began to see exactly where he wanted to go.

It kind of shocked him, but as it settled in, he knew it was right.

BEFORE BLAIRE EVEN opened her eyes she knew where she was. She'd been in the hospital before, and the odors plus the steady beeping of equipment placed her firmly in her present location.

As she surfaced slowly from the drugs, memory returned. Being shot, the insane ride through the woods that she would have been smarter not to do, helping Gus capture the bad guy. The ride in the Stokes basket up to the helicopter. Then nothing.

She moved a little and felt that her wound had changed. Probably surgery, she thought groggily. Yeah, her throat felt raw, so there'd been a breathing tube.

It was over. She'd be fine. She didn't need a doctor to tell her that. She'd been in worse condition once before from a roadside incendiary device. That time she'd been saved by luck as much as anything, being on the far side of the vehicle.

"Blaire."

A quiet voice. Gus. He was here. Warmth suffused her, and a contradictory sense of happiness. Lying post-op in a hospital bed seemed like an odd place to feel that warmth.

At last the anesthesia wore off enough that she could open her eyes. They lighted instantly on Gus, who was sitting beside her bed.

"Blaire," he said again, and smiled. A wide, genuine smile that communicated more than words. She was okay and he was happy and relieved about it. Then she sensed him gently taking her hand.

"Welcome back," he said. "You're fine."

"What was that all about?" she asked, her voice thick. "The guy. What was he doing?"

He told her about The Hunt Club, about how the man they had captured had been forced into committing two murders by threats against his life.

"Sport?" That almost made her mind whirl. "They were doing this for sport?"

"Two of them, evidently. They've been rounded up. The full truth will come out with time, but right now the man we caught seems eager to talk."

"Good." Then she slipped away again, still under the influence of surgical medications.

She had no sense of how much time had passed, but when she came to again, her shoulder throbbed like mad. "Damn," she said.

"Blaire?" Gus's voice again. "What's wrong?"

"My shoulder hurts worse than when I was shot."

"I'm not surprised. No adrenaline now, plus I guess they had to do some work inside you. One of the docs said you were lucky your lung didn't collapse."

Those words woke her up completely. "What?"

"You were bleeding internally. Next time you want to ride a horse when you've been shot, please reconsider." Then he pressed a tube into her hand. "Top button. Call the nurse for some painkiller."

She certainly needed some. She pressed the button and a voice came over the speaker over her head. "Nurse's station."

"Something for pain, please."

"Be there shortly."

Then she dropped the tube and her fingers reached for Gus. He replied by clasping her hand.

"Listen," he said. "You were tough. You *are* tough, as tough as anyone I've known."

Something important was coming. She could sense it. All of a sudden she didn't want that nurse to hurry. She wanted to listen to him.

"I know we've avoided this," Gus continued. "But I refuse to avoid it any longer. Nearly losing you… Well, it kind of yanked me out of stasis."

"You, too?"

He nodded. "We don't have long. I'm sure you're about to get knocked out again. But tuck this away for when you're feeling better because I don't want to take advantage of you."

"How could you?" She thought she heard the nurse's rubbery steps in the hall. Her heart began to accelerate. "Gus?"

"I love you," he said simply. "And if you don't mind, I'd like to marry you. But don't answer now. Just put it away until you're back on your feet. I promise not to pressure you. I just needed you to know."

Just as the nurse wearing blue scrubs appeared in the doorway, she felt her heart take flight. "Pressure away," she said. Then the needle went into the IV port. "I love you, too," she said before she vanished into the haze again.

A MONTH LATER, they stood before Judge Wyatt Carter and took their vows. They'd agreed to keep their jobs, to feel out their path into the future.

And they'd promised each other they were going to attend the trials of The Hunt Club. A game? Just a game had cost five lives? It was an appalling idea. It appalled Blaire even more to recognize Jeff Walston and remember they'd served briefly together. A man known to her!

But that faded as they stepped out of the courthouse into a sunny August morning. The bride wore a street-length white dress and the groom wore his best Forest Service uniform.

A surprising number of people awaited them outside and began to clap. Turning to each other, they kissed, drawing more applause.

They had friends and had found love and a new way of life.

"Upward," he murmured. "Always. I love you."

* * * * *

COMING SOON!

We really hope you enjoyed reading this book. If you're looking for more romance, be sure to head to the shops when new books are available on

Thursday 5th September

To see which titles are coming soon, please visit

millsandboon.co.uk/nextmonth

LET'S TALK
Romance

For exclusive extracts, competitions
and special offers, find us online:

 facebook.com/millsandboon

🐦 @MillsandBoon

📷 @MillsandBoonUK

Get in touch on 01413 063232

For all the latest titles coming soon, visit
millsandboon.co.uk/nextmonth

MILLS & BOON

MODERN

Power and Passion

Prepare to be swept off your feet by sophisticated, sexy and seductive heroes, in some of the world's most glamourous and romantic locations, where power and passion collide.

Julia James
Heiress's
PREGNANCY SCANDAL
MILLS & BOON
MODERN

Jennie Lucas
Chosen as the
SHEIKH'S ROYAL BRIDE
MILLS & BOON

Kim Lawrence
A WEDDING on the **ITALIAN'S DEMAND**
MILLS

Sharon Kendrick
The
SHEIKH'S SECRET BABY
MILLS & BOON
MODERN

Eight Modern stories published every month, find them all a

millsandboon.co.uk/Modern

MILLS & BOON
Desire

Indulge in secrets and scandal, intense drama and plenty of sizzling hot action with powerful and passionate heroes who have it all: wealth, status, good looks… everything but the right woman.

JOIN US ON SOCIAL MEDIA!

Stay up to date with our latest releases, author
news and gossip, special offers and discounts, and
all the behind-the-scenes action
from Mills & Boon...

 millsandboon

 millsandboonuk

millsandboon

It might just be true love...